Moment Of Truth

Presidential Press Secretary Guy Pompey is trapped in the most agonizing decision of his life. He must commit himself to what might be one of the most infamous acts in history—or a deed of supreme patriotism.

The countdown begins as Pompey assembles his small band of co-conspirators: his girl friend Gail Sorrell, ranking intelligence agent Harvey Gordon, Secretary of Defense Ralph Jacobs, and alcoholic left-wing columnist Peter Amory Street, who was once the President's close friend.

Tension runs high as time runs out—the five must take the perilous gamble to its inexorable and cataclysmic finale. . . .

Avon Books by Burt Hirschfeld

FIRE ISLAND

CINDY ON FIRE

BEHOLD ZION

Moment Of Power

BURT HIRSCHFELD

AVON PUBLISHERS OF BARD, CAMELOT, DISCUS AND EQUINOX BOOKS

This is the first publication of *MOMENT OF POWER* in any form.

AVON BOOKS
A division of
The Hearst Corporation
959 Eighth Avenue
New York, New York 10019

First Avon Printing, December, 1971

Printed in the U.S.A.

The least considerable man among us has an interest equal to the proudest nobleman, in the laws and constitution of his country, and is equally called upon to make a generous contribution in support of them;—whether it be the heart to conceive, the understanding to direct, or the hand to execute.

To the Printer of the Public
Advertiser, March 19, 1770
—Junius

I do solemnly swear that I will faithfully execute the Office of President of the United States, and will to the best of my ability, preserve, protect and defend the Constitution of the United States.

—Inaugural Oath

CONTENTS

INTERCONTINENTAL NEWS BUREAU
SPECIAL TO ALL SUBSCRIBERS

PEKING—MARCH 14,

PREMIER LIN CHEN-FU CHINESE PEOPLE'S REPUBLIC DISCLOSED THIS DATE THAT A MUTUAL DEFENSE PACT HAS BEEN CONSUMMATED BETWEEN UNITED STATES OF AMERICA AND THE SOVIET UNION IN SECRET MEETINGS HELD AT AN UNIDENTIFIED LOCATION ON THE BLACK SEA . . . LIN WAS QUOTED IN PEOPLE'S DAILY AS FOLLOWS—

> " . . . ANOTHER COWARDLY BETRAYAL OF THE PEACE-LOVING PEOPLES OF THE WORLD BY IMPERIALIST GANGSTERS AS THEY PLAN FOR GLOBAL WAR . . . THE PEOPLES OF THE WORLD WILL NOT BE DECEIVED BY HOLLOW TALK OF PEACE AS PREPARATIONS FOR WAR ARE MADE . . . THE IMPERIALISM OF MOSCOW AND WASHINGTON WILL BE MET IN CONCERT BY FREEDOM-LOVING PEOPLES EVERYWHERE IN RESPONSE TO THIS SHAMEFUL CONSPIRACY WHICH AIMS AT THE DESTRUCTION OF A PEACEFUL AND PROGRESSIVE CHINA . . . LET THE MONGERS OF DESTRUCTION AND DEATH BE WARNED—CHINA STANDS READY AND ABLE TO DEFEND ITSELF AND EVEN NOW OUR DEFENSE FORCES HAVE RESPONDED AND ARE PREPARED TO FIGHT TOOTH AND CLAW AS THE TIGER FIGHTS TO DEFEND HER LITTER AND HER LAIR. . . ."

THE CHAIRMAN INDICATED HE EXPECTS AN INVASION OF HIS COUNTRY BY THE COMBINED FORCES OF THE

SOVIET UNION AND THE UNITED STATES WITHIN THE NEXT NINETY DAYS AND CALLED FOR THE UNALIGNED FREEDOM-LOVING PEOPLES OF THE WORLD TO INTERVENE ON THE SIDE OF PEACE AND JUSTICE. . .

—MORE TO COME—

Moment Of Power

One

Pompey's Day

I

It began for Pompey on a Tuesday morning.

He deposited the black Mercedes roadster in the garage in E Street, joked briefly with Walter, the Negro attendant, then set out for the White House, three blocks away.

It was a fine day and different. Overnight, winter had fled, leaving in its place the first hopeful signs of spring. The early sunlight felt pleasant, and squads of government girls stepped along with a bright, bouncing sexuality that made Pompey smile to himself.

A willowy redhead came out of the Willard Hotel and turned toward him. She moved in that way some women have, smoothly athletic, engagingly feline, her legs lean and strong, round at the calves. Pompey marked her down as an excellent skier. Their eyes met, her glance bold and good-humored, a woman used to being looked at and enjoying the fact.

She measured Pompey over the closing distance and liked what she saw. Most women did. At forty, he still retained a muscular leanness, despite the growing infrequency of his appearances on the Yacht Club tennis courts; there was a quiet masculinity about him, a man at first glance comfortable in his own skin. Except for his eyes, which were large and almost black, his features were undistinguished, a face swart and self-consciously poised, more attractive than its parts.

Pompey wanted the willowy redhead, the wanting physical, a taste in his mouth, a spreading hollowness behind his navel, a reminiscent desire. When he was younger, his needs more insistent and closer to the surface; it had been this way and almost always after leaving one bed he had sought another. No one woman seemed able to gratify him, and the craving became more powerful with each succeeding experience.

But that had been a long time ago, before his marriage to Betsy. Then, in the years after their divorce he had slipped back into the old pattern. Until Gail. Once they became lovers, there were no other women. Not that he had stopped looking, for the desire was still there, and a part of him craved every pretty girl he saw.

Now, as the redhead approached, he experienced a vague guilt, as if he was being unfaithful to Gail, and imagined her as he'd left her, still asleep. She was a splendid girl who gave freely—more so than he did—and certainly she would have made him a good wife. He shrugged the thought away. He wasn't ready for marriage again. Not yet.

The redhead came abreast of him, mouth curled expectantly. Pompey looked away and moved on.

He crossed 15th Street and circled the massive Treasury Department Building. On East Executive Avenue, tourists were beginning to collect outside the black iron fence, lining up for the public tour through the Executive Mansion.

Pompey greeted the uniformed guard at the East Gate by name and in return received a casual salute. He was aware of the tourists watching him with curiosity and respect. He liked that. He was proud of himself, of the job he held, of how far he had come from St. Louis where his immigrant father had owned a small *trattoria;* and he remembered with no pleasure the long, hot hours spent working in the kitchen during college vacations.

He considered his undergraduate years at Northwestern. Not one of his friends of those days, boys of good families with roots deep in the American tradition, not one of them had attained a comparable success, a comparable prominence. Press Secretary to the President of the United States! A rising sense of triumph tempered by uncertainty took hold, for he still found it difficult to believe all the good things that had happened to him.

He forced such thoughts out of his mind and headed for his office in the West Wing. His secretary, Margaret Reilly, greeted him with professional restraint as he entered the anteroom, not looking up from her typewriter. "The boss wants to see you," she said without emphasis. "First thing."

"Early start. Must be spring fever."

She placed her hands carefully in her lap and looked up at him. She disapproved of his levity. Margaret Reilly took her work seriously. She had joined the White House office staff during the first Eisenhower Administration, had seen press secretaries come and go. This one was better than some and not as good as others. Easy-going, glib, he had got along pretty well with the press corps, though he did have a tendency to let certain procedural matters slide past, to overlook details. It was this that caused her concern. A strict Catholic upbringing had imbued Reilly with a respect for hard work and personal discipline; and privately she scorned Pompey's professional laxity—and his casual attitude toward the True Church into which he had been born.

"What's happening?" he said.

"You don't know!" she said, unable to disguise the challenge in her voice.

That boyish smile fanned across his mouth and she turned away; he was too charming, too attractive. All of them were, she sniffed to herself. Italian men. A dangerous breed.

"Come on, Maggie, give. There's so much I don't know. I depend on you."

Maggie. She hated the diminutive and he knew it. She flipped the starter switch on the IBM Executive and it began to hum. "He wants *you,*" she said stiffly. "I'm only your secretary."

Pompey gave up. When Reilly set herself, nothing would move her. "Call downstairs to the Navy mess," he said, taking a yellow legal pad and a schedule of the day's activities from her desk. "Some coffee and toast."

Her mouth turned down. "That isn't much of a breakfast."

"I should be back by the time it gets here."

He stepped into the corridor, heels clicking on the tile floor. An Army warrant officer sat in a chair outside the President's office, in his lap the black box containing the codes which the Chief Executive would use should it ever become necessary to order a nuclear attack. There were five of these warrant officers, one always on duty with the code box in close proximity to the President.

Hank Luplow suddenly appeared, a glum expression on his elongated face. The speech-writer had been with the President. He directed a bony forefinger at Pompey and, typically, began speaking in mid-sentence.

". . . Changing the entire principle. A totally destructive approach, fruitless, bound to elicit strongly negative responses and undermine the efforts of our friends. Such a modification can't possibly do any good. I mean, it's absurd. Virtually a major policy change. So unlike Gunther. Thinking differently, wrongly. Not himself at all."

"Nice morning," Pompey said lightly. "Spring, cherry blossoms, girls. Why isn't a nice boy like you married?"

"Funny man," Luplow said. He gazed down at Pompey from his great height with no change of expression. "Do you know what he wants me to do?"

"Another time. The man wants to see me."

"You don't care," Luplow said sadly.

"Later," Pompey said, brushing past him. "I never keep Presidents waiting."

II

The President was not alone. Six men were seated around the spacious oval office. Pompey recognized them all, nodded a perfunctory greeting. At what impossible hour had the President dragged them out of bed? Gunther's propensity for early-morning meetings was well known.

Harrison Leo Gunther stood in front of the three tall windows looking out at the President's Park and the Ellipse beyond, the sharp, clean shaft of the Washington Monument, and farther still, across the Tidal Basin, the Jefferson Memorial. He stood stiffly, hands clasped behind his back.

"Good morning, Mr. President," Pompey said.

"Good morning, Pompey," the President said, without turning. Even now, after three years as Press Secretary, Pompey felt awed in this room with its implicit and visible evidence of tradition and power. Underfoot, the worn green carpet with the Green Seal carved into it; the Presidential banner and the American flag draped in front of the windows; the portrait of George Washington over the mantle; the painting of Andrew Jackson; the deep, comfortable couches on either side of the fireplace; and the rocker—was it Kennedy's or the one Lyndon Johnson had used? There was continuity here, emphasizing for Pompey the importance of the Office, more so than the man.

"A lovely day," the President said. "Soon the Rose Garden will start to bloom."

Pompey concealed his smile. There was *that* about Gunther, his variety of tastes and interests, the range of his knowledge, his frequent concern for the seemingly insignificant, sometimes surprising even those closest to him. He would have fit perfectly into ancient Greece: philosopher, political strategist, athlete, esthete, mystic, sensualist. He was all of these and more.

"You know everyone, Pompey," the President said, still gazing to the south through the three-inch bulletproof plate glass that shielded him from any would-be assassin sniping from a half mile away. "Have you met Dr. Tolchin?"

Milton Tolchin, liaison between the National Aeronautics and Space Administration and the White House. He was a stocky man who assessed the world through black-rimmed glasses with steady, searching eyes. Pompey nodded to the scientist, allowed his eyes to range over the other men present, greeting each by name: Jonas Keefe, Secretary of State, mild-mannered, diffident, more administrator than creator of policy; General Alton Miller, Chairman of the Joint Chiefs of Staff, weathered and serious, dedicated to the military and to the nation; General Arthur B. Quirk, Chief of the Air Force, bemedaled, proud, aggressively patriotic; Daniel Crowell, the physically small Director of the Central Intelligence Agency, his darting eyes missing nothing; and Ralph Jacobs, the tough-minded Secretary of Defense.

A thickening air of tension gathered under the lofty ceiling, and all at once Maggie Reilly's challenging *"You don't know!"* came spinning into the fore of Pompey's brain. What *was* happening?

"Would you like to tell us your opinion, Pompey?" the President said, still staring out the window.

Pompey hesitated. He had spent the night at Gail's apartment, and a bad night it had been: they had argued, gone to bed angry. As a result, he had slept poorly, had woke unrested and troubled, had hurried back to his own apartment for a quick shave and shower, a change of clothes, not bothering to listen to the morning news broadcasts. What had he missed? His brain was a jumble of information, bits and pieces to be considered, then discarded, until a likely subject clicked into place.

"You mean the manned flight to Mars, of course." He spoke with an assurance he did not feel.

"The Mars shot," Gunther said noncommittally, coming away from the window.

To Pompey, he looked the way a President should look. An imposing, slightly bowed elegance, all strength and confidence, moving with easy articulation, traces of youthful handsomeness still lingering, the features defined and enhanced by the furrows of time and experience, gray scoring the thinning, sable-colored hair. Pompey perceived so much in this man, a prescience that evoked respect, an aura of authority, a luminosity; he was a shaper of events, a creator of ideas, a leader of men, confirmation of the theory of natural selection.

The President stood behind his large desk and stared at Pompey, the brown eyes alertly curious, the way a predator might be curious about an always threatening environment. And in that brief span Pompey realized that his attempt to mislead Gunther had failed. The President's voice, though quiet and even, was ominous when he spoke.

"The Mars shot," he said, lowering himself into the green leather swivel chair. He stretched his right leg beneath the desk and arranged his fingers in a steeple, appraising Pompey across the apex. "You are aware, Mr. Pompey, that our space agency launched a two-man craft yesterday morning aimed at attaining an initial landing on Mars?"

Pompey flushed. He supposed all Presidents sooner or later wielded sarcasm as a weapon, but it was a fairly recent addition to the Gunther arsenal—and the first time it had been directed at him. "I know about the Mars shot, sir. We watched it together on television. At breakfast, in your quarters."

"So we did. How nice if you had extended yourself enough to listen to this morning's reports. "Dr. Tolchin," the NASA representative stepped forward, "be good enough to bring our Mr. Pompey up to date. It would be helpful if my Press Secretary were privy to such matters."

Tolchin began to speak, his manner pedagogic, the words spaced as if difficult to choose, issued with some reluctance.

"The launch was perfect, Mr. Pompey, and no corrections were required during the first hours of flight. Accordingly, there was every reason to anticipate complete success. At midnight, however, the computers at the space center in Houston recorded some minor deviation. We checked the command pilot, and though we were unable to account for the course change, we were able to make the necessary adjustments. Three hours later, the computers foretold another deviation upcoming. Every attempt was made to prevent this from happening; but despite our best efforts the spacecraft lurched off-course, and less than a minute later veered again. Severely."

"An unusual procedure, Dr. Tolchin?" the President asked, eyes closed, head resting against the high back of the chair.

"Decidedly, sir. We did what we could—and efforts are still being made to correct the situation—but the space vehicle continues to proceed on an infinite flight trajectory."

Pompey felt his stomach go hollow. "Does that mean the astronauts, that Worthington and Sprague are heading into space without any controls?"

The President straightened up. "You begin to understand the dilemma."

"How could that happen?" Pompey said.

"It was no accident." The President spoke the words coldly.

Pompey swung around, awkward and uncertain. He watched the President snap his fingers in command, saw the huge Alaskan sled dog, Ketza, bestir himself, rise from his place against the far wall, and pad slowly, reluctantly almost, to where the President sat. The dog was thick-furred, tan and white, with slanted eyes that gave his massive visage a foxlike expression. He raised his huge, flat head and gazed up into Gunther's face. The President scratched absently at Ketza's ears.

"No accident?" Pompey said, a faint uneasiness spreading along his nerves.

"Exactly," the President said. "The spacecraft was deliberately misdirected, turned off its course, deliberately sabotaged, those two fine, young Americans sent to a lingering and pointless death."

"Mr. President," Ralph Jacobs said.

"Who——?" Pompey muttered.

"The Russians," the President said, his voice thin.

"Mr. President," Jacobs repeated, coming forward.

Pompey's head swung to him, as if seeking an explanation. Weakness took hold of his knees, moved upward, and he wanted very much to sit down. To rest.

"I must disagree, Mr. President," Jacobs said, moving in front of the big desk.

The Secretary of Defense was a slender man, pale, his movements deliberate, precise, with a style of speech to match. There were many people who considered him the strongest individual, the most competent man in the Administration, forceful and brilliant; others, however, characterized him as an animated calculating machine, cold and dehumanized, oblivious to the human element in government.

"There is no hard evidence," he said, "that the Russians or anyone else sabotaged this flight."

The President shoved Ketza aside and leaned forward, eyes fixed on Jacobs. "Mr. Crowell. Will you inform us as to Soviet capabilities in this matter?"

Daniel Crowell, Director of the CIA for seven years, had already become one of those institutionalized government men seemingly beyond criticism, public or private. He cleared his throat and spoke in a softly melodious voice.

"The Russians own highly sophisticated equipment capable of misdirecting any one of our space efforts. It's a fairly simple matter. Naturally, we have reason to believe that Moscow has been observing our progress in this area quite closely, that they were in fact tuned in on all our communication once the vehicle was launched."

"Come off it, Dan," Jacobs said crisply. "The whole world's been tuned in. And watching, too. Our television networks have been broadcasting the entire thing. Nobody had to spy on this project."

"I assume, Mr. Secretary," the President drawled, "that there are aspects of our government with which you are not conversant, that in matters of space you do not consider yourself an expert."

Jacobs ignored the sarcasm. His manner was mild and controlled, and Pompey decided that only he was not at all intimidated by these surroundings.

"If there is concrete evidence that the Russians have interfered with our spacecraft," he said, "I would like to hear it. There is no logical reason for them to take such a step, especially since the treaty——"

The President shoved himself erect, the aristocratic face pink. "Two boys are going to die for no good reason! Face it, Jacobs, the Soviet mind is unfathomable, and despite every political turn they are committed irrevocably to Marx's theories of world revolution and to the destruction of capitalism as practiced in these United States."

"A thing of the past," Jacobs said. "The Soviet Union has almost achieved material parity with us, Mr. President. Their people, for the first time in history, are well fed and comfortable. Their lives are easier. They have greater incomes than ever, more leisure, more automobiles. They are committed to the Limited Test Ban Treaty, as are we. They stand actively opposed to nuclear proliferation. Like us, Russia fears the aggressive and warlike postures assumed by Red China. There's no sensible reason why the Kremlin would interfere with our Mars shot. Again I refer to the Mutual Defense Pact——"

The President waved him silent. "Yes, the treaty. I went after it with both hands. You all know how hard it was to work out, how demanding the Soviets were, but I stayed with it."

"And the world will be forever grateful, Mr. President," Jacobs said.

The President grunted. "Perhaps. But perhaps I made a mistake, listened to the wrong advice. I had hoped that Moscow was sincere about wanting peace, about wanting to cut back on the armaments race, about standing against China. Now I wonder. The Russians make a lot of noise about peace, but when the money's on the line they always revert to those old, hostile attitudes."

His voice became thin, querulous. "Oh, yes, I feared the Chinese, feared that China might wreck the peace of the world. But I am no longer so sure of that position. I met with Premier Grishin myself. And I made concessions, and God knows how many votes that'll cost the party next election. And Jonas Keefe has done little else but pursue the treaty for almost a year. I fought members of my own party over it, and the opposition, and still there's no certainty that the Senate will ratify. My political future hangs in the balance in this matter, but more important, gentlemen, the security of our country. I submit *that* for your consideration, Mr. Jacobs. Do you think I would accuse the Russians of sabotage if I were not pretty damned sure?"

He was breathing hard, eyes flickering from Jacobs to the others. Seconds later, the tension washed out of his face. A small, crooked smile spread across his mouth, the famous Gunther grin that had done so much to get him elected. He sank back in the green leather chair and spread his hands.

"Okay, Ralph. It's proof you want, and you'll get it. Dr. Tolchin. Will you explain?"

Pompey held himself very still. He had been startled by the outburst. During his three years in office, Gunther had seldom displayed anger, and on those few occasions it had been controlled, directed at a proper target, emotional support for a virtually unassailable position. Stupidity would anger him. Or slothfulness. But never a request for additional information, for a fuller explanation. Nor had he ever objected to those who disagreed with him, always ready to explore viewpoints other than his own. Dimly, Pompey heard Tolchin droning on, and such terms as electromagnetic interference and attitude control thrusters registered. There was a reference to proper radio equipment and a knowledge of frequency codes.

"Theoretically," Tolchin was saying, "the space vehicle could have been manipulated and turned off-course. You gentlemen will recall that the English were able, without difficulty, to pick up radio signals from a Russian moon shot in the sixties and thus, uh—appropriate their moon photos. Also, remember, if you will, the difficulties experienced by Astronauts Armstrong and Scott during the Gemini 8 flight while trying to dock with the Agena target rocket. There was an unusual and not totally explained amount of pitching and yawing."

"Do *you* claim sabotage, Tolchin?" Jacobs asked, almost disinterestedly.

When the scientist hesitated, the President spoke. "It might have been sabotage, Jacobs." He enunciated each word with great precision. "Consider the possibility, if you will."

Pompey thought he saw a shadow of uncertainty pass across Jacobs' face. "I hope, Mr. President, that this Administration will do nothing to endanger ratification."

"You echo my deepest concern, Jacobs." The President's smile was quick and fleeting. "Tell you what, let's bring this affair out into the open. I would like to know what those people in Moscow are really thinking. Pompey, call a press conference for eleven this morning. State Department auditorium. TV, radio, the works."

"Do you intend to raise this issue of sabotage publicly?" Pompey asked. "It would make rich editorial grist for some of the anti-treaty types."

"Maybe they've got a point," the President said. He rubbed absently at his stiff right knee, a memento of college football. "Keefe, I'll want you at this conference to make soothing noises about peace and tranquillity. You too, Dr. Tolchin."

Tolchin flushed. "What will I say?"

The President smiled warmly in his direction. "What you said here this morning. The truth, that's all. Secretary Jacobs is right, of course. We have no conclusive evidence, so we will not charge sabotage. We will simply tell the press and the voters what it is we do know." He glanced around the room. "Dan," he said to the CIA chief, "I'll want you too. Lend the authority of the intelligence community to things. Pompey, put together some kind of a statement for me to read, something about those two boys sacrificing their lives in the cause of freedom and in the advancement of science. Have it mimeographed. I guess that's it, gentlemen. Let's all get back to work." The men began to file out. "Oh, General Quirk," the President said. "Stay, please. There's a question I want answered."

In the reception room, Charley Hepburn, Chairman of the National Committee of the President's party, was waiting for his nine o'clock appointment. This would be the first of many such talks between the two men about the following year's election. Pompey greeted Hepburn, a small, tight man with a narrow head and an intense manner, who was known for his tough competency and his ability to raise campaign funds. The door to the President's office opened and he peered out, winked slowly, and grinned at Pompey who couldn't help smiling back. He crooked a finger at Hepburn.

"Charley, my man," he said in mock reproval, "do you plan to spend all day out there? Matters of state to attend to, matters of state."

Pompey ducked across the corridor to his own office, dwelling briefly on the odd personality mixture then in with the President—Quirk, the military martinet, a political Neanderthal, and Charley Hepburn, the pragmatic political technician. He wondered what they could possibly have to discuss. But there was no time for speculation; he had work to do.

Hank Luplow was perched on the corner of Margaret Reilly's desk. He swallowed the last of Pompey's toast and took a long gulp of his coffee.

"It was getting cold," Luplow said happily.

"Just some coffee, Maggie," Pompey said, going into his own office. "But first come inside."

Luplow followed close behind, established himself in a chair and heaved his feet up onto Pompey's desk.

"Yes, Mr. Pompey," Reilly said.

"Hey, Guy," Luplow mumbled, "what's the pitch with Gunther? Is it my imagination, or is the man jumping the gun?"

"Knock it off, Hank." Pompey turned to Reilly. "Press conference at eleven this morning. State Department auditorium. Full list, including TV and radio. I'll do a handout. Is there time enough to mimeo?"

"I'll make time."

"Okay. And the coffee."

"Yes, sir." She went out and closed the door behind her.

"What's the scoop, Scoop?" Luplow asked.

"Go away, Hank. Write a speech."

Luplow straightened up. "That's just it, the speech. Let me tell you . . ."

Pompey pulled the typewriter table toward him and rolled a sheet of paper into the machine. He frowned thoughtfully.

"What was that bunch doing with Gunther, Guy, first thing in the a.m.? Something hot?"

Pompey sighed. "The Mars shot went screwy."

"I know that."

"And two good men were lost."

"Tough." He considered the situation. "Was that enough to get a couple of Cabinet officers and two generals down here before breakfast? Unuh. It must be something else. Besides, why the changes in the speech?"

Pompey kept his face blank. "What changes?"

"I told you. He wants a rewrite of the Peace Now Foundation speech for Saturday week."

"He's the boss."

"Sure. But the whole idea was to make a strong public plea for support, letters-to-your-Senator kind of thing. Everybody knows that unless Gunther pushes hard for ratification it won't come. Hell, some of these mossback types on the Hill—they're still trying to turn back the French Revolution. The idea of a Mutual Defense Pact with Russia—well, it bugs those Fascist nuts."

"Spare me your Cambridge Square socialism," Pompey said thinly. "Sure, some Senators will vote against ratification, but they honestly hold it not to be in the national interest. Everything that happens isn't a Communist conspiracy or a Fascist plot. There are still men around who think and act for themselves, and out of conviction."

Luplow heaved himself erect, aimed a bony finger at Pompey. "Thanks for the civics lesson." His long face sobered. "What bugs me is that he wants the speech rewritten in such a way that it will be little more than a threat to the Russkies. The way Gunther wants it, either they act like nice, accommodating boys or we'll scrap the whole project, go back to that cold war nonsense. *How come?* is what I want to know. What changed him? He's been acting kind of peculiar, strained, a different man, trying too hard. He needs a vacation."

Pompey stared glumly at the blank sheet of paper in the typewriter. He felt unsettled, discomforted, as if there was something he should remember, something that had passed earlier; but it refused to come into focus, existing just out of range.

"The man had second thoughts, Hank. He got sore. He's got a right, when things go wrong."

"Okay, buddy. So our science people goofed a space shot. And we lost a couple of good guys. Tough. But he's the President and if he doesn't keep his perspective, who will? A thing like that isn't enough for this country to start issuing warnings to Russia, challenging her integrity, threatening atomization. The way he wants to wave around our nuclear capability makes him sound like Foster Dulles."

"You made your point."

Luplow never stopped talking. "Face it, man, Premier Grishin has his own troubles. He has to fight off his own warhawks, and this won't help his position in the Kremlin. And it sure as hell isn't going to win any votes to ratify."

A thought surfaced and Pompey swore under his breath. The reception at the British Embassy that night. The way the day was shaping up, he wouldn't have time to retrieve his dinner jacket. He glanced at his watch. It was still early; Gail would not yet have left for work. He dialed her number. It rang six or seven times before she came on, voice weak and irritable. It wasn't like her to sleep this late.

He said, "Are you feeling all right?"

"Just fine. What do you want?"

"Something bothering you?"

"I'm all right." Her voice contained a petulant undertone. "What do you want, Guy?"

He had hoped that a night's sleep would wash away whatever it was that was bothering her, whatever had caused last night's unpleasantness. There was no reason why their relationship shouldn't continue as before, steady, comfortable.

"Sorry I woke you," he said. "It's one of those days down here. Do me a favor?"

"What?"

"My dinner jacket. It's at the cleaner's. You know the one. I thought I'd change at your place. All right?"

There was a long silence. "All right," she said "Anything else?"

"I hope you're feeling well," he said stiffly.

"I'm fine. I'll see you later. Good-by."

He replaced the phone in its cradle. They would have to talk, he and Gail, discover what had gone wrong between them, straighten it out. Pompey was convinced that any problem could be solved, once it was identified and faced up to, squarely and sensibly.

"That's a fine-looking lady friend you got yourself, buddy," Luplow offered cheerfully. "Better than an old lecher like you rates."

Pompey laughed a self-satisfied laugh. It pleased him to know that other men envied him Gail Sorrell. She was young and beautiful, and most men who saw her desired her.

He remembered their first date, three years earlier. He had wanted very much to make a powerful, lasting impression; and so, when he had taken her home, he had kissed her, a kiss he was certain she would not forget, passionate and skilled, ignoring her protests, her struggles futile against his strength. And remember, she had. But he had never guessed that she had considered not seeing him again because of that kiss, because of his insistence, his disregard for her feelings, that she had seen him again only because he had been such an excellent contact for a beginning reporter on the *Post*.

By the time she had been transferred over to the society page, none of that had mattered; by then she had been in love with him.

"Hank, get the hell out of here. I've got work to do."

Luplow scowled. "Worried about the speech."

"Forget it. The President's put in too much time and effort to let anything damage the treaty now. He wants ratification so much he can taste it. Okay, so the man's nerves are on edge. It's the nature of the job. Maybe I'll mention it to Dr. Corso, have him suggest he take a vacation. *After* ratification." He escorted Luplow to the door. "We've got sixty-two certain aye votes, Hank, and two strong probables—Salisbury of Alaska and Marsden of New Mexico. Okay. That means we need only three more to ratify. And we'll get them. You know the kind of political genius Gunther is." A thought made him grin with renewed confidence. "That must be the reason he had Charley Hepburn in to see him this morning. Charley will toss his weight around up on the Hill, let some of those Senators know that they might just find reelection difficult if the National Committee withheld a certain amount of the usual campaign money. So relax, buddy, we're home free. Depend on it."

"I hope you're right," Luplow said. He brightened perceptibly. "Sure. There's nothing to worry about. Russia and the U.S., ass-hole buddies. What a relief that will be. And won't Peking have conniptions?"

"They already are. But it won't do them much good. The squeeze will calm them down, like a bucking horse at a rodeo, gentled between two big saddle ponies."

"Right," Luplow said. "That's the way it's going to be."

After Luplow left, Pompey settled down behind the typewriter and struggled to concentrate on the statement the President wanted. It came slowly, his mind preoccupied with the events of the morning, with the scene in the oval office. There had been some disturbing difference, a shadowy quality that defied identification. Despite his best efforts, the vague uneasiness returned, bringing with it a single, pervasive thought, a sense of oncoming danger.

III

Northwest Washington is a succession of hills and ravines. Rock Creek snakes through the district, its bed studded with fragments, its banks steep and wooded. Here, the streets are laid out in no ordered pattern, a confusion to the uninitiated, houses obscured and difficult to locate. Extending diagonally from Dupont Circle is Massachusetts Avenue, and on it, beyond the Islamic Center with its towering minaret, on the slope leading up to Mount Saint Alban, is the British Embassy, an English manor house that might have belonged to Queen Anne.

In a city noted for its extravagant galas, receptions at the British Embassy were always well attended. Not only were the Ambassador and his lady personally charming, but the quality of their food and drink was always superlative. At eleven o'clock guests were still arriving—envoys from various embassies, Senators, Congressmen, Cabinet members, industrialists, lobbyists.

"It's quite a show," Pompey said.

He and Gail had paid their respects to the Ambassador, had spent the required number of minutes with this important guest and that one, had laughed when expected to and had appeared suitably and solemnly impressed when such was in order. The ritual fulfilled, they had withdrawn to a place along the curved wall of the wide reception foyer, silently watching the new arrivals.

Pompey was tired. It had been a long, difficult day spent fending off reporters, denying rumors, hewing to the official line regarding the Mars shot, attempting to correct misunderstandings about the President's attitude toward the Mutual Defense Pact. There had been too many loaded questions at the press conference, insinuations that the President had altered his position on the pact, which indicated an information leak in the White House; Pompey suspected Hank Luplow, and meant to do something about that.

Adding to his weariness was a spreading sense of dissatisfaction directed toward Gail. Not that she had said or done anything out of line. Hell no. Proper in every word and gesture,—that was Gail—proper, cool and distant, all warmth gone. He'd apologized for his part in the night before, and that should have ended it, brought back her usual high spirits. It hadn't. Instead, tension all evening. His attempts to lighten the atmosphere all failed and he became resentful.

There had always been something about Gail, about their relationship, that had caused him to feel unsure of himself, defensive frequently. And that troubled Pompey. For so much of his life he had functioned with surety and confidence, a man who had accomplished much, who had gathered considerable prestige and the rewards of a successful business. A man still moving forward. Upward.

And there was his current status. Few men ever reached such a high level. Perhaps he lacked the aggressive authority of a Jim Haggerty or the cool competence of a Billy Moyers; still, there was no need for apology. He did his job well, better than average, lived his entire life that way. There were times when he was convinced Gail thought otherwise, viewed him as some kind of a glorified failure, a man who had never fulfilled his potential. Well, to hell with that nonsense! A man did what he could. A man *was* what he *did,* neither more nor less. It was time she recognized that.

As for any difficulties between them, it was time Gail grew up, viewed life practically, assumed her share of the burden when matters went wrong between them. And he intended to tell her so. Later, back at her apartment.

"Some good names tonight," she said quietly, as she made notes. For Gail, this was a working assignment.

He studied her clean profile, the graceful arc of her neck. She was wearing a short, silver-colored, metallic evening dress that drew attention to her full, young body. At once he wanted to hold her, to make love.

"I like that dress," he said.

"Thank you," she said, not looking up.

"You look beautiful tonight, Gail."

She continued her note-taking.

Gail Sorrell was slender, delicate without being fragile, with a rounded, balanced figure, the kind that drew admiring glances from men and envious ones from women. Her face, neatly structured, featured large, Tartar eyes of a pale green that at times seemed almost yellow; her sculpted mouth was inclined to slow, shy smiles; her black hair was cut short, worn in kind of a monk's cap, stepping across an intelligent forehead in jagged bangs. Even in repose, there was an expression of energetic curiosity on that face.

"Would you like something to eat?" Pompey said. He felt impelled to breach the barricade which had been erected between them, offended by it, threatened.

"No, thank you."

An Under Secretary from the Ghanaian legation appeared, on his way to the main room. He greeted Pompey, exchanged inconsequential remarks, and moved on. Pompey turned back to Gail.

"This isn't the place to talk," he said quietly, "but don't you think you're overdoing it?"

She turned her face in his direction, the Tartar eyes direct and disconcerting.

"You're right. This isn't the place to talk."

"Then act civilly, for Chrissakes."

"How long, Guy?" Her voice was quiet, controlled, and her failure to display any emotion agitated him further.

He frowned. "What?"

"How long have I been your mistress?"

He flushed. The outdated word was somehow charged, condemnatory. She cut short his protest.

"Three years." A smile broke across her face and she responded to the greeting of the Iranian Ambassador, passing in native costume. When he was out of range, she went on. "I'm tired of being a mistress. I want to be a wife."

It was as if his vertebrae fused into a solid, inflexible rod. The professional, cordial expression on his face was a restraining mask. "Why the change? I thought you were in no hurry for marriage. You wanted a career. You were satisfied with things the way they were."

She stared at him steadily. "Not anymore. I'm twenty-five years old and I want a home of my own, a family, all the things I used to mock, to consider dull and mundane." She turned back to her notes. "I want a man who belongs to me," she finished.

"We'll talk about it later."

"I suppose we will."

There was a new, enigmatic note in her voice. He scowled. "What is that supposed to mean?"

"Later," she said.

A quick, emotional retort forced its way into his throat; but he spied Ralph Jacobs, the Secretary of Defense, picking his way toward them, moving in that distinctive style of his, placing each foot with cautious precision, and so he swallowed his resentment. Jacobs was unimpressive physically, his face narrow and pale, thinning brown hair brushed flat against a long head, with inquisitive blue eyes that never blinked.

"Pompey," he began. He inclined his head to Gail. "Miss Sorrell. How nice to see you again." There was no animation in his voice. He gazed at her notebook. "Surely you're not still working."

She was almost as tall as he, their eyes at a level. "My informants tell me that Ralph Jacobs does little else but work, Mr. Secretary, that the lights in your Pentagon office burn late into every night."

"Exaggerations." He arranged his flat mouth into a

small, humorless smile. "Still, in a city such as this, it is difficult to compartmentalize one's existence. Work frequently overlaps other activities, such as this party."

"That isn't the way I intend to go on living," she said with no particular emphasis.

"Good for you. For a lovely young woman, Miss Sorrell, life holds much more than mere work." The smile lingered, a cool arc, the blue eyes reflecting no warmth. "May I borrow your Mr. Pompey for a few minutes?"

"Of course," she said. "I should circulate, get some quotes for my story."

"See you later," Pompey called after her. She gave no response as she disappeared into the main room.

Jacobs took Pompey's elbow in a grip surprisingly strong for such a slender man, directed him toward a remote corner of the reception foyer.

"This morning," he said quietly, "an interesting exchange in the President's office."

Pompey slid automatically into the role of Press Secretary, a bland ambiguity on his tongue. It was a technique he had learned years before, during his first job on Madison Avenue: to suspend his critical faculties, to substitute an ingratiating caution that allowed nothing meaningful to be said. Protect yourself, and the client, at all times, had been the guideline to live by. And prosper. He arranged the old public-relations-man smile on his mouth.

"It was interesting," he agreed.

Jacobs looked at him without blinking. "Have there been many such performances lately?"

"Performances?"

"Dammit, yes." For a man who's been breaking his back to bring about a détente with Moscow, the President is too aggressive for my taste."

"The President had cause to be upset, sir. The loss of the spacecraft and the two astronauts. His feeling for people——"

"Save it," Jacobs said. "This morning I got the

impression you were troubled, Pompey. Was I wrong?"

Pompey stiffened. The uneasiness returned, almost a physical distress, a light-headedness, a weakness in his extremities. "I'm afraid I don't understand, Mr. Secretary. Nothing is troubling me. Nothing."

Jacobs measured Pompey as if marking off his strong points and weaknesses, as if aiming himself at the most vulnerable portion of Pompey's anatomy. Before he could speak again, they were interrupted by Peter Street. Obviously Street had drunk too much champagne, though he managed to transport himself with a kind of dissipated elegance; his lean face was flushed, the handsome features somewhat corroded, his smile unsteady but winning. The J. Press dinner jacket he wore draped off his high shoulders with a kind of sculpted arrogance, as if he alone had been created for such finery.

"Gentlemen, good evening," he began. "Mr. Pompey. Mr. Secretary." He drained the glass in his hand, handed it to a passing waiter, and helped himself to another. He grinned at Jacobs. "Learn to drink, Ralph. It makes all this passable. Passable. Only that." He followed his own advice, gesturing with his free hand. "See them all, the preening peacocks and their cackling hens, the controllers of men's destinies, the shapers of the world, the keepers of our fate. The intellectually deprived elite. What a farce all of this is!"

Jacobs almost smiled. "We do our best, Peter."

"*Your* best is quite good, Ralph. But these others—which of them has your brain, Ralph, your sense of dedication, your grasp of historical imperatives?"

Jacobs smiled. "Your academic credentials are showing."

"Would that others were so equipped. Perhaps, if some here owned a wider sense of the past, we might indeed profit from history. Sadly, we learn no lessons from our mistakes and are doomed, it seems, to repeat them."

Pompey tuned them out. He knew Street's personal and professional history had marked him as one of those men who are always kept off balance by life's left jab, unable to cope or to win.

At twenty-seven, Peter Amory Street had been a full professor of Russian history at one of the Ivy League universities, had been published three times in book form, and in most of the esteemed political journals. He had been the glittering hope of the academic world, more than a scholar, a political realist, a man with a firm grasp of international dealings and a brain capable of penetrating to the core of a problem, able to cut through the camouflage men and nations used to conceal their true aims. Even more, he had owned the ability to invent solutions that were both different and practical.

No one was surprised, therefore, when Harrison Gunther's predecessor in the White House appointed Street to be an Under Secretary in the State Department. Two weeks later, Street came up with the plan that ended the Pakistani-Indian dispute and that subsequently was incorporated into the Darjeeling Agreement.

Around Washington, Street was lionized, but his glory was short-lived. Four months after his arrival in Washington, there was a scandal having to do with the fourteen-year-old daughter of a Nebraska Congressman. Street denied knowledge of the girl's true age, had insisted that she had come uninvited to his office late one night, had seduced him. There were those who believed him, for the girl had already established a notorious reputation. It didn't matter. The Secretary of State had to ask for his resignation. Though no charges were leveled and the incident received no public airing, Street's career in government had ended.

But, severely infected by the political virus, Street was unable to return permanently to academic life. He spent a year at Berkeley and another year at the University of Virginia, the time totally unsatisfying. One day, unannounced, he appeared again in Washington, employed as a writer for an ultraliberal newsletter of limited circulation and influence, a post that still allowed him to function on the fringes of the world that had become so important to him.

A friend of Harrison Gunther,—they had been roommates at college—Street had hoped for a resurgence of his political fortunes when Gunther was elected President. The dream was soon shattered. Gunther, too political a creature to risk the stain of Street's record on his Administration, kept his old comrade at a distance, never drawing on his knowledge of Communism nor of Communist politics, not inviting him to any official functions, pointedly ignoring him whenever their paths accidentally crossed. In time, Street's writings became increasingly critical of the Gunther foreign policies, as well as of the man himself, and it was generally agreed that Street had lost all objectivity.

So it was that at forty-seven, Peter Street was looked upon as another of the many charming, if slightly notorious, males around Washington. Admittedly, he drank too much, though he seldom lost control, remaining always an entertaining talker, an attractive extra man, always available to fill out a guest list.

"That press conference this morning," Street said to Pompey, "a fiasco by any measure. Those wild statements by General Quirk. Why does Gunther allow it, Pompey? Surely he recognizes Quirk for what he is, a man anxious to turn us back to the peak of the cold war. Gunther must know better, unless he's gone absolutely beserk. It's your job to advise him on such things, Pompey."

"I'm the Press Secretary," Pompey said, "not a Cabinet officer."

"The Russians are sensitive to the dangers of war, of nuclear destruction. They want no part of it. Ever since Khrushchev, they've been moving toward peace. The current Kremlin hierarchy is not the Bolshevik revolutionists of old. Not like those wild men in Peking. Those people grew up on Mao Tse-tung's philosophical excesses, the Red Guard come to maturity. And we're stuck with them. But Premier Grishin is a reasonable and wordly man who wants to provide his people with the material rewards of their labor. That's why he's gambling on the defense pact."

"No more so than the President," Pompey said.

Street finished his champagne. "Why allow Quirk to shoot off his mouth? He virtually accused Moscow of sabotaging that Mars shot."

"It's possible," Pompey said, "that the Russians did—"

"Nonsense!" Jacobs said. He broke off, his attention drawn by a flurry of excitement at the front entrance of the embassy. A murmur rippled through the crowd, and there was a smattering of applause.

Street turned and a grudging laugh escaped his mouth. "It's Harrison, up to his old tricks. He loves to play this game."

It was the President, pushing his way through the crowd behind a pair of worried Secret Service agents, grinning that crooked grin, shaking hands, calling out to friends, managing to appear perfectly at home in an ordinary gray business suit.

Pompey started forward. The President had sent his regrets to the British Ambassador declining his invitation, claiming the press of business; yet here he was in a typical Gunther ploy, showing up when least expected, creating a greater excitement for doing so, claiming center stage—he often used such seemingly unplanned appearances as a forum to give voice to new ideas, to test the impact of some fresh program, to gain a response to a change in policy.

The President spied Pompey and waved, spoke his name. Moments later, the British Ambassador, a smile of welcome splitting that impressively mustached visage, was claiming his attention, expressing his delight, offering champagne.

Toasts were proposed, and there were the usual bantering exchanges as the Ambassador escorted the President toward the main room where most of his guests were waiting. An anticipatory murmur went through the crowd, and a wave of applause as the President came into view. Pompey watched admiringly. Street was right. The President enjoyed his role, enjoyed the emotional response his presence kindled, enjoyed seeing the effect his prsonality had on people.

The crowd pressed forward; and as the crush around the President increased, the Secret Service agents tried to clear an area around the man they were sworn to protect. A futile effort. Men of stature shoved forward to grasp the President's hand, to exchange remarks with him, to laugh with him. And women, too, strained to get closer, to touch him, to bathe in the warmth of those penetrating eyes.

Abruptly, as if on signal, the sound level fell off; there was a subdued murmur, and that too expired. In the silence, Mikhail Sokoloff, Ambassador of the Soviet Union, flanked by two of his aides, trundled forward, bowed stifflly. The President's response was a small, tight nod. The brown eyes were suddenly veiled, wary, and a strained tautness lined his face.

From where he stood, Pompey imagined he could detect a deepening of those grooves from nose to mouth, a new set of lines curling around that aristocratic chin, a general coarsening of features. The job, Pompey acknowledged silently, was too much for any one man; with each succeeding administration it heaped greater, more oppressive responsibilities upon the man who occupied the oval office.

Without preliminary, the President's voice cut through his thoughts, loud and firm, each word enunciated with clarity. And Pompey knew that this was why Harrison Gunther had come; and the Press Secretary was afraid.

"How good it is, Mr. Ambassador, that we can still meet in peace among friends."

Sokoloff was a squat man with a flat, Slavic face, his eyes small and upturned. He had a short neck and a wide mouth, and reminded Pompey of a sea turtle. He smiled agreeably.

"Soon our two nations will stand as allies against the terror of war and for peace for all mankind, Mr.

President." He spoke in a gravelly voice, heavily accented, and his little eyes remained inscrutably still.

"We must drink to that," the British Ambassador said. A waiter appeared. "To the Mutual Defense Pact," the Englishman toasted. "To peace. The hope of men everywhere." There was a murmur of approval.

The President handed his glass back to the waiter.

"You do not drink, Mr. President?" Sokoloff said.

"It is difficult for the President of the United States to toast idly when two of his country's finest young men are speeding to a cruel and slow death in space."

Sokoloff clucked sympathetically. "I understand, Mr. President. We Russians have also had our space failures." He chuckled softly "But I must confess we publicize them less than your people."

"The difference between freedom and . . ." He hesitated, " . . . a dictatorship."

Sokoloff's broad head seemed to shrink deeper between his bulky shoulders. The wide mouth twisted as if a great struggle was being fought internally. His shoulders slumped and after a moment his head came up. "The leaders of all great nations carry immense burdens, and there are times when events conspire to sabotage their best efforts."

"An excellent choice of words, Mr. Ambassador."

"I do not understand, Mr. President."

"Sabotage. There is reason to believe that our space vehicle was sabotaged, deliberately diverted from its course by a foreign power."

Sokoloff stared up at the President for a long, silent interval, the peasant face placid and without guile. "I will not believe that a nation civilized enough to develop and operate such advanced equipment would act in a manner so dishonorable."

"Is any Russian in a position to discuss honor?"

There was an audible gasp.

"Russians may claim honor as do other peoples," Sokoloff retorted with a kind of resigned heaviness. He seemed about to speak again, then stopped.

A sound that might have been a laugh died on the

President's lips. His voice was harsh, serrated. "I negotiated the treaty in good faith. Now I begin to question. Too often the Soviets have failed to respect their international obligations. As for Russian honor—"

"Mr. President!"

"There was little honor in Budapest—or in Prague—and not even a fanatic would characterize Stalin as an honorable man. And what honor was to be found in the Soviet-Nazi pact, or in the placement of missiles in Cuba and lying about it, as Khrushchev did in 1962?"

Gail Sorrell frantically made notes. This exchange would rate front-page placement, and she didn't intend to miss a word. There was movement to her left, and a quick glance revealed Peter Street leaving, face pained and anxious. She couldn't understand how he could turn away from this dramatic moment. Here was history in the making.

"So!" Sokoloff said thickly, voice low and muffled. "It is honor you wish to discuss. Very well. Explain, sir, the bombers you have in the air at this very moment, armed with nuclear devices, ready to destroy the cities of my country. And the missiles. Talk of the honor in the Bay of Pigs, of Eisenhower's lies about the U-2 spy planes, of the Doninican Republic, of Vietnam. The catalogue of American *dishonor* is fat with citations. It is easy to speak of peace, not so easy to act upon the word."

"Give us concrete evidence of Russian good faith and we will act accordingly. Until that day, it is the duty of the President of the United States to defend the nation, and this President will do just that. To do otherwise would justify my impeachment."

"You think we Russians are fools, sir?" Sokoloff's accent thickened as his agitation increased. "I am aware of General Quirk's aggressive remarks at your press conference today, virtually accusing us of interfering with your space program. I deny such allegations most emphatically, and name them for what they are—provocations, incitements to war. You talk of peace while your generals prattle of war and of America's arsenal. The Soviet Union desires peace, and labors only to that end."

The President's eyes were veiled, and his mouth worked silently. Secretary Jacobs pushed through the crowd to his side. He spoke with quiet urgency.

"Gentlemen, this exchange can profit no one. Neither of our nations has a monopoly on peaceful intentions or good works. Let's end this fruitless discussion."

"You forget yourself, Mr. Secretary." The President spoke sharply. "I will attend to Mr. Sokoloff." He turned back to the Russian. "You say it is peace Russia wants. Then explain this—two days ago the Federal Bureau of Investigation rendered inoperative a Soviet espionage apparatus in this country. Its aim was to subvert our Doomsday Launching System, our ultimate defense system against a sneak attack. Arrests have been made and there will be more. Let Premier Grishin reconcile Soviet protestations of peaceful intentions with such a warlike act. I, sir, cannot."

Pompey felt drained, ill, physically weak. He had heard nothing of a spy ring. Perhaps the FBI coup was being kept on a need-to-know basis for the time being. If so, the security had been breached; it would be all over the front pages tomorrow.

When Skoloff replied, the words came from deep in his barrel chest, rumbling out emotionally. "I have no such information, Mr. President. You have my word on it."

The President started to speak, checked himself, and turned away. The crowd fell back as he strode out of the embassy, the Secret Service agents hurrying to keep up.

Pompey watched him go. Gradually he became aware that he was standing stifflly, joints locked, literally holding his breath. He forced air into his lungs and tried to will the tension away. A blunted ache settled into his shoulders; he yearned to close his eyes, to sleep. From where he stood, he could see the expression on Ralph Jacobs' face. It was concerned, grim. A pulse began to leap erratically in Pompey's temple.

IV

Pompey wheeled the Mercedes 230-SL across the Arlington Bridge and onto the Mount Vernon Memorial Highway. He made the seven miles to the outskirts of Alexandria in about as many minutes, cruising slowly through the local streets to the garden apartment complex where Gail lived. Neither of them spoke until they were inside her comfortably furnished apartment.

"Coffee?" she said, kicking off her shoes, padding into the kitchen.

He tossed his jacket onto a chair and undid his tie, then sprawled out on the couch. His eyes burned and he squeezed them shut. Too much smoke, too much champagne. He was beginning to enjoy the social whirl in Washington less and less.

"What about that debate between Sokoloff and the President?" she called. A moment later she appeared, reaching for the zipper of the silver dress, disappearing into the bedroom. "So strange." Her voice reached him as if from a great distance, removed, somehow unfamiliar. "Frankly, I was disappointed that Gunther would make such a public display."

Pompey offered no reply. In the lidded darkness, his brain spun on its axis, a whirl of impressions, memories, snatches of conversation. Two days, the President had said, since the FBI had broken the spy ring. Forty-eight hours, and not a whisper had reached Pompey, and that in a city which nourished itself on gossip. Of course there were national secrets to which he was not privy, but this one lacked that urgency. Besides, as Press Secretary he should have been informed, for sooner or later the story was bound to surface, and it was to him the White House correspondents would turn first.

"You knew about it, I suppose." It was Gail, calling again from the bedroom, the remark emphasizing his vulnerability.

"What?" he made himself say.

"The spy thing. When I phoned, my editor wondered why it had been kept so hushhush. He's checking it out." A nagging doubt took hold of him, blurred and unidentifiable, but before he could isolate it, the sound of her laughter dispelled his apprehension. "Won't the phones at the FBI be busy tonight? My hunch is Gunther didn't intend to let out the news, that it was supposed to be kept quiet for some reason, that he slipped."

Pompey doubted that. Such a mistake would be out of character. In three years, Pompey had never known the President to issue any public statement that said either more or less than he intended. He functioned with a rare and impressive intellectual and verbal precision. Still, upset about the loss of the astronauts, deeply angered at the Russians, he might have blundered.

Pompey cleared his mind. Washington was like this, no end to the job, to the ramifications of government work, to the constant intrigue. Politics was a twenty-four-hour, seven-day occupation, and his interest in it was sharply diminished from those exhilarating days when he had first come to the Executive Mansion.

Looking back, Pompey had come to understand that it had been no accident. No lucky confluence of forces. He had wanted to be a delegate, had worked for it, had gotten what he wanted. And having achieved that much, he had reached for more.

The party powers had selected Philadelphia as the site for the convention that year. Philadelphia in August was a terrible burden. It was an incredibly hot and humid month and people talked as much about that as they did politics and they were all afraid that the air conditioning in the hall might fail. But it didn't.

It seemed like a good idea, becoming involved in politics, a potentially profitable idea. As head of one of New York City's most active public relations agencies, Pompey was always on the hunt for new accounts, always anxious to establish contacts with important and influential people. The political arena appeared to be the place to do just that.

The New York delegation came to the convention uncomitted. There had been some talk of going for the Governor on the first ballot as a favorite son, and even more talk about the Senator as a serious Presidential candidate. Some of the delegates were excited about the chances of South Dakota's Walker but that soon expired. And a few of the more passionate delegates were working for Harrison Gunther.

Pompey marked him as a loser. In Pompey's view, Gunther lacked stature. To begin, he was too damned good looking, overbred almost, too charming and refined. Pompey was convinced that any man so graced owned comensurate character flaws, though he was unable to define them. In fact, Gunther gave every indication of being a man who voted on the correct side of every issue, whose every public statement seemed concerned with the good of the Republic and the people.

Presidential balloting began at 10:15 that Wednesday night, and no one accumulated the necessary number of votes. As soon as the totals were announced, the New York delegation was summoned to one of the caucus rooms by the Governor. He was a paunchy man with thinning gray hair and a suggestion of a smile always on his pink face. He waited for quiet.

"Ladies and gentlemen," he began. "I appreciate the support given me, but I have never been and am not now a candidate for the Presidency of these United States. With that in mind, please vote your consciences with the concern of our great country in your minds and hearts. There is continued unrest in the nation and in the world and . . ."

Pompey stopped listening. Seated in one of those hard wooden folding chairs, he was aware of every slat and every crack under him. If only his bottom were more amply padded. He folded his arms across his chest and allowed his attention to wander. In the row ahead, to the left, a woman sat so that her profile was turned to him. Her features were irregular, but cleanly etched, and her auburn hair was a glittering cloud. She made him think of Betsy; but his ex-wife had been more delicately formed and owned darker hair. Still, there was that same lofty tilt of chin, the same set to the mouth. He wondered what this woman would be like in bed. There had been that about Betsy, a marvelous lay no one better.

He must have been staring. The woman with the auburn hair turned and looked at him. He nodded agreeably and gave her his best smile. She held his eyes for a beat or two then looked to the front without acknowledgement. Pompey grinned to himself. That was a start. Of course, she wouldn't turn again, but she was aware of him, would continue to be, would expect him to make a move in her direction. She would keep, he assured himself, until the right moment. He directed his attention back to the Governor.

"In such perilous and sensitive times," he was saying, "It is imperative that the man in the White House be trustworthy and dedicated, dependable, skilled in the arts of govenment, that he possess not only the experience and talents that make for a good politician but those personal characteristics that make for an outstanding human being, a good man. I know of one such person and, ladies and gentlemen, I present to you my candidate for the Presidency of the United States of America, Senator Harrison Gunther . . ."

Pompey had never seen Gunther in person before. He was even more impressive than on television. He stood up at the front of the caucus room waiting for the applause to fade away. The lean, intelligent face was somber, the eyes raking the room deliberately, as if measuring each delegate in his chair. Pompey liked what he saw, the slightly stooped elegance, the confident easiness, hands relaxed at his sides. He gave no suggestion of the inevitable pressure.

"Well," Gunther started out, grinning that quick, angled grin of his. "You're asking yourself—what makes this character so special that he should be President. Well, all right. In your place, I'd be asking the same question." There was a smattering of laughter. Pompey slumped down in his seat and stared at the woman with the auburn hair. Now Gunther would catalogue his credentials, the laws that bore his name, his voting record, the kind of Governor he had been, his executive abilities. As long as he didn't get cute; Pompey hated cuteness in politicians.

"Well," Gunther said. "If this man is special it is up to you to decide so. I figure it this way—by now you've been inundated with information about each of the candidates, from when they were weaned to the kind of drinkers they are. I won't add to that avalanche of information." The laughter was louder and there was some good-natured applause. "Here it is. I think I'm the man for the job, if any man is for that job. I judge myself to have the intellectual and emotional disciplines necessary. I have no intention of promising you the millenium but I will promise to give you, to give the people of our country, one hell of a run for glory." The applause was loud and there were cheers.

Pompey straightened up in his seat. *A run for glory.* He liked that. No political particulars. No vague promises. No modest ambitions. A run for glory. There was the ring of dedication to it, the kind of thing the Founding Fathers might have said. It spoke of Gunther's hopes for the nation. Pompey tuned in fully.

Gunther held up his hands for quiet. It came finally. "You are in some degree all politicians, else you wouldn't be here. But you are also the people. You expect and are entitled to a candidate who represents certain philosophies and attitudes. Well, this is your chance to pin me to the mat. Fire away. Ask questions and I'll do my best to answer straight."

"Have you settled on a Vice President yet?" a little lady in a flowered hat asked.

Gunther bowed from the waist. "Have you chosen a President yet, madame?" The lady laughed and applauded happily.

A burly man in a black suit and brows to match rose. "I want to know how we're going to protect our soldier boys posted around the world. There's been too damned much shilly-shallying with the Commies, and I want to know what you're going to do to keep our boys safe while they are protecting democracy."

Gunther layed a forefinger alongside his nose. "I'm going to give those boys the best insurance policy I know of. And that goes for all of us, the world itself. I will do my very best to keep the guns still, sir, to maintain peace, to stop wars and threats of wars. I know of no better way to save lives and to that end I dedicate all my strength and energy and intelligence."

The cheering was spontaneous and loud this time. After that, the questions came with increasing frequency, and Gunther's replies seemed more deliberate to Pompey, more thoughtful, as if the candidate was reluctant to encourage any more outbursts.

Pompey glanced at the woman with the auburn hair. She seemed completely captivated by Gunther, hanging on his words, quick to laugh or cheer or applaud. At once, Pompey wanted to bring her attention back to himself, to impress her. He rose.

Gunther recognized him. "You, sir."

"Government is larger and more complex than ever," Pompey said. "The men who head the various agencies and departments are more vital since in many instances they have become almost autonomous. I don't mean to press you for names but——"

The woman with the auburn hair turned and looked up into his face, listening intently. Silently urging him on, Pompey was certain. He paid no attention to her.

Gunther broke in, grinning, nodding. "—But you want to know about Cabinet member, other appointments?"

"Yes, sir," Pompey said, unable to keep from grinning in return.

"Well, you're entitled, Mr. . . .?"

"Pompey. Guy Pompey."

"Mr. Pompey, I won't give you specific names because I don't have them. But this nation is rich in all its resources, human and otherwise. Once nominated, I will concentrate a good deal of time on that problem. I intend to request . . ." He broke off, ducking his head. "Hell, no," he said. "I intend to demand, *demand,* the services of the best men in behalf of America. Excellence exists from sea to sea, and I will utilize it."

There was more, but Pompey had made up his mind. He was Harrison Gunther's man. After the candidate had left, a vote was taken. It was overwhelmingly for Gunther. While the Governor counted upraised hands, the woman with the auburn hair turned to see how Pompey had voted.

When they filed back onto the convention floor, Pompey took a route that brought him alongside her. "He's quite a guy," he said conversationally.

"Mr. Gunther, you mean?" she said seriously.

"Mr. Gunther."

"Do you think he'll get the nomination?"

"And the Presidency."

"Oh, I hope so."

Pompey introduced himself and asked her name.

"Carla Gilbert," she said. "Mrs. Gilbert."

She was from an upstate county, and her husband owned two drugstores and took no interest in politics. She had two children and this was her first visit to Philadelphia. Pompey made a joke about spending a week in Philadelphia one night, and she laughed and touched his wrist in approval. He asked her to have a drink with him when the session was over.

She avoided his eyes and said something about the bars being closed early.

"That's no problem," he replied easily. "I've got a bottle of first-rate Scotch in my room."

"Oh."

"Perhaps you don't like Scotch?" he went on.

"It's all I drink."

"Then we have a date, to celebrate Gunther's nomination?"

"Well. I suppose one drink would be nice."

She had four drinks and stayed the night and went back to New York with him and remained for an extra day. One of the fringe benefits of being a delegate, he told himself, though she was not nearly as gratifying as Betsy had been.

Three days after the convention, on a Sunday morning, Pompey was awakened by a phone call from Jake Rubin. Rubin, his District Leader, was a former State Senator.

"Guy," Rubin began, wasting no time on preliminaries. "We have got a tough job on our hands, putting Gunther across in the state. The opposition is powerful and well financed. I need your help."

"I'll put a check in the mail," Pompey said.

"Good, but not good enough. I expect more from you."

Pompey yawned. "Come on, Jake. There's the agency. That's a twenty-four hour proposition."

"I want you to handle the publicity on Gunther's campaign in the State. That means speech-writing, releases, organization, the works. It's up your alley, Guy, and I want you to donate the services of your agency. For the good of the party. And the country."

A new excitement gripped Pompey. He sat up in bed and reached for a cigarette. "Now, Jake," he said, thinking that a political campaign would be a welcome respite from the sameness of his work routine. More, it would place him in an excellent position to make additional contacts, line up some new accounts.

"I insist that you say yes, Guy," Rubin went on. "I need you. Gunther needs you. He wants you."

"Oh?"

"Sure, kid, he told me to get in touch with you."

That one question in Philadelphia. Pompey was flattered, but wasn't about to make an impulsive decision. "Give me time to think, Jake."

"I'll give you today. I want your agreement tomorrow morning by eleven."

"I'll call you."

He considered what it would mean, exploring all areas, all possibilities. He wished there was someone with whom he could discuss it, someone who cared, and so would understand his ambitions as well as his fears. Too bad he wasn't still married—that drew a harsh sound out of him. He thought back to Betsy's reaction when he had decided to open his own agency, to strike out by himself.

"Marvelous," she had crowed, voice heavy with sarcasm, that beautiful face a mocking mask. "You'll become the most important buttondown man on Madison Avenue."

"What kind of a crack is that?"

"Keep your cool, sweetie. After all, I'm your wife."

"That doesn't give you the right to put me down. This is a big step."

"Okay, I'm impressed, sweetie."

"Don't call me sweetie, dammit. Save that for those phony actor friends of yours."

Her sigh was elaborately manufactured. "Shall we not argue, Guy. I've got an audition tomorrow and lines to learn. You will forgive me . . ."

Betsy, he reflected, would not be much help now. All that had ever mattered was the theater. No, he corrected. Not the theater, not acting. Just *her* career. *Her* place in that glittering scheme of things.

On Monday morning, Pompey phoned Jake Rubin and accepted the job. Within a week, he had so organized matters at the agency that he was able to concentrate almost all his time on the Gunther campaign.

Those first weeks were in many ways routine. Yet they were also exciting, exhilarating. He discovered that he cared, was involved in a larger purpose, a *cause*, with the result that he worked harder and more effectively. And when he spoke or wrote about Gunther, it was with the deepening conviction that he was on the side of the Just.

Early in October, with the campaign turning into the homestretch, Jake Rubin called to say that Harrison Gunther wanted to speak to him, face-to-face. That meant a trip to Dallas, where Gunther was speaking that night. Pompey caught an early plane and met the candidate in his suite that evening. Gunther was dressing for the rally and Guy sat on the edge of the bed and watched and listened.

"You know Stuart Wanger, my press representative?"

"We met once."

Gunther turned away from the mirror, slid his tie into place. "Stuart's out." Pompey displayed his surprise. "Fired, by me. Stuart drinks too much, and though I take no moral position I can't indulge that kind of weakness when it affects a man's work. Stuart wasn't getting the job done." He put on his jacket. "Can you get the job done, Pompey?"

Pompey hesitated, suddenly afraid, and desperately wanting to take advantage of the opportunity.

"You'll have to travel with me for the remainder of the campaign," Gunther was saying. "It's a twenty-four hour job, turning out releases, helping with the speeches, catering to the press boys, radio, TV. But it's an important job, maybe the most important at this stage. Jake Rubin tells me you're a top man and there have been other good reports. More, I like the feeling I get from you. I want you, Pompey. Say yes and we'll get to work."

Pompey said yes.

The weeks that followed were frenetic, tiring and immensely satisfying. And finally election night, with the returns making Gunther a winner by a modest but clear margin.

As expected, Pompey added some new names to the client list of the agency. What he hadn't expected, was a job offer from Harrison Gunther.

"I want you for my Press Secretary, Pompey," Gunther said, the day after the election, phoning from his parents' home in Kansas City.

Pleased and flattered, Pompey hesitated nevertheless. "I'm not sure I'm the man for the job," he said, meaning it in part, in part wanting to be convinced.

"I disagree," Gunther said, "and I want you to consider the offer, then accept it."

And accept it Pompey did. He had been a newspaperman for seven years, reporter and feature writer, before going into the public relations field. That had been a vital move for him, and even bigger had been the decision to open his own agency. Now this, the biggest challenge yet, the greatest reward; a burgeoning sense of pride and elation took hold of him. He thought of some of his reporter friends, so quick to disparage his PR activities, to make light of his success. He savored the envy they would feel.

And Betsy, not even Betsy's caustic tongue would be able to lessen this triumph. This was the big time, the major leagues. She would have to be impressed.

How much time had passed since he had last seen her, or had even spoken to her? Four years. Nearer to five.

She had called him, about a week after *Paradise Here* was released. In New York on a publicity tour, she invited him to have dinner with her at her suite at the Plaza. The food was superb, paid for by the movie company, and afterwards they got pleasantly high and made love. She stayed in New York for three days and they slept together every night, and the sex was as good as it had ever been. But when she left, he was glad.

That was the last time he saw Betsy. She phoned once, after receiving star billing in *Happy Life, Lover*; something about a tax problem, wanting to know whether he still claimed her as a dependent. That was before the divorce was final. With all the money she was now making, Betsy had learned to concern herself with financial matters. Perhaps, had she considered his economics with equal fervor during the marriage, he pondered, there might never have been a divorce. But gradually he had come to know better.

"I think the pressure's getting to him."

Pompey's eyes rolled open. For a brief moment, he couldn't remember where he was. Gradually, Gail came into focus, standing in the center of the room, gazing down at him expectantly. She was wearing a long green velour robe that heightened the grape-green of her eyes. He reached for her. She avoided his hand, moved toward the kitchen.

"What the hell is wrong?" he muttered, heaving himself erect, going after her. She arranged cups and saucers on the round, white-formica table and poured the coffee. They sat across from each other.

"I thought the President was going to battle for ratification," she said finally.

"He is."

"From the way he talked tonight, I'd say the fix is on."

"Very funny." He sipped the coffee. It was hot and, as usual, too weak. He lit a cigarette. "Tonight was a mistake. Okay. We all make them. The strain is too much. That job is a killer." He brightened briefly. "Tomorrow he'll probably phone Sokoloff and apologize, sweet-talk him dizzy. Let's face it, everybody knows Gunther's always been conciliatory toward the Russians, sympathetic to their problems. Sokoloff knows it, too. So does Grishin."

"Maybe. But it looked as if Sokoloff was about to erupt this evening." She sipped her coffee, made a face. "I can write a fine feature story, drive any car ever made, ski like a pro, play a fair game of tennis, and I broke one hundred my first time on a golf course. Why can't I make good coffee?"

"It's fine," he said automatically. His mind reached back to a scene he had witnessed a week earlier. He had been invited to breakfast with the President in the oval study adjoining his quarters to discuss editorial reactions to the defense pact. Toward the end of the meal, the mess attendant had accidentally spilled some coffee. Gunther had barely been touched on the back of one hand. His reaction, immediate and violent, had startled Pompey. He had leaped erect, snarling obscenities at the frightened man, ordering him out of the room.

"I've always felt that the man in the White House," Gail was saying, "whoever he was, was a special sort of person, with special intellectual and emotional equipment, keen insights, highly disciplined, always able to maintain his sense of balance."

"Gunther's not Superman."

"Right. And it's naïve to expect him to be. Maybe I want Big Brother taking care of the country, so the rest of us don't have to worry." She sipped her coffee. "Tonight, Guy. *That* frightened me. He was saying things I believe shouldn't be said in public. For a minute there, I had the feeling that he wanted to destroy the treaty."

"Ridiculous. It's *his* treaty."

"The President I saw tonight was different from the public man we've come to know, different from the private man you've described to me, a stranger, another person."

"Another person," he repeated scornfully. "You and Hank Luplow should compare notes. The moment the President doesn't come up to your expectations both of you begin to see ghosts."

"How did Hank get into this?" she said easily. "All I'm saying is that the President acts differently."

A faint throbbing came into being behind his left eye. It grew more intense. He blamed it on too much champagne. He wanted to turn off his mind, to stop thinking, and wished Gail would end this pointless conversation.

She smiled reminiscently, went on softly. "When I was an undergraduate at Michigan, there was a boy named Telfer who had a twin, a student at the University of Illinois. Identical, both of them. The same size, coloring, everything. One semester, after Easter vacation, they decided to switch, change campuses, each assuming the other's identity."

"Oh," he said automatically.

"They went to each other's classes, spent time with each other's friends, even dated each other's girls. Everything." She paused.

"And?"

"It worked out fine," she said evenly. "No one ever knew."

"I see." He looked at her. "How did you find out?"

She returned his gaze with no change of expression. "Freddy. The one who really belonged at Michigan told me, after they switched back."

He started to ask her a question, thought better of it and fell silent. "Well," he said, "the President doesn't have a twin." He laughed uneasily. "At least, I don't think he does."

After a while they began to talk again, absently, trying to bridge the uncomfortable silent gaps, so larded with stress. In time the gaps became more extended, occurring more frequently, and their verbal efforts grew increasingly awkward. At last Gail rose and carried the dishes to the sink and rinsed them. She spoke without turning.

"Are you staying?"

In tone and content, the question disturbed him. He went over to her, placed his hands on her narrow waist, feeling the soft beginnings of her round hips. He kissed the back of her neck.

"It sounds as if you wouldn't mind if I left."

She walked out of the kitchen. "That's up to you."

He trailed her into the bedroom, watched as she turned down the bed. They were both tired, he told himself, and this was not the time for a serious discussion. Besides, it all came down to one thing: she wanted to get married and he didn't.

"We won't talk about it now," he said.

She stripped off the robe and turned to face him. As always, when he saw her naked, desire skittered along his nerves. And now in the soft glow of the Tiffany lamp—the loving lamp, they called it—he wanted her very much. She moved toward the bed, tall and graceful, belly a gentle curve, the taut flesh gleaming. She lay down and pulled the covers to her shoulders.

"You know how I feel, Guy," she said. "You don't want the same things I want. You prefer this arrangement. It suits your needs. You have all the conveniences and you're still free to come as you wish."

"That's not fair. There's been no one else."

"It might be better if there was."

"I don't understand you." The Tartar eyes seemed unusually bright and he hoped she wasn't going to cry. "You mustn't crowd me, Gail," he said quietly.

"It was so good when we first met, Guy. I needed a man like you."

He misunderstood. "An older man, you mean?" The words came out waspishly; lately the fifteen-year difference in their ages had begun to trouble him.

"A man who was patient," she replied softly. "And understanding, who was able to wait until I felt safe and could learn to be a woman. You were so handsome and I was so proud to be your girl." Her eyes closed, and a small, sad smile came onto her mouth. She looked up at him. She was crying, soundlessly, trying to suppress the tears, knowing that any emotional display upset him. He took a step toward her. "No," she said quickly, wiping at her eyes. "You did a fine job, darling. But now I am a woman and I want everything a woman is entitled to. You won't, or can't, or don't want to give me those things."

"Do you mean you want to end it? Now? This way?"

A sigh expired on her full mouth. "I'm saying that I want to get married to a man who will love me and give me babies. You don't understand about babies, Guy, about how much a woman can want to have children."

"I'm sorry," he said. "I just don't feel ready."

She shifted into a sitting position and the covers fell away, exposing her breasts. "I wasn't going to tell you," she said. "I was just going to break it off between us, to go away and have it done by myself, like pulling a tooth. A slight unpleasantness that must be attended to. I've already made some inquiries."

A fluttering fear came alive in his gut, spread quickly. He was angry suddenly, resentful, and wanted to strike out.

"What the hell are you talking about?"

"I thought about it and decided it wasn't right. I owed it to myself and to you to tell you."

The throbbing behind his eyes grew worse and he blinked in a futile attempt to ease the pressure. "What are you trying to say?"

"I'm pregnant, Guy. I'm going to have your baby."

Later, much later, when time had dulled the memory and the impact of her words, there would be a variety of reactions on his part; but in that moment he responded viscerally, aware that in her belly was a life that his seed had created, and he was proud. He embraced her and made small reassuring sounds; after a moment she began to tremble and the tears came. It was a long time before she stopped crying. She wiped her cheeks and blew her nose while he lit cigarettes for both of them.

"I'm sorry," she said, trying to smile. "It's my fault. I was careless."

"You're sure?"

She nodded. "I went to the doctor. The tests are positive." Her voice was girlish, her smile brief and penitent. "I'm sorry."

"There's nothing to be sorry about. I'm not." He made himself smile at her. "Looks as if we're going to get married after all."

She shook her head from side to side. "No. No, I couldn't do that. Not this way. I know us both too well. You'd always resent me, and the baby." She cut short his protests. "And I'd never be sure that you really loved me, really wanted to marry me. There's only one thing to do. I'll get an abortion."

A dark, swinging terror broke over him, a surging sickness, mingled with relief. "I hate the idea . . ."

"So do I," she said calmly. "But it's the only way for us. Now," she went on solemnly, as if all problems had been solved, all decisions made, holding out her arms to him, "will you please take off thosc silly clothes and come to bed and make love to me." She giggled and lowered herself into a more comfortable position, tossing the covers aside. "There's nothing to worry about now."

Somehow, crazily, it was better than it had been for so very long, wild and free, a soaring excursion into nearly forgotten regions, a passionate advance up a steep incline, and finally the peak, a compulsive, lingering spasm of pure sensation. He lay in her arms, warming himself against her firm flesh, sluggish in the embrace of a misty gratification, distantly aware that for him no better woman could possibly exist, knowing at the same time that he wanted to continue the search.

Two

A Question of Policy

I

Ralph Jacobs left the British Embassy alone. He settled into the deep back seat of the Defense Department limousine while the chauffeur circled the Naval Observatory to Wisconsin Avenue, drove south to Georgetown. Jacobs stared sightlessly into the darkness as he reviewed what had passed between the President and Ambassador Sokoloff.

A public display was out of character for Harrison Gunther, and was in Jacobs' estimation unforgivable, a disservice to the nation. Yet how significant was it? Presidential outbursts were hardly unknown in Washington: Truman had erupted in public on more than one occasion; Eisenhower and Johnson had owned monumental tempers, though both men had concealed them in public. Gunther had done likewise, until recently; his equanimity in the face of the most extreme provocation was a strong point, and his patient intelligence in winning the opposition to his position had evoked wide respect for his diplomatic and political skills. In recent weeks, Jacobs could recall a gradual lessening of restraint—obsessive outbursts at Cabinet meetings or during the weekly gatherings of the National Security Council. There was a smoldering impatience in the President these days that erupted with increasing frequency. As for this night's tantrum—and Jacobs found it impossible to use a softer word—surely it was the most damaging, so lacking in purpose. No President could afford that kind of self-indulgence, Jacobs decided unhappily.

And Soviet espionage. Surely this was a matter for the Secretary of Defense, yet he had received no prior information. Could this be Marshall's doing? There was no love lost between the Director of the FBI and himself, but he was convinced Marshall would not permit personal differences to influence his official attitudes. Such a lack of procedural orthodoxy was bothersome.

Jacob's thinking advanced with a precise orderliness. He dealt with ideas as if they were figures, adding and subtracting with unhurried thoroughness, never making an arbitrary decision—action always the end product of the objective processing of all available data.

He extracted a small notebook—the kind that could be purchased in any stationery store for a dime—from his inside pocket and began to enter his observations, printing swiftly and neatly in lower case. By the time the limousine turned into the street where he lived, Jacobs had completed his note-making. The car slid to a smooth stop and he waited for the chauffeur to open the door.

Jacobs enjoyed living in Georgetown with its visible symbols of tradition, its respect for what was good in the past. The distinctive character of the district was strictly maintained; no high-rise apartment buildings were permitted and commercial enterprises were rigidly zoned. This street, with its red-brick, smooth-fronted houses of the Federal period, reflected a quiet graciousness, so different from Jacobs' beginnings in the noisy and crowded streets off Southern Boulevard in the East Bronx.

That neighborhood had been almost exclusively Jewish in those days—which had changed nothing for the boy. Jew among Jews; Jew among Gentiles; it had all been the same to him. But not to others. He had been criticized for behavior that was either too Jewish or not Jewish enough.

The way of the world, he had decided during those early years, was to label and categorize—intellectual short cuts. In that regard, he saw little difference between life in the highest echelons of government and diplomacy in Washington, and the way it had been in the East Bronx. Here too men sought easy ways to circumnavigate thought and understanding.

The three-story house in Georgetown with its walled-in garden was a sanctuary against all that. A quiet, private place to be. It was a pleasant place to live and, sometimes, late at night, when it became difficult to sleep, he would stroll through the narrow streets down to the Potomac, or over to the University, pleased to be a part of this tradition, to play a role in the continuing history of his country.

He went up to his third floor bedroom and undressed. Clad in white pajamas and a blue silk robe, he padded across the hallway to his study. By the soft glow of the desk lamp, he poured his nightly snifter of Courvoisier. Next, he removed a thin brown cigar from the humidor on the desk and—copy of the *Racing Form* in hand—settled into the big maroon leather chair. He sucked contentedly on the cigar, smoke drifting about his head, and allowed himself a tantalizing sip of the brandy. He put the glass aside and began to dope out the next day's winners at the various eastern tracks.

Jacobs never actually bet his choices, but he found it relaxing to pit his mind against the odds. And he considered himself something of an expert, basing his selections on the times turned in by the various mounts at the tracks in question. Horses-for-courses was his handicapping philosophy, and he owned the record to show for it.

On this night he found it difficult to concentrate, and after a while he put the racing paper aside, took another taste of the brandy. All this was designed to help him relax, to wash away the tensions of the day. Tonight it didn't work and he became acutely aware of the dark silence of the house.

He lived alone, and preferred it that way most of the time. But there were moments when he craved the presence, the attention and concern of another human being. He considered such yearnings clear evidence that he had not yet learned to fully control himself, signs of weakness—as were the stomach pains that sometimes kept him awake.

This was the only time of the day that he allowed himself either alcohol or tobacco. He enjoyed both, but discovered during his early manhood that they interfered with his concentration and control; and so he rationed himself accordingly, a program from which he had never deviated. One drink and one cigar before bed. Never more.

Again he began to sift the events of the day that had begun in the President's office that morning. And again instinct warned that something was wrong; a fragment of the puzzle out of place; it was being forced to fit. He went into his bedroom and studied the entries in his notebook. The facts were clear enough; but what did they mean? He returned to the study and picked up the telephone, dialed. It rang six times before the familiar rasping voice came on.

"Yes."

There was no timidity in that single word, only the crisp sound of competence. Jacobs liked that about Harvey Gordon. The Defense Intelligence Agency man was economical in deed and word. He wasn't the most creative of men, but then imagination was seldom required of him in his work; he was a technician, highly trained and efficient, an intelligence agent able to perform as needed, a mechanic first, a man only then—the perfect spy. Jacobs found it incongruous to consider a life for Gordon outside his work, to think of him as having ambitions and dreams of a private nature. Yet surely that was the case. There was a wife, Jacobs knew, and two children, both boys; but Gordon as a husband and father created no particular impact.

"I wake you, Harvey?" Jacobs asked.

"Yes, Mr. Secretary. You did."

Jacobs grunted under his breath and sucked on the cigar. It had gone out.

He reached for the box of kitchen matches. "At the British Embassy tonight," he lit the cigar, went on, "the President and Sokoloff went round and round."

"I heard."

"What do you know about this Russian espionage apparatus?"

"Nothing."

"Nor do I, Harvey. And that troubles me. If the DIA possessed such information, the Secretary of Defense would be told, wouldn't he?"

"Yes, sir. At least, that's the way things have been up till now."

"This thing bothers me, Harvey."

"And me, Mr. Secretary. All field reports come across my desk. I've seen nothing on this case."

"Could the FBI have worked on this without informing the DIA?"

"Possibly, but it's unlikely. There's conflict between our agency and the CIA over preeminence in certain areas. But there's no trouble with Marshall's people."

"Besides," Jacobs said, "I have a private pipeline into the FBI."

"I know."

Jacobs couldn't keep the surprise out of his voice. "How do you know?"

"My private pipeline informed me, sir."

Jacobs grunted. "Yet neither of us heard a word. I'm unhappy, Harvey, to be excluded from anything this vital. Would you like to scout around, see what's happening?"

"Will do."

"If this could happen without DIA knowing, Harvey, we'll have to take steps to upgrade the agency."

There was an extended silence as both men considered the situation. The DIA had spread an efficient network of trained operatives throughout the world, yet now it appeared as if a major weakness had been revealed in its own back yard. The irony of the situation was not lost on Jacobs. Nor the danger.

"Anything else?" Gordon said.

"The Mars shot. The President seems to think it may have been misdirected via an outside radio signal. Get a reading from the scientific people, here and overseas."

"Right."

"And, Harvey, be quick about it."

"Yes, sir," Gordon said. He hung up.

Jacobs went back to his chair and his brandy. He appreciated Harvey Gordon, perhaps more than any other man he knew, felt closest to him. Which was odd, he thought, for they seldom saw each other, and then only in an official capacity. Perhaps that was the basis of the feeling, the perfect blending of their talents and professional need of each other. Nothing else interfered.

Long ago Jacobs had organized his life to exclude personal entanglements, to eliminate debilitating emotional relatonships. He had no friends and wanted none. Oh, there were times when he speculated idly on what it would be like to truly care for another person, and to be cared for in return, to be able to confide in someone, to reveal his private fears. Perhaps even to cry. How long had it been since he had shed any tears? His mind easily spanned the years to the time when he had lived with Mendelsohn. There had been a Mrs. Mendelsohn, but she hadn't mattered. Only Mendelsohn had left an impression.

Jacobs had been eight years old, and on this particular day he had come running back to that dismal Simpson Street apartment crying, his mouth cut and swollen, nose bleeding, humiliated in a fight with an older boy.

Mendelsohn had asked for no explanation, had offered no sympathy. Instead, his great, fleshy hand shot out, landing heavily on the boy's cheek, hurting much more than any blow taken in the fight.

"Do what you want," Mendelsohn said. "Kill yourself, for all I care. But don't cry to me. The noise gives me a headache."

Jacobs never cried again.

Jacobs extracted a still, private pride from the knowledge of how far he had traveled since then. Mendelsohn, and all the others who had offered nothing, given nothing—were they still alive? He hoped so. He hoped they all knew what Ralph Jacobs had accomplished.

By *himself.*

Always alone. There had been no older brother or father to help. Nor anyone else. Jacobs had never known his parents, and his first memory was of an aunt, broad-shouldered and forbidding, with black, accusing eyes. His presence had never pleased her and she soon arranged for him to live in a succession of foster homes, for a price; and in none of them was he ever offered an embrace or a kiss or a word of affection or encouragement. The world, he decided before long, was a place where each person had to look out for his own interests, depend only upon the equipment, the few talents with which he might be gifted. He began to analyze himself, anxious to discover those areas where he could function best.

In time he realized that he owned a singular skill with numbers. There was an order to them that he approved of; the sums always made sense. Before his sixteenth year, he began working in an accountant's office, checking tax returns. Within a year, it was generally agreed that Jacobs was the sharpest tax man in the firm. At twenty-one, though lacking even a high school diploma, Jacobs owned his own accountancy firm, employing six people, all college graduates, including the secretary. There was a certain amount of satisfaction in this, but not so much that he failed to recognize the advantages of formal education. He then went back to high school, graduated, and enrolled at City College. It took eight years of night classes, but he got his degree.

This done, he selected the hardest-working, most unimaginative of his accountants, a man with limited prospects for the future, and presented him with a twenty-five-percent share in the company, trusting him to oversee the day-to-day affairs of the business. Two weeks later, Jacobs attended his first class at the Columbia University School of Law.

Seven years later, Jacobs was a partner in a Wall

Street law firm which recognized his commitment to hard work, appreciated his attention to detail, his ranging imagination. Clearly, Ralph Jacobs was a man with a mission.

Also, a nervous stomach.

Jacobs never learned how to make friends, or to take pleasure outside of his work but he did teach himself to draw up an unbreakable contract, to spot flaws in any brief prepared by another lawyer—and to recognize the hidden economic potential of companies long dormant and considered worthless.

So it was that on his thirty-eighth birthday, Jacobs gave himself a gift—he bought a dilapidated machine-tool factory for a down payment of only twenty thousand dollars, plus a short-term bank loan for an additional eighty thousand. Two years later, he refused to sell the factory for two million dollars; instead he went public.

With the money from the stock issue, he began to diversify: electronics, plastics, hardware. He made changes, merged less successful operations with other companies, using the strengths of one firm to shore up the weaknesses of another. When his electronics company developed a transistorized fire-control system smaller but more efficient than any other then on the market, Jacobs began doing business with the Department of Defense.

The generals with whom he dealt considered him a strange one. He refused to court them, to supply them with women, to entertain them, insisting that the products he made sold themselves. And he was right. He rode herd on his managers until they produced higher quality merchandise for sale at lower prices; generals continued to resent his blunt manner, but they were obliged to do business with him. As his reputation for honesty and reliability spread, he accumulated a number of enemies, but he also acquired one important admirer, Harrison Leo Gunther, then junior Senator from Missouri, and a most vocal member of the Senate Armed Forces Subcommittee. One week after the election, Jacobs received an invitation to meet with the President-elect at his winter home in Key West.

"You're going to be my Secretary of Defense," Gunther began.

Jacobs liked that approach, and he was complimented. But he wasn't looking for that kind of trouble. He thanked Gunther and refused the job.

"Why?" Gunther stared at him, those lambent brown eyes unblinking, curious, anxious to hear Jacobs' arguments, prepared to eliminate them one by one.

"I'd cause trouble, for myself, and for you. I think you'll be a good president, maybe a great one. I'd get in your way. People don't take to me, especially politicians."

Gunther had grinned that crooked grin of his and Jacobs found it almost impossible not to smile back. "Jacobs, I want a man to run Defense who will demand quality from the contractors, and from the military, too. Someone to keep those generals in line, a secretary who can face up to nosy politicians, tell them off, and make it stick. I believe you're the man to do it. What do you believe?"

Jacobs did grin then. "I believe you're right."

Those first six months were tumultous, unsettling, nothing like it ever having been seen before around the Pentagon. Sacred cows were put to pasture, myths laid to rest, shibboleths shattered. Officers settled behind comfortable desks were shipped out to field jobs; men with a propensity for playing it safe were uprooted; systems were modified, traditions broken, classifications changed; purchasing methods were streamlined and tight price controls instituted, with multiple checks. Shrill objections went up all over the country, from post commanders, from the Reserves, from defense manufacturers, from Capitol Hill. Seven times during that period Jacobs was hauled before the Senate Armed Services Committee, twice in executive session, to account for his actions. He was assailed with opinion and history and patriotism and passion. None of it did much good.

The senators found that he came well armed, his brain an inexhaustible storehouse of information, of statistics, of facts, his logic irrefutable, almost obsessively thorough. There were some who characterized him as arrogant and opinionated; Jacobs never faltered, never became ruffled, responded always in the same detached way, his words considered, saying only what he chose to say, exactly what he meant, indicating the flaws in his opponents' positions, supporting his policies, turning aside the conveyed wrath of those generals and admirals to whom the military establishment had long been a private province.

And in the end, politicians, top brass, and citizens, all learned that the Department of Defense was again under civilian control and that civilian's name was Ralph Jacobs. No one else.

Jacobs swallowed the last of the Courvoisier in the snifter. He would have liked another drink, but denied himself, fighting against a rising loneliness. It was the price paid for becoming the kind of man he was, self-sufficient, isolated, dependent only on himself. There were times—and this was one of them—when he wondered whether or not the price was excessive. The phone ended his ruminations. It was Alton Miller, Chairman of the JCS.

"Sorry to disturb you at this hour, Mr. Secretary," Miller said.

Jacobs was grateful for the interruption. "What's on your mind, Alton?"

"I'm sorry, sir," Miller said. There was an apologetic whine in his usually crisp voice. "Would it be possible for us to talk, Mr. Secretary?"

"Now?"

"It's important, sir. Something's happened and I don't understand."

Jacobs crushed out his cigar. "Where are you, Alton?"

"At the Pentagon, sir. I could come to you."

"Stay there. I'll be along as soon as I can. Your office."

Jacobs dressed quickly, sorry that he'd dismissed

the chauffeur. He'd have to drive the Buick himself and he disliked driving. He took some small consolation in the lateness of the hour—traffic would be light.

He headed into Virginia over the Key Bridge and south on the Mount Vernon Highway, considering Alton Miller. The general had been *his* man, his nominee for Chairman of the JCS. And equally the President's choice. Much decorated as a company commander during World War II, Miller had led an infantry regiment in Korea and commanded a division in Vietnam. His grasp of strategy and his ability to lead and inspire men had stamped him early as an officer of infinite potential.

To Jacobs, Miller was more than a first-rate military man. He owned a solid understanding of global realities, understood that war, as a political weapon, as an extension of national ambition, was obsolete, that a soldier's primary task had become defensive, always seeking to widen the peace. During his slightly more than two years as chairman, Miller had become a bulwark against the entrenched establishment within the military who still viewed the world in prenuclear terms.

Moonlight sparkled off the Potomac as Jacobs pulled the Buick into the Pentagon lot near the river entrance. He was oblivious to the sight, as he was to the institutional plainness of the Pentagon itself with those endless rows of windows marching around its five sides. Had he wished, Jacobs could have recited a litany of statistics about the huge structure: sixty percent of the personnel working in it were civilians; there were 280 rest rooms and 1,900 toilets; each of the sides was 921 feet long; and each day more than 270,000 calls came over 24,000 telephones. There was more.

The guard at the reception desk snapped to attention as Jacobs strode through one of the tall wooden doors, nodding his recognition. The Secretary continued swiftly down the long corridor, shoulders characteristically thrust forward, rubber heels beating a sibilant rhythm on the highly polished floor, until he came to the E Ring offices of the Joint Chiefs of Staff. Here admittance was by authorized credentials only. He displayed his to the man on duty, then moved on to Alton Miller's office.

The general, beribboned blouse properly buttoned, came to attention when Jacobs appeared. The Secretary settled himself into a chair in front of the huge desk.

"Alton, it's past two o'clock. Sit down and stop playing soldier."

Miller nodded and his shoulders slumped. As Jacobs watched, that ruggedly masculine face, like seamed and weathered copper, appeared to melt, all color drained off, grown old suddenly. A nerve began to twitch in the pouched skin under his right eye. He rubbed it instinctively.

"Sorry to drag you out at——"

"Alton, you look terrible. What's going on?"

Miller's eyes darted about, lighting nowhere. "About an hour ago. The President called me about an hour ago. You see, I was here working on the Chinese Contingency Program in terms of our deep-water antimissile system, the Pacific Perimeter. There are some bugs that I'm concerned——"

"Get on with it, Alton. The President called you. About what?"

Miller couldn't hold his gaze. "He demanded my resignation as Chairman of the Joint Chiefs. Effective immediately."

Jacobs hadn't expected that. What had he expected? Some kind of special report, perhaps. Or information for the new budget. A complaint over some real or fancied military shortcoming. But to fire Alton Miller! The announcement stirred a dark fear in Jacobs' private heart.

"What did he say?"

"He gave no reason. Only that he considered it in the national interest. I was stunned. I couldn't speak. I stuttered like a frightened schoolboy."

Jacobs searched his brain for some possible explanation. "Was there any warning that something like this was in the wind?"

"No."

"Anything you said? Some speech, maybe. Something in opposition to Administration policy."

"Nothing."

"And he gave no explanation?"

"None."

"Did he say who he intends to appoint in your place?"

"Only that he wants my resignation in the morning."

Jacobs suppressed an oath. "Not before I talk to him. I want to know what this is about. Dammit, he's the boss, but I don't like this kind of thing happening to my people. There has to be a good reason. There has to be." He went to the door, turned back. "Alton, you keep this quiet until I've talked to him. I'll be in touch with you tomorrow."

"Yes, sir."

Jacobs hurried along the corridor to his own office, leafed through his secretary's directory until he found the home number of Bill O'Brien, the President's Appointments Secretary. O'Brien came on sleepy and annoyed.

"This is Ralph Jacobs, Bill."

The annoyance drained away. "Yes, sir. How may I help you, Mr. Secretary?"

"I want to see the President, first thing tomorrow."

There was a pause and Jacobs envisioned O'Brien reaching for his appointment schedule. "Well, about tomorrow. A particularly bad——"

"I *must* see him, O'Brien." There was no mistaking the hard edge in Jacobs' voice.

O'Brien cleared his throat. "I suppose I could squeeze you in before breakfast. Lately, he's been taking an early morning swim."

"What time?"

"Seven-thirty. I'll leave word at the West Gate."

"Good."

"I can let you have only about ten minutes, Mr.

Secretary," O'Brien said apologetically. "Senator McCandless is coming for breakfast and . . ." Jacobs hung up.

He drove slowly back to Washington, across the Arlington Bridge. He was confused and troubled. Fire Alton Miller? Why? The absence of logic was offensive. Something was going on about which he was ignorant, and that bothered him. He strained to solve the riddle, only to come up empty.

At the Lincoln Memorial, he impulsively braked the Buick to sit gazing at the floodlit monument, so impressive in its magnificent simplicity. Tomorrow, thousands of tourists would mount those wide steps, past those fluted Doric columns, to stand before the huge statue of Lincoln; would any of them make a meaningful connection between that brooding stone portrait and their own lives?

He looked out at the reflecting pool which stretched in the direction of the Washington Monument. Jacobs had come to love this city with its statues and memorials, all reminders of the country's growth and change, of its living strength—the first city in the world designed expressly to be a nation's capital. He considered it to be the most beautiful of cities, and at this time of year particularly, for spring brought not only the cherry blossoms, but a host of other blooms, to perfume the air and color the landscape. Yet it was also a city that kept people strangers, and at that moment he was acutely aware of his own apartness.

He reached for the ignition and saw the woman. She was alone, advancing slowly, her expression serene in the reflected light. Her glance swung toward him, and as she came abreast of the Buick she paused, leaned forward, smiling. It was a pleasant face, unspectacular, but with a beauty of its own, the mouth generous, the eyes silently offering.

"Hello," she said.

"Good evening." He arranged himself so that his face was in the shadows. It would not do for the Secretary of Defense to be seen with a streetwalker.

"We're both alone, it seems."

"I'm on my way home," he said formally. The scent of her drifted into his nostrils and he experienced a sudden yearning, a swift emptiness.

"To your wife?"

"I'm not married."

"Neither am I. Not anymore." Her smile was wistful. "Perhaps you would appreciate some company. My company."

He took a long breath. No one need know. She was a pleasant woman and it had been so long. He deserved some satisfaction, some relief. He was about to invite her into the Buick when he remembered the single cigar he allowed himself each evening, the one brandy, and he knew that he would not indulge himself to this extent.

"You're kind," he said, an efficient briskness coming into his voice. "But I must go."

She drew back. "It could have been so nice." There was a sad note in her voice that he put down to professional disappointment. He released the brake and drove back to the house in Georgetown alone.

II

The President stroked powerfully back and forth across the small basement pool that Franklin Delano Roosevelt had built. He moved easily through the water, arms and legs meshing smoothly. Jacobs stood at the edge of the pool watching, admiring the coordinated effort, the admiration of a nonswimmer for one who has conquered an alien environment. He made a silent vow to someday master his fear of the water.

The President heaved himself out of the pool, toweled his wet skin vigorously. He was lean, his shoulders broad and strong, bands of muscle ridging his torso. He was in every way, Jacobs told himself, an exceptional man.

"You swim well, Mr. President," the Defense Secretary said.

"My only exercise these days. Never enough time, I'm afraid." He shoved his feet into a pair of wooden clogs. "Well, Jacobs, what crisis brings you down here so early?"

Jacobs made a conscious effort to smother the unrest that slithered along his nerves. A Secret Service agent extended a blue terrycloth robe to the President. He put it on and started toward the elevator.

"General Miller tells me that you asked for his resignation as Chairman of the Joint Chiefs."

Jacobs trailed the President into the narrow elevator. The crowded, mirrored proportions of the lift accentuated the physical contrast of the two men, the one tall and casually elegant, the other a head shorter and neatly unprepossessing. The differences were lost to neither of them.

In the bedroom of the third-floor living quarters, the President tossed the robe over a chair and stripped off his swimming trunks.

"Miller's out."

"Why?"

"He's the wrong man for the job." Gunther disappeared into the bathroom and a moment later the tattoo of the shower made conversation impossible. Jacobs waited until he returned and began to dress himself.

"I don't understand. When the appointment was made, we both agreed Miller was the ideal man for the job. As recently as last month you commented on what a good choice it had been. What has happened that disqualifies Miller now?"

"I've talked with him, privately, in the last few weeks. His opinions and my own no longer jibe. I want a Chairman with whom I see eye-to-eye."

Jacobs withheld comment. The President had often spoken of the disadvantages of not limiting his advisers to men who agreed with him, claiming it was the nay-sayers who extended him to the limits of his resources, forcing him to exercise his imagination fully. Now this.

"And frankly," the President was saying, "I think Miller's lost the confidence of the Joint Chiefs."

"My impression is to the contrary."

His shoelaces tied, Gunther straightened up, one corner of his mouth tugging up in that crooked grin. "Okay, Ralph, you want to know why I'm firing Miller and you're entitled to know. It's the Pacific Perimeter. He's totally committed to the project, gone on record before Congress and in the press. Only last week he sounded off about it on TV, said it was the single most important item in the upcoming defense budget, said that not to erect the perimeter was tantamount to committing national suicide."

"So?"

"So this." The President's face sobered, the brown

eyes steady, the voice toughly thin. "I have decided to scrap the entire project."

Jacobs reacted instinctively. "You can't do that!"

The President issued each word with tough emphasis. "The . . . hell . . . I . . . can't." He turned to the mirror over the ancient Victorian bureau and began to knot his tie. When he spoke again, the easy warmth had returned to his voice. "See my point of view, Ralph. The perimeter is superfluous. When you think about it, really think about it, you begin to understand that it is based on a false premise. First, it's too damned expensive. Billions of dollars planted in the continental shelf to no purpose. And it's strategically unnecessary. Face it, Ralph, the Chinese aren't about to launch a long-range missile attack against us. Which means that such a complicated and costly defense system would waste time, manpower and money, diverting us from the real danger. It's Moscow we have to worry about."

Miscellaneous information flashed through Jacobs' mind. It was Harrison Gunther's enthusiasm that had turned the idea for an underwater antimissile missile barrier along the West Coast into a distinct reality. It had become feasible with the perfection of the Hummingbird rocket, which operated on a sound-heat-light principle that made it the most reliable weapon in the American arsenal, able to home in on any target, no matter how swift it was or how high it flew, within a matter of seconds. Work on the Pacific Perimeter had been scheduled to begin in August and once the Hummingbirds were in their nests, the United States would be virtually immune from missile attack.

"We know," the President was saying, "that, popular opinion to the contrary, the Chinese lack the ICBM capabilities to launch a missile attack against us. We have little to fear from them. The Pacific project would mean erecting barricades when there's no chance of the Indians attacking from that direction." He swung around, expression set. "Miller refused to be convinced and continued to come out *for* the perimeter. I see no reason to tolerate opposition at that level." He put on his jacket and headed for the door, Jacobs following.

They entered the President's office through the secretarial cubicle. Sarah Harris trailed them inside.

"Are you ready for me?" she said.

"Not quite, Sarah," the President said, taking his place behind the big desk. "Is General Quirk here?"

"In the reception room."

"Send him in." The President snapped his fingers to Ketza; the sled dog heaved himself erect without enthusiasm and padded across the oval room, raising his massive head searchingly. The President scratched absently at the dog's ears. "Good morning, General," he said, as Quirk entered, resplendent in a custom-tailored uniform studded with battle ribbons.

"Mr. President. Mr. Secretary."

"Sit down, gentlemen, please."

Jacobs settled into a chair, trying to inhibit his emotions, to clarify his thinking, anxious not to anticipate, yet certain he knew what lay ahead.

"Mr. President," he began.

"Mr. Secretary," the President mimicked, and laughed shortly. "Ralph, I assume you intend to hold to your enthusiasm for the Pacific venture."

Jacobs hesitated, decided to plunge right in. "If I do, will you ask for my resignation?"

That laugh came again, a humorless sound that ended abruptly. "You're the best Defense Secretary since McNamara, Ralph. Everybody says so. Said so myself many times. Now, how would it look if I fired you? No, you'd make too tough an enemy. I want you to continue in the job, Ralph, to give me your support. I need it." He leaned forward and there was a boyish helplessness in his face, a silent plea that evoked concern and sympathy. It reminded Jacobs that the President always had been a difficult man to resist. "Look at it this way—I'm convinced I was mistaken about the Chinese and equally mistaken vis-à-vis the Soviets. Moscow still can't be trusted."

Jacobs shook his head as if to clear it. "The Russians have made clear overtures for an end to the cold war, for a meaningful peace."

"Propaganda. They're not reliable allies and break any agreement when it suits their mood. Only by opposing them do we advance the cause of freedom. Wouldn't you agree, General?"

"The Russians always violatc their treaties, sir. That's traditional. I never trusted them. Never." It was said with pride.

Jacobs ignored the general, aware of his frozen political views. "The Mutual Defense Pact which you promulgated . . ."

The President shrugged. He made a steeple of his fingers and gazed into infinity. Ketza, too long ignored, lumbered apathetically to his place along the far wall and collapsed with a sigh. "Why should I believe Grishin will respect this pact any more than he has other treaties? The Kremlin tears up any agreement when they think they can get away with something."

"Mr. Secretary," General Quirk put in, voice smugly satisfied, "information from our intelligence community warns us that the Russians, hope to suck us off balance. They'd like us to lower our guard, to fall into a euphoric condition so that when they embark on their next set of aggressive moves we will be in no position to oppose them."

Jacobs measured the Air Force officer. To him, Quirk personified the worst kind of a career soldier. His strong point was limitless energy and he used it to overwhelm people rather than persuade, to outlast them if not outflank them. He owned no imagination and Jacobs was certain that he hadn't had an original idea since he joined the military.

"Perhaps, General," Jacobs said, "you have information which I don't receive."

"Now, Ralph," the President interrupted. "Let's keep ego out of this. Quirk is a soldier trying to do his duty. Patriotism is not a bad word around this house these days."

"Thank you, Mr. President," Quirk said.

The President smiled briefly.

Jacobs selected his words carefully. "No such intelligence reports have come across my desk. Nor is there any objective reason to suspect the Russians of anything but sincere intentions. The active threat to world peace today, as it has been for many years, is an overly aggressive China."

"I hesitate to contradict the Secretary," General Quirk said, "but China has made no overt moves in our direction. Let's face it, the Chinaman never put troops into the field in Vietnam, and he crossed into Korea only when MacArthur threatened his border at the Yalu."

"Nonsense, General. Such an approach ignores the indirect hostility of the Peking regime. You make no mention of their savagery in Tibet, or their continued violations of the Indian border, or of the hundreds of confrontations between Chinese and Russians along the Manchurian frontier."

Quirk laughed, a loud, harsh sound. "Well, don't expect me to get mad over those two dogs fighting."

"I agree with General Quirk," the President said. "His position finds wide support among the top military people and in the highest echelons of industry, as well as with some of our diplomats whose thinking I prize most highly."

"Does this mean you don't intend to continue fighting for ratification?" Jacobs said quietly.

The President stared at the Washington portrait above the fireplace. "The treaty stands for itself. I'm certain the Senate will give it the consideration it merits."

None of this seemed real to Jacobs, but as though seen through a shattered glass, a remote witness to a carefully practiced charade.

"The treaty is a good one," he said. "Premier Grishin wants it. He's proved that he intends to live up to its provisions by granting on-site inspection of nuclear plants and missile pads. He fears Peking even more than we do."

"As *you* do, Jacobs," the President said.

There was a note in his voice that sliced through the Defense Secretary's defenses and triggered ancient unnamed terrors. Jacobs broke sweat. "About General Miller . . ." he said.

The President stood up. "That's settled. Miller's out. I'm appointing Quirk to be the new Chairman of the JCS. I expect you will indicate to the press that you are pleased with the appointment. Thank you for coming by this morning, Mr. Secretary. It's always instructive to listen to your views. . . ."

Later, alone in his Pentagon office, Jacobs reviewed the morning's happenings. He made additional entries in his notebook, studied them. He was particularly exercised by the introduction of patriotic clichés into the President's conversation, by his dogmatic attitude, by a new and disturbingly intense passion. Harrison Gunther had never been a man for verbal excesses. Even more bothersome were the indicated policy changes.

Without Presidential assistance, the treaty would never be ratified. And that would injure American prestige, undermine confidence in the Administration, and cast the Secretary of State, so active in furthering it, into the role of diplomatic jester.

It would also humiliate the Soviet Union in front of the entire world, would rekindle Russian distrust of American intentions and sincerity. Only Peking could profit from this sequence of events. No longer would China feel squeezed between the two great nuclear powers and she would once again be free to continue on an increasingly aggressive path. Jacobs was convinced that China's leaders had long been preparing for war, an undeclared nuclear attack, to be launched when her military position justified the action. A time not far off, he knew. The Chinese, with their singular vision of violent revolution, were prepared to sacrifice hundreds of millions of people in order to achieve their political ambitions. Failure to understand this, Jacobs was convinced, meant failure to understand the true nature of international politics and so negate all possibilities of peace.

Granted the rightness of his logic, Jacobs wondered what had caused the President to change his mind about the treaty, about China, to embark on a course diametrically opposed to his earlier beliefs. Perhaps it was the pressure of the job—had it become too much for Gunther? Was his mind giving way under the strain? Had he surrendered his grip on reality, lost the ability to make a decision based on hard information, pursuing instead political ghosts and misty conspiracies, anxious to eliminate them in one master stroke? Was it possible that Harrison Gunther was no longer in control of the situation, no longer in control of himself?

These possibilities failed to satisfy Jacobs. An unsettling doubt continued to plague him, convinced him that he had overlooked some salient point, failed to total up all the figures—the conclusion simply not proving out.

An oath broke out of him. He had to know more. He made a decision and signaled his secretary on the intercom.

"Get me the Soviet Ambassador," he said. "At once."

III

Pompey walked out the East Gate of the White House, on his way to the National Press Club. He regretted having allowed Warren Gilbert to talk him into this lunch date. It had been a difficult morning with many interruptions, and a mountain of work remained to be done. And there was, of course, Gail.

It all seemed so unreal, a suite of blurred images stuttering across the screen of his mind, his emotions equally unclear. As the day wore on, it was resentment that he felt mostly, resentment that she could be so careless, so blatantly self-destructive. To forget the pill! Slowly, out of the resentment grew hope, hope for an error, a laboratory mistake that would correct the situation and turn everything back in time to where it had been. Pompey felt helpless, adrift, unable to direct his existence. He was wondering about the chances for a miscarriage when she called to say that she had contacted a doctor in a small city in West Virginia.

"He's been doing these things for years," she said, "and I understand his reputation is excellent. A hospital situation with a general anesthetic, a nurse and antibiotics. Everything."

He wanted to ask about money and felt ashamed. "Did you make an appointment?" His voice was low, conspiratorial, and he realized for the first time that they were going to break the law, to commit a crime, and he hated being forced into this position.

There was regret in her voice. "He can't do it. The girl who gave me the doctor's name told me that periodically he stops operating, goes away on a vacation. He's an old man."

"What do we do now?"

"Oh, it's all right. He gave me another name and a phone number. In Baltimore. I'm to phone this evening between five and seven and make an appointment." She hesitated. "Shall I go ahead?"

A spasm of terror came into his middle, an almost painful acuteness, and then was gone. He longed to act decisively, to be courageous, confident in this as he was in all things. What had happened to his confidence? Lately he too often felt unsure, as if some vital part of his being had been sliced away and replaced with nothing. Where had it gone, the belief in himself, the belief that had allowed him to create the agency, to turn it into a success against all odds? During those years he had always known who he was, what he wanted, where he wanted to go.

So much of that was gone now, diminishing progressively ever since his arrival in Washington. It troubled him. Was he out of his depth here, involved in a game too demanding, a game that required skills superior to those he owned, a manhood superior to his own? No. He couldn't believe that, wouldn't allow himself to believe it. If he'd lost any part of himself, he'd reclaim it, shore up areas of weakness. He might not yet be the man he wanted to be, but he was on the move, changing, growing stronger.

As for this problem with Gail, any man would have been troubled by it, disturbed, uncertain. After all, he was sensitive and wanted to do the right thing.

"Well," he heard her say faintly, "What shall I do?"

He stiffened and forced his attention back to her, made himself speak without emphasis. "If we're going to do it, we might as well get started. The longer you wait . . ." He broke off.

"Yes," she said. "I'll call and make an appointment."

"Shall I come over later?"

"Oh, yes." Her response was almost too quick. Then after a moment's hesitation. "I'll make some dinner for us."

"Don't go to any trouble."

It was difficult to clear all that out of his mind and he was in no mood to fend off Warren Gilbert's anticipated cross-examination. Gilbert, whose column was syndicated in more than 300 papers domestically and a dozen or so more overseas, had a strident public voice and a tough, insistent manner of gathering information. He was a humorless, aggressive man with an inflated sense of his own importance, and Pompey knew that there would be nothing relaxing about lunch.

The National Press Club occupied the two upper floors of the building on 14th Street. Pompey discovered Gilbert holding court in the celebrated bar, regaling three young reporters with tales of his news gathering exploits in a loud voice, his big-feathered face animated, his gestures oversized. Gilbert was a huge man with a great round chest and powerful shoulders. His arms were long, his hands broad. It was said that his physical strength was limitless and in his youth he was given to proving it frequently. In his later years, he had become more tranquil and the only public exhibitions of muscle-flexing he made were in his column.

Spotting Pompey, Gilbert left his audience and steered the Press Secretary to a comparatively secluded corner table in the dining room. On the wall above them were stereotype plates of famous front pages. They ordered drinks.

"Pompey," Gilbert husked out, trying to keep his voice low, "it's about time you and I had a private talk, eyeball-to-eyeball, so to speak."

"Sure, Warren." Pompey sipped his martini.

"You know I've been picked up in San Francisco, Seattle and Omaha. And next Monday I start running in Honolulu. Not bad for an old sports reporter."

"You've come a long way, Warren."

"Give the public the truth. None of that intellectual crap. Just plain, straight-from-the-gut truth. That's what I am—just an ordinary joe doing a job that needs to be done. People appreciate."

Pompey said nothing. Gilbert had become the most widely read political columnist in the country through a combination of gossip, innuendo, speculation and muckraking. His predictions were often wrong, a fact few of his readers were allowed to remember as he blatantly called attention only to those of his forecasts which came to pass. Now he tugged at his long, thick nose and glared at Pompey from under bushy brows.

"Level with me, baby," he rumbled. "What was that scene all about last night? Between your boss and Sokoloff."

Pompey studied his martini. "You know as much about it as I do."

Gilbert scowled and grunted and pressed his thick thumbs together. "Knock it off. I want to know why. Looks to me like Gunther's trying to shoot down his own treaty. What's his game?"

"Warren, you know Harrison. He wants only one thing, peace. The pact is his brain-child."

They continued the discussion through lunch, Gilbert raising disturbing questions that Pompey had asked of himself, or fought against asking. And now he found himself defending the President, trying to rationalize his actions, to explain away Gilbert's doubts. And his own. It couldn't be done.

"What about General Miller?" Gilbert said suddenly, over dessert and coffee.

"What about him?"

A slow, satisfied grin turned the big fleshy mouth upward. The eyes glittered happily. "*You* didn't know," Gilbert said accusingly. "Gunther canned him, dumped him, fired him. He's appointing General Quirk as Chairman of the JCS."

"Quirk!"

"That's it. A forty-five-caliber brain in a thermonuclear age. How come it's all so hushhush? Did you know that Ralph Jacobs only found out about it *after* Gunther dumped Miller? It doesn't figure, Jacobs going along on this. Quirk is not his cup of tea."

"Secretary Jacobs supports the President's actions." Even to himself, Pompey sounded pompously defensive, uncertain, and he longed to recall the words.

Gilbert snorted. "Jacobs doesn't go with anybody unless he thinks they're right. And you know as well as I do that the Quirks of the world give him a pain in the rump. Now fill me in, Pompey. What's happening?"

Pompey shrugged and tried to appear casual. "The President runs the executive branch, Gilbert. He makes decisions in accord with his policies and it isn't my place to——"

"Crap on that noise. I checked out that spy ring. Nobody's talking, for publication, that is. No information and no names. Oh, sure there's whisperings about people being taken into custody, but who the hell are they? Even my contacts at the FBI won't open up. Like the heat's on them."

Pompey made himself laugh. "Security, Warren. Those people are hipped on it." Gilbert grunted. "Relax, Warren. Let the President take care of the country."

"That'll be the day. I never bought that Big Daddy jazz. Not from Ike and not from Lyndon. We all piss in the same way, buddy, and they got to prove it to me." Gilbert clicked his teeth and eyed Pompey speculatively. He issued the words softly. "What do you hear about the cancellation of the Pacific Perimeter?"

Pompey leaned back. Gilbert was off base this time and he told him so. "This is the President's pet defense project."

"Maybe. Maybe not. All I know is certain contracts that were let for materials and deep-sea diving teams have been canceled. Does that sound as if he's going ahead with it? And if not, it means this country will remain vulnerable to attack from China. That's insanity, or worse."

"Oh, come on, Warren! You're going too far. There's always been a difference of opinion regarding the defense posture of the country. Remember that flap during the last Administration between Defense and Congress over manned bombers, and——"

"Okay. But you know that China is a growing danger to us. They've been turning out A-bombs and H-bombs at an increasing rate each year. My sources tell me that Peking has almost 900 of the big ones."

"But not the delivery system."

"They've had intermediate range rockets operative for some time. They could blast just about any Pacific target. Include Australia in that. Also, Japan, the Philippines. India. I have reason to believe that an effective intercontinental ballistic missile system is within reach for them. And once they get it, baby, they could launch an attack against any point in the U.S. And us without an effective defense."

"You're exaggerating."

"The hell I am! You want statistics, baby? San Francisco, Los Angeles, Seattle, Dallas, Chicago, Detroit. Maybe the whole East Coast from Boston to Richmond—all wiped out. *All of it.* Seventy, eighty major cities leveled. A hundred million people dead in the first few minutes. More later from fallout. Everything contaminated. No water. No food. Nothing. Nobody left but some idiot hermit in Minnesota or someplace, and he wouldn't last very long."

"Okay, Warren. You made your point. We all know what a nuclear attack could mean. And so does the President. You can be sure he isn't about to jeopardize the safety of the nation."

Gilbert signed his name to the check. "You better be right, for all our sakes. The way I figure it, time is running out. But fast. And I intend to say so in my column."

Pompey walked back to the White House slowly, trying not to think about the frightening prospects raised by Gilbert, peering back into some deep portion of his brain for an elusive image that barely fluttered into being, fading away before he could identify it. The now familiar uneasiness took hold of him. There was something he should do, something he should know. If only he could remember what it was.

IV

The Defense Department limousine carrying Ralph Jacobs rolled across the Rochambeau Bridge and past the Washington Monument. The lengthening rays of the late afternoon sun reflected off the aluminum cap of the soaring obelisk, which appeared to have taken root and grown naturally out of the grassy knoll on which it stood. Traffic was heavy, slowing the limousine, and Jacobs impatiently beat time with his right heel. He made himself stop, sat erect, facing straight ahead, hands folded in his lap.

It had not been a good day. His morning meeting with the President had been but the first discordant note. There had been others. The Army's Criminal Investigation Division had uncovered a case of collusion between an automotive manufacturer and a purchasing officer, revealing three million dollars worth of faulty truck parts. And in the Marine Barracks at Paris Island, a charge of brutality had been leveled against a lieutenant colonel heading a training battalion. And Harvey Gordon had reported back that he had come up empty, had discovered no new information. No sooner had he hung up than the President was on the wire again insisting Jacobs make no public comment regarding the treaty, the Pacific Perimeter, or the appointment of General Quirk that might be construed as being in opposition to his own position. Before Jacobs could voice his objections to being muffled, the President hung up.

Thus it was a bitter, frustrated Secretary of Defense who was on his way to meet Peter Street before keeping his date with the Russian Ambassador. When

Jacobs said he wanted to bring Street to the Meeting, Sokoloff merely grunted his assent, as if it mattered very little who was present or what they discussed. It was this attitude, closed and remote, that troubled Jacobs, made him anxious for Street to be present. Street was more than an authority on Russian history and Russian affairs; he had a deep intuitive grasp of the Russian personality, understood the complex emotional reactions of the Kremlin's representatives toward their Western counterparts, and, since he held no official position in the Government, he owed no allegiance to any particular policy and so could offer opinions uncolored by personal interest.

Traffic continued to move slowly and Jacobs struggled against a rising agitation, using all the internal controls he had learned to lessen the tension, to calm his seething emotions. By the time the limousine drew up at Farragut Square, where Street was waiting, all outward manifestations of his unrest were successfully concealed.

"What's this all about, Ralph?" Street said, as the car got under way. His smile was sly and Jacobs decided he had been drinking. "Does Harrison know you invited me along for this little session?"

"The President doesn't know about this meeting. It's unofficial."

Street's brow crinkled and he uttered a short, satisfied laugh. "The man is going to be unhappy with you, Ralph. I'm persona non grata."

Jacobs stared briefly at Street before speaking. "This is no game. You're here because I need your advice, your professional opinions. Whatever is said today, by either myself or Ambassador Sokoloff, is strictly confidential. It stops with you. Is that understood?"

"You can trust me, Ralph."

Jacobs turned to the front. His trust of Street was limited, as it would have been toward anyone else with the same degree of self-indulgence. But this was no time to consider Street's shortcomings; he was present because of his strength, his experience and his knowledge. Jacobs made his voice conversational.

"You've known Sokoloff for some time?"

"Oh, yes. We met years ago at a disarmament conference in Prague. We even spent a couple of nights arguing the merits of Russian vodka versus the American brand, sampling each, I might add. A steady man, Mikhail, all Russian, stolid and unshakable. One of those Georgian peasant types like Khrushchev."

"I want you to judge his responses to what I say. Is he lying, concealing something, dissembling? Can you do that?"

Street smiled as if he had discovered a secret. He leaned forward and Jacobs detected the stale-sweet smell of alcohol on his breath. "Don't tell me that the Secretary of Defense, the omniscient man, is unsure of himself, needs help."

Jacobs made no response. He was aware of his public image, but he had no intention of defending himself, not now, not ever. He would continue to do what he believed was right.

"Your help, Peter," he said, "is what I want. Do I get it?"

Street leaned back and closed his eyes. "Of course," he said softly. They drove the rest of the way in silence. When the car stopped in front of the Soviet Embassy on 16th Street, they got out.

"That scene last night," Street said. "It troubles you as much as it does me." Jacobs made no answer. "What are you after, Ralph?"

Jacobs glanced up at the façade of the embassy. It was a massive building of ornate design, and he thought that it would not have been out of place in the center of Moscow's Red Square. Ironically, it was very much a product of a capitalistic mind, built in 1910 for the wife of the gentleman who made his fortune by designing and manufacturing sleeping cars for America's railways.

"You listen, Peter," Jacobs said, "and observe.

Later, I'll put one or two questions to you. Just go along with me."

"Why not?" Street said, as they were admitted. "The vodka has always been first rate here."

Ambassador Sokoloff received them in his office, a room of no particular distinction, being neither opulent nor Spartan in its furnishings. An aide, a somber man in a dark, double-breasted suit, offered refreshments. Street had a double vodka; Jacobs nothing. The ritual of hospitality fulfilled, the aide withdrew. Sokoloff, silently standing behind his desk observing, now seated himself. His upturned eyes swung toward Peter Street.

"It has been some time since last we spoke."

"Too long, Mr. Ambassador."

Sokoloff arranged his fleshy mouth in what passed for a smile. "I am pleasantly surprised that Mr. Jacobs brought you along." Sokoloff glanced at Jacobs. "Over the telephone, Mr. Secretary, you said it was important that we meet in private to discuss a matter vital to both our nations. Please proceed."

Jacobs felt Sokoloff was curious, perhaps apprehensive, made more cautious because of the previous night's encounter with the President. He was aware also of his own ambivalence about this meeting; if the President knew about it he would undoubtedly disapprove, characterize it as a disloyal act. The evolving situation regarding the treaty was disturbing, puzzling, and he failed to understand what the President was trying to accomplish. Yet that hardly justified meeting with the opposition in this manner. Jacobs derived a small measure of amusement at the internal conflict, this attack of conscience, the question of higher loyalties. He told himself that he was acting in the best interests of his country and turned his attention to the present. He wished there was some way to discover what message had been dispatched to the Kremlin by Sokoloff in the diplomatic pouch that morning. It was hardly likely the Ambassador would provide the information. He filled his lungs with air, and the corners of his mouth tugged upward in a pleasant smile. He was going to have to convince Sokoloff of his own good intentions.

"About last night . . ." he began.

The flat face gathered together and Sokoloff's tiny eyes almost disappeared into the folds of skin that surrounded them. He looked up at the high carved ceiling and made a baritone sound in his chest. "What is there to say? Your President impugned the honor and peaceful intentions of my Government. That he should do so at this time perplexes all of us and is distressing. We have given him no cause for such an attitude."

"The espionage apparatus——" Jacobs said.

Sokoloff silenced him with an abrupt slicing gesture. "There is no such apparatus, Mr. Secretary. Certainly, it was possible that I might not know of such affairs and so I made an investigation. There are in this embassy, as in all embassies, people who know about such things. Also, I spoke to certain people in Moscow last evening after the reception, importantly placed people. I have been assured that there is no apparatus. No spies. None." He exhaled deeply, almost a sigh. "Ever since the treaty negotiations were begun between our two countries such activities have been suspended. There are no secrets in such matters between us, Mr. Secretary. Yes, we have conducted espionage against you as you do against us. But no longer. Oh, it is true that some Soviet personnel study your scientific periodicals and analyze statements made by your public people. All very routine. Certain persons, professional agents, you might call them, have been transferred from the United States and no replacements made. Or else they remain, their covert lives dormant. Your President obviously doesn't believe this."

"The President spoke of the FBI breaking the ring, of people being jailed."

Sokoloff snorted and waved one pudgy hand in distress. "To imprison people, those of the lower echelons, would be simple enough. They are always vulnerable to arrest by counterespionage agencies such as the FBI. In Russia, all the couriers are known, all those who labor for your CIA and if we wished . . ." He stopped. "To go on with this is nonsense. You know it all. I repeat, there are no spies."

"And the Mars shot. Consider those two men floating helplessly until they expire——"

"Mr. Secretary! Science in the Soviet Union is as highly developed as it is in the United States. We have long possessed the means to divert rocket flights. Our technicians know all about electromagnetic interference and have labored for some time on methods of protecting our own flights from sabotage. Oh, it can be easily enough arranged. But we have not done this thing, not this time nor any other. Once more, sir, I can offer no evidence but my word and that of my Government."

Sokoloff rose and circled behind his chair. He turned swiftly and Jacobs saw anger, and something else, in his face. The Ambassador balled his stubby fingers into a fist and held it aloft, a symbol of the power packed into his short, squat body. His voice was throaty and emotional.

"Gentlemen, this matter disturbs me. The Soviet Union desires peace. Only peace. There has been little of it since 1917. First the Germans; then the Allies, including American Marines, at Archangel and Siberia, trying to suppress our revolution; then the Nazis; and after that, this absurd cold war, the constant arming, the constant alert, the constant wearing threat of annihilation."

"The United States also desires peace," Jacobs said.

"Then let us have it!" Sokoloff cried. "The treaty is drawn, the terms finally hammered out. At last our people and your people have been able to sit down, to understand each other, to work for a common end, a common good. And then, last night! What is the matter with your President? Is this a step toward peace, to paint my people as evil, as international villains? Nothing could be less true.

"Why should this be? Your country and mine, they have much in common. Our peoples are very much alike. A good number of your citizens come from Russia. We know that now the good life is possible because of modern technology, but we are also aware of the terrible destiny that awaits a world plunged into nuclear disaster. We fear the power of the bomb. We want none of it." He sucked air noisily into his lungs. "It is not the Soviet Union that your President must fear, but China, as must we ourselves. China has been altered little by the teachings of Lenin. Their leaders still think like warlords of an ancient time, hoping to expand their power by force and by guile. We Russians know them, for we own a long unhappy border in common and still suffer their incursions."

"We recognize your problem here in Washington."

"Yet my country is slandered, accused of dishonorable actions! In Moscow, the generals know their place. They are subordinate. They obey orders and attend to matters that are military, technical, and leave policy to others. Here, matters seem quite different." His voice echoed raspingly in his full, round chest. "Your General Quirk, a man out of his time, a man dedicated to war with Russia. Frequently he meets with certain executives of the CIA, which is almost a government unto itself. Who can say what insidious plots they devise even now? We can point to the past, to Guatemala, to the use by the CIA of faculty members of Michigan State University in Vietnam in 1955, to the Bay of Pigs, and more. This Quirk, now your foremost military leader. I cannot believe that this appointment could be made without *your* approval, Mr. Secretary, and my Government must look upon such an appointment as a hostile act."

Jacobs kept his voice flat. "General Miller resigned for personal reasons, Mr. Ambassador. The President chose General Quirk as the most experienced man for the job. There is no deviousness in this matter." The expression on Sokoloff's face told Jacobs that his words were met with disbelief.

It was all repetition after that. Sokoloff's resentment would not be softened, and though he spoke in the ambiguous language of diplomacy, it was clear that he intended to hold to a hard position. They parted with each man stating his hope for trust and understanding, for a peaceful future.

Neither Street nor Jacobs spoke for a long time after leaving the embassy. It was Street who finally broke the silence, a doubting, suspicious tone edging his voice.

"What was it all about, Ralph?" he said. "You could have anticipated Sokoloff acting the way he did, speaking the way he did. And you asked him nothing probing, nothing new. Why did you go there tonight?"

"To let Sokoloff know that there are some people in the Government still working for ratification."

Street remained unconvinced. He studied the Defense Secretary in profile, the molded line of the high forehead, the crested nose, sharp, thrusting, the tough angle of the chin. All spoke of Jacobs' intelligence and firmness, yet here he was equivocating, avoiding answers. It was out of character and heightened Street's curiosity. He realized that he had been brought along as a specialist, required only to offer an expert but limited opinion. The role of outsider was not to his liking, however, never had been; he yearned to be worthy again of total trust, of all the facts, welcome in the highest councils. Once it had been that way and he still craved it desperately.

He could have told Jacobs to take his bare bone with its reminiscent scent of glory and find another boy, or else be completely open with him. It was a risk he didn't dare take. Even that meatless bone so tempted him that if necessary he would accept it, grateful to be allowed back inside the fold in the smallest way.

He crushed out the cigarette he was smoking. How far removed he was from the bright, young intellectual who had been graduated from Princeton with the certainty that there was nothing wrong with the world that could not be fixed. Especially by Peter Amory Street. A wry smile fanned across his finely detailed mouth. Perhaps it had all been too easy in those early years. Answers had always come quickly, so quickly that often there had been no need to think, no need to consider, to entertain all the ramifications. A certain cerebral glibness had been substituted for contemplation with the result that there had been errors of omission and commission, errors that a less gifted, more prudent man might not have made. In those days, cloaked in a kind of arrogant certainty, he lent his name and prestige to various causes, various organizations, only to discover that often he was being used. His efforts to conceal his mistakes, to cover his tracks, had usually made matters worse.

That's when the heavy drinking had begun. The liquor softened the disappointments, shadowed his inadequacies, bolstered his ego. Before too long, it became a necessary support to getting him through each day. He wondered how different life might have been had he remained a teacher, but that route had been studded with dangers. All those young girls, so bright and lovely, so lush and beguiling, so inclined to experiment, seldom helping him to resist. He remembered too many of them, faces and names, the soft firmness of their bodies, the sweet, warm scent of them in the darkness. And the memories allowed him no peace.

The limousine drew up in front of the house in Georgetown. Jacobs led the way up to his study and offered Street a drink.

"Bourbon," Street said.

Jacobs handed him a glass, watched him take a long swallow. "Now let's talk. How would you characterize Sokoloff's attitude?"

"Deeply troubled, I would say." He pursed his lips thoughtfully. "Mikhail has never been a devious sort. When following the official line, he's always assumed the posture of the tough peasant—which he is. A direct man, utterly without fear."

"Was he offering his own opinions?"

"Partly. But also the Kremlin position. A Soviet diplomat can't do otherwise, of course."

"Of course."

"But Sokoloff wants that treaty. There was deep

emotion in him today, that classical tragic concern, the kind of alienation you find in the Russian novelists. They've all got it, you know. A sadness for the people who've always lived under tyrants and been deprived. The way I see it, Mikhail's been going out on a limb with his superiors, emphasizing Harrison's hope for peace, for an accord. Suddenly, this about-face. He's confused and resentful, and he's got a right to be. His career's on the line."

"The spy ring."

"There is no spy ring," Street said flatly. He finished the bourbon. He went over to the bar and refilled his glass.

Jacobs waited until he returned to his seat. "He could be bluffing."

Street considered that. "I don't think so. He admitted previous espionage activity here. When did you ever hear a Soviet official confess to that? It was his way of underscoring the truth, as he knows it."

"Could such an apparatus exist without his knowledge?"

"Perhaps, but I doubt it. A Soviet Ambassador knows just about everything that goes on in the country to which he's assigned."

"Then you believe his talk of wanting peace?"

"Absolutely. Ralph, the Russians don't want war. They'd be insane if they did, and they are above all a practical people. They have as much to lose as we do and more than most other peoples."

"And the Mars shot. He denies interfering with it."

"Again, I believe him. The Russians don't do things unless there is a sound reason behind it. What would they gain from diverting the spacecraft?" He answered his own question. "Absolutely nothing."

Jacobs nodded, considered what he had been told, decided he had no further questions and stood up. He arranged his mouth in a cool smile. "I appreciate your help, Peter."

Street downed the remainder of the bourbon and rose. "I don't suppose you're going to tell me what this is all about?"

Jacobs started for the door of the study, Street a step behind. "You've been very helpful, Peter."

"If I knew what was going on I might be more helpful. My experience with the Russians, my understanding of the Russian character . . ."

Jacobs recognized the plaintive note in the other man's voice. He resisted an impulse to lower the barrier. Nothing of what he felt showed on his face. He opened the front door. "Shall I phone for a cab, Peter?"

Street stared at Jacobs, shorter by almost a head, pale and physically slight.

"You're so strong, Ralph," he said. "So damned strong."

Jacobs had long ago decided that explanations served no purpose, were in fact self-defeating for a man in authority. There was no reason to confide his thinking to Peter Street, no reason to voice his suspicions. At this stage, everything was still too vague and unformed. It was information that he was after, a body of evidence that would in its own time provide its own conclusion.

He held out his hand and Street took it. "Thank you for coming, Peter."

Street wet his lips and the aristocratic face seemed to sag. "Anytime, Ralph. I mean, it's a pleasure to be admitted back into the club, if only for a little while. I think you understand. If you can use the few small skills I possess . . ."

The jangling of the telephone interrupted. They said good night and Jacobs went into the kitchen in the rear of the small house. It was Harvey Gordon.

"I tried you earlier," the DIA agent said. "You'd already left your office."

"What have you got?"

Gordon responded briskly. "I checked both matters as completely as possible, under the circumstances."

"All right. Fill me in."

"The Mars project seems proper enough. Our scientific people are convinced something went wrong in the guidance system, and that loused up the automatic correctional devices. The possibility of outside interference is remote. Unlikely, I'm told. You'd have to know wavelengths, particular codes and so on. They're changed regularly."

It jibed with Sokoloff's protestations of Soviet innocence. "And the other matter?" Jacobs said.

"Something odd about it," Gordon said. "My pipeline into the FBI is all clogged up. I had to push a lot to find out anything. Security is tighter than I've ever seen it. This is Marshall's personal baby."

"Go on."

"He's running this show by himself. It seems that there *were* some arrests made. Mostly domestic Commies who still cling to the bromides of the thirties about the revolution of the proletariat. Frustrated girls with bad teeth and angry men."

"Okay. Save the analysis."

"Right. Some couriers, a guy running a drop in a tailor shop in Detroit, a traveling salesman from Toronto, a naturalized citizen from Latvia—which lends a nice middle-Europe touch to it all. But no important fish. Truth is, there hasn't been any big-time Soviet espionage in some time. This treaty—"

"Are you saying there is no spy ring?"

"I'm saying some little people were gathered in the net. No one worth spending time with. Messenger boys. That's all. The way I hear it, most of them have been dormant for months, years in some cases. I tried making contact, but it was no go. They're all being held incommunicado." He paused. "That bothers me. I should have been able to break through."

"You still haven't answered the question. Is there a spy ring?"

"Some people were arrested, that's all. Few of them were connected to each other. The FBI is holding on tight, and what bugs me is that no one in our office knew anything about this until after it was over. Nobody knows much now."

"Was the CIA in on this?"

"Doesn't look that way."

"What else?" he said.

"Nothing," Gordon said. "Anything else you want me to do?"

"No. Forget the entire affair."

"Sure," Gordon said.

Neither of them would be able to do that.

After leaving Ralph Jacobs' house, Peter Street hailed a cab and gave the driver his own address. Halfway there, he changed his mind.

"Drop me off in back of the White House."

Slowly, thoughtfully, he strolled around the old mansion on Executive Drive, head down, hands deep in his pockets, looking up only occasionally. He allowed his mind to turn to Harrison Gunther and what had once existed between them. They had been friends, and more. Street had been a valuable adviser, a man whose knowledge and opinions were esteemed and sought after. But that had been long ago and was now only a memory, a fading memory that cause Street sometimes to question whether it had actually been the way he remembered it. He paused and looked through the black iron fence. Lights still burned in the West Wing. Men were at work, making vital decisions, getting things done. Peter Street should have been a part of that process. *Should have.*

"You've been very helpful," Ralph Jacobs had said to him.

How had he helped? What had he actually accomplished? Street punished his brain in pursuit of an answer. Why had the Defense Secretary taken him to the Soviet Embassy? What was Jacobs after and what was Street's contribution? No answers came.

"You've been very helpful. . . ."

Oh, God! How much he wanted to really help, to become involved once again. No role would be too insignificant, no job too minor. To belong. To do. To be what he had been designed to be. A tortured cry was smothered behind his clenched teeth. He swallowed it, and the lingering taste of Ralph Jacobs' fine bourbon took its place.

Moving rapidly with long strides, he turned away

from the White House. *"Shall I phone for a cab, Peter?"* Damn Jacobs for being so strong, so much in control. Damn him for not being less than he was and thus needing Street more. Damn him. A shudder rode down Street's spine as he remembered. He had begged and hated himself for doing so. *"If you can use the few small skills I possess . . ."* And Jacobs had dismissed him as one might dismiss an irritating child.

Someone bumped Street and he was jolted back to the present. He was in the downtown area now, the lights harsh and abrasive, the streets crowded and noisy. Without direction, he turned into a quieter avenue. He entered the first bar he came to. It was dimly lit and cool, with only a few, solitary, drinkers at the bar and two or three couples at tables in the back. Little of that registered as Street ordered a bourbon, and then another.

His mind shifted backwards. How pleased he had been when Ralph Jacobs had invited him to go to the Soviet Embassy. How excited he had been, the old sense of importance swelling up in him.

But Jacobs had kept him outside, squinting through a soiled glass in a futile effort to see the sweet prizes contained within. He resented Jacobs' secrecy, for not telling him what it was about. He made an effort to figure it out for himself. A new treaty with the Russians, perhaps? Or another joint effort to settle the Middle East problem? No firm answer came. Street finished his drink. Whatever the Defense Secretary was up to, it clearly depended upon continued good relations with the Soviets, that much was clear.

Jacobs. How difficult to penetrate and understand him. He had developed a hard shell that deflected all efforts to peer through to the core of the man. The shell was an effective shield that kept its wearer apart and alone. Street wondered if Jacobs ever felt lonely, the way he did so often. It was difficult to visualize the Defense Secretary longing for human companionship. He was tough and resolute, not like other, lesser, men. Not like Peter Street. He called for another bourbon.

A girl materialized out of the shadowed darkness at the rear of the bar, floating up to Street with a wistful smile on her wide mouth. She was slender, with lusterless yellow hair that had been bleached too many times and wide eyes that were probably green. She seemed unsure, mouth tremulous, one hand fluttering tentatively.

"Excuse me," she began.

The barman brought the bourbon. "Listen, lady," he said, his boredom laced with an undertone of toughness. "This ain't no pickup joint."

"Oh," she said, uncertain, backing off. "I didn't mean . . . I'm not what you think. I'm sorry," she directed to Street. "I'll go away."

"No, wait," Street said. He spoke to the barman. "The lady and I are old friends. The daughter of a friend," he amended, impelled to explain away her pale youth.

The barman shrugged. "Whatever you say, mister." He started away and Street called to him.

"What will you drink, my dear?" he said to the girl.

She wet her lips. "A . . . scotch sour, please."

She sat on the stool next to Street and looked at her hands. The barman brought the drink and left. She lifted it and gazed at Street over the rim of the glass. "Here's to life," she said shyly.

He nodded and watched her drink.

"It isn't that way," she said after an interval. "The way the bartender thinks. I'm not a . . . a whore."

"Of course not."

"My name is Linda."

"And mine is Peter."

She nodded and looked to the front. Her features were precise, small, her neck graceful; and under the white blouse she wore, her breasts were outlined, neat and heavy. She looked very young and he told her so.

"I'm twenty-one," she said, without conviction.

He finished the bourbon and ordered another. "Why me?" he asked.

"What?"

"What made you choose me? There are other men here, younger, more attractive men."

She looked up at him. "Not more attractive. Besides, you were the nicest, the way you're dressed and all."

"Expert tailoring is the secret. That, and the right university . . ." He grew solemn. "But the truth is, you were sorry for me, an older man alone and moping in his bourbon."

"I was the lonely one. I really wanted to talk to *you.*"

"That's hard for me to believe. You're so pretty. And so young." She had said twenty-one but he found it difficult to believe, didn't want to believe it. "You must have an army of boy friends."

"Boys," she said scornfully. "They're all the same."

"How is that?"

"All the same, clutching at you from the start, thinking a girl is only good for one thing."

The scent of her sifted through the cavities of his skull, and there was a stirring between his legs. He changed his position and smiled at her.

"You're very nice," she said. "I could tell from looking at you that you would be."

"You live with your parents?" he said, not knowing what to say.

She gazed at him in disbelief. "Are you kidding!" Then, more softly. "I'm all alone now."

"There was someone. A husband?"

"His name was Lenny. I was living on a farm in Ohio." She made a face. "It looked like I was going to spend my whole life on that farm, cooking and cleaning for Daddy, never getting to live at all."

"And then Lenny came along?"

"It sounds corny, I know. But it's true. He was so smooth. Good-looking, and he was good to me then."

"You left the farm with Lenny."

"I had to get away. Lenny brought me to Washington."

"What happened to your husband?"

"Oh, we never did bother to get married. Lenny kept saying we would but we didn't." Her eyes fluttered. "I suppose I shouldn't be telling you all this, but there's something about you that makes me want to talk to you."

He patted her thigh. "Feel free to tell me everything."

She leaned forward and spoke confidentially. "I've never been all alone before. It's kind of fun. Only sometimes it gets sad, like I want to cry, you know."

He wanted to touch her thigh again. It bespoke a youthful strength and he wondered what she would look like naked. He wished she were younger.

"Where is your friend now?" he asked.

"Lenny! Screw him!. The bastard split on me and took my money. I had saved almost a one hundred dollars and he lifted it. I been working in an office filing and such, and he just up and left with my money."

The profanity disturbed him. He preferred young girls to look and act innocently. To be perfect. "Are you able to support yourself?"

She shrugged. "Just about." A transformation took place in her face and she jerked around to face him. "Say, what are you driving at? You better get things straight! I know what you're thinking."

"I'm not thinking anything particular," he said soothingly.

"The hell you say! I'm a nice girl, Peter. And you better believe it. I'm not a hooker. I'm *not*. Just because I live alone and wanted to talk to you, is no reason for you to think . . ."

He wanted to silence her. "Please . . ."

"You have no right. Sure, I live alone now. But that don't mean I do bad things. I loved Lenny, and that's why I went off with him. But I'm no bar girl, no matter how it looks." She slid off the stool.

"Don't go," Street said, touching her arm. "I didn't

mean to upset you. I didn't mean anything, in fact. Just that you're so young and alone. It must be difficult."

There was a petulant expression on the pale face. "I get by. It's not as if I live in some kind of a pigsty. My place is neat and clean. My mind is clean. My body is clean," she recited. "You don't believe me?"

"I do!"

She frowned. "No. You think I'm trying to hustle you. Well, all right, Mr. Peter. I'm going to prove to you how wrong you are. Come on," she said, tugging at his sleeve. "My place is just a few minutes from here. Come on. And see for yourself. You'll see."

He went, telling himself that he shouldn't, and knowing that he wanted desperately to be alone with her. He vowed silently that he would stay for only a few minutes, that he would do nothing to worsen the situation. She was, after all, a child, an innocent, and thus the source of all his difficulties.

She was right. Her room was neat and clean. Small, with papered walls and a minimum of furniture, it might once have been servants quarters in the old renovated town house.

"You see!" she said triumphantly. "I live decently."

"Of course you do."

She looked up at him and the challenge seemed to wash out of her eyes. She made a swift, aimless gesture with her hand. "Well. You're here. Why don't you sit down?"

There was a single, straight-backed chair with one short leg that made it tilt. He sat in it.

"I have some drinking whisky," she said in a low voice. "It's rye, if you want . . ."

"That would be very nice."

She brought him a water tumbler half full, then went over to the bed and sat down, knees locked against the revelations of her miniskirt. He felt out of place, not sure what was expected of him. He asked her what it was like for a girl alone in Washington; and she said it was terrible, all those government girls competing for the few available men. She wanted to know about Princeton and he told her about the beer parties and the pranks, and made her laugh. When his glass was empty, she brought the bottle and refilled it.

He put his hand on her waist. She stiffened at the touch. He withdrew the hand. "I'm sorry. It's just that you're such a pretty girl."

She wet her lips. "You mustn't think that I don't like you, Peter. I do like you. Very much. But if I let you, you would think I was just another cheap girl and I couldn't stand that, you see."

He swallowed half the rye and put the glass on the floor.

"Now I've gone and hurt your feelings," she said.

"I wouldn't say that."

She knelt in front of him and took his hands in hers. "Oh, Peter. I didn't mean to hurt your feelings. Honest. I do like you. But a girl meets all kinds of fellows, and if I was to give them all what they wanted . . ."

"You can't be expected to please everybody."

She laughed. "That would sure keep me busy." She placed her hands flat on his thighs and rose. She leaned over him. "If you would like to kiss me, Peter, I reckon it would be all right with me."

He felt stupid and awkward, engaged in a child's game for which he owned no talent. Yet he preferred not to disengage. He kissed her lightly on the mouth.

Her laugh was brittle. "That's not so much of a kiss, Peter. Maybe I can teach you something." She took his face between her hands and lowered her mouth to his. Her lips were soft and moist, tasting of too-sweet violets. He heard her sigh. He put his hands to her waist and drew her into his lap.

When she made no objection, his tongue went between her lips. Her teeth were locked in place. After a moment, they parted. Her hand stroked his cheek.

He touched her breast and she shivered. He traced the full, heavy underside, cupped, caressed and squeezed. He discovered the nipple stiffening to his touch. She moaned his name and drew back.

"Oh, Peter. Please. You're going to think I'm bad, that I was lying to you."

"You're so lovely. Lovely."

"You'll do it and go away and not come back."

"That's not true. I'll come back as often as you allow me."

"I'd like that a lot."

He kissed her again and his hand went under her blouse. He fumbled with the brassiere and she maneuvered so it was easier for him. The warm mounds were everything he had imagined, firm and smooth, exciting. He pulled the blouse out of her skirt and kissed her navel, worked his way higher. He found one nipple and it became a sweet axis on which he spun, a rising mist descending.

Without knowing when, or how, they went to the floor, rolling on the musty imitation Oriental rug. Hands were everywhere and clothes were flung aside. He studied her as if from a great distance. The fullness of hip, the thighs thick and youthfully strong, the pale yellow wedge that drew him deeper into a dark vortex . . .

"Ah, Peter . . ."

There was nothing else. No place else. Only here and now. A deeper darkness, whirling and tilting, straining for release, a blur of inner sound clogging his ears, and the pounding heartbeat, louder—and a strange voice crying out in fierce anger.

"I'm gonna kill you!"

A man loomed over them. He was big and swarthy, and owned huge shoulders and clawlike hands that were made into rocky fists.

"Oh, Jesus!" Linda cried. "Lenny!"

It unfolded in halftime to Street. Angered at his role in this silly charade, without dignity in his shirt and tie and stockings, some unknown, interior strength caused him to sit up. The girl, naked and afraid, retreated to the far wall.

"Go away, Lenny!" she muttered. "You got no right barging in this way."

"You're my wife!"

"No," she protested. "You went off and left me."

"You're my wife," Lenny insisted.

"Now, look here," Street said, trying to clear his head, to force his brain to function in a more orderly fashion. "You aren't legally married to Linda. You deserted her."

"Shut up, fella," Lenny growled. He put his hand into his jacket pocket. "She lied to you. We was married legal and proper—and more than that, she's just a kid, mister. She's only seventeen."

Street looked at Linda. There was terror on the young face, the young, unlined face of a child. He knew that Lenny was telling the truth. Street turned back to the big man. There was a knife gleaming in his right hand.

"Oh, my God!" Street muttered.

"I am going to fix you, mister, once and for all. You ain't going to put horns on anybody else, I tell you true."

Street took a backward step. "This is ridiculous," he managed.

"Lenny, don't do it!"

"And when I'm through with him," Lenny gritted, "it's going to be your turn."

The thought came into the forefront of Street's sodden brain, and with it the ability to act. The courage. He charged, coming at Lenny from the side, reaching for the knife hand.

Lenny cursed and spun around, elbow driving into Street's chest. He went to the floor, gasping, the pain above his heart acute. Lenny went after him, knife poised.

"Lenny!" the girl shrieked. "Don't kill him."

Lenny hovered over Street. "She's right. Taking a murder rap for you, it ain't worth it. But you ain't going to get away with this. I'm calling the law. You committed statutory rape, mister. Contributing to the delinquency of a minor."

Street experienced a fear greater than the fear of being injured or killed. A fear of exposure. A duplication of what had gone before, of what had brought him down to this, of destroying whatever remained of his life. An image of Ralph Jacobs illuminated his mind, and he knew that his final link with the world he cherished and needed would be shattered. The only world in which he could exist.

He came up onto his knees. "Wait," he said. "I didn't know she was so young. I didn't know she was married."

"Don't give me that."

"It's true, Lenny," Linda put in.

"You big dealers in government," Lenny bit off. "You smooth characters with your fine educations and dough. You think you can do whatever you want, and get away with it. Well, you can't. Not this time."

Peter reached for his jacket, pulled out his wallet. It contained more than two hundred dollars in cash. He thrust the money at Lenny. "Take it. Please. It's all I've got with me. Take it, please." He put the money in Lenny's hands and quickly pulled on his trousers. "None of us want any trouble." Jacket in hand, he went to the door. Lenny made no effort to stop him.

Outside, Street paused only long enough to put on his jacket, to straighten his tie. From behind the closed door, he heard their voices. They were laughing. Both of them. And in that moment, Street knew that he had been manipulated, used. He ached to go back, to avenge the indignity, to reclaim his money. He wanted to. But didn't dare.

V

It was a shining day, the sun bright, the crocus and narcissus beginning to bloom, the air warm and caressing. Pompey stood off to one side of the South Portico watching the President greet a trade delegation from New Zealand. This was the Harrison Gunther he was used to, high-spirited, laughing easily and quickly, joking with members of the delegation, sparring lightly with the press photographers. Pompey's mind reached back to that conversation with Gail, to the lingering uneasiness, to the insane suspicion that had clogged his brain. The product of an unbalanced mind, he told himself scornfully, the thinking distorted; he should have known better than to so indulge himself, and vowed to wipe his mind clean of such ideas in the future. A voice at his shoulder drew his attention. It was Bill O'Brien, the Appointments Secretary.

"How's it going?"

"Beautiful," Pompey replied. "He's really something, the way he handles people."

O'Brien nodded happily, jowls shimmering in the sunlight. "A slick one, this President. Charm you out of your pants if you're not careful."

He moved forward to remind the President of his next appointment, and Pompey returned to his own desk. Fifteen minutes later, he was summoned to the oval room.

The President was alone. He looked up when Pompey appeared, his face showing nothing. He extended a sheet of paper to Pompey; six names were scrawled on it in the President's hand.

"New appointees," the President said. "I've indicated the posts next to each. Get out a story on it this afternoon." He paused while Pompey ran down the list. Two names leaped off the page, and the surprise he felt showed in his face. "Any comment?" the President said, a hard, warning note in his voice.

"No comment," Pompey said.

Harrison Gunther leaned back in the green leather chair. "There'll be questions from the press. I don't intend to discuss it with them. Can you handle them?"

"I think so."

Ketza rose sluggishly from his place near the tall windows where he had been sunning himself, padded past the President to Pompey, and lifted his massive head to be petted. Pompey reached out automatically, began stroking the soft, furry underside of the dog's throat. Ketza gazed up at him with soft-eyed approval. And there was that split second of recognition, as if this moment had happened before, as if Pompey was repeating some vagrant ritual, faulted and blurred, an error compounded and calling for correction.

"That will be all, Pompey."

The dismissal was curt, the usual Gunther warmth absent. Pompey moved toward the door and already the image had faded away.

"Do this right, Pompey," the President said, a mirthless angle to his mouth. "Some of these appointments will be considered controversial by my enemies, but they're *my* choices—and I'd like them given a full measure of editorial support."

Back in his office, Pompey rolled a sheet of paper into his typewriter and began to compose a news release. He wrote the lead paragraph, was dissatisfied, and wrote it again. It lacked incisiveness. He leaned back and lit a cigarette. He rang for Margaret Reilly, and when she appeared he read the six names to her.

"Get me whatever biographical material is available, the kind of stuff that justifies their appointments."

"Yes, sir."

He stared at the list in his hand, at Harrison Gunther's strong scrawl made with an old-fashioned, thick-nibbed fountain pen. A lot of questions would be asked and Pompey was expected to field them. He decided to get it over with as quickly and painlessly as possible.

"Schedule a press conference for this afternoon in my office," he told Reilly. "The regular White House correspondents. That'll give me time enough to write this story. I'll indicate where I want the biographical stuff entered, Maggie." He brightened slightly as her mouth flattened out disapprovingly at the use of the diminutive. "Think you can excerpt a short paragraph on each man? You know the kind of thing."

"I imagine I can do that," she said stiffly, and marched back to her own desk.

It was not quite three o'clock when the reporters gathered in Pompey's office, talking among themselves. They drifted in, in twos and threes or by themselves, ignoring the Press Secretary, who was on the telephone with a publisher of a weekly newspaper in a rural community in Oklahoma. About thirty of them took up positions around the spacious office, casual, bored, anticipating nothing monumental, aware that presidential press secretaries seldom make announcements of shattering importance, nevertheless content to break the routine of an otherwise dull day.

His call completed, Pompey swung around to face them, waiting until they quieted down. "I've got a short release here, some new appointments."

A soft, disappointed moan sounded in the back of the room. "Is that all?"

Pompey laughed. "Sorry I can't give you boys some big, black headlines, but I only hand out the news. I don't make it."

"Let's have the names," someone said.

Pompey read them off. "Reilly has copies of the release. It includes a short professional sketch on each man."

"Justifying the choices?" Kyle Tavis, of the *Times* Washington Bureau, asked.

"*Supporting* them," Pompey responded mildly.

"That Kenneth MacMillan," Tavis persisted. "Wasn't he one of Gunther's instructors at college? In political science, I think."

"As a matter of fact, yes," Pompey said, hurrying on. "Now I also have tomorrow's activities. It's a full schedule. The President will be seeing——"

"I don't get it," Tavis said. "MacMillan is more of an extremist than Joe Stalin, a kind of socialistic primitive. Why should the President want him around?"

It was a question Pompey had asked himself. MacMillan, only a few years older than Gunther, was a known radical whose political pronouncements were more often in sympathy with Peking than Washington. During the Vietnam War MacMillan was one of those who had announced that he wanted the United States defeated. This then was the man the President was appointing to the newly revived position of State Department Under Secretary of Security and Consular Affairs, a highly sensitive post.

"What about this Edgar Bookman?" the man from the St. Louis *Post-Dispatch* asked. "My God, Pompey, he's the original eighteenth-century man, a religious Fundamentalist and the worst kind of reactionary. Doesn't the President know he was one of the organizers of that crackpot Bunker Hill bunch—the nut who tried to set up training camps to defend us from a Communist invasion?"

Pompey had expected this. Edgar Bookman was generally acknowledged to be one of the extreme spokesmen for the right wing, an articulate man congenitally opposed to anything less than total war on all Communist countries and on all social reforms. Bookman's glib tongue and quick answers, cloaked always in obscure language, delighted his followers and had made him a sort of a glamour figure, something of a TV personality. He was to be Special Assistant to the President on Foreign Affairs, with an office in the West Wing of the White House.

"What's the President thinking about?" Tavis asked.

"Yeah," the Chicago *Tribune* correspondent said. "Does Mr. Gunther have so little respect for the American public that he's also appointing hard-line Commies like MacMillan now?"

"Mr. MacMillan," Pompey said patiently, "is a respected member of the academic world with authentic credentials. His advice has been sought frequently by——"

"By kooks and fellow travelers."

"If we're gonna talk about kooks," the UPI man put in, "what about Bookman? I remember when that nervous Nellie ran for Congress on a platform that called for the removal of all business taxes, a doubled defense budget and elimination of the draft. His answer to the civil rights problem was to use nuclear weapons on Harlem."

An appreciative laugh went up. Pompey felt himself react, emotion clogging his middle. He tried to control the feeling, warning himself to join the laughter, to make light of the criticism, aware that editorial support for such extreme appointments would be divided and so for the most part nullified. He couldn't remain detached. The appointment of MacMillan and Bookman troubled him as much as it did any of the newspapermen, and he didn't understand Gunther's motives in choosing them. Pompey felt trapped between conflicting forces, afraid to show his back to either. He lit a cigarette.

"Okay," he said shortly. "Let's knock it off. These are good appointments of good men, thoroughly qualified. You don't have to like them, but neither do you have the right to class them as nuts or weirdos."

"Oh, ease off, Pompey," Tavis said. "You sound premenstrual."

"Funny, Kyle," Pompey said, when the laughter died out. "But this is a serious business. Now all of you, out. That's the story. Reilly's got the release for you. I have work to do. Out. Everybody."

Tavis waited until the others had left, came back to Pompey's desk. "Sorry to put you on, Guy, but face it,

MacMillan and Bookman are pretty far-out people. What's the President trying to prove?"

Pompey resented being placed in this position, having to defend people like MacMillan and Bookman. But the job demanded it of him. He took a deep breath, kept his manner light.

"Harrison Gunther is President of all the people, Tavis. You know he goes after advice of all shadings. These two men are patriotic Americans. They're entitled to their points of view, no matter how unpopular."

"Sure. But are they entitled to influence the direction of government from positions of responsibility? I say no, and so will many other citizens."

"You're going overboard."

Tavis went to the door and turned around. His sagging, bloodhound face looked sadder than usual. "There are few politicians I trust, Pompey. Experience has taught me that. I've also learned that men who want power go after it while the rest of us sit on our hands. And when they get it, they exercise it for their own ends. The President is handing over some of that power to MacMillan and Bookman, and I would like to know why."

He left. Pompey sat staring at the paneled door, trying not to ask himself the same question, afraid of the answers he might get. An increasing irascibility took hold of him. He felt out of touch with what was happening, suddenly a stranger in a once familiar landscape. He signaled Reilly.

"Yes, sir?" she said over the intercom.

"Get me Charley Hepburn," he said, "and then Miss Sorrell."

When the call to the Chairman of the National Committee came through, Pompey spent no time on polite preliminaries. "Charley, there's something on my mind. Could you spare me a few minutes? Today?"

There was a brief pause. "What's it about, Guy?" The politician's voice was metallic, almost challenging.

"I'd rather not say over this phone."

Another silence, then, reluctantly: "Very well. Five o'clock all right? The Round Robin at the Willard suit you?' '

"See you later."

As soon as he hung up, Reilly came on to say she was holding Gail Sorrell on one of the other lines. He pushed the appropriate button.

"Gail?"

"Guy, I'm on my way out on an assignment. Can you call me later?"

"Are you feeling all right?"

"I'm fine," she said, but there was no animation in her voice.

"Have you made that call yet?" He hesitated. "To Baltimore?"

She had phoned the previous day, had spoken to a man named Al, who had told her that the operation would cost five hundred dollars, that the abortionist performed only one evening a week, each week a different night, and that she was to contact him the next afternoon to make an appointment. At that time he would supply all necessary details.

"He's only there between five and seven. It's a special phone. I guess they have to be careful, protect themselves."

"I guess. You'll call later, then?"

"Yes."

"Shouldn't we get together afterward, this evening, and talk about it?"

"What is there to talk about?"

"What are you going to tell him?"

"I'll make an appointment to have it done."

"Oh," he said.

She responded aggressively. "That's what you want me to do, isn't it?"

"It's not what I want," he protested. "It's just that—look," he said, almost pleading, "if we were to get married now, it would be a mistake. I mean, neither of us would ever be sure."

"That's right. So I'll make the arrangements."

"Why don't I come by later? Some dinner. We can talk about it then. You'll know everything . . ." His voice trailed off.

Her breathing was audible over the wire. "All right. About seven, if you wish. I've got to go now." She hung up.

He understood her cool defensiveness, the resentment she undoubtedly felt. But the rudeness was unnecessary. This damned situation, unfortunate, upsetting, but not of his deliberate doing. As a matter of fact, had he so chosen, he might have disclaimed all responsibility. The error was hers.

He resolved not to deal in recriminations. After all, they were in love and owned a long and meaningful mutual history. It wasn't as if he was evil, as if he had made no positive contributions to the relationship. To her life. With no great effort, he was able to assemble a catalogue of benefits brought to her by Guy Pompey.

From the start, he had sparked her existence with an excitement and importance it had never before known. He had induced her to a world where attractive and influential people functioned, had placed her near the center of things; and because of him, his contacts, his ability to open doors for her, to arrange meetings and interviews, her career had flourished. And so had she. In many ways.

Not that he intended to make less of her. She had always possessed an abundance of affirmative qualities. She was exceptionally good-looking for one thing. More than merely pretty, her face promising provocative depths and shadings.

He'd first seen her at the Peruvian Embassy reception for the new Ambassador. She wore a pale green cocktail dress that intensified the green of her Tartar eyes and managed to make her seem rounder than she was. Plump, almost. Less than sophisticated. Her hair had been long then, pulled back in a ponytail, and her fine mouth would have benefited from a change of hue. From where Pompey stood, she was just another of those nearly beautiful girls one discovered in Washington, the daughters of minor government officials or admirals or foreign attachés. Girls in expensive clothes with excellent manners and first rate educations. They were never quite at ease, such girls, never quite intelligent, never quite in fashion.

But such girls offered other rewards. They were anxious, desperate even, to please a man and frequently made their bodies available at first request. This one, Pompey had thought, appraising Gail from across the embassy ballroom, promised more than most. The slightly Oriental cast of the eyes, the lush, overdone mouth, the full body, all gave her the look of a sexual athlete. A waiter appeared and Pompey lifted two glasses from his tray. He carried them over to where she stood and extended one.

"Not to drink at a Washington cocktail party," he said, giving her his best smile, "is sinful and may result in repressive legislation."

She gazed up at him as if from behind a protective screen. A slow turn of the full mouth gave her an added dimension and made him less sure of himself.

"I don't drink," she said.

"What else is wrong with you?" he said, grinning so that she'd know he was making a joke.

She made no reply and that surprised him. Most Washington girls were masters of the quick repartee that got them from the receptions and dinners and parties to the bedroom with a minimum of conflict. This one wasn't playing the game.

He said his name and saw her eyes respond with interest.

"You're the President's Press Secretary!"

Ah, so that was the key! He would turn it. He put his hands up in mock surrender. "I plead guilty." He looked down the front of her dress. Under the green chiffon, her breasts were white and enticing, with a complex of orange freckles. He lifted his eyes. "Who are you?"

She couldn't meet his gaze and he decided that she was going to be easy, after all. A sitting duck, overwhelmed by Guy Pompey, Presidential Press Secretary. Well, not just that. There was more to him than the job. He was, at thirty-seven, darkly handsome, with a face that looked much younger and rugged enough to be trustworthy. He was tall and had good shoulders and a small waist and that devastating smile. He turned it on her now and asked her name again.

"Gail Sorrel."

"Well, Gail Sorrel, I am going to take you out of here, to dinner. And while we're eating, I shall drink wine in great amounts and convert you to the benefits of alcohol."

"Oh," she said blandly, "I drink wine, Mr. Pompey."

He took her to a Spanish restaurant that was illuminated only by candles and ordered a delicious paella and white wine and concentrated his attention wholly on her. It was an effective technique he had developed years before. Make them believe there was no one else. Never could be. And he placed no pressure on her, letting her make the decision to leave, to go home.

At the door, she surprised him, turning, extending her hand, saying good night with a tranquil surety that left no room for him to maneuver. It occured to him that she might be much more than she seemed.

He thought about her the next morning, tried to categorize her. There were girls who functioned on a sexual schedule, he knew. First date, nothing. Second, an invitation to a nightcap, some tentative necking. After that, a gradual relaxation of defenses. And eventually, surrender. All right. It was a game he could play.

But she didn't play according to the rules, as he knew them. They saw each other ten times during the next month, and except for a few antiseptic kisses she held him off, growing silent and distant whenever he became too aggressive. Yet she never sent him away, and his curiosity and desire were heightened. He vowed to seduce her and made plans to that end.

He would play it cool, crowding her not at all. She

would begin to question his remoteness, his lack of interest, question her own desirability.

It didn't work. On their next date, he intended to leave her at the door. But she walked into the apartment, leaving the door ajar, giving him little choice but to trail after her. She sat on the couch and he took the big easy chair, determined to keep his distance. After a few minutes, she came over to him, lowered herself into his lap. Her mouth came down on his, gentle, soft, with lingering interest.

"I think," she mumured, after a while, "that I have been awfully dumb."

He was acutely aware of her flesh, the thick, sweet smell of her, the way in which her buttocks, accommodated themselves to his thighs, the feel of her waist under his hands. She wasn't plump, he thought idly. Not at all.

"What do you mean?" he said.

"Making you wait so long. Making us wait."

He hesitated. He realized what she was offering and wanted to respond. Yet at the same time, a vague resentment formed in his gut. He was annoyed because she had destroyed his strategy, had not allowed him the triumph of winning her according to plan, had appropriated his cherished control.

She guided his hand to her breast and shivered at the touch. "Don't you want to love me, Guy?"

"Of course, I do," he said, without conviction, frightened suddenly, feeling no strong passion, fearful that he was about to fail.

"If you'd rather not . . ."

"Don't be silly."

He kissed her mouth, thrusting his tongue between her teeth. He reached under her dress and squeezed her breast. He removed his hand after a while and put it between her legs. She admitted him. Her thighs were vaguely damp.

His voice was harsh when he spoke. "Let's get undressed."

She stood up and obeyed.

He took off his clothes. When he finished, he

turned. She was standing naked, chewing her lower lip, but making no effort to conceal herself from him. She had loosened her hair and it cascaded across her shoulder in a a thick, black fall that made her seem very young.

He went to her and held her close. She was trembling. He kissed her hair, her cheek, her shoulder. He held her bottom. She didn't move.

"Listen," he said. "Is this the first time for you?"

She giggled. "I'm not a virgin, if that's what you mean."

"Yes. I think that's what I meant. What do you mean?"

"I'm not terribly experienced."

"How experienced are you."

She considered that. "Well, there was my seducer."

"Yes."

"And one other. That's two times."

"Two men."

"Yes."

"How many times do you think you did it with them?"

She brightened. "Oh, I know exactly. Once with each."

"Holy Christ! Is that all!"

"I'm sorry."

He sat down on the edge of the couch and studied her. She had a magnificent body, the flesh tight over her bones and beautifully proportioned. Her breasts were neither too large nor too small, and her legs were finely shaped and smooth. The belly thrust, the dark feathered place. All perfect. All wasted.

"What in hell have you been doing?" he said tightly.

"Nothing, I'm afraid. She took a single step forward. "Oh, please, Guy, don't be angry. I'm sorry I'm so inexperienced."

"So am I. I never enjoyed being a teacher."

"Couldn't you make an exception in my case?" she said, smiling shyly.

"I don't understand, a pretty girl like you."

"Neither do I," she said intently. "Nobody tries. Nobody I like, I mean." She looked away and back again. "I had to ask you."

He looked at her wonderingly. She was much more than he had supposed. And much different. He would have to wipe away all the impressions, learn what she was really about.

"Here we are," he said quietly. "Talking like two reasonable people. Quite civilized and intelligent. Except that neither one of us is wearing anything."

"I noticed that."

He felt a twinge, a shifting of flesh. "Did you?"

Her eyes traveled downward, then quickly away. "Yes."

He stood up. "Come here."

The kiss was extended and she clung to him desperately. "It's so nice," she said finally. "Being close like this, feeling all of you."

"I have an idea."

"What?"

"Let's go to bed."

She laughed. "A marvelous suggestion!"

In the bedroom, she pulled back the spread and folded it neatly, turned down the blanket, the sheet, finally faced him uncertainly. Laughing, he directed her between the sheets. He kissed her mouth, her breast. She held herself very still, eyes closed, lips parted.

"You like that?"

"It makes me want to shiver."

"Is that good?"

"Beautiful."

"In that case . . ." He found the other breast.

"Guy," she said. "You know so many nice things to do."

"Give me a minute, I may be able to think of something else."

He stroked her thigh, his hand coming to rest between her legs. A low moan broke out of her and she reached for him.

That first time, it was less than satisfying for them

both. Her passion was tempered by fear and there was physical pain. She insisted that there must be something physically wrong with her, that she was too small or deformed in some way. Twice, he stopped to reassure her and the second time was unable to suppress his anger. And in the end, he was forced to withdraw because she was unprepared. As was he.

Afterwards, they lay side by side without touching and he wished it had never happened. What a mess! It made no sense to get involved with an inexperienced woman. Too damned much trouble. He decided that he wouldn't see her again.

"I'm sorry," she said, breaking the silence.

"Be still."

"It wasn't very good for you."

"It was fine."

"It should be fun. Shouldn't it?"

He agreed that it should be fun.

She came up on one elbow. "If you'll teach me, Guy, I'll try to be better. I mean, I want to learn and I'm really quite bright. I learn new things rather quickly," she ended seriously.

He laughed. "Incredible."

"What?"

"You. You're incredible."

"Why?"

He pulled her down. "Don't you have a diaphragm?"

She blushed and shook her head.

"Well, get one," he ordered.

"Oh. I'd be too embarrassed. To go to a doctor to be fitted. After all, I'm not married."

"Get a diaphragm," he said presently.

"All right."

But when he saw her next, she had done nothing about it. He tried to make her understand. "You could become pregnant. You don't want that to happen."

"Oh, I would love to have a baby. My own baby. But not yet. Not this way."

A thought surfaced and he frowned. "I am not a man for marriage."

"I know that, Guy."

"I've been married."

"I understand."

"I just wanted to make sure that you did."

"I do, believe me."

He nodded and wondered why he felt so discomforted. "You've got to get a diaphragm."

Her brow wrinkled in thought, the Tartar eyes narrowing. "Guy, couldn't you buy some of those . . . things? Condoms?"

"Just do what I tell you! Rubbers are no damned good. It's like wearing a raincoat in the shower," he said, remembering the old Army joke.

"What are they like, Guy? I've never seen any."

"What difference does it make?"

"Would you get one, Guy, just so I can see it? Please."

"All right. If you promise to go to a doctor to get fitted."

"I promise."

And she kept her promise. And the next time they were together, she insisted on showing him the diaphragm, explaining insertion procedure, despite his protestations that he wasn't interested. Later, it took nearly twenty minutes to place it, and by the time she returned to bed neither of them felt like making love. The next time they were together, only ten minutes were needed.

"I've been practicing," she explained proudly. "I'm getting much better."

"At everything," he said. It was true. She was freer these days, aware of her own flesh and the pleasure it could get and give. He would have preferred her to be more aggressive, to initiate more sexual activity, but he expected that in time she would be.

Soon they were seeing each other four or five times a week and he stayed at her apartment overnight, except when the demands of his job made it impossible.

"Sleeping together," she told him. "That's almost

the nicest part of it all. Being able to cuddle and knowing there's somebody with you who cares."

"I care," he said, and meant it.

"I know."

"How do you know?"

"I can tell." She paused, then: "Whenever I have a bad dream, Guy, the way you touch me, reassure me. You put your hand on my fanny. Or take me around. And I know Guy is there and it's all right. That's very nice, you know. Very nice."

He never was certain of the exact moment that he realized that he was in love with Gail. It seemed to have happened in bed, one night when it was almost unbearably good, a pulsating kind of joy that permeated his flesh and caused his head to spin. But that had been transient, elusive, though repeated with greater frequency. He felt himself drawn into her as if his will had been subverted and his responses determined by her needs, her desires.

But the love was more than the bed. It had to do with the way she looked and spoke, the pleasure she took in life, the way she laughed. Her laughter was a free, rising sound that erupted spontaneously and often without apparent provocation. She found amusement in words and events that eluded him, and he made a conscious effort to study her, to see what she saw, to hear what she heard, and to understand. And in time, his senses became more acute, his responses freer.

One night, in bed, smoking and touching and talking softly, he was telling her about his day. There had been a bad moment with the Senator from Illinois, a pompous and vain man. The President had catered to the Senator's prejudices, to his intellectual shortcomings, to his known predilection for straight gin and government-paid expeditions to exotic places around the world. Without warning, Gail began to laugh.

"What's funny?"

She tried to explain, but he failed to see the point. He fell silent, sullen and resentful. She made an effort to restore his good humor without success. She bent over him and kissed his chest, his stomach. He set himself against her, but his body betrayed him.

"Ah," she murmured, shifting closer. "How pretty he is!" She kissed him.

"You never did that before."

"You like it?"

"Yes."

"I've been thinking about doing it. I want to, Guy."

"For me?"

"And for me. To please us both."

His body arched under her attention, straining for gratification. She swung into a position astraddle him and at once they were joined. She pounded down at him with unrestrained ferocity, hips swinging in an extreme arch that threatened to sunder the coupling. But never did.

He fought back, rode her high into the air. She cried out joyfully and forced him back down to the bed. Only muffled sounds came out of her now, attenuated exhalations. They squirmed and twisted until she was on her back, and they had never parted, flesh slapping wetly together in a beat that sent them marching toward a spasmodic flood, left them limp and full.

"I love you," he told her the next morning.

"Guy."

"I really love you."

"And I you, Guy. So much. I didn't think it would be this way for us. Love, I mean. I'm so glad."

He was too. Glad and afraid. But he made no mention of his fear. They saw each other almost daily after that; and when he could arrange it, they would take weekend trips to New York or to the shore. Four months later, she missed her period.

"Are you sure?" he asked, the fear gripping him fiercely.

"I keep a calendar."

"How it could happen?"

She chewed her lip,"I spoke to a friend of mine, an older woman. She said the diaphragm could be incorrectly placed. Or could move, if we made love very actively."

"Have you gone to a doctor?"

"No," she said, very softly.

"Dammit! Well, go! Find out what's happening, what we have to do."

She made an appointment and failed to keep it. Made another appointment and missed that too. A week passed with nothing being done. Fury and fear rising, he insisted that she see a doctor. She said she would. But he didn't believe her. There was a private quality to Gail. A disturbing remoteness. It was almost as if she were challenging him, threatening him, rejecting him.

He arranged to go with her to the doctor. The appointment was for Tuesday afternoon. They would have a late lunch and go together. At eleven that morning, she phoned him.

"It's all right," she began.

"What?"

"I'm bleeding."

At once there was relief, a lightness; all emotion except weariness drained away. "You're sure?"

She laughed gaily. "Of course, silly. A veritable flood. Everything is all right. You can stop worrying."

"Yes," he said. Then, more slowly: "I want you to keep the appointment. Ask the doctor about birth control pills. Let's not take any more chances, darling."

"I hate pills," she protested.

The anger flared quickly in him. "Don't you know how lucky we were! Next time we might not be. Now do what I tell you!"

"Yes, Guy. But don't be mad at me."

For a long time after she began taking the pill, there was a constrained, almost mechanical, quality about their love-making, as if both of them were distrustful of her body and wary, afraid to allow their emotions full range. After a few weeks, the restraint evaporated and he became aware of a new aggressiveness to her. She was more adventuresome, more willing to experiment. That troubled him for a while, as if he had lost some vital but unnamed portion of himself. Eventually, he stopped worrying and surrendered to her desire and abandon and learned to enjoy it.

Pompey arrived at the Round Robin a few minutes after five. The cocktail lounge was already crowded with government employees, and as Pompey picked his way toward the corner table where Charley Hepburn waited, he overheard snatches of talk, gossip, criticism of superiors. He had heard it all many times before.

Hepburn greeted him with the firm handclasp of a professional politician and guided him into a seat. A waiter materialized and took their order.

"Well, Pompey," Hepburn began, eyes bright and curious, "you're a veteran of three years in the Washington theater of operations. You're battle-tested and bloodied. Have you made peace with the vicissitudes of political life yet?"

Pompey had long ago marked Charley Hepburn down as the most direct and uncomplicated politician he had ever met, at the same time recognizing him to be a complex man. He was insightful, shrewd and daring, and as devious as might be necessary to gain his ends. Pompey decided that these first words were a thinly veiled bit of advice—*Don't go overboard too quickly. Don't become too concerned by that which is at first glance incomprehensible. Whatever the problem is,* Hepburn was probably saying, *it will dissipate itself if given enough time.*

Pompey couldn't wait. "There are times, Charley," he said, selecting his words with care, "when I wish I were back on Madison Avenue."

Hepburn smiled and his narrow, bony head bobbed as if in agreement with whatever thoughts swirled around behind his pale, almost translucent brow.

"A jungle, that Madison Avenue. But with limited goals. Money, mostly. This is where they separate the men from the boys. Here is where the real power lies."

Pompey agreed. "It's surprising that more people don't lose control down here, the constant pressure, the problems."

"Many do. I give you the late Mr. Forrestal. Few of them go that route, of course, but their grasp on life is loosened, made less certain, and men who once functioned on a cool, cerebral plane find they have surrendered control and begin to react emotionally, often, sad to say, obsessively."

Pompey fingered his drink. "Suppose that were to happen at the top, in the White House?"

"It has, my friend. This country has operated with less than total authority on Pennsylvania Avenue, but we managed to survive. We always do." He faced Pompey, his expression stony. "The burden of the Presidency can only be carried by a superior human being and we're fortunate to have such a man running the show right now."

Pompey stared at a point beyond Hepburn's left ear. "Those appointments he made today," he said. "MacMillan and Bookman. How do you reconcile them with what the President is supposed to stand for?"

The blue eyes glittered. "It's not my place to reconcile them. Nor yours. MacMillan and Bookman. Bad choices, both of them, and I told the President so. Political liabilities, from my point of view. Y'know, with election coming up next year he's been clearing all appointments with me."

"Then why those two?"

"I argued against them, but he convinced me."

"He did?"

Hepburn almost smiled. "His argument is worth considering. Harrison's a locked-cinch to be reelected, but we want to sweep the Congress too, be able to push his program through. That means a broad political censensus. So he's widening the appeal of the Administration. Right wing, left wing. What difference does it make? Harrison Gunther ramrods this outfit, and everybody knows it. The rest of us are just spear-carriers."

"Still——"

"Consider it, Pompey. This pulls the extremes of the party together. Those rockheads on the right are going to have to go along now with Bookman on the team. I know Edgar. He's an ambitious man and he'll swing his weight around. There's a lot of big money over there, oil money, for example, and a political party can always use some of it. As for MacMillan, we all know what he stands for, and the President will put that professor through his paces like a trained seal."

The words added up, made sense, but only if the world was a political stage and the players puppets to be manipulated. Pompey felt no reassurance. Government had become too big, too complex, and often decisions made at lower levels took root and grew until they were embraced as national policy, come into being from neglect rather than purpose. Hepburn, like so many in politics, was a craftsman, concerned only with means, seeing men and events as instruments needed to win the next election, to assume power and so be able to distribute the benefits of that power. To Pompey politics was more, laced with such heady concepts as duty and honor, words he hesitated to voice, was embarrassed even to consider.

By the time Pompey left the Willard, his brain was a tumbling bog of alcohol and conflicting ideas. He'd turned to Hepburn hoping to be convinced that the appointments of MacMillan and Bookman were an expression of political expediency only, rather than a basic change in policy. He wanted very much to accept Hepburn's assurances.

He drove the Mercedes carefully across the Arlington Bridge, dimly aware that he'd had too much to drink, his reactions slowed, his vision blurred. By the time he reached the apartment complex in Alexandria where Gail lived, it was nearly 7:30. She admitted him, and a cloud of annoyance gathered in her eyes.

"Sorry I'm late," he muttered, brushing past her,

weaving his way into the living room. "Hell," he blurted out challengingly. "It was business."

He sprawled out on the couch, head back, eyes closed. There was a lack of synchronization among his various parts. A dull ache moved into place between his shoulders, reached out for the muscles leading into his neck.

"Obviously, we're not going out to dinner," she said.

"I don't feel well."

"Perhaps you should go home," she said, after a moment.

The darkness behind his lids was in action, gray and smoky, on the move, without direction. A moan trickled across his slack lips.

"Are you really ill, Guy?" He said nothing. "Do you want a doctor?"

"I'll be all right."

She waited for a long time before speaking, not certain how to proceed, not sure what it was that she wanted, yet convinced that some violent change was necessary, anything to save herself from the insistent bog that sucked threateningly at her.

"I made the call," she said.

It took a great effort to open his eyes, to sit erect. "And?" he said.

"I made the appointment." Her voice was charged with suppressed emotion. The Tartar eyes peered narrowly at him. "I'm to be in the railroad station in Baltimore on Tuesday night at 9 o'clock. The Charles Street entrance. This man, Al, will meet me."

"How will you know him?" Pompey heard himself say.

"He'll know me. I told him what I would wear." She blinked but didn't cry. "He said it would take about four hours, traveling to wherever they're going to take me, the operation, and back again."

Four hours seemed like such a long time to Pompey. Shades of terror illuminated his mind.

"He said to bring the money, five hundred dollars, in cash, in an envelope."

"I'll give it to you."

"I want to pay for it myself," she said.

"No!" The word was a fiery eruption. "No," he repeated, more quietly.

"It was my fault. I was careless."

He was sober now, and the ache between his shoulders had settled in, deeply painful. "What else?"

"He said that the operation would be performed by a medical doctor, and there's going to be a nurse in attendance and an anesthesiologist." She tried to smile. "Isn't that nice?"

"They must know their business."

"Oh, yes. I'm not at all worried."

"Good."

"Al . . . he said I wasn't to worry, that everything would be all right."

"And it will."

"Yes," she said, then: "He said it would be all right if I wanted to bring someone along. To the depot."

"Well, of course," he said with forced heartiness. "I'm going along. Tuesday at 9 o'clock. I'll make the necessary arrangements to be free. Everything will be fine, you'll see."

"I know it will."

He looked up at her, wanted to say something reassuring, to tell her that he loved her, wanted to marry her, but no words came. This affair, this abortion; it was a growing danger to him, a threat. If word of it got out, he'd be finished in Washington. It would mean the end of his political career. The President would never tolerate such a situation; Pompey would be fired and everything would be spoiled, his future stained.

He shuddered and was ashamed. To consider himself, to be preoccupied with his own welfare at this time, when it was Gail who needed help, *his* help. He struggled to focus only on her and what lay ahead, but was unable to rid himself of other thoughts, as if something terrible was about to happen, something ominous and threatening, agonizingly out of reach.

He made himself smile at her and said that he intended to stand by her until the ordeal was over. He intended to do the right thing.

"Of course," he said, "we'll have to be careful that none of this gets out."

She stared at him briefly, then turned away, and he knew that he was alone.

VI

Jacobs frequently worked late in his Pentagon office. The job had become more complicated each year, reaching into new areas, making more stringent demands on his time and energy, encasing him in more and more details. Though most of these were assigned to subordinates for execution, he insisted on being kept aware of their final disposition. This meant poring over reports, budgets, tables of organization, projected plans of defense and attack, submissions from various military strategy groups, assessments of the daily intelligence reports, as well as considering the most recent technological advances.

The telephone interrupted. "Jacobs," he said brusquely into the mouthpiece, making no effort to conceal his annoyance.

"This is Guy Pompey, Mr. Secretary."

A vision of the Press Secretary faded into Jacobs view. He saw Pompey as a man blessed with abundant gifts, gifts in large degree nullified by a limited desire to utilize them. His earlier success in the public relations business was typical of the man. On Madison Avenue, his charm and good looks, supported by talent for writing and a fine imagination, carried him to the apex of his profession. Once in Washington, however, he seemed unwilling to use his talents fully and soon settled at a lower level than he was capable of achieving. It was too bad, Jacobs thought, for had Pompey wanted to, he might have risen high in government, using himself for his own and the public good. Jacobs decided that he was a man more afraid of success and its attendant responsibilities than he was of failure. Men like Pompey saddened the Defense Secretary. He hated waste.

"What is it, Pompey?" Jacobs asked.

"Mr. Secretary," he began uncertainly. "I must talk to you."

Jacobs flipped open the appointment calendar on his desk. "Tomorrow's out. I'm due before the Senate Finance Committee. That might take all day. The day after? Eleven-thirty in the morning."

"No. That won't do at all." The sharp response surprised Jacobs. There was demand in it, the sound of authority, a sound he had come to recognize, a spine of strength possessed by men who maneuvered others to do their bidding. Perhaps he had underestimated Pompey. "I must see you today."

Jacobs looked at his watch. He had promised Pamela Holliday that this time he would arrive punctually for her dinner party.

"I'm due in Chevy Chase in ninety minutes," Jacobs said. "I must go home and change clothes. Where are you calling from?"

"A booth in Alexandria."

"Fine. Pick me up and drive me home. We'll talk along the way."

Pompey surprised him again. "No. I don't want us to be seen together. I'll go to your house."

Jacobs agreed. He wondered what it was Pompey wanted to discuss. And, wondering, he knew with a deepening certainty. And, knowing, he didn't want to know, wished he had been out to Pompey's call, wished he could turn his back on what lay ahead. He should have realized that the same unanswered questions that bothered him would sooner or later trouble someone else—the same disturbing hints, the suggestions of something out of place, of a picture unchanged yet somehow different. That it was Pompey who had responded surprised him.

A sigh passed across his lips. There would be no avoiding what lay ahead, no matter how distasteful. He had turned the corner. Now came the ultimate test of the man he had made himself into. He collected his papers and shoved them into a battered brown briefcase and marched out of his office.

When he arrived back at the house in Georgetown, Jacobs dismissed the chauffeur. Pompey would drive him to Chevy Chase.

While waiting, Jacobs prepared for the evening. He placed the trousers of his tuxedo on the bed, carefully attaching the white braces and placing the cummerbund alongside. He arranged his patent-leather evening slippers on the floor in front of a chair, draping a ruffled dinner shirt over the back. From an antique velvet-lined jewel box, came his cuff links and studs. He did these things automatically, a man who cared little about clothing, yet nevertheless was always perfectly groomed. He dressed well because it insured unobtrusiveness and because the skills of a first-rate tailor guaranteed a high degree of comfort, allowed him to concentrate on more important matters.

By the time Pompey arrived, Jacobs was arranging his shaving equipment on the broad glass ledge adjoining his bathroom sink. He punched a signal button to admit Pompey. Jacobs spoke into the communication system he had installed when he bought the house.

"Upstairs, Pompey. The second floor."

He greeted the Press Secretary on the landing, noting the vertical crease between his dark eyes, the somber expression. They shook hands.

"What's on your mind?" Jacobs went back into the bathroom and Pompey stood in the doorway. He lit a cigarette and puffed quickly, watching as Jacobs washed his hands and face. He applied a hot, damp face cloth to his cheeks. "You sounded . . ." Jacobs searched for the right word, ". . . concerned over the phone."

For Pompey, there was criticism in those words. He felt awkward, stupid, a schoolchild who had impulsively volunteered, only to discover, too late, that his brain contained no answer.

"I don't know how to explain."

"Is this official?" Jacobs applied shaving cream to his face with a brush.

Pompey took a deep breath as Jacobs opened an old-fashioned straight razor and placed the blade against the line of his sideburn.

"I'm concerned," he said.

"Yes?"

Pompey held himself still. "About the President."

Jacobs wielded the razor like a baton, directing it over his cheeks to an inner tempo.

"Go on," he said.

"It all seems so stupid now. I don't know where to start. For some time I've been troubled. I tried to synthesize it for myself, to come to some solid conclusion, but without luck. I can't name what's troubling me, can't isolate the . . . the fear."

Jacobs worked over the curve of his small, hard chin. This was the delicate moment. If he was to cut himself it would be here, now. Seconds later it was done and there was no blood. He rinsed the razor, patted it dry, returned it to its place.

"I'm listening," he said, trying to conceal his interest, *his* concern, unable however to soften the tone of command in his voice. Pompey reflected his own unrest, his own indecisiveness, his own inability to arrive at a satisfactory conclusion. He began to brush his teeth.

"There's something about the President," Pompey said at last. "Something strange, different almost. Whatever it is, I'm bothered by it; and what makes it worse, I don't know why, or what it is that bothers me. It's as if I should know, be able to touch it almost. But I can't." He was embarrassed, and he tried to avoid Jacobs' eyes. "I guess I shouldn't have come," he ended lamely.

"Harrison Gunther is a complex man, many-faceted, given to a variety of moods."

"Yes," Pompey said. Was it that simple? A deep man, reacting under continual pressure, displaying long-concealed aspects of his personality, refracting a unique experience in a unique way. Pompey remembered something. "I was with him at breakfast a few weeks ago and the mess attendant accidentally spilled some coffee. It barely touched the President. Just some coffee on the tablecloth. Nothing more. He became furious, literally screamed at the man." Pompey reached back for the scene. " 'You stupid black . . .' . . . bastard, I suppose he was going to say. But he caught himself and smiled at me and at the messman, and said something about not sleeping too well."

"He didn't actually curse the man?"

"Not in so many words. He caught himself in time, but I have no doubt——"

Jacobs cut him short with a gesture. "Never mind half-spoken words. I know Harrison Gunther, a man totally without racial bias." He rinsed his mouth, looked up. "Is that all that's on your mind?" It was a flat challenge and Pompey was aware of the implied rebuke.

"The other morning, in his office. The way he lost his temper when you questioned his assertion of sabotage on the Mars shot. That was unlike him."

"Presidents and kings, Pompey. Neither are like other men. The good ones have monumental abilities which are often matched by monumental tempers. Johnson, Kennedy, Ike, Truman—they all let go on occasion."

"But not Harrison Gunther," Pompey said quickly. "He always retained control. Only recently has he shown anger. Always before, he was able to sublimate it in some way. That was part of the secret, part of his ability to get things done, to get people to do things for him. Three years, and I never saw him bully anyone. He enticed people, the same way that a beautiful woman entices men, to get them to act in her behalf. He had that quality."

"All right, we agree the man lost his temper once or twice."

"He was wrong about the Mars shot, you know."

"So?"

"Has he ever mentioned it again to you? Apologized?"

Jacobs measured Pompey. The man *was* more than he appeared to be; at least the potential was there. Their roles had been reversed, and he felt the Press Secretary boring in for the knockout. Under other circumstances he might have resented it, but not now. Pompey was riding his instinct, certain he was closing on some special truth. Jacobs wanted to help him.

"You've forgotten that exchange with Sokoloff," Pompey said. "That was completely out of character."

"What else?" he said.

"There have been other tantrums. Toward Sarah Harris, twice in the last week or so; and he chewed Hank Luplow out over some detail in a speech Hank's writing."

Jacobs nodded coolly. "Have you considered this—that a President has intense pressure focused on him all the time. None of us, no matter how intimate, can ever really understand that pressure. For all the time you spend in his presence, for all you believe you know about him, for all you recognize about the rigors of the job, I say you know nothing. Nor do I. Nor anyone else, except those who have held the job. He's the *only* man involved in everything, aware of everything, responsible for everything. There are no respites for a President, no way he can remove himself from the demands of the office, not if he is going to be a good President. Sooner or later it all piles up, and at that point any man is liable to let off a little steam, lose his temper. You would, Pompey. And so would I. So would Harrison Gunther. Face it, he's only human."

Jacobs stripped off his robe and stepped into the enclosed shower. A moment later steam began to rise, clouding the glass-paneled doors. Pompey stepped back into the bedroom and lit another cigarette. Dissatisfaction drifted through the hollows of his skull. Was this a mistake? To have turned to Jacobs, so cold, and aloof, so much a part of the Establishment; to seek help from such a man was naïve. The Defense Secretary was no different from any other political creature, essentially cautious and self-protective.

To make matters worse, Pompey was sure he was handling the situation badly, unable to express what he felt, what he knew. *Knew?* The word was much too strong. He went over the facts in his mind and was embarrassed at the weak case he presented, assessed himself from Jacobs' point of view, and wished he had been able to compile an accurate and detailed dossier of intelligence. His sense of inadequacy increased when he considered that Jacobs, with that sharp, probing mind of his, would soon begin dismantling this house of cards he had so loosely constructed.

Perhaps he would call it off, apologize, claim he was not himself, a man under unusual strain. *Gail and her pregnancy.* Of course! Jacobs would understand and sympathize. Any man would. No. Not Jacobs. He would frown and stare, his disapproval clear. Ralph Jacobs would never have allowed himself to get into that kind of a situation. He was much too careful, too precise in shaping his environment. Get out, Pompey told himself. Risk Jacobs' wrath for wasting his time, but don't plod deeper into this mire which his own disordered mind had concocted.

But the by-now-familiar uneasiness settled back down over him, and Pompey knew that he couldn't stop. Not yet. He made a massive effort to clear away all distractions, to think clearly.

The shower stopped and Jacobs called to him.

"Pompey. You can go on now."

Pompey again placed himself in the doorway to the bathroom. He watched Jacobs towel himself dry, surprised at the wiry body, the pale, thin arms strong and corded, the chest deep and firm, legs hard and well formed, the thighs heavily muscled. Pompey had always thought of Jacobs as an indoor man, an extension of a desk, at home with a column of figures, a sedentary creature. Yet here was the body of a physical man, an athlete perhaps, and he made an effort to visualize Jacobs taking part in some violent activity.

Pompey began to talk about his lunch with Warren Gilbert. "He's been asking about General Miller's resignation and the appointment of Quirk as Chairman of the JCS. He claims there's something phony about it. He's convinced the President has given up on the Mutual Defense Pact and is now working against it."

"How do you feel?"

"I'm not sure. The President no longer talks like a man who intends to fight for ratification."

Jacobs finished drying himself and applied after-shave lotion to his cheeks, quickly combed his hair. Satisfied, he went into the bedroom and began to dress.

"And there's the cancellation of the Pacific Perimeter."

Jacobs spoke in a mild manner. "I'm for the perimeter. But the opposition makes a strong economic and political argument."

"The President was for it! Enthusiastically. And now this switch! It makes no sense. I hear the Chinese are close to perfecting a long-range rocket delivery system. What's to stop them from launching a sneak attack against us? Oh, sure, there'd be an automatic retaliatory attack on our part, but they're prepared to risk a certain amount of destruction, a certain number of millions of dead. They've got almost a billion people. We haven't, and without a foolproof defense system can we stand up under a full-scale nuclear attack? From what I hear, the answer is no."

"And you believe the President's current attitude will invite such action?"

"I'm concerned," Pompey said. "Worried."

Jacobs made a small noncommittal sound back in his throat. A glob of resentment formed in Pompey's gut. He wanted to attack Jacobs, punish him for remaining so detached, force him to become involved. This was no classroom exercise. This was power politics in a world where the slightest mistake in judgment could set off a terminal holocaust.

Pompey spoke in a tight, thin voice. "You should be worried too."

Jacobs placed the cummerbund around his waist, slid it into place. He reached for his tie.

"Do you know how to tie one of these things? I always have trouble."

Pompey began to tie the bow. He felt increasingly uncomfortable under the close measuring stare of Jacobs' eyes. There was activity in some normally silent portion of his brain, an idea stirring fitfully, nagging. He reached for it only to have it dissolve into blackness.

"And those recent appointments," he said. "MacMillan and Bookman. Men from the political poles."

Jacobs stepped back and studied the tie in the mirror. It was perfect. "A bone to both extremes. They cancel each other out." He shrugged into his dinner jacket. "As for the perimeter, would you deny a President the right to change his mind?"

"Of course not."

Jacobs strode out of the bedroom. Pompey went after him. Halfway downstairs, Jacobs began to speak. "Harrison Gunther has a probing mind, always seeking answers, always open to new ideas, to a fresh approach. Very well. Maybe he's mistaken, misguided even. Nevertheless, there are men in government, substantial men, who agree with this new position." At the bottom of the stairs, Jacobs turned, his face a pale mask, remote, inscrutable. "Okay, Pompey. Put it into simple English, man. What are you trying to say?"

All strength drained out of Pompey. Jacobs was crowding him, making demands he wasn't able or ready to fulfill. And now he had allowed himself to be maneuvered into a cul-de-sac. All his life, no matter what the situation, he had provided a ready avenue of retreat. Jacobs refused to allow him that and he hated him for it.

"What's eating you, Pompey? Are you here to criticize Presidential policy? If so, you're out of line. You're supposed to be the President's man and it's your job to support him, to transmit his decisions to the press, to shield him from unnecessary harassment. Instead, it seems to me, you're at the head of the pack."

"It's not like that!"

Pompey searched for a way out. Jacobs was forcing Pompey to support his doubts, to prove his case. And in that moment Pompey understood that Jacobs too was afraid; and that knowledge terrified him, for he had always viewed Jacobs as a man without fear. It was this that had drawn him to the Defense Secretary. Of all the Cabinet members, he alone evoked confidence in Pompey. Of all the Presidential advisers, only he seemed to possess the strength and character to face any problem, and solve it. Next to the President himself, Pompey ranked Jacobs as the single most reliable, most effective man in Washington.

"You're frightened, too," Pompey said, as they got into the Mercedes.

"Concerned," Jacobs amended. "In an open society, the chief of state seldom embarks on a change of policy, a major change, without consulting his closest advisers. I checked with other Cabinet members, and the President has discussed cancellation of the perimeter with none of them, not even the Secretary of State." They drove in silence for a while. "Did you know that the President has begun taking morning swims?"

This obvious irrelevancy irritated Pompey. "How does that concern the treaty?" He turned into Wisconsin Avenue and pressed down on the accelerator. The Mercedes moved smoothly ahead.

Jacobs stared into the onrushing night. "He never was much of a swimmer. As a young man, football, basketball. Later on, handball. Swimming was too slow to him. Not enough action." He twisted around to loom at Pompey. "What else has been bothering you? About the President, I mean?"

A vein leaped wildly in Pompey's temple. He gripped hard at the steering wheel. "He's different." And even as he spoke, the words were reminiscent. What was it Hank Luplow had said? That Gunther seemed strained, different, trying too hard. "Yes," Pompey repeated. "Different, not himself, as if he's under a strain." He summoned a vision of the President to mind. "And physically it shows—there's a tautness around the eyes, and the lines from his nose to his mouth are deeper, more pronounced." He anticipated a mocking response. There was none.

"The job changes a man."

Pompey knew that. It had killed FDR and given Ike two heart attacks. No man who held that Office remained untouched. Still, there was something else, something conclusive, irrefutable, but tormentingly elusive.

"It's time," Jacobs said quietly, "for us to define precisely what it is we're talking about. You're leveling some kind of a charge against the President. Name it. Merely a change in policy position? I think not. That wouldn't be enough to get you this agitated. Whatever it is, you haven't put it into words. Perhaps you haven't formulated it in your own mind. Perhaps you don't dare." Jacobs waited and when Pompey made no response, he went on. "Either we move ahead at this point, Pompey, or we forget this conversation ever happened. *You must say it now.* Are you accusing the President of incompetence? If so, resign your job, fight against his reelection. That's your right and your duty. Incompetence in the White House is no crime. Unfortunately, I can tick off a number of names.

"If not incompetence, then what? Insanity, perhaps? I doubt it. And we all know about the Wilson situation, how his wife virtually acted as President while he lay helpless in his bed. And of course Garfield was incapacitated for a long time after he was shot, leaving the country without a Chief Executive. And perhaps Eisenhower was in no shape to stay on top of things following that first heart attack. Granted, Pompey, anything is possible. Presidents, like all of us, display a propensity for human frailty. Are you suggesting that Harrison Gunther is no longer able to dispatch his duties effectively?"

"No, dammit! No!" The Mercedes swerved and Pompey struggled with the wheel. He regained control and glanced at Jacobs. The Defense Secretary sat rigidly, staring through the windshield, a whiteness accentuating the corners of his flat mouth.

"Stop the car," he said.

Pompey pulled onto the shoulder. After a moment, Jacobs began to talk in a low, steady voice. "A body of opinion and supposition is what you offer, laced only lightly with facts. From this I'm supposed to draw some conclusion, one which suits you. The obvious conclusion is that you may not be fit to hold your present post. Your thinking is muddled and your dedication less than total. You turn to me, hoping the burden will be lifted from your shoulders, that I will assume command, that I will commit myself where you are reluctant to do so—"

"All the proof—"

"No proof. No evidence. Nothing a lawyer could bring into a court of law. Oblique suggestions are what you offer, bits and pieces that fail to make a complete picture. You dangle this before me, hoping that I'll take a stand where you fear to do so. You take no risks, while trying to entice me onto thin ice."

"I thought you could help."

"How?"

Pompey chewed at his lip. "Perhaps we could go to someone, to the Vice President."

Jacobs snorted disparagingly. "With what? To hint of fears and suspicions and nothing more? Not for me. Realize that this already stinks of conspiracy, and there are those around who would gladly apply a stronger word to it—treason."

Pompey shivered and wanted this to be a dream from which he would soon awaken. But this was *his* reality, and he could not escape it. And as if in confirmation, in the thick, ominous silence that followed, the memory he had tried so hard not to remember, settled firmly into place. He peered at it from different points of view, unable to diminish its importance, unable to make it disappear. It was nothing and everything, a small observation that forced him to know at last what it was he feared.

"The dog," he said in a soft voice.

Jacobs' expression never changed. "Ketza?"

"Ever since those Eskimos gave the President the dog during that Alaskan trip two years ago, Ketza has spent his days in the President's office. He's a lazy beast, phlegmatic, nothing bothers him. I've seen the dog lay that big head of his in the President's lap a thousand times, look up into his face, asking to be fondled."

"Get on with it."

Pompey sighed. "Ketza always offers his throat to be scratched, the underside of his throat." Jacobs turned his mind back into the oval office, pictured Gunther absently caressing the huge animal. "These days," Pompey went on, "the President scratches Ketza's ears, always the ears."

It was true. It had registered in Jacobs' mind like a thousand other observations, large and small, filed away as being of no immediate use. Swifty it came back, vivid and compelling.

"It's a small thing," he said to Pompey, prompting. "Of no consequence."

"No," Pompey said. The words came tumbling out. "It was an instinctive act, never thought about, an automatic response. Why do it differently? There was no good reason. The dog *wants* his throat rubbed, prefers it that way. Gunther wouldn't change, not consciously. Nothing happened to cause him to change. Except that *he's* different. Someone else. Another man. Not Harrison Gunther, an impostor posing as the President of the United States. . . ."

Three

Jacobs' Way

I

Ralph Jacobs held himself very still and stared at the man behind the steering wheel. Pompey's words ricocheted around his brain, echoing insistently. *An impostor in the White House.* It was a wild idea, mind-boggling, hallucinatory, laughable. But he didn't laugh, knew that he never would, that this improbable conclusion was precisely the one he had been reaching for himself, that this was the inevitable end product of the neatly entered observations in his notebook. In that moment, Jacobs hated Pompey, wished the Press Secretary had not sought him out, had not placed him in this absurd position. But Pompey *had* come to him, had finally and clearly spoken, and there was no ignoring it. Not now.

Conflicting thoughts ebbed and flowed and Jacobs tried to sort them out. That it should be the dog! A small thing, always the small things that could not be foreseen. His orderly mind was able to envision the preparation that must have gone into the project, lengthy and awesomely detailed, refined and rehearsed, studied and modified, created in that way a sculptor creates, bit by laborious bit, until the whole is achieved. Yet for all the skill and intelligence, all the thoroughness, they had erred and the mistake was costly.

They?

Who was *They?*

Was there in fact a *They?* The possibility made him shudder. Fear settled in his bowels, and a succession of tiny shock waves traveled along his nerves; the thin, pale hairs on his forearms trembled, and his eyes burned. He blinked and brought Pompey back into focus.

Did *he* understand what this meant? The ramifications were threatening beyond imagination. The President not Harrison Gunther! Who then? Who was the man in the White House? Where had he come from, and at whose command? On what plan was he embarked, and what did it foretell for the United States? For the world?

And Harrison Gunther? Where was he? Alive still? Held somewhere as a hostage? Or dead? The questions came in rapid-fire order, half-formed and biting deeply, frightening; and Jacobs couldn't guess which were valid even to ask.

If true, if the President was indeed an impostor, if the duly elected choice of the people of the Republic no longer governed from that green leather chair in the oval room, if he had been replaced by the agent of an unknown master, if the surrogate was intent on leading the nation along a dark road to some terrible end, what could be done about it?

Jacobs recoiled from further thought. He was a rational man, a man of figures and facts, of reasonable conclusions, a man prepared to consider all the choices open to him, and then act. But *this*. Solutions stunted and fluttered into view and dived on past, flawed always, until only a single mad idea remained, so outrageous, so dangerous, that he closed it out of his mind at almost the precise instant it appeared.

A huge interstate trailer came speeding toward them, its brilliant headlights illuminating the interior of the Mercedes for a long span. Jacobs shivered in the glare, and for the first time since leaving Georgetown he could see Pompey's face clearly. It was taut, anticipatory, and made Jacobs aware that he alone carried the burden, that though Pompey might serve as a subordinate, he was incapable of acting on his own. His strength had been enough to bring him this far, to consider the fact of an impersonation. He would go no further. Not alone. Jacobs was sure that

Pompey had not dared to consider the next step, should his suspicions be confirmed.

Jacobs forced breath into his lungs and imagined the reconstituted blood flushing his arteries, rejuvenating his weary limbs, stimulating his sluggish brain. He began to review everything that had been said, to compare it all with his own observations. He sought to respond to each point and dispose of it, to see each as an isolated example, unimportant in itself, a change of thinking on the President's part, a modifying of a previously held position. Yet when each point was linked to the others, a pattern became clear. And even if everything else Pompey had said was ignored, there was still the dog.

Jacobs swore silently. He had never felt much kinship for animals, and especially not for dogs, so docile and anxious to subordinate themselves to their masters. He would never have owned one; a cat was more to his liking, independent, wary of other creatures, acting out of instinctive self-interest, true to its nature.

His lungs ached and he exhaled slowly. At last, reluctantly, mournfully almost, he made the admission to himself—there was no avoiding any of this; it would have to be diligently pursued. Later, when it proved out, *if* it proved out, he amended with little optimism, there would be time enough to consider corrective methods. He straightened up, sharp features implacable.

"A wild, improbable charge," he said. "For your sake, I hope you've made it to no one else."

Pompey's tongue moved sluggishly. "No one."

"Anyone less generous might direct you to a psychiatrist."

"Am I imagining it all?"

"You are not to mention this to anyone else. Is that clear?"

"Yes, sir."

Jacobs turned to the front, concentrated on the Mercedes star atop the grille. "Your thinking is slovenly, Pompey. Have you considered where you would take this insane accusation of yours? Assume that you're right, that the President is not in fact the President. What next?"

Pompey resisted a rising panic. "He's got to be exposed, the truth brough out."

A simple, noble solution. Very well, Pompey. Expose the impostor, if he be one. Will *you* stand face to face with that man and accuse him of not being Harrison Gunther?"

A bead of perspiration rolled down the length of Pompey's spine, into the hollow of his back. He shivered. He wanted to speak, to protest, to explain. No words came. No ideas. His brain was frozen, the cells lifeless, drained of all energy. A sound seeped through. Another. Jacobs was speaking, his voice piercing a succession of filtering screens.

"Proof is required, concrete evidence that will stand up under examination, not by lawyers, but by the eyes and intelligences of the entire world."

A groan came from afar. Pompey knew it had risen out of the despair locked in his middle.

"Consider, Pompey, you have accumulated a body of satisfactory evidence. What next? No procedure has been established to cope with this situation, no formal tribunal. To whom do you present it? The Supreme Court? The Congress? The FBI? Regardless, be certain there will be those who will shred your case, will never be convinced."

"The evidence——"

"You anticipate men acting in a consistent and rational way. Nonsense. They won't. They will believe what they choose to believe, what they *want* to belive, a truth that supports their prejudices. After Dallas, there were those who were convinced Oswald had been a tool of the extreme right wing. Others were equally certain he was an agent of the Communists. Others spoke of domestic plots to advance the political ambitions of this man or that one. The conspiracy theory of history was dusted off, and no amount of evidence, no line of logic, could shake the *believers* loose of their certainty."

"You mean we can do nothing?"

"I'm saying forget it. And I will too. I'm saying learn to harness your imagination, put it to work in more constructive ways." He hesitated. "You might take a rest. A vacation. Sunlight and a gentle surf. Your friend, Miss Sorrell—a pretty girl, I'm told—goes far to replenish a man's energy."

Pompey felt helpless, on the edge of panic. Not since Korea, had he been so afraid. That long night on post came back to him, shadows flitting through the darkness, the gutting terror. He fired more than one hundred rounds, challenging the night aloud, sure that his fright had given birth to the enemy.

In the morning twenty-two dead Chinese soldiers were found within fifty feet of his position, and a general pinned a Silver Star on him and told him he was a hero. He was proud, but not so proud that he forgot the fear, the terrible, watery fear. This, now, was worse. Much worse.

"I'm late for my appointment," Jacobs said softly. "Are you ready to drive me the rest of the way?"

"Yes."

When they pulled up in front of Pamela Holliday's white colonial mansion in Chevy Chase, Jacobs got out of the car. He closed the door and looked in at Pompey.

"Go home," he said. "Try not to dwell on this, though of course you will. Remember, you are to mention it to no one. Is that clear?"

"Yes, sir."

Jacobs reached for Pompey's hand. "Good of you to bring me," he said gravely. "Don't worry about me—someone will give me a lift back to town. Good night."

Pompey watched him move lightly up the steps fronting the wide, unrailed veranda, disappearing a moment later into the house. Pompey drove carefully back toward Washington. He didn't want to have an accident.

II

Ralph Jacobs gazed without emotion across the tops of the microphones at the squad of United States Senators facing him. It was a familiar scene, ritualistic. The names might change, but the performances remained static; and many of the faces were constant, fixtures in the Capitol as much as the bronze Statue of Freedom atop the great dome. Jacobs allowed his eyes to trail over his questioners: the Pedant, the Economist, the Drone, the Professor, the Patriot; all were present and anxious to display to their constituents that the Republic stood strong and secure while each of them served. Jacobs wondered if somewhere in the bowels of the Capitol there didn't exist a secret training school designed to equip Senators for their roles, even as actors were trained to project their voices, or policemen to direct traffic, of window-dressers to arrange their wares. It was an intriguing idea but he lacked time to pursue it further, for Lucas Abernathy, senior Senator from Missouri, Chairman of the Finance Committee, was speaking to him in that country-boy drawl of his.

"There are items on your proposed Defense Department budget, sir, that offer little or no indication of how they will be utilized. It is my belief, Mr. Secretary, that the people of these United States are entitled to an honest and accurate accounting of the ways in which their tax dollars are to be spent. Now, let us look at the matter of this DIA of yours. Well, Mr. Jacobs, we Americans have the CIA and NATO and the Secret Service and the FBI and SEATO and the TVA and now this DIA, whatever creature it may be. I would surely like to know, sir, as I am certain the voters of my state would like to know, just what that DIA of yours is up to, and how much good American money they are spending, and on what, sir. On what? Mr. Secretary, I imagine you would like to enlighten?"

Jacobs was enervated. He had allowed Pamela Holliday to seduce him into remaining until the last of her guests had departed. Only then had she agreed to drive him home. She had chattered all the way, gossip to which he had listened with only a small part of his attention, filing the information, nothing wasted for a political man. Then she had insisted on having a nightcap, trying to convince Jacobs that he needed a wife and a hostess, and that she qualified on both counts. It had been difficult, for Pamela was a persistent woman, but eventually he had gotten her to leave. Sleep had come reluctantly, his mind active, ranging over the events of the evening, a muscle leaping sporadically along the inside of his right thigh.

So it was that he was weary and irascible this morning, and these Senators strained his patience with questions to which they already possessed answers, wasting time with their blatant politicking forcing him to cover ground best not emphasized. He loathed the public charade he was forced to be a part of each year in order to obtain an adequate operating budget. It was time better put to productive uses. He reminded himself that this was democracy in action, and submitted.

"Senator," he said, "our defense program—to be kept viable—must be supplied not only with men and matériel, but with a constant and current flow of information. Intelligence. The Defense Intelligence Agency does that for us."

"Surely, Mr. Secretary," Senator Abernathy droned, "the CIA can supply your . . ."

Jacobs ignored the interruption, and the Senator fell silent. "Senator, I'm not prepared to discuss other agencies, other bureaus. Let me remind you that when the DIA was established in 1961, it was out of need, the then Secretary of Defense having decided to consolidate the various military intelligence groups. It made sense then; it makes sense now."

"The additional funds . . ." Senator Abernathy began, stopping abruptly. He smothered a grin as Jacobs leaped into the verbal gap.

"The CIA spends an estimated eight hundred million dollars each year. Like that agency, our budget is a concealed item within the total money-picture of the Department. For the good of the service and the nation, it must continue that way."

So it went, the questions rambling and disjointed, often statements of position, the answers to the point, abrupt. At 1 o'clock Senator Abernathy adjourned for lunch, ordering Jacobs to return at 2:30 for further questioning. Annoyed, he stood up and began stuffing papers into his briefcase. His advisers, an Under Secretary and a pride of generals and admirals, began to talk at once. Ignoring them, he marched toward the double doors at the front of the committee room. He turned at the sound of his name to see Senator Abernathy approaching, a conciliatory smile on his florid, jowly face.

"Mr. Secretary," he muttered, "hope we haven't spoiled your appetite."

"These hearings only disrupt my workday, Senator. The affairs of Defense won't always wait."

Abernathy chuckled softly. "All things wait, Ralph, and those that don't, seldom cause monumental disasters." The smile widened and he ran stubby fingers through his great shock of snow-white hair, carefully unkempt. "Join me for lunch, Ralph. Appreciate your company."

Jacobs' mind turned over swiftly. Abernathy wanted to discuss the budget further, to justify his own line of thinking, to try to convince Jacobs to act in a more cooperative manner. To hell with that, he thought. The budget was reasonable and accurately reflected Departmental needs.

"Senator, you can't buy national security at bargain rates. It just won't cut."

Abernathy nodded ponderously. "Certain you're right, Ralph. Now let's get us something to eat and talk about it."

More time wasted, Jacobs thought, time better spent reviewing plans for reorganization of the Mobile Tactical Force which had seemed clumsy and outdated during the last All-Army maneuvers. He was about to refuse the invitation when he remembered that Senator Abernathy was closer to the President than any other member of Congress, that Abernathy was a frequent guest at the White House, was said to be privy to Presidential thinking on most matters.

"My pleasure, Senator."

They rode the subway from the Senate Office Building to the Capitol restaurant. They were led to a table in the center of the high-ceilinged chamber, under one of the cut-glass chandeliers.

"A little more privacy, Senator?" Jacobs said quietly. Abernathy nodded and indicated an empty table in the far corner, in front of one of the tall windows with its green draperies and potted plants.

"I know you're not a drinking man, Ralph," Abernathy said, "so you won't miss a cocktail. But I certainly do wish these Congressional dining rooms served some hard liquor. Have some bean soup, Ralph. Traditional, you know."

They ordered and after the waiter left, Abernathy leaned back in his chair, hands folded on the edge of the table. "Unhappy with your treatment this morning, Ralph?"

"Senator, you make a witness feel like a defendant. Some of your colleagues act as if it's a mortal sin for a Cabinet member to know his job."

Abernathy laughed back in his throat. "Does seem that way sometimes. Guess most people get sort of unsettled by too much efficiency. They ain't that used to it, and it frightens them when they meet a man who is. You are something special around this city, Ralph. Real special. You do your work proper without frills, currying no favor, not making like you're a buddy, not playing politics. Not playing politics in

Washington, Ralph—that sets people's teeth on edge."

The bean soup came. It was excellent.

"Senator, you're up for re-election next time around."

"Funny, Ralph, that you should keep up with that kind of thing."

"You were running pretty good this morning, Senator; at my expense."

Abernathy rocked his massive head and the white hair danced in gently flowing rhythm. "Try not to be too hard on us elected officials. We do the best we can, only there are times when we fall from grace, especially when our jobs are on the line. There is a so-called reform movement going on in my state, a bunch of fired up young wolves who believe only they have the welfare of the country at heart. They figure they got an inside track to all the answers and that an old type like Lucas Abernathy has got to be put out to graze. They're talking fusion and they might just whip me. Then again, they might not. With the precious assistance of Harrison Gunther they may find me too tough to digest." A slow smile turned his mouth."Guess I *was* talking for the home folks this morning. You see, Ralph, you can always go back to those companies of yours, but not me. I'm only a small-town boy struggling to get by."

"Senator, you're fantastic."

The smile widened. "Why thank you, Mr. Secretary. I believe you're complimenting me."

Jacobs nodded briskly and all the lightness was gone. "Senator, leave the DIA out of the hearing from now on. You'll get no more information out of me than I gave in Executive Session, and this line of questioning can lead to nothing productive. It could be damaging."

"Be patient with me, Ralph. I'm an old man and weary." The big head rose, eyes solemn, penetrating. "I will never short-change Defense, but there are things going on that I don't like, and I intend to make sure that the proper steps are being taken in the national interest. You saw the morning papers, Ralph?"

"The latest Chinese blast against the treaty?"

"Yes. Now you tell me how those people got that information. First, they found out about negotiations before they were made public, and now this. They were able to accurately spell out plans for the joint military command of the merged Armed Forces of the two countries. Well, now, you know the kind of a furor that is going to kick up in this land of the free. Dammitohell, I already had a couple of dozen phone calls before I could get out of my office this morning. Newspaper people, politicians, some California oddball who wants to annihilate everybody in the world except the Baptists—and me a Methodist. I know what Harrison's after and I'm all for him, but it would have been better if the details had been kept quiet until after ratification. Ralph, this is what worries me—is their intelligence operation so good that they can find out this sort of thing before our own people know?"

The waiter brought the entrées, and Jacobs toyed with his salad. He kept visualizing the President seated in that green leather chair, idly scratching Ketza's ears. Not the ears, he pleaded silently to the vision. Not the ears. Nothing changed, and after a while the image faded away.

"I don't know where they got the information, Senator."

"And that business of exchanging nuclear secrets with the Soviets. Now that kind of thing makes people nasty, Ralph. Our folks have been hating the Soviets for a long time now."

"There are no nuclear secrets, Senator. Never have been."

"Not even production short cuts?"

"Not any more. Oh, maybe some fine point, but nothing that ever really mattered. Check the record. The Russians produced their first atomic bomb in 1949, years before our scientific people thought they could. Same for China. Once people knew that it could be done . . ." He let it hang.

"Kind of like the four-minute mile."

"Exactly."

Abernathy sliced his steak into neat bite-sized chunks. "I suppose that Russia isn't the enemy anymore, hasn't been for years. But the hating habit is tough to break. Folks got to be educated. Take China, a bunch of hardheads, just rooting around looking for a fight. What's the word shrinkers use for people who are always suspecting everyone else?"

"Paranoiacs."

"A fine word. Guess we just got to hold them off till their people get fat and sassy, the way the Soviets did, and realize that there ain't no more profit in making war."

"The pact ought to slow them up."

Abernathy laid aside his fork. "That's what's making me fret, Ralph. Old Harrison, he ain't been himself lately. Generally, he's got his little old finger on the pulse up here on the Hill, and he's always in there pitching, laying on the grease, pressuring this one and that one until he gets his votes. That man has a way of sweet-talking, and backing it up with muscle. Not very complicated either. A little-bitty old dam goes to some water-hungry state, and a new military airfield to another, or whatever. A first-rate political man, but with tone. Real tone. Only he seems to have lost belly for this fight. Ralph, I'm worried about that treaty. It's liable not to get ratified."

"That can't be allowed to happen."

"He's a changed man, and not for the better. Reckon I'll try and coo some into one of his ears someday soon. Get him off and on. Been doing my best for the treaty, but it's his baby, and he's got to put out to make it happen." He picked up his fork and speared a crisp square of steak. "Now Ralph, you just got to have some of that delicious, flaky apple pie they serve here. You just got to."

But Jacobs didn't.

III

Pompey struggled to hold his thoughts. The night before he had slept little, despite two Seconals and a double shot of good Scotch. He had drifted off, only to be jolted back to wakefulness by some random thought, body and mind gripped by tensions.

And now, irritable and weary, he sat behind the desk in his office and struggled to concentrate. He was scheduled to deliver a background briefing that afternoon on the new bracero agreements with Mexico. One of his assistants had assembled all the facts and figures, and he tried very hard to digest them, making notes from which he intended to deliver his speech.

Nor was that all. There was an article promised to the Sunday *Times Magazine,* due in three days, and still in need of revision. Add to this press releases not yet written. It was going to be one of those long, bad days. Reilly came on the intercom.

"What is it?" he said curtly.

She made no effort to disguise her displeasure. "It's the Meet-The-Press people. They would like you to appear on this Sunday's program to discuss what they call the information gap. They——"

He cut her off. "It's impossible."

"They want to talk to you personally."

"Tell them I'm in a meeting, but make it clear that I can't do the show. No time. No time at all." He clicked off. The job was becoming too much—despite the corps of helpers, despite the computerized, transitorized, specialized system, too many details came to his attention. Somebody should do an article, he thought, perhaps for *Harper's*, about the increasing work load in all areas of the White House. It seemed like a good idea and he made a note to gather some research material. Then he turned his attention to the speech.

But it was impossible to keep from thinking about the man in the oval room. And Ralph Jacobs. And the trip to Chevy Chase, and what had passed between them. Pompey was convinced he had done himself irreparable harm by revealing his suspicions to the Defense Secretary. Jacobs was not the man to allow matters to go unfinished. At the very least, in the future he would keep Pompey under close surveillance, anxious to determine whether or not he was still capable of performing his duties. One serious blunder, and Jacobs would descend heavily upon him, ruin his career in the name of good government, of patriotism, perhaps blacken his reputation to such a degree as to prevent him from resuming his public relations activities in New York. He wondered if it wasn't time to resign, get out now, before the world collapsed around him.

On the other hand, Jacobs had rejected his thoughts, had indicated that for him they bore no merit, were not worth pursuing. Pompey wanted to believe that Jacobs was right. It was a mad idea, and he must have been mad to mention it to anyone else. Perhaps he would be lucky and it would end with Jacobs; he vowed to think about it no more. He picked up the telephone and called Gail.

He said hello and asked how was she feeling, and she said that she was feeling fine.

"You know what I mean," he said confidentially.

She said, "I know what you mean. And I feel fine." There was no warmth in her voice.

"What is it?" he said, feeling clumsy and stupid. "What's wrong?"

"Should something be wrong?"

It was difficult to find the right words. His mind was cluttered, his emotions in the way. If only he knew what he wanted; but nothing was clearly defined, nothing was simple. He searched for some phrase to bridge the awkwardness. A short laugh escaped his mouth, a reflexive exhalation, without gaiety.

"Look," he said. "Why don't I come by this evening? About eight. We'll go somewhere for dinner. Some place nice and——"

"I'm sorry, Guy. Not tonight. I'm busy."

He wasn't sure he understood. "Later then?"

"Tonight I'm busy."

It penetrated slowly, escorted by disbelief, by a widening resentment, by fear and finally relief. "You've got a date!"

"I'm busy."

"I don't understand," he began, congestion thick in his throat. "That's all right. I mean, it's your affair. But we ought to talk. About what's going on. It's not the kind of thing that can wait forever." He sucked air deep into his lungs. "Why don't I come over afterward? After your friend has left."

"That wouldn't be fair, Guy."

The words came ripping out of him. "Oh, you're something! With my baby in your belly, you can't wait to screw some other guy. What have you got to lose now? Does he know you're pregnant? Do you talk to him about me?" He broke off, frightened and uncertain. At last alone.

"All right," she said very quietly. "Come at 11 o'clock. Not before."

"I'm sorry. I didn't mean to——" She hung up.

Senator Abernathy adjourned the afternoon session at 4 o'clock and Ralph Jacobs went directly back to his Pentagon office. He yearned to release all the accumulated energy and frustration. He struggled to immerse himself in his work, and for a while it served its purpose—until now. With the Pentagon rapidly emptying of its daytime population, the irritability returned, deep and persistent.

Work was impossible. His thoughts were occupied with the man in the White House; Harrison Gunther, political strategist, historian, activist, a complex man, subtle, devious when necessary, but always aware of his purpose, of his goals, the President of the United States.

Or was he? Jacobs grimaced. Pompey had raised an army of ghosts that refused to stop marching. Past events, commonplace, routine, rose to haunt him, shaded to support the absurd charge. Ordinary conversations became pointed in retrospect, fraught with concealed meanings; and the day-by-day backing-and-filling, so much a part of the political scene, was transmuted into something insidious, murky, its motivations unclear. Ominous.

Once again he went to the small notebook. No single entry was conclusive, and totally they formed less than a positive picture of treachery on Pennsylvania Avenue. Why then had he kept the record? This was not Pompey's doing. In fact, he had been disturbed for some time. By the identity of the President? No, the question had never arisen. Rather by his course of action, the changes in temperament, in outlook, the unsettling ways in which he had begun to function, his goals suddenly blurred and strangely altered. Gradually, reluctantly, the two began to slide into sharp focus, Pompey's fears and his own.

Such troublesome speculation had to end, a finite identification made, an unimpeachable stamp of approval given. Who could supply it? Charlotte Gunther? Jacobs smiled at the thought of the wispy First Lady, remote, vague, always out of place, belonging nowhere with the single exception of her precious Rose Garden. She could offer little.

Who else was there?

There were areas of the President's private life about which Jacobs was knowledgeable, areas he was reluctant to explore. He entered Charlotte Gunther's name in the notebook. He thought for a moment. Then, Anne Lockridge. Peter Street. Dr. Corso. *Of course!*

Jacobs phoned the White House and asked for the President's personal physician, was told he could be reached at his private office. He dialed again. A female voice came on, Corso's nurse. Jacobs gave his name and waited.

"Hey, Ralph," Dr. Corso began. "Good to hear from you. Friend is this call professional or personal? I don't want to rush you, but unless it's serious, come around tomorrow. I'm off to play handball."

Jacobs smiled grimly. He had been right to call. "You still play, Tony?"

"Regular. You know what a nut I am about exercise. Trouble is, when men get to our age, they let go and soon begin coming apart at the seams. Violent exercise. Keep the blood circulating, get it out of the extremities, force it back through the heart so the old pump doesn't have to strain to do the work. Keep fit, keep young. I believe in it."

"Yes, Tony."

The doctor laughed. "Worst happens, it tires you out so you sleep without worrying. And that adds years to a man's life. I wish the President had time for more exercise. For him, too many tensions. Activity relieves that. At least he's swimming these days."

"Was that your doing, Tony?"

"*Quién sabe, amigo.*" Corso laughed, a loud, open sound. "He used to play handball with me pretty regular. At the Spartan Club. They've got four courts over there. But a few weeks ago he began to beg off. Too much business, I suppose. Anyway, he substituted swimming. Never knew he liked the water that much." Again that hearty laugh. "You know what the head doctors say about water, a womb symbol."

"They mean the ocean."

"Oh," Corso said, then brightening, "same thing, I guess. Now I got to go, Ralph, otherwise I'll never find a partner."

"Tony, would you like an easy mark for that game of yours?"

Corso laughed happily. "That's what I need, friend, to reinforce my ego. Ever since Harrison ripped me four in a row, I've been nursing my wounds. Meet you at the Spartan in half an hour. Okay?"

Jacobs found Dr. Corso waiting in the locker room, already in gym shorts and a T-shirt. He was a stocky man, thick through the middle, with no hint of flabbiness. Dark and hairy, heavily muscled, there was about him the bulging look of suppressed power. He was quick-moving and volatile, emotions close to the surface, without guile.

Corso had been a handball enthusiast since high school, and it was through handball that he and Harrison Gunther first met. Both were from Kansas City, and both had entered a local tournament during summer vacation from college, facing each other in an early round. Corso won handily and Gunther vowed revenge. As their handball enmity intensified, their friendship ripened. When Gunther was elected President, he insisted Corso give up his practice, transfer his medical activities to Washington, serve as White House physician.

Jacobs put on his gym clothes and laced up his sneakers. It had been six months since he was last here, and he found the stale-sweet smell of perspiration invigorating. He was glad he'd come, anxious to move around, to swing his arms, to feel the small, black, hard-rubber ball sting his palms. He stood up and grinned at Corso.

"I'm going to whip you, Tony."

The swarthy face creased into a brilliant smile. "For how much, friend? For how much?"

They were lucky. Upstairs, they found a vacant court. Corso switched on the lights and closed the door, and they were alone in that rectangular box of a room with its polished hardwood floor and white walls. There was something about four-wall handball, about being enclosed, isolated, excluding everything, everyone, but your opponent. This was a world apart, contained, singular, the very silence possessing a special quality of its own. They warmed up, the ball thumping solidly off the walls, biting at their hands through the gloves. Jacobs felt good moving around, and after a few minutes he stopped thinking and allowed his reflexes to take over. Soon he broke sweat.

"Whenever you're ready, Tony."

They played a game. Jacobs had never played enough to become really good at handball, but he liked the idea of pitting himself one-to-one against another man, liked the speed, the action, the strain on his body. It was a game in which a man could rise above his physical limitations, using his brain and his guts to prevail.

He was quick, both his feet and his hands, with a tendency to move toward the front wall too readily, anxious to meet his opponent's return, and thus frequently found himself being victimized by Dr. Corso's hard passing shots or deep lobs.

They split the first ten points, then Corso pulled ahead, winning easily. The doctor was not breathing hard.

"You're getting soft, Ralph. Should get out more often. Take care of yourself. Maybe this game is a little too tough for a desk type like you."

Jacobs grinned tightly and gestured for Corso to serve. He compensated for his errors, holding back more, trying to keep the ball in play, to allow Corso a chance to make mistakes, forcing the action. They had a number of long volleys, but Corso won each point. By now Jacobs' hand was swollen, and each time he hit the rock-hard black ball the pain was acute. An easy kill glanced off the heel of his hand and Corso laughed. Jacobs accepted it silently; winners, he had long ago learned, always laughed.

He braced himself and returned the next service low and hard to the front wall. He anticipated the kill and pulled up. It was a mistake. Corso flashed into view from the left, right hand reaching, hitting the ball high and deep. Jacobs turned and ran for the rear wall. He leaped, swung as hard as he could and barely got a piece of the ball. It bounced weakly off the front wall and Corso was there. He put it away. He ran off the next seven points and the game.

"Enough?" Corso said, black eyes glittering.

"Enough. You're right. I'm in miserable condition."

They went back down to the locker room, and

Corso smoked a cigarette while they stripped off their sweat-soaked clothes. "You're a pretty fair player, Ralph. But you'll really never be good till you stop trying to power every ball. Oh, you'd have to work yourself into playing shape, legs, wind, arms. But given the physical attributes, this becomes a head game, which is what a lot of people never realize. A smart player will out-brain a muscle man all the time."

The shower room was large, stalls providing privacy behind locked doors. The sting of hot water was invigorating, and Jacobs luxuriated under the fine spray long after he had finished soaping himself.

"That's my trouble," Corso said, when he finally appeared.

"What?"

"Too many muscles and I'm always trying to use them. You gotta know yourself. I mean, it took me years to realize that though I thought my arms were of equal strength, they weren't. Sometimes I try shots with my left hand that I never will be able to pull off, shots that would be a cinch for my right."

Jacobs finished drying himself and wrapped the towel around his middle. "How good is the President?"

"Interesting. I've played with that guy for years, ever since college. And I could always take him. Why? Because I had the power and he always catered to my strength. He used to make the same mistake you made today, returning my serve to the front wall when it can't be put away. Result—an easy kill. See?"

"I see."

They moved back into the locker room, began to dress. "Always did have Harry's game pegged," Corso said. "Always could take him. The few times he won, I wasn't putting out or didn't care. When I wanted to, I beat him easy. Until lately."

Jacobs concentrated on buttoning his shirt. His tone was casual, matter-of-fact. "What was different?"

"He beat me, that's what was different. All of a sudden he pulled a switch and beat me."

"Maybe you're getting old, Tony."

The physician snorted. "Nah. It was the switch. He used to play a slashing game, constantly attacking, moving forward. I could anticipate his moves and drive him back. You see, he never knew how to take a shot out of the air. The last few times were different. He changed. Wised up, I guess. Obviously, he had been thinking about it, figured out what he was doing wrong and what I was doing. Just like that, he began to lob me to death. Just like that, a soft-ball artist. You should have seen it. He took control from the start; lobbed and lobbed and lobbed some more. Forced me away from the front, set me up like a pigeon, and *wham!* put it away. I mean, he really worked me over."

"Probably a bad game for you."

"No," Corso said thoughtfully. "Happened too often, maybe a dozen times over three or four playing days. No. He worked out a complete change of strategy; his approach to the game turned around, and he stuck to it."

Jacobs went over to the mirror and combed his hair and did his tie. "Does he still beat you?" he asked.

"Nope."

A surge of disappointment went through him, the theory shattered before it had really taken hold. "You made some adjustments in your own game?"

"Nope. We haven't played for over two weeks. The last time he beat me I complimented him. Said I was glad he finally had smartened up, even if I was getting whipped, said it was like playing against a different man and I'd have to sharpen my tactics. We made a date to play again that week but he broke it—the next day, I think. Guess he's been too busy since."

"Well," Jacobs said, "from what you tell me, there's no need to be concerned about the President's health. Sounds as if he's in first-rate condition."

"Better than ever. His reflexes are excellent, his

heart strong. A slight rise in blood pressure, but nothing to worry about. The job, you know. Even his muscularity seems to have improved. People say the Presidency is a man-killer, and I suppose it is. But Harry's a different breed. He thrives on it."

Different. The key word, the word used over and over, a word to gambol tauntingly around Jacobs' brain.

Pompey left the White House and crossed East Executive Avenue, heading for the garage on E Street. He hesitated before entering. Where was he going? He had no intention of returning to his apartment. He glanced at his watch. A few minutes after eight. Nearly three hours before he was to meet Gail. Walter spotted him and greeted him by name.

"Want the Mercedes, Mr. Pompey?"

"No, thanks, Walter. Think I'll have a little dinner first."

He went to O'Donnell's and drank two Gibsons on the rocks. He ordered a center cut of striped bass, a baked potato and cole slaw. He wasn't hungry, but made himself eat, chewing carefully, determined to finish it all. Halfway through, he gave up and ordered coffee.

It was not yet nine o'clock when he left O'Donnell's. More than two hours to kill. He went to the Variety Club and drank Scotch and talked about the Senators' chances in the American League that season. The barman agreed that the team's chances didn't amount to very much. Another customer summoned the barman, and Pompey took the opportunity to gaze around the room.

He spied a vaguely familiar face, a pretty secretary who worked for a Congressman from Nebraska. She was sitting with an elderly man who appeared to be delivering a lecture, waggling a forefinger under her chin. From his place at the bar, Pompey saw her flush. She fought back, eyes flashing, lips working swiftly.

Abruptly, the exchange ended. The secretary made

a gesture of dismissal, and her companion rose and left. The girl sat back in her chair and lit a cigarette. Pompey noticed that her hands were steady. On impulse, he joined her.

"Hello," he said. "You work for George Luchan?" She nodded coolly. "I'm Guy Pompey."

"I know. I'm Sylvia MacDonald."

At close range, it was apparent that she was at the peak of her attractiveness. In her middle twenties, there was still a freshness to her, the features clearly defined. Before long, excess weight would pad her out, and she would grow soft and puffy. But that lay in the future. Now, face framed by carefully arranged crimson hair, she was more than just pretty.

"I remembered your name," he lied.

She shook her head. "I don't believe you. There are thousands of girls like me in this town. You must meet most of them. But there's only one Presidential Press Secretary."

He sat next to her. "And here I am."

"How nice for me!"

"Your friend, is coming back?"

"He's no longer my friend and he'd better not come back."

"You're a hard lady."

She shrugged and finished her drink. "A girl either takes care of herself or she goes under." She lifted her glass. "Buy a drink for a lady?"

Pompey signaled the barman; he brought them each a drink.

"You come here often?" Pompey said.

"No. My friend . . . my ex-friend likes this place. He makes this out to be a swinging scene, all that show-bussiness jive. Also, his wife isn't likely to spot him here."

He asked her where she was from, and she began to talk about herself. She spoke swiftly but without strain, an outpouring of detail that demanded little or no response from Pompey. When her glass was empty, he ordered more drinks. She continued to chatter. Pompey looked at his watch.

"You got to go?" she said.

"I've got an appointment."

"Is she pretty?"

He wondered if Sylvia knew about Gail. In official Washington, there were few secrets, and gossip was elevated to a fine and efficient art form.

"Business," he said.

Her brows rose and she spread her voluptuous lips. "So late!"

"Later," he grinned. "At eleven."

"Monkey business."

He laughed. "I won't argue."

"Listen," she said slowly. "There's still plenty of time. Wouldn't you like to take me home. I live only a few minutes away and——"

"Let's go."

She lived in a studio apartment, the walls smooth and white, the furnishings very modern, sleek. She directed him to the couch and urged him to make himself comfortable. He took off his jacket and sat down, put his head back and closed his eyes. A dark swirl, a shifting perspective, settled around his brain. Through the swirl, and the gray darkness, there was something else. Movement. Another presence. He forced his eyes open. Sylvia had settled next to him, the pretty face closed and remote. She stroked his cheek.

"Don't go to sleep on me, honey."

He grunted.

"You know, honey, you're one of the most talked-about guys in this town."

He focused on her.

"All the girls have it for you. Why not? You're good-looking and close to the top. I mean, who wouldn't like to make it with you!"

Her hand on his stomach began to move in a small tight circle. She leaned closer, her perfume faintly unpleasant, distasteful. He leaned back again.

"A few of us were talking about you, wondering how come you never tried to date anybody. I mean, with the shortage of real men, most girls are not ex-

actly hard to get. They can't afford to be—you fo
I mean, a groovy character like you could have a ba
all the time."

"Does that include you?"

"Try me."

He touched her lips. They closed softly on his middle finger. She sucked wetly, staring into his eyes. A twinge of excitement came and held. How would it be, he wondered. It had been so long since he had had another woman, a woman other than Gail.

She slid her hand under his shirt, onto his bare chest. "Ah, nice. You got hair. I like that, a man with hair on him." She laughed thickly. "I figured I'd take a chance getting you, when I saw you at the bar."

"What about your friend?"

"I got rid of him easy enough. Picked a fight and dumped him."

"I'm flattered."

"You like me, honey?"

"Sure," he said, thinking about Gail. Where was she at this moment? And with whom? He visualized her in a man's apartment, naked, making love, doing the things that for so long had been reserved only for Pompey, saying the words she had spoken only to Pompey. He straighened up.

"Is something wrong, honey?"

He hooked his hand behind her neck and drew her face down to his. Her mouth was gaping, her tongue fleshy and wet. He felt for her breast. It was larger than Gail's and softer. Flabby almost.

She pushed against him, maneuvering until she was on her knees facing him. She yanked her skirt higher, striving for greater mobility. Her crotch pressed against his waist with competitive urgency, and her breathing was asthmatically noisy and feverish.

"Jesus!" she cried, rotating her middle against him. "I like the way you do things. And the way you kiss. You've got a great mouth. Here," she said, guiding him to her spread thighs. "Idle hands make for mischief, my mama used to say."

The flesh was loose and warm. She planted her

his and held it there for an extended pe- en she rose quickly.

ome on." She began to undo the fastenings of her dress. "Let's get down to it. We don't have a lot of time. There's that appointment of yours. I wouldn't want you to be late." She laughed.

He took off his shoes. Standing, he slipped off his jacket and hung it carefully over the back of a chair. Next, his tie and shirt. He stepped out of his trousers.

Naked, she came at him, breath rasping, hands grasping. The slight sag of her heavy breasts was provocative and he watched with approval as she dragged his undershorts off. She kissed his stomach, his chest. She drew him back to the couch, coming down on him.

She raised her head. The red hair fell in strands and the lipstick was smeared and there was a voracious gleam in her eyes, the cheek puffy. Her laugh was a triumphant wail.

"Know what I thought, honey? With you not making it with any of the girls. That you were gay. Isn't that a riot! You a fag! We figured that girl you were supposed to have was just a cover, a beard, see. That you really made it with boys. This town is loaded with that action." Again the rising laugh. "But I know better. You're for real, honey, the real action."

Her mouth played along his rib cage, across his stomach. She shifted lower, working down past his swollen manhood, chewing his thigh, traveling along his leg, stopping finally at his stocking tops.

He watched, peering down the length of his body, gripped by a detached interest. The heavy breasts hung freely, suddenly seemed to be without shape, streaked and stained by a complex of blue veins, undernourished. The belly drooped loosely and shimmered as she moved. Her buttocks and upper thighs were dimpled, and he noticed stretch marks on her hips.

She was back astride him soon. She tugged and manipulated, fiercely demanding. Painful. Her mouth was insistent. "Oh," she complained. "What is it?

Where did it go? Make it come back, honey. Make it." A thick sound filled her throat. "I'll do it. I'll make it come back. You'll see what I can do, a little loving . . ."

He felt nothing. The swirl enveloped him once more, and his brain dipped and tilted. A distant light came into view, growing brighter, taking shape. A face, the features faintly reminiscent. Gail's face, the expression disappointed, forgiving. He looked at his watch.

"You're not trying," Sylvia complained, sitting back on her haunches. "You got to do better. I know you can. Come on, now."

He stood up, started to dress.

"Hey! What do you think you're doing? What in goddamnedhell do you think you're doing?"

He looked at her, then turned away.

"I asked you a question," she bit off toughly. "You can't just walk out on me!"

"This is a mistake," he said. "I'm sorry. I shouldn't have come. A mistake."

"Just like that!" She stared at him for a long beat. "You're really going to split, just like that. Well you can't. You just *can't*. What about me, the way I feel. You can't leave me this way. You can't."

He adjusted his tie and put on his jacket, ran his fingers through his hair. "I'm sorry, I said. This isn't going to work."

"Bastard!" she shrilled, as he went toward the door. "I was right about you. Right! You're queer, a rotten, perverted faggot!"

He left trying to retain some sense of dignity, aware of the absurdity of the moment, and his role in it. He went back to the garage and climbed into the Mercedes. He lit a cigarette to help remove the taste of Sylvia MacDonald from his mouth. Two puffs and the dizziness returned. There had been too many Scotches. His mind was thick and ponderous, his vision unclear, his senses blurred. He wanted very much to hit somebody.

He drove slowly, carefully, concentrating on the

road ahead, trying not to anticipate the confrontation with Gail. He parked fifty feet from the entrance to her building and lit a cigarette. It was 10:45. Had she returned? Even now she might be alone with her date in the apartment. He struggled to turn his mind to other things without success, kept imagining her with another man, her body arched in that way she had, the stranger's hands roaming across her flesh. He cursed himself for being a fool.

A white Thunderbird turned into the curved street, drew to a stop in front of the building. Gail went inside, followed by a tall, well-dressed man. Ten minutes passed before the tall man reappeared and drove away. Pompey climbed out of the Mercedes. He was very tired.

He rang her bell and waited. Rang again. Finally, she admitted him. She had changed clothes, was wearing a floor-length hostess gown of maroon silk with a Mandarin-style collar. It enhanced the Oriental set of her eyes.

"I'm making some coffee," she said.

"I want a drink."

She glanced sidelong at him. "Coffee would do you more good." She disappeared into the kitchen. He went over to the bar and poured some Scotch into a glass. He went into the kitchen for ice. Her back was toward him. He put a hand on her waist. An almost imperceptible movement was enough to dislodge it.

"Shall we go inside?" she said, moving ahead of him.

In the living room, he established himself on the couch and was annoyed when she took her coffee to a straight-backed chair across the room.

"You wanted to talk," she said. "All right."

His brain pitched and yawed, and out of the heaving he wanted to punish her, to cause her pain.

"Who was that man?"

"Does it matter?"

"How long have you been dating him? While we were seeing each other?"

"This was the first time." She spoke evenly, her manner controlled and distant.

"How do I know?" he said, wishing he could hold back the words. "How do I know you're not lying? That he hasn't been around all this time? Maybe he's the one, not me."

It rose up into her throat—a glob of emotion, the accumulated resentment, his rejection of her and her baby, his failure to be strong when she most required strength of him, his failure to love her enough, to love her as she loved him, his inability to make room in his life for her and her child, his refusal to provide the continuity she yearned for and needed.

"I think you'd better go." She stood rigid and resolute, at the same time vulnerable. There was a kind of waxen immobility to her features that made him unsure.

"I didn't mean that." He lurched erect, took a step toward her.

She backed away. "Don't touch me, Guy."

He sat back down, a faint trembling rising up from his knees. He brought the Scotch to his lips with an unsteady hand. His brain was jittering from side to side like some rubbery mass, unstable, formless. He wanted very much to close his eyes, to shut out everything. He stumbled to his feet, face mottled and straining.

"Listen, Gail," he began. Abruptly all color drained out of him, and he went running into the bathroom. She heard him being sick and tried not to feel compassion. She had to take care of herself, had to keep from being hurt even more, had to keep from being used. There was no future for them together.

She went into the kitchen and filled a cup with black coffee. When she returned to the living room, he was spread out on the couch, wan and weak.

She placed the coffee on the low table. "This may help."

"I'm sorry," he murmured.

"It's all right."

"This thing has got me crazy," he mumbled. "Not

knowing is the worst of it. Not knowing what's happening."

"It will all be over in a few days," she said, trying to reassure him. "There's nothing to worry about. I went to my own doctor. He said that I was strong and healthy, and nothing bad could happen to me. When I come back, when it's done, I'm to call him at once and he'll examine me, take care of me. So you can see there's nothing to be frightened about."

His eyes rolled in their sockets and she was afraid he was going to be sick again. He stared through her. "Not knowing," he sputtered. "And not saying. Not able to talk to anybody, to be sure."

"I don't understand."

His eyes clamped shut and his head fell back. "The President," he mumbled, almost inaudibly. "Not Gunther. Not him. Ketza knows. Ketza."

"Ketza?"

"His dog. The dog knows."

"What are you saying?"

". . . Dog wants his throat rubbed . . . throat. He won't do it . . . won't do it." He came erect, face distorted, eyes staring. ". . . Isn't the President . . . not him at all . . . somebody else taking his place. An impostor . . ." He fell back and a moment later began to snore, a soft staccato.

Gail sat in the chair across the room and gazed at him for a long time, trying not to believe what she had heard.

IV

It was a monumental hangover. The pain across his forehead made Pompey know he was awake; it came and went in alternating waves, searing deep into the tissues on the underside of his skull. His eyes were swollen in their sockets, throbbing, his mouth corrupted. A moan trickled across his parched lips. He moved. And fell off the couch.

Gail came hurrying into the living room. He lay still, eyelids fluttering.

"Are you hurt?" she said.

"I," he managed after a moment, "am going to die."

"I doubt it," she said dryly. She went back into the kitchen and reappeared moments later with tomato juice and black coffee. She set both on the low table near him. "I must get ready for work," she said.

After a while, he managed to come up into a sitting position and reached for the tomato juice. Swallowing was difficult. By the time Gail finished her shower, he was able to turn his attention to the coffee. When she returned to the living room, wearing a green wool challis dress, he had made it back onto the couch.

"I love you," he said.

"Not enough," she said without bitterness. "And this way is no good for me. You better shower now and dress. It's getting late."

"I prefer to stay here and die," he muttered with dignity.

"Outside, please. In the streets, where nobody'll notice."

"You're cruel, lady." He forced himself erect and stood swaying, dizzy, pleased by the sensation. He made it into the bathroom without falling. A shower helped. Afterward, he swallowed four aspirin and shaved, using the razor she kept for him. When he returned to the living room, she was seated primly on the straight-backed chair. Another cup of coffee was on the table.

He started to speak, but she interrupted. "Last night you said something about the President."

He concentrated on the coffee. "I was drunk."

"It couldn't be true," she said.

Jacobs had warned him to make no mention of this matter, and so he had promptly gotten drunk and done exactly the reverse. Her expression was serious, brow grooved with worry. Gail, he assured himself, was dependable, trustworthy. Then, second thoughts. Was anyone to be trusted in a situation so explosive, so close to disaster?

"I was drunk," he repeated.

"You said the President was not Harrison Gunther, that he was an impostor."

"A bad joke."

The Tartar eyes were slitted, wary. "It couldn't be true. It simply couldn't be."

"I was drunk, trying to be funny."

"I didn't laugh. That isn't my idea of a joke, and I don't think it's yours."

"You've lost your sense of humor."

She wanted to end it, to put the idea out of her mind, to believe she had heard only the mutterings of a man drunk and trying to be amusing. But such an explanation was too glib, too easy to accept.

"Have you told anyone else?" she asked.

"Oh, please, leave it alone, Gail."

"Who?"

There was a growing urgency to share the burden, to tell someone and so ease the pressures he felt. He needed a confidant, someone close, someone who cared about him and would identify with his torment, the growing terror. Gail would understand. He wet his lips.

"This is getting us nowhere," he said.

"You've told someone. Who was it?"

He sighed. "He didn't believe me either. So you see, it doesn't matter."

"Who did you tell?"

"Ralph Jacobs."

"Oh, no! Not Jacobs! You fool! You damned fool! Do you realize what you've done? You're finished now, your career, everything. They'll hound you, punish you at every turn, allow you no rest."

"You don't know what you're talking about. Jacobs said——"

"Jacobs isn't going to let it go. You know the kind of man he is. He'll pursue it until he's satisfied one way or another. A thing like that, he could never ignore it. Not Jacobs. He'll try to prove that you were wrong or right. And you're not right! You couldn't be. Oh, damn! Guy, where did you ever get such a wild idea?"

He tried to explain, to tell her everything; she cut him short. Never before had he seen her this agitated.

"I don't want to hear it. None of it. The man in the White House *is* Harrison Gunther. *Must be.* He must . . . Do you know what it means if this is true, what it means to the nation, to everybody in the world?"

"That's just it, Gail. I mean . . . oh, damn! I care about the country . . ." He breathed deeply and tried to smile; it wouldn't hold. "All right. I told you. I suppose I had to tell someone, to get it out. Now you've got to promise you'll say nothing to anyone. You can see, nobody must know."

"You didn't have to ask. I wouldn't tell anyone. I *couldn't*. This is too wild, too insane. Nobody would accept it. It's too much, and I don't want to think about it."

"Then I can trust you?" He peered searchingly at her.

"Trust me?" she said quietly. She almost laughed. It was not her reliability that should be questioned, but his own; and she considered the times he had failed her. How odd, she thought, that at a time when such a singular and terrifying piece of information had come to her, she still managed to remain concerned with her private affairs. Perhaps that was part of being female; biology, she dimly recalled reading somewhere, determines destiny.

"I'm depending on you, Gail," he said.

She looked up at him. "I will keep your secret."

They stood facing each other with the room separating them, and she experienced a resurgence of feeling for him. Love? No. That was all past, and she would not allow what still lingered to direct her any longer. Compassion was what she felt. Understanding, perhaps. Pity, although she loathed the sentiment. But no more love. Love for Guy Pompey had trapped her, had planted the seed of a new life in her belly, a life he did not want, a life she dared not bring forth. And she was deeply afraid of what was going to happen, and of how she was going to feel afterward. No more love for them.

"I must go," she said firmly. "I'm doing a series of articles about some of the private gardens in the area. I've scheduled an interview with Mrs. Gunther, about the Rose Garden. She's done some wonderful things, you know. I've got to go. You stay as long as you like."

She turned at the door. He appeared forlorn and wasted, smaller somehow. "I don't want to hear about it again. Never. I mean it, Guy."

He nodded.

"One more thing," she said. "I made the arrangements. Tomorrow night. In Baltimore."

He felt himself go cold.

"This man, Al, he'll pick me up at the railroad station, the Charles Street entrance, at 9:15."

"Well, I'll get the money for you. Five hundred, in an envelope." He stood up and filled his lungs with air and arranged a small smile on his full mouth. "I'll drive you, of course. We can stop off somewhere and have a nice dinner. Maybe at—"

She shook her head and he saw her lips tighten. "No dinner, please. Just drive me there. I appreciate that. And about the money—I'll pay you back some day."

"No!"

"I *want* to, don't you see? This is as much my fault, maybe more."

"We'll talk about it another time."

Her mouth curled upward at the corners in what was not a smile. "I'll expect you tomorrow about eight."

"Yes."

She turned back at the door. "Guy," she said. "I'm terribly frightened."

When he arrived at his office, Pompey found a message from Ralph Jacobs asking him to call at once. He was reluctant to talk to the Defense Secretary, yet felt he had to. "Get him for me," he told Margaret Reilly and sat down behind his desk, aware of a spreading tension in his loins.

Jacobs wasted no time on preliminaries. He came on curt and to the point. "At my house at 7," he said. "This evening. We've got some talking to do."

The peremptory summons shook Pompey. There was disapproval in Jacobs' voice, an implicit threat. He tried to anticipate Jacobs' thinking, the action he would take. He considered the matter from every angle, and decided that Jacobs intended to force him out of the White House, out of government. The flaw in the system was to be eliminated.

Well, all right. It was time to go back where he belonged, to the agency, to New York. The rewards would be greater and more varied, the demands fewer and less wearing. As for the time he'd spent in Washington, his record spoke for itself.

That evening when he arrived at the house in Georgetown, Pompey was ushered to the upstairs study. Jacobs, though clad in a velvet smoking jacket and slippers, seemed no less intimidating, his manner stern and unbending. He motioned Pompey to the big maroon leather chair and took his place behind the desk.

"Some refreshments?" Jacobs said. "A brandy?"

Pompey declined. His stomach stirred uneasily, the memory of the previous night too vivid. He watched Jacobs open a small, inexpensive notebook and spread it flat upon the desk, briefly study the contents.

"I've been considering what you said," he began.

Gail had been right, Pompey recalled unhappily. Jacobs couldn't allow such an unlikely charge to go unanswered or unproved. Pompey was going to be the target for the full force of the Defense Secretary's fury and power, victim of his own impulsiveness, his own undisciplined imagination.

"Your charge," Jacobs said, "stands unproved, a wild premise, far-fetched, isolated and difficult to believe, impossible to accept." His head was tilted against the high back of the chair, and his eyes closed. "Almost impossible," he amended. "But not quite."

The words seeped into Pompey's brain, took on meaning. A pulse began to throb irregularly in his temple.

"Then you believe me—that the President is an impostor?"

Jacobs kept his eyes closed. "I believe only that the possibility exists. Nothing more. Most likely, it is all convergence of circumstance, absurd for the most part, without foundation, a devastating condition if true. I expect it will prove out to be nonsense and in retrospect laughable."

That was it—a very bad joke. But the fact that a man of Jacobs' stature and intelligence would give it even this much consideration was alarming. And at the same time, vaguely reassuring. Jacobs would determine the truth and that would end the matter; and then they—only the two of them—would be amused as they reflected on how they had supposedly held the fate of the nation in their hands. His smile widened.

"I guess we'll just have to solve the problem," Pompey said.

"Yes," Jacobs said glumly, "we will."

If only, Jacobs reflected, men were the rational

beings they liked to consider themselves. This man, this Guy Pompey, educated, worldly, accustomed to associating with people of substance, a man of accomplishment, a sophisticated man, yet willing to give credence to an idea so outrageous that, if true, could uproot governments, cause death and destruction, radically alter the course of history; yet Jacobs doubted that Pompey had, for even a millimeter of time, considered what action should be taken if his suspicions were confirmed.

Sitting immobile behind his desk, immutable, eyes steady and flat, Jacobs considered the problem. There was no provision in his experience for this mad moment, at first glance so reasonable and civilized on the surface, so tumultuous and violent in the deep. By Jacobs' unstated beliefs, a man scratched and squirmed in the struggle to survive and prevail, he pursued goals, shifting positions, changing directions—often only barely within the laws of man and of God, but constantly alert not to harm other people, for human life was sacrosanct. Paradoxically, he headed an establishment capable of vaporizing a large majority of the world's people in a matter of minutes. There was an unsettling twinge in his duodenum.

"Given," he said, "an impostor sits in the White House . . ."

Pompey felt easier. This much acceptance was enough to save him, to protect him, restoring his belief in his own sanity. He felt in tune with the world now, certain all questions would soon be answered. That relief and comfort should come at such a moment did not strike him as odd.

"To accept the possibility," Jacobs said, "is one thing. To prove it, an entirely different matter."

Pompey edged forward. There was a growing excitement about all this, a rising confidence in his own judgment. His swart skin glowed in the soft light, and his dark eyes were bright.

"This is no child's game," Jacobs said. "The risks are tremendous. Have you thought that, if there is an impostor, it means that somebody has stolen the real Harrison Gunther?"

The vertebrae of Pompey's spine seemed suddenly to fuse into a rigid line of bone. "That means someone has him now. . . ."

"Or more likely, has disposed of him," Jacobs said.

"Murdered the President!"

"Accept the initial premise, and that seems likely," Jacobs said dryly. "It's also reasonable to assume that same someone would kill both of us, should our suspicions become known."

A chill of despair pimpled Pompey's skin. He brought his attention back to the Defense Secretary, still talking in a flat, expressionless way.

"A scheme of this magnitude—it would require a tremendous effort. Planning, time, money, people highly trained—especially the double."

Pompey felt overwhelmed by the situation, so immense and terrifying. It was insane, all of it. Only a man unbalanced and out of harmony with his environment would have entertained such an idea.

"To begin," Jacobs said as he reached for a pen and began to make notes, "we have to put ourselves in the kidnapers' position, reconstruct the plot, consider the various possibilities."

Pompey began to stutter. "It might have been anybody, anybody in the world."

"Not at all," Jacobs said briskly. His brain was alive, seeking information, assembling data, attempting to formulate a train of logic. He enjoyed this in the same way that he enjoyed solving a mathematical problem or plotting the races. He almost smiled. "Consider. To make such an impersonation come off, it would be necessary to virtually reproduce Harrison Gunther, physically and otherwise. A monumental project. Assuming they were successful, there had to be the right combination of coincidence and hard work, a long and trying effort. Where would it begin? When? How?"

Pompey fought against the panic in his middle, forced himself to attend the problem. Obviously, all this had begun after the election, for there had been no certainty Harrison Gunther would be elected. In truth, he almost had been defeated, his margin of victory less than two hundred thousand votes.

"*They* began with the discovery of a double," Jacobs was saying. "I would imagine just before or at about the time of the election."

"Who are *They*?"

Jacobs shrugged. "It could be a gigantic criminal plot, an attempt to extort a huge sum of money or disrupt the normal functions of government. But I doubt that. Politics appears at the root."

"The Russians?"

"Or the Chinese. Or someone else. Why not one of the smaller, unaligned nations hoping to direct this country's policies in a more favorable path? The possibilities are endless. Though, at this point, it doesn't matter too much. In time, I suppose we'll get to it. For now, we have to decide to our own satisfaction whether the man in the White House is Harrison Gunther or not—and without arousing public suspicion or fear. No one must know what we are about. The slightest hint would have a calamitous result. Understood?"

"Yes," Pompey said, remembering Gail. He made himself listen. Jacobs was talking about Dr. Corso and the President's apparently increased muscularity.

"And this change in his handball game," Jacobs said, "it involved a different strategic concept, an alteration in his thinking. We know that men play games mostly on instinct. Thinking precedes action. Once play starts, it's almost always an intuitive reaction."

"Couldn't the President have considered the game, how Corso always beat him, and adapted himself accordingly?"

"Yes, though after so many years, it seems unlikely. The President was too smart not to know why he was being beaten. All along he continued to play his own game. Call it ego, or faith in himself, whatever you want. In any case, he intended to win or lose in terms of himself. I don't believe he switched. And if so, why did he suddenly cease playing with Corso when the doctor pointed out the change in style?"

"Wasn't it possible for the impostor to have known the kind of player the President was, played that kind of game?"

"Perhaps." Jacobs fell silent, then: "Maybe his own competitive instinct came into the picture. More likely they overlooked this. Some things were bound to be missed, no matter how thorough the preparations. The dog, for example. His informants, agents, never spotted that. The same with the handball game. Perhaps there have been other oversights. We'll see."

"How?"

Jacobs' brows tugged together and the high, pale forehead ridged over. Pompey had fallen comfortably into place in the rear rank, awaiting instructions, his brain turned off. It was a situation Jacobs had come to expect.

"The President's parents," Jacobs said. "They're still alive?"

"Yes. Still living in Kansas City."

Jacobs made a note. "Someone will have to talk to them," he said. "And to his wife."

Pompey recalled what Gail had said about a gardening series, about interviewing the First Lady. He hesitated, then told Jacobs.

"Could you arrange for Miss Sorrell to ask certain questions of Mrs. Gunther? Of course, you won't be able to explain why."

"I think so," Pompey said.

Jacobs reached for a yellow legal pad. He wrote for ten minutes, tore off the sheet and folded it neatly into quarters, handed it to Pompey. "These questions. You're not to show them to Miss Sorrell, or mention me or this discussion. Merely suggest that you have private reasons for wanting the information, phrase the questions in your own language, *read* them to her. The point is to elicit information that may be known only to the President's wife. Agreed? Now, who else must we interview?"

Anne Lockridge. The name lit up Pompey's brain. Gunther's affair with the actress was no secret in high places in Washington. It had been going on for years, and upon his election Anne Lockridge had moved into an expensive apartment in the Meridian Hill Park district, available whenever he wanted her. Any investigation would have to include her, and that presented certain dangers, for the very nature of their affair displayed her intense protective concern for the President.

As if reading Pompey's mind, Jacobs spoke. "Anne Lockridge. Have you ever met her?"

"Once, briefly. During the campaign. She was on tour with a play, and Gunther was in Detroit for a speech. He asked me to bring her from the theater to the hotel so that no one would see her."

"How did you manage?"

"It was a strange experience. Sneaking through the service entrance, through thc basement, bribing an elevator operator to let me take his car while he waited downstairs, hiding in corners until people passed us by. But no one saw her."

Jacobs put Pompey's initials next to her name. "Speak to her. See what you can learn. Personal things. I imagine she'll be difficult, but you must make her talk."

"About what?"

Jacobs glared at him, hard and unbending. "Has she noticed any recent changes in behavior, the kind of thing a mistress might be sensitive to? Anything at all. No point in preparing questions for her. You'll have to be alert to your opportunities."

"I'll try."

Jacobs made a noncommittal sound. "I'll talk with Peter Street. He and Gunther used to be close, he might be helpful. Also Julian Dawson."

Pompey allowed himself no visible reaction. Julian Dawson was the chief of the White House Secret Service detail, a man sworn to sacrifice his own life if necessary to protect the Chief Executive, a man tough and suspicious. He had a way of looking at people that disturbed Pompey, made him feel vaguely guilty.

It was 10 o'clock when Pompey arrived back at his own apartment. He was tired and craved a woman. He thought about Gail and knew that she would never accept his attentions on this night. Then he remembered the questions Jacobs had prepared. He phoned. She indicated no pleasure at the sound of his voice.

"How do you feel?" he began.

"I'm fine."

"Try not to think about it," he said.

Her reply was swift, charged. "I *want* to think about it, Guy. For the rest of my life. Tomorrow I'm going to kill my baby, Guy, and I don't want ever to forget it."

He suppressed a quick retort, then: "I know, darling. I understand."

"No. No, you don't understand. You couldn't. No man does, who allows a woman to do this thing. Let's not talk about it anymore. Please." Her voice grew lighter, more casual. "Now, why did you call?"

"To say hello, and good night."

"I see."

"By the way," he went on, wishing he didn't have to involve her. "Are you going to interview Mrs. Gunther tomorrow?"

"Yes."

"I'd like you to do me a favor, put a few questions to her." The sheet of paper Jacobs had given him lay open on his lap.

Her voice was small and frightened. "It's not over, is it, Guy? You still think it's true?"

"Please. Let me read the questions to you. Write them down. Just leave it at that."

"You and Ralph Jacobs. You've been talking to him again. That means he believes it too."

He fought a mounting annoyance. "I want you to do me a favor. Must you dramatize it?" He put a smile into his voice. "Ask Mrs. Gunther these questions, darling. She likes to talk. Just get her started.

She's kind of a far-out type and chatters on about everything."

"It's true," she murmured, "about the President being an impostor?"

"For God's sake, Gail, do what I ask! Believe me, it's important."

"Oh, Guy, I'm frightened."

"Do this for me."

"Secretary Jacobs," she said. "He believes you. It must be true," she ended weakly.

He exhaled. "No. Not yet. He doesn't believe it yet." He felt himself go limp, muscles sagging, his spine flexible. "He doesn't know. Neither of us does. Gail, we've got to be sure."

"What's happening?" she whimpered into the phone. "The woods are on fire and nobody's doing anything."

"We're trying," he said desperately. "That's why you've got to help."

"All right," she said after a long interval. "I'll ask the questions. But afterward, when you have your answers. What then?"

"It depends on what we find out. There are other people to talk to." He hesitated. "You're not to mention this to anyone. No one. Jacobs doesn't know that I've told you."

"Tell me the questions."

She sounded strained and lifeless when they finally said good night. He told himself that when everything was over, this affair with the President, the abortion, when she'd had time to regain her strength, her sense of proportion, she'd understand that he was doing what had to be done. She'd be proud of him. When she was feeling better they'd go out to dinner, some place expensive, where the lights and the music were soft. After drinks and a good meal she'd be ready for anything. That was worth waiting for.

V

Pompey tore the sheet of paper out of the typewriter. He balled it up and threw it toward the wastebasket in the corner. Missed. He swore again and rolled another sheet into the machine.

Last night he had slept fitfully, and now the cavities of his skull felt swollen, his thought processes ponderous and slow. This story on the President's welfare program—he'd been working on it for two days and still it was wrong. The bill was holed up in committee in the House, sat on by Representative Simons who fancied himself to be the last bastion of Federal economy, a man who frequently sounded a call to what he termed Christian principles, principles that always managed to ignore the increasing hordes of impoverished people in the slum areas of the dying cities. This story, it was hoped, would arouse public indignation and so pressure Congress into acting soon.

Earlier, Charley Hepburn had phoned Pompey, stressing certain points he felt should be made, underscoring the political value of passage in this session, a strong weapon to be used in next year's elections. But the story failed to jell, was confused and without direction. Pompey made a mighty effort to organize his ideas, to begin again. He made no attempt to conceal his annoyance when Margaret Reilly appeared.

"What is it?" he said.

"I'm sorry," she said. "Sarah is outside with the Time Right Society delegation."

He swore and Reilly tried not to hear the words.

"The President wants you to see them," she said

with a certain amount of satisfaction. "Sarah says something's come up."

That should have alerted him, but sudden changes in the President's schedule were not unusual and delegations were frequently directed to other White House aides in an effort to distribute the work load.

"I understand," Reilly continued, "that General Quirk and Secretary Keefe went in to see him, some others. I wonder what's going on?" she ended brightly.

Pompey did too. He was more than mildly curious. "Scout around, Maggie. See what you can find out."

"Yes, sir."

"And send Sarah's people in."

There were six of them, four ladies and two men, elderly, with thin, parchment skin, their mid-Western faces bland and scrubbed, gold-rimmed glasses glinting. Pompey welcomed them with professional cordiality and explained that the pressure of the national interest prevented the President from greeting them in person.

"The President knows you understand," he closed, smiling his most charming smile.

They did indeed. "We wouldn't want to disrupt things around here," a little, plump lady in a blue-and-white flowered dress gushed, hands fluttering. Her wide-brimmed white hat bobbed excitedly as she spoke. She took one step forward. "Mr. Pompey, we don't want to take up too much of your time with our little problem. But it is the right of an enlightened citizenry to petition for grievances . . ." She giggled and blushed. ". . . And we do have out little grievance." Her round face lengthened, grew serious. "We feel this is *très* important to us all, to you, to the nation at large, Mr. Pompey."

"I'm sure it is. Mrs.—Toland, isn't it? Tell me what's on your mind. I'll convey your thinking to the President myself."

It was a matter of time. Daylight saving time, to be exact. Mrs. Toland blurted out breathy sentences, as if unable to inhale while talking. Occasionally she would pause, a kind of momentary desperation, her ample bosom heaving for air. During these interludes, the other members of the delegation interpolated their support.

"The days of summer are long and sweet."

"They needn't be longer."

"Amen to that. Winter needs the extra time."

Winter, Mrs. Toland explained, was when the days were grim, the period of light too brief. An additional hour tacked on to each day would add much to life, would have a practical, constructive quality.

"Cut down on crime, Mr. Pompey, most of which comes in the dark, you know."

"And diminish auto fatalities. Yes, sir. It would. People speeding around at night are more likely to come to no good end."

"And consider morale. Folks are just naturally more sprightly when out in God's own bright daytime."

Pompey allowed them fifteen minutes before he maneuvered them out of his office, past Reilly at her desk, and into the corridor, promising to plead their case.

"Was it very bad?" Reilly asked when he returned.

He grinned at her. "Not really. They've got a good idea. Daylight saving time in winter. Not bad." He sobered swiftly. "Did you find out anything?"

"I spoke to Sarah. There's trouble in a place called San Carlos. They're talking about it in the Cabinet Room."

San Carlos. A small Central American country, ruled by a military junta, almost totally dependent upon United States' economic support. There had been rumors of unrest for some time, of an impending revolt. Nothing new in that. Rumors grew thick in that area. No one ever lent much credence to them. Why this sudden activity? The telephone rang and Reilly answered.

"It's Sarah," she said. "You're wanted at the meeting."

The Cabinet Room, separated from the President's office by the secretarial cubicle, was a large, light room, the scene of a succession of historic decisions in recent years. The Jouett portrait of Thomas Jefferson gazed down from its place over the fireplace on the large, coffin-shaped table around which sat the President and a dozen of his advisers. Flanking the President were Secretary Keefe and General Quirk. Also present were Edgar Bookman, Kenneth MacMillan, Daniel Crowell, the Senate majority and minority leaders and their counterparts from the House of Representatives, members of the National Security Council, and two White House Special Assistants on Latin American Affairs. Seated in the black leather chairs against the wall opposite the yellow-draped windows, which looked out on the Rose Garden, were a clutch of generals and admirals. To Pompey, it seemed they had been poured from a single mold, somber men with flat, down-turned mouths and pale eyes that stared at some remote point in space. The President was speaking when Pompey entered, his voice crisply metallic. He waved the Press Secretary to an empty chair at the far corner of the big table.

"When this mess breaks out, Pompey," the President said, "there'll be questions on top of questions. You should be acquainted with my thinking, to speak —when you do—with my voice. Here's the rundown, quickly. We've learned that Moscow is seeking to provoke a rebellion in San Carlos, another of their people's revolutions. They've been sending arms and military advisers to rebel bands, Communists all of them, and an outbreak in hostilities is expected momentarily. Okay, gentlemen. Let's go from there."

Pompey stared at the President, elbows resting on the table, fingers intertwined. The aristocratic face was animated, the brown eyes shining, as if this moment would inevitably lead to acute and even more pleasurable gratification.

"Ken," the President said, "give us the benefit of your expert thinking on Communist tactics."

MacMillan was a heavy-set man with broad shoulders and a pugnacious set to his jaw, an aggressive image contradicted by a voice feathery soft; his speech was slurred and it was difficult to understand him. Pompey strained to hear; at the same time his glance was caught by a movement outside the windows.

He saw Gail, with the First Lady, strolling through the Rose Garden. Gail's lips moved and Mrs. Gunther laughed gaily, leaned forward confidentially to speak, laughed again. He wondered if Jacobs' questions had been asked yet; and the answers? He forced his attention back to the table, eyes ranging swiftly around the room.

Where was the Secretary of Defense?

". . . No question in my mind," MacMillan was saying. "Typical Russian behavior pattern over the years. When least expected by the West, they seek to advance their strategic position, taking very real risks, certain we won't respond with force. Witness Khrushchev's missile gambit in Cuba. Same kind of thinking went into this coup, a move obviously designed to achieve for them a firm foothold in the hemisphere."

"You may be right," Secretary Keefe said in a mild voice. "Still, I would appreciate additional information. We know too little. Has Juan Ginastera contacted us officially? It may be that he can cope with the situation on his own."

Daniel Crowell cleared his throat, smiled tolerantly in Keefe's direction. "Let's be realistic, Mr. Secretary. Ginastera is a dictator who depends entirely on military strength to keep himself in power. I put the question to you—who can ever be certain what path the army will take in one of these banana-republic shoot-ups? No, Mr. Secretary, this is going to be our show sooner or later, just like Santo Domingo, just like Vietnam, just like the others."

Keefe glanced around the table furtively, as if seeking assistance. He found none. "You may be right, of course. But isn't it within reason that this is an indigenous revolt, genuine? I mean, after all, I'm not talking out of school when I say that this fellow Ginastera is an absolute tyrant. He's corrupt and cruel and——"

"This trouble is sponsored by the Communists," Crowell said, staring fixedly at Keefe. "The Russians are behind it all."

"Well?" Keefe said. "Well, that's possible, of course. But you remember that when the difficulty began in Santo Domingo your agency reported Communists all over the place." A nervous laugh sputtered out of him. "And if you remember, there were really very few——"

"I hope you're not questioning the competence of the CIA, Jonas," the President said. His voice, though kept soft, cut through the silence in the room. "We're getting swift and accurate reports, intelligent interpretations. These CIA people are first-rate professionals, Jonas, first-rate."

"I'm certain of that, Mr. President——"

"Good, Jonas. Then you must come to the same conclusion I have. Once again the Russians are dealing from the bottom of the deck. I trusted them. The defense pact, the trade agreements I've fostered, the cultural exchanges, my open-sky offer. Let's face it, Jonas, those people make it impossible to be friends. This latest Soviet move is aimed at weakening us by putting a second Communist government into power in the hemisphere."

"Cuba's an annoyance, Mr. President. I grant that. But hardly a threat."

Pompey watched the President's face firm up, saw the mouth curl.

"I will not stand by idly, Mr. Secretary, and watch freedom wither away in North and South America. A victory for the Kremlin in San Carlos would be a world-wide blow to our prestige. I don't intend to let it happen. The CIA has supplied detailed information. We know what we're up against, gentlemen. The only question is what form of action do we take? At what point do we intervene?"

Fear flowed out to the ends of Pompey's nerves. Jacobs should have been here, to speak out against this, to put up forceful opposition. He alone of all the Cabinet members owned the personal strength and prestige to stand against the President. And at that moment Pompey was certain that the Defense Secretary's absence was no oversight.

The discussion continued, those pressing for early and violent action clearly in the President's favor.

"Gentlemen," the President said at last. "We will not act precipitously in this matter. I intend to preserve our options. Therefore, we shall continue to watch and study. If, however, President Ginastera asks for help we are obligated to provide it. With this in mind, General Quirk will make the necessary standby arrangements for an air-borne division, plus whatever supplementary forces are required. I want them ready to fly into San Carlos on short notice."

"Yes, Mr. President."

"And everything that has been said in this room is to remain among us. There will be no leaks to the press, no talk of hawks and doves. You will respond to no conjecture. In this affair, we speak with one voice. I hope that is clear. I shall be very disturbed should anyone betray my trust."

The President rose and there was a shuffling of chairs. He marched across the diamond-patterned green-and-yellow carpet toward his office, Kenneth MacMillan at his heels.

Pompey struggled to make sense out of what he had heard, longing for an orderly world, a world in which men and nations lived within the guidelines, obeyed the rules. He stopped trying to understand when he reached his desk. He phoned the Pentagon.

Ralph Jacobs tried to recall the last time he felt so unsure of himself. Not since his childhood when he had been shuffled from foster home to foster home, helpless, a victim always. Once again he seemed to have become the pawn of outside forces embarked on a course of action designed to achieve some unknown end.

Pompey's phone call had left him deeply troubled. For him, for the Secretary of Defense, to be excluded from anything as immediate and serious as that San

Carlos meeting could have only one meaning—the President intended to replace him, had already launched a campaign to undermine his status in the Administration. Soon the campaign would extend into the public areas with veiled allusions to his diminished position in newspaper columns, hints that he had outlived his usefulness, speculation about his replacement. In the beginning, no names would be mentioned, but the detailed accounts of how the President had turned his back on Ralph Jacobs would leave little doubt as to the identity of the Cabinet member referred to; and in time Jacobs would be forced to confront Harrison Gunther with the reports, forced to demand public support and, failing to get it, he would tender his resignation. It would be accepted with regret and he would be relegated to a back bench in the hall of history, simply another observer.

For most of the day, Jacobs remained alone in his office, seeing no one. He repressed his initial impulse to contact the President, to demand an explanation, wary of an emotional response that might only worsen an already disintegrating situation. Nor did he seek any additional information about San Carlos, though he was disturbed by the lack of comprehensive reports and evaluations.

What value was there in having a large and expensive military intelligence community when the Defense Secretary was screened off from the most recent crisis? Obviously some serious malfunction existed in the sprawling apparatus. In the normal course of events, anything sensitive—and the San Carlos situation was so much more than that—would have been brought to his attention immediately. As he measured and considered and assessed, a conclusion began to form that was at once wildly illogical and dangerously reasonable. He decided that a cold, professional appraisal was required. He reached for the phone.

Three minutes later, Harvey Gordon shuffled into Jacobs' office, hands in his pockets, looking diffident and ineffectual. He was a dark man with a face that appeared to be a mistake, the features squeezed together without regard to balance or composition. The forehead was broad and low, the hairline intruding irregularly, the nose stubbed, the chin long and wide, split by an expressive mouth. The overall impression was that of a preoccupied student, a cover Gordon had often used, his ability to pass unnoticed as a national of this country or that one adding to his effectiveness.

These days Gordon operated for the most part behind a desk in the Pentagon, evaluating reports, dispatching men to various parts of the world, coordinating certain top-secret activities. If he was displeased with this more sedentary life, he gave no indication. It occurred to Jacobs that he didn't know Gordon's reactions to his new assignment, that the DIA agent seldom revealed his feelings on anything even remotely personal. Gordon was prepared to execute the policy of those who commanded him, a man of action as needed.

Looking at him, Jacobs wondered how many men like Gordon there were in Washington; and, wondering, he knew the answer. Almost every high official had at his command someone similar, a quiet man who came and went on order, living unobtrusively, doing what he was told to do without fuss, an instrument of public and private policy. Such men lived in the shadows, their places on government rosters camouflaged with misleading titles, the moneys they received concealed in the budgets of innocent agencies. Jacobs knew that every capital city in the world had its populations of Harvey Gordons. They were necessary men.

"What do you know about San Carlos?" Jacobs began.

Gordon crossed his legs, uncrossed them, and crossed them again. He adjusted the thick, loose knot of his red knit tie. He ran a hand through his long, unruly hair. The generous mouth turned up at the corners.

"I read the same reports you do, unless you're getting some additional material."

"Something's happening."

Gordon grunted and shifted his position, searched for a place to put his hands, finally folded his arms. "'Course there's talk. The usual sort, arms smuggled in, explosives, unrest among the colonels. Standard procedure down there."

"Any of it involve our Soviet friends?"

Gordon shoved one hand into his trouser pocket. It seemed like a good idea and he repeated the gesture with the other hand. "They have a couple of men in the country, that we know about. A travel agent, for one, and a priest. Of course, there's the standard complement of embassy people who do intelligence work. We know all of them, and they know who our people are."

"Very friendly."

"Oh, well," Gordon said reassuringly, "there are spooks who are completely underground, so to speak. I mean, we have ours and they have theirs. Nobody talks about them, of course. They have it rough, spend a lifetime in a place, take all the risks and get none of the credit. But most agents do only routine work, see who talks to whom and where they go, study periodicals, analyze political trends. Who they are doesn't matter; it's the conclusions they reach." He retrieved his hands and folded them in his lap. "That's not why you wanted to see me. San Carlos, you said."

"The word I get is that there's a revolt imminent. Russian-backed. Including some of their people. Maybe."

Gordon held himself very still and Jacobs waited for him to consider the possibility. "No," he said finally. "No Soviet people. What's the point? Equipment, supplies, arms. Maybe. People, no."

"Are you sure?"

Gordon shrugged. "I'm sure," he said; then with a quick, shy smile: "but I didn't say absolutely."

Jacobs made no response to the old joke. "Look into it, will you?"

"Yes, sir."

"Today, Harvey."

Gordon untracked himself, rose slowly to his feet. He glanced sidelong at Jacobs. "I could make a phone call. Anything else?"

"Nothing else."

At the door, Gordon turned. "Where will you be? This may take a while."

"At home."

It was past midnight when the call came. Jacobs was in the study with his brandy and cigar, laboring for a solution to the Navy's personnel problems. With each passing year, it had become more difficult to recruit the kind of men needed to man a technologically advanced fleet, the Navy unable to compete with the high salaries being offered by private industry. Obviously, increments would have to be steeply upgraded. Would that be enough? What else could be offered to the type of man required, men educated and imaginative, men seeking a challenge? He found no answer, anxiety dulling his thought processes, and the call was a welcome interruption.

"Jacobs here."

"Mr. Secretary," came Gordon's familiar voice, more military over the wire. "I'm calling from a phone booth, sir, and I'd like very much to talk to you in person."

"You think that's necessary?"

"I do."

"Well," Jacobs muttered. Gordon was taking no chances that his telephone might be tapped. Jacobs knew that even at his level such things happened. He recalled the trip to the Orient taken by then Vice President Humphrey in 1966; security agents had discovered his private quarters bugged more than once. And later that same year, it was revealed that two Czechoslovakian agents had attempted to place a listening device in the State Department. With the development of transistorized electronic equipment, privacy was increasingly difficult to insure. "Where shall we meet?" he said.

"Be in front of your house. In fifteen minutes."

Gordon was prompt. Jacobs liked that; he hated waiting. He climbed into the seat alongside the driver and they rolled through the streets. Gordon's three-year-old Ford station wagon would attract no particular attention even at that late hour.

"We'll ride around town," Gordon said.

"What have you found out?"

"Well, you know about the competition between the CIA and our company. Those people out at Langley resent us."

"Get on with it, Harvey."

"Our people don't get much cooperation from them."

"Your point is?"

"Simply this. If they came across something big, or were working on an operation of their own, they just naturally wouldn't let us in on the secret."

"San Carlos."

"Right. That situation stinks, my man tells me. He reports there are a lot of guns being moved. Rifles, automatic stuff, grenades. The kind of hardware you need if you're going to make a revolt in a small country like that. And all of it's been breaking out in the last day or two. That's why we heard nothing before."

"The real thing?"

"Right. Somebody's about to pull the pin."

"Who?"

"That's what bothers my man. From what he told me, we're sending a lot of stuff. Or at least the CIA is. Here's the screwy part. Ginastera is getting all of it."

"You mean we're supplying arms to the Government?"

"On the sly. The stuff is coming off boats in out-of-the-way harbors."

"I don't get it."

"There's more. Up in the hills, and on the plantations, bands are forming. They're arming themselves with good automatic weapons and lightweight artillery. There's also talk of armored vehicles."

"Where the hell are *they* getting it from?"

"Russia."

Russia. Then the President was right! Moscow was not to be trusted and an aggressive defense posture toward the Soviet Union made sense.

Jacobs struggled to piece it together; nothing fit. Why would the Russians plot a rebellion in San Carlos at this time?

Was it possible that all the talk of peace, of hoping to reduce their military expenditures, of easing the pressures of the cold war, was simply a ruse, a device to get the United States to lower her guard? Was the Kremlin leadership still dreaming of world revolution, of undercutting the American position by force?

"Can Ginastera suppress a rebellion, Harvey?"

"Not the way things stand. His support is shaky. The people are almost totally opposed to him, and so are many of the military people."

"Would we go in if he was in trouble?"

"We might. And it would be a mistake. Our prestige would suffer, and it would turn most South American countries against us just when they're getting over the idea that we operate as if they're our private preserves."

Jacobs frowned. Was the world doomed to teeter on that slender strand between peace and nuclear obliteration for all time?

"Where's the logic in such a move by the Russians?"

"I don't know. I have no answer. All my information supports the theory that they want no trouble at this time. Oh, hell, do we really know what goes on in the Kremlin?"

"I hope we do," Jacobs said slowly, then: "There was a meeting in the White House this morning. About San Carlos."

"I heard."

They were cruising along Constitution Avenue. At 23rd Street, Gordon turned, and moments later they circled the Lincoln Memorial. A reminiscent wave broke over Jacobs as he gazed at the massive monument, so impressively serene at this late hour. He reached back, visualized the woman who had approached him, asked for his company. Hers had been a nice face, warm and gentle, friendly and a little sad, as he remembered. Had he made a mistake? She might not have been a whore, only a woman alone and seeking companionship, needing human contact. Talking to her could have been rewarding and pleasant. With such a woman, a man could do things, stroll alongside the reflecting pool perhaps, and enjoy the spring blossoms. Gordon's voice drew him back to the present.

"Is Number One going to dump you?"

Jacobs smiled in appreciation of the agent's grim bluntness. "I think so."

Gordon made no reply. Long ago he had made peace with his own limitations. A technician, he reached for the outer limits of his efficiency, while avoiding the inhibiting influence of politics. Politicians came and went, and little was changed because of the coming and going; it was the hard core of professionals who provided governmental continuity, who made things happen.

"Something else you should know," Gordon said. "Rumor says the CIA has ordered surveillance flights resumed over Soviet territory. Specifically over those sections of Kazakhstan where the Russians planted their long-range missile silos."

Jacobs swore. "Why? The Samos satellites provide detailed information. My God, we can tell from fly droppings how much garbage comes out of their mess halls and how many men they're feeding. What's the point? The damned U-2, even the drone model, is outmoded and at best can only duplicate . . ." He stopped abruptly. "Harvey, it's a deliberately provocative act."

"Whatever you say, Mr. Secretary."

Jacobs measured the other man, the profile irregular, a series of unmatched thrusts and angles. "Let me put a question to you, Harvey. Not connected with this discussion."

"Yes, sir."

"Give me your professional opinion." Jacobs stared

straight ahead at the moving concrete ribbon. "Would it be possible to arrange an impersonation of a head of state for any length of time?"

"Replace the top man, you mean, with an operative?"

"Exactly."

Gordon considered the question. It was an intriguing technical problem. He knew that the Germans had used a stand-in for Hitler during World War II, and the English did likewise with Churchill. But these were only physical doubles for certain public functions; they took no part in making or executing policy. There had been an effort made by the Egyptians to overthrow a bordering sheikdom by replacing the ruling prince with a surrogate; but he was found out after a week and given a state funeral in place of the real sheik who had been killed. It was said that the coffin had been sealed with the impostor still alive.

"Be quite a trick," Gordon said finally. "A real long shot. It would take a lot of planning, study, endless amounts of rehearsal, learning everything about the real leader. Naturally, you'd need a substitute with a very close physical resemblance, and he'd have to be a guy dedicated and determined. A pretty quick thinker, too, ready for anything that might happen."

"Could it be done?"

"I suppose, given the right circumstances."

Jacobs shifted around to face Gordon. "And what would you do if you discovered such an impostor?"

"That's easy," he said in a mild voice. "I'd kill him."

At about that same time, in Baltimore, Pompey came back to the railroad station. The Mercedes was parked near the Charles Street entrance where he had left it, and for an instant it seemed as if nothing had changed during the last few hours. He knew that wasn't true. Somewhere in the city, Gail was different. A stranger had violated her, had scraped out of her the life that had been there, had killed her child. *His* child. Despite the hot thickness of the night, Pompey shivered. The abortionist was his delegate. He lit a cigarette.

All of it had been so strange and unreal, the mounting fear, the knowledge that they were breaking the law, the physical risk to Gail. Pompey looked at his watch. Nothing registered. He looked again. More than three hours had passed since he had arrived at this place with Gail. According to instructions, they sat on the bench just inside the depot entrance, close to each other, but not touching, trying to remain calm, keeping their occasional comments superficial and gay. But as time dragged on and Al failed to appear, all gaiety evaporated.

9:15 came and went and no Al. "This is the worst part," Gail had said. "Suppose something went wrong. Suppose he doesn't come. After all, they have to be careful."

He squeezed her knee and tried to reassure her. A pair of railroad workmen ambled by. They looked knowingly at the man and woman on the bench, and one said something, and they both laughed. Pompey removed his hand.

The pressure was alive, an expanding force focused at his diaphragm, an increasing weariness as if that muscle had been too extravagantly used. He forced himself to sit erect and breathe with deep regularity. It didn't help.

It was almost 9:30.

"What are we going to do?" Gail said, helplessness sounding in her voice.

He almost called it off then. He'd had enough and so had she. It wasn't fair. This was more punishment than either of them deserved. There was no reason to endure more. They'd leave, go back to Washington. They'd be married. Gail wanted that and he loved her. He did. But he said nothing.

A few minutes later, Al appeared. He was a mild-mannered man with a pleasant smile and large ears, wearing a colorfully checked sportshirt that was somehow reassuring. He pumped Pompey's hand energetically and assured him that there was nothing to worry about, allowing him to accompany Gail to the car outside the Charles Street entrance. It was only after the light-blue Buick disappeared, that Pompey realized there had been three other women in the car.

Al drove without speaking and the women in the Buick said nothing. Each of them sat stiffly, staring to the front, hands folded in laps or brushing at stray hairs.

Gail was ashamed and wanted to hide her face, to fade into oblivion. She had failed to consider this part of it, the practical aspects, the coming and going. The arrangements. She had assumed it would all be carried off in privacy, her identity kept secret. She had worried about the physical danger and the legal aspects, the fact that she was breaking the law, that she would be destroying her baby. But she hadn't thought it would be this way. So public and casual, a social enterprise.

"This ain't the best part of the town," Al said, his manner jovial. "But don't worry. There ain't nothing to be afraid of."

Gail glanced at the girl alongside. She was very young, very pretty, very frightened. Her face was pale, her mouth tremulous, eyes fluttering reflexively. Gail looked away.

The car pulled over and stopped. "This is it, girls," Al said. "Everybody follow me."

They entered a building of no particular distinction, found themselves in a long, carpeted hallway. Al indicated a coatrack. "Hang your things and wait in the living room." He pointed, then disappeared through a door at the far end of the hallway.

The living room was spacious and needed painting. The furniture, though ancient, was comfortable and in good repair. There were some magazines on the coffee table, but no one seemed interested.

One of the girls lit a cigarette, and Gail decided that was an excellent idea. She offered her pack around but the others declined.

"I gotta admit," the girl who was smoking said, "I expected a lot worse. Some sleazy back room with a poker game going on up front, you know." She laughed harshly. "I came a long way for this, so I had lots of time to anticipate."

"Where are you from?" Gail heard herself ask. The steadiness of her voice was surprising.

"San Francisco."

"So far!"

"My friend," the girl drawled. "My good and very dear friend isn't the kind of stud to take any chances, you know. Not close to home, you know. There's a wife and a couple of kiddies to protect. And a business. This made a lot more sense."

"Did he come with you?"

"You must be kidding!"

The pale girl who sat next to Gail in the car straightened up. She tried to smile and failed. "My fiancé is waiting for me downtown. He rented a hotel room and we're going to stay overnight."

"Hotel rooms are what got me into this," the girl from San Francisco said abrasively.

"Milton thought it would be better," the pale girl said, "if we stay overnight, so I can rest. He's very considerate."

"Sure he is," San Francisco muttered. "All of them are. What about you?" she said to the fourth woman.

The woman stared at her. "I'm here. Doesn't that say it all?"

"Sorry. Just trying to kill the time."

"Sorry," the fourth woman said, looking off into space. "I've got a husband."

"Doesn't he want children?" the pale girl said. "I don't understand people who aren't just crazy about kids."

"It isn't his," the fourth woman said.

"So don't tell him," San Francisco said. "He'd never know the difference."

"He'd know. My friend is black."

A nurse appeared in the doorway. She arranged a cheerful smile on her broad mouth. "Well, doctor's all ready now. Who's going to be number one?"

"Oh, my God!" the pale girl said.

Nobody moved.

"Let's go," the nurse said curtly. She pointed at the pale girl. "Okay, lady, you're it. Follow me."

"Oh, my God!"

"Go on," Gail said encouragingly. "Waiting will only make it worse."

The pale girl stood up and started out of the room. "Oh, my God," she said, as she disappeared down the long hallway.

No one said anything after that. After a few unmarked minutes, the nurse reappeared. "Next."

San Francisco stood up. "I'm your victim, sweetie. Tell me, you enjoy your work?"

The nurse made no reply.

Gail lit another cigarette. When the nurse returned, she glanced over at the married woman. "Would you like to go first?"

The woman smiled her gratitude and left.

Gail held herself very still, fighting against the fear that slithered along her limbs, that churned in her stomach, that made her want to scream and run and hide.

"Ready for you," the nurse was saying.

Gail stood up.

"Last but not least."

Gail followed the white-garbed woman down the hallway into a room set up as a surgery. A black leather examining chair dominated the chamber. Two men in white surgical gowns and masks were present, the surgeon and the anesthetist.

"Take off your girdle," the nurse ordered.

"I don't wear one," Gail said.

"Lucky you," the nurse said. "Panties, then."

Gail turned her back to the men.

"Let's get on with it," the doctor said, in a bored tone. "Into the chair, feet in the stirrups."

Gail obeyed. It was an awkward position and made her feel helpless and vulnerable. A mask came down over her face and the panic set in as her arms and legs were strapped into place.

"Breathe deeply and count backwards from ten."

"No worse than having a tooth pulled. Ten, nine, eight, seven."

She spun off into space, alone, angry and ashamed. Worst of all was the shame. The shame.

The hours that followed had been difficult for Pompey to fill. First, a coffee shop and an attempt to read a newsmagazine. His mind kept wandering. He strolled through the downtown area of the city. Baltimore, a brown city, stained and dirty. The stuff of slums, all of it, colorless, blighted, waiting to expire. Nor did the newly built glass towers improve matters. Instead, they seemed to assume the dull façade of the dingy row houses, the sullen expressions of the inhabitants, the meanness of the streets. A city for losers, he thought. A proper place to kill a baby.

Loew's Century Theater. A banner announced that it was cool inside, air-conditioned. He bought a ticket and found a seat in the orchestra. He watched the flickering figures on the screen without interest, unable to follow the action, not caring. After a while he got up and left.

He walked without purpose and eventually found himself on a street patrolled by raucous men and overdressed women, a street of garish signs and blaring music, of one small nightclub after another. A drink seemed like a good idea. He went into the nearest club and stood at the bar and ordered Scotch. This was a blue world, made so by dim, revolving lamps studding the ceiling.

On the small stage behind the bar, a thick-bodied blonde moved about in the blue light, disrobing with contrived sensuality. She was no more than thirty, but already the signs of disintegration were present; her thighs were flabby, dimpled at the back, and stretch marks scarred her gross hips. He finished his drink and left.

Back at the depot, Pompey peered at every passing

car. Suppose something went wrong, what would he do? He had heard of such things, of women butchered and left to die alone. What if Al failed to bring her back? The police.

The police! That would mean publicity, notoriety, the end of his career. The President would never stand for a scandal in his Administration. That had been made clear in his attitude toward Peter Street. A despairing moan trickled across Pompey's lips. There was no help anywhere.

Five minutes later, the light blue Buick eased to a stop in the driveway. Gail got out and the Buick drove on away. The corners of her mouth lifted in a wan smile, and she moved uncertainly toward him, holding one hand aloft to forestall questions. He guided her to the Mercedes.

He got behind the wheel and lit a cigarette and offered it to her. She shook her head in refusal, peering up at him out of eyes veiled and unfocused.

"Are you all right?" he said.

She nodded. When she finally spoke, it was in murmured fragments. "The anesthetic. . . . I'm fine. . . . Don't worry about me. . . . I'm fine. . . . Very good. . . . Everybody . . . very professional. . . . Experts at their jobs. . . . Little weak . . . and tired. . . . That's all."

He placed his hand on hers and squeezed gently. She closed her eyes.

"Poor Guy," she sighed. "It must have been . . . so hard for you."

"As long as you're all right."

"Oh, yes. Fine. Just fine."

"Let's not go back tonight. We could stay in a motel. You'll be stronger in the morning."

"Nooo. I want to go home . . . sleep in my own bed. Please. But drive carefully . . . slow over the bumps. . . . I'm a little tender, you see."

He started the car and turned toward Washington.

"Please, Guy," she said presently. "Stay with me tonight. Sleep with me. I don't think I want to be alone."

"Of course," he said, and quickly, "I love you."

Her head fell back on the seat and she closed her eyes. He concentrated on the road ahead, glad it was over at last.

VI

The President was annoyed and it showed. The fine-boned face was drawn together and the sculptured mouth was downturned.

"Damn Warren Gilbert," he burst out. "People like him just don't understand."

Pompey stood in front of the big desk in the oval office and listened. Editorial cries for ratification of the Mutual Defense Pact were increasing with every passing day. Even some of the more conservative journals were beginning to suggest that an alliance with the Soviet Union might be rewarding; they reasoned that it would bring about diminished government spending and might eventually result in a lower tax burden.

"Trouble with writers is they sit in their ivory towers and dream up answers. They have no responsibilities beyond the next day's edition. I must answer to the Congress, to the electorate. I must be concerned with what actually happens."

"A lot of people believe it would be a good thing if Russia and the United States got together finally."

"Well, dammit, man, don't they know that I want peace, that my bones ache for it? That I'd do anything to achieve it? If only the Russians could be trusted. You know what's happening, Pompey. The trouble is those people . . ." He broke off abruptly and grew thoughtful. "Are many of the White House press boys around?"

Pompey looked at his watch. It was nearly eleven o'clock. "Most of them, I imagine."

Canadian Black Velvet.

We think everyone should enjoy a higher standard of living it up.

Now that you have a book for the weekend, we can give you a weekend for the book.

Bermuda, Puerto Rico, Jamaica, the Caribbean Miami, Mexico at weekend-sized prices. Call us or your travel agent.

EASTERN The Wings of Man.

The President stood up. "Come on, Pompey. We're about to do a little impromptu propagandizing."

The President was at his best with the White House correspondents, charming and amusing, presenting his point of view effectively, eliciting laughter from most of his listeners by baiting such journalistic institutions as the New York *Times* and the St. Louis *Post-Dispatch*, two of his most vociferous critics.

Back in the oval room, he grinned at Pompey. "How'd I do?"

"They were eating out of your hand."

"You too, Pompey?"

The Press Secretary shifted uneasily. Those soft brown eyes seemed to peer beneath his skin.

"You were very convincing, Mr. President."

The President settled back in the green leather chair. "That's the kind of thing I should do more often, the personal touch. The press boys seem to like it, and it brings me a little closer to them. Bound to reflect in their reports."

"I agree. It's a good idea."

"Too bad you didn't think of it," the President said. His expression was guileless, but Pompey felt the critical thrust implicit in the words.

"Anything else now?" he said.

"Not a thing."

In the corridor outside the President's office, Julian Dawson was talking to one of the agents on duty. Pompey waited for him to finish.

"Come into my office, Jules," he said. "I haven't seen you in weeks."

Dawson, a solidly built man of Pompey's height, had a thick, veined neck and a face larger than it should be. He moved with the cautious concern of a man who was afraid he might break something.

"How goes it, Jules?"

"This job only looks easy," he complained. "Always a sweat. Each week, hundreds of nut letters and phone calls. Threats against the President. We got to consider every one of them and sometimes we check out a couple of dozen or more. It's not easy."

"I believe you, Jules," Pompey said. He invited the other man to sit down.

"You know what I need?"

"What do you need, Jules?"

Twice as many men and four times the dough they allow me."

Pompey laughed. That was the usual plaint of all Washington department heads, and he said so. A hurt expression came onto Dawson's oversized features.

"You don't understand. You, you're on the inside. Not me. Me and my men, it's like we were pickets in that iron fence around the White House. As long as the job gets done right, nobody pays attention. But let something go wrong and everybody becomes a critic. Investigations, committees, everybody blaming everybody else." Dawson studied his wrist watch, an oversized stainless steel affair of dials and levers and buttons, a match for his own proportions. "In a few minutes, I'm supposed to see the man and finalize the details of the New York trip. We're flying all the way, this time. 'Copter from the White House to the airport, and 'copter into Manhattan, the Pan Am Building. You realize how complicated this kind of thing can be."

Pompey made sympathetic sounds. "You must have to spend a lot of time with the President when there's a trip coming up."

Dawson scowled and cracked his knuckles. "When he'll see me. This President runs hot and cold, know what I mean? Mostly he hasn't been interested in my problems, always pushing into crowds, anxious to shake hands, insisting on that open-topped car of his, going here and there without warning, not letting me set things up. Lately he's wised up a little. I been working on him. Face it, he can't do anybody any good dead."

"Not much chance of that happening."

The big face, ridged and bony, lengthened. "In my business, how can you tell? There are a couple of hundred million citizens out there. Some of them got grievances, real or fancied. Some of them are crazy, you know, the true believers, set on saving the country, the world. All you need is a particular kind of grudge and a particular kind of mind. When the two come together, somebody takes a crack at the President."

"Your men are trained and whenever you travel——"

"Sure," Dawson interrupted. "I get police cooperation, and even the Armed Services when I want. None of it helps much against one determined man. Oswald, for example." Dawson looked grim and cracked the knuckles of his left hand. "Take this Peace Now Foundation dinner on Saturday. Exactly the kind of thing I'm talking about. A couple of thousand people, maybe, crowded into that Foundation Building. You know the place? An architectural mess. Oh, sure, we'll check it out and post our people. But no matter, if some crackpot wants to, he'll figure a way to get to the President."

"How?"

"How do I know? If I did, we'd plug up the loophole. That's the kind of bind we're in. No matter what precautions we dream up, some fanatic with a wild imagination will come up with a way to crack them. And in a crowd, if a man's willing to gamble, lay his own life on the line, there's no way he can be prevented from getting close to the President and doing the job." Dawson heaved himself erect. His broad upper lip lifted in what passed for a happy smile. "Yeah. It's a problem. People just don't realize. But life is simpler now." He lowered his left eyelid in a slow, insinuating wink.

"What do you mean?"

"His *friend*. That's all over, y'know. She folded her tent and went back to New York. And that didn't make me a bit sorry."

Pompey sat quietly behind his desk after Dawson left. Anne Lockridge back in New York, her affair with the President ended. The knowledge was doubly interesting, for he had heard nothing about it; and Washington was not a city where such information remained secret for long. At the same time, he felt strangely disappointed. He remembered Anne Lockridge as a spectacularly attractive woman, with a stylish manner and the ability to find humor in the circumstances which surrounded her.

The affair had been a long one, beginning before Gunther became President. After his election, she had ended her acting career to live in Washington, to be near him, providing a private place where he could escape his office and its pressures. Pompey wondered why it had ended, if it bore in any way on his suspicions. He wanted to discuss it with Jacobs and reached for the phone, withdrew his hand, reluctant for the call to go through the White House switchboard.

It was past 1 o'clock before he was able to get away from his desk. He hurried downtown and ducked into the first available public phone booth. Jacobs was having lunch in his office; Pompey told him what he had learned.

"I'd like to know more," Jacobs said. When Pompey made no response, Jacobs continued. "It might be a good idea if you went up to New York and spoke to the lady. Tonight. It could be rewarding."

"How will I justify such an intrusion on her private life? She might not talk to me."

"Invent a suitable cover story, Pompey. I'm confident you can use that public-relations imagination of yours." He hung up.

Pompey glared at the instrument in his hand, slammed it resentfully into its cradle. Jacobs had no right to speak to him in such a peremptory manner, to treat him as if he were a mere messenger.

Resentment soon gave way to anticipation. This was beginning to appeal to him. A touch of drama, excitement and intrigue, the flavor of mystery. And more, Anne Lockridge was a damned fine-looking woman.

He found a sandwich shop that wasn't crowded and ordered, devising a story while he ate, simple and logical, one that should convince her. His lunch finished, he located another phone booth and placed a call to her.

He identified himself when she came on and told her that he would be in New York that evening, asked her to dine with him. She hesitated, and a wary note crept into her voice.

"I'm doing an article for a magazine," he said hurriedly. "It's all very speculative at this point, but what I have in mind is a broad character sketch of the President. I'm hoping to gather impressions from a wide variety of people who know him."

She tried to hold him off, protesting that she had nothing of consequence to contribute, that her private life must remain private. Pompey persisted. He pointed out that history obligated men in his position to provide information for future generations, stressing that he was after nothing more than a reflection of her attitudes and impressions, promising her name would never be mentioned. In the end he prevailed, and she agreed to meet him that evening.

Then he phoned Gail. She said she was feeling surprisingly strong and intended to return to work the following day. That made him feel better, his concern diminished.

"I'm not going to be able to come by this evening," he explained. "I've got some advance planning to do on the New York trip and I'm running up there."

"That's all right," she said. "I understand."

She sounded detached, almost as if she welcomed his absence.

"I'll call you tomorrow," he said.

At first thought, he was pleased that Gail was taking it all so calmly. But this was soon replaced by doubt, and he grew alarmed. That she displayed so little emotion wasn't natural. The more he considered the situation, the more troubled he became until finally he thrust it out of his mind. He would think about it another time. Right now there were more important things to attend to.

Pompey arrived in New York a few minutes before eight and taxied up to Anne Lockridge's address on

Second Avenue in the Eighties, one of those white brick apartment buildings.

He remembered her as a woman of impressive tranquillity, functioning out of a center of balance that permitted her to view the grotesqueries of the world with detached amusement. She had changed. Now, as she admitted him to her apartment, she seemed stretched tight, eyes darting anxiously, expression uncertain as if she were expecting bad news.

She was tall, with round hips and a full, heavy bosom, her face a series of planes, brow flat, eyes level, the mouth wide and too quick to smile. There was a tentative tilt to her head, giving her a perpetual look of curiosity.

She had mixed a batch of martinis, and now poured one for him and another for herself. "It is surprising," she said, seating herself on the deep satin couch, motioning him to a chair opposite, "how much an occasional martini can do to help a lady get through the day. Gin has remarkable narcotic qualities."

He wasn't sure how to respond. "It's good to see you again, Miss Lockridge."

She crossed her legs and tugged at the short skirt of the black sheath she wore, and Pompey tried not to look. She drained half her drink and murmured into the glass. "How strange that in my almost three years in Washington you and I met only once, and that actually prior to my moving there." Her voice, throaty and caressing, was a fine instrument for an actress. "Or perhaps it isn't so strange after all, considering my position, and your own."

They made conversation about Washington, of the social life, the constant partying, to which she had remained aloof. She confessed that during those three years there had been an almost perpetual loneliness, a sense of being apart, an outsider always waiting, unable to direct her own life.

"Even when I was with him," she said, with a quiet bitterness in her voice, "the loneliness was there, always waiting for him to leave and never knowing when he'd come back. *If* he'd come back. It must be that way for a dog, any pet. Its master leaves, and there's no way of knowing whether or not he'll return. Total dependency. Nothing can be more horrible. You feel so helpless. So helpless." She looked up and smiled wistfully. "No human being should be made to feel that way. Nobody should be made to wait all the time. Nobody . . ."

They met in Vietnam at a forward-area camp.

She was with a USO entertainment unit. Though she had never ranked herself highly as a singer, she rendered a few songs and served as a foil for the comedian who headed the troupe. There were two other girls along and they wore miniskirts, provided the obvious sex appeal. Anne Lockridge avoided that. She appeared in a sedate gown, acting the sophisticated lady that in fact she was.

They did two shows at that camp and afterwards ate dinner with the enlisted men. There were so many of them. And so young. Eager to talk, to tell her their names, where they came from.

"Horner, Miss Lockridge, from Missouri."

"Gilbert, Miss Lockridge, from Vermont."

"Dade City, Miss Lockridge. That's in Florida."

The names and faces flowed together and a spreading weariness and despair took hold of her. She thought of them fighting and killing, being killed, and she could find no good reason why it should be that way.

So she sat with them through the evening and let them look at her and tell their jokes, and she explained what it was like to be an unknown actress in the New York theater. She told them about her ambitions and how she had worked and studied, had sacrificed many of the rewards of life to get even this far professionally. They sympathized and said it sounded like a very tough way to earn a living.

Finally, too tired to continue, she excused herself, headed back to her tent. She was halfway there when the tall man caught up with her. He was lean, slightly stooped, and looked more like a college professor than a soldier. He wore no insignia of rank on his fatigues, but because of his bearing and the fact that he was older than the others, she assumed that he was an officer.

"I enjoyed your performance very much," he said, turning an angled smile her way. "It means a lot to these boys."

"You're kind to tell me."

She moved on and he fell into step beside her. "My name is Harrison Gunther," he said.

There was one in every camp, she supposed. One with more nerve than the others, a greater willingness to risk rejection, determined to discover for himself if the Anne Lockridges were available. She supposed some were.

In front of her tent, she thanked him for escorting her back and turned to go in.

"Are you going directly home from here?" he asked.

"Two more dates, then back," she said, over her shoulder.

"When?"

"Next Wednesday."

"To New York?"

"Yes."

"A new play?"

Now she did turn. "I can't afford to miss out on the part. I need the job. To pay my bills, you see."

"I see," he said, grinning. "What's it called, the play, I mean?"

She couldn't help but smile in return. "Are you planning to see it, soldier?"

He jerked his head in cheerful assent. "Wouldn't miss it."

She sobered quickly. "I hope it runs long enough . . ."

He laughed, open and engaging, his eyes never leaving hers. "I'm heading back to the States in a few days myself. I'm not a soldier, Miss Lockridge. I'm a member of the Armed Forces Committee and we're investigating . . ."

"A politician?"

"A United States Senator."

"You don't look like a Senator."

"Oh?"

"I imagined they were all elderly and paunchy, men with jowls and not to be trusted."

"Do you trust me?"

"Not especially."

He laughed cheerfully. "You haven't told me the name of the play."

" 'To Each His Own Pain.' " She grimaced. "A little precious. But with luck . . ." She broke off and extended her hand. "Nice talking to you, Senator."

"Gunther. Harrison Gunther."

"I'm not very political."

He nodded once. "Good night, Miss Lockridge. I'll see you again."

Lying on the Army cot later, unable to sleep, a nerve leaping erratically in her thigh, she considered Harrison Gunther. He was, she decided, the most attractive man she had ever met. Thoroughly charming. Dangerous therefore. She doubted that he would remember either her or the play. Doubted that she would ever see him again. But she hoped she was wrong.

From the first day of rehearsal, Anne Lockridge was discouraged about "To Each His Own Pain." There was a lack of dramatic life to the script. And to make it worse, the director failed to take command, to state guidelines, to indicate a dramatic purpose. At the end of the first two weeks of rehearsal, there was uncertainty on the stage. The leading actor did not yet know his lines, and the blocking was incomplete.

Two days later, the director was fired and a new man was brought in. He was short, intense, with hands that were never still. His record didn't promise much, three failures in three attempts on Broadway, but he asserted his authority from the first moment.

"In nine days," he began, "we open in New Haven. And open we shall, in better shape than what I witnessed here yesterday, from a seat in the balcony. In all kindness, the performances were horrendous. But that's in the past. As of now, matters improve. There are eight days left to us. To make the most of that time, we shall eliminate discussions and exchange no philosophies about acting or interpretation. I shall tell you what I want and you will give it to me. Fail to do so, and you will be replaced at once. Very well. We begin. The first act—it stinks. To lessen the odor, Miss Lockridge will appear on stage earlier wearing as little as the law and my conscience dictates . . ."

Anne started to protest, but thought better of it.

The director went on. "If we can't be good, we can at least be attractive . . ."

They were greeted in New Haven by unenthusiastic reviews and tepid audiences. The word went back to New York—another flop.

The director refused to quit. He worked with the author at night, and huge sections of dialogue were completely rewritten or cut entirely. The second act was tightened and the third act was discarded, a new one written with a different ending.

As a result of the changes, Anne had two new scenes in the second act and appeared on stage during the whole of the last act. This meant a new contract and a larger salary and featured billing. In Boston, the critics treated her kindly, but little hope was offered for the play itself.

The director went back to work. The new third act was cut and reshaped, dialogue added. Anne was given a confrontation with the star that allowed her to display a full range of emotion.

They opened in New York on a Thursday night. That same day, the newspaper printers went out on strike. There were no reviews. It was generally agreed that it was just as well. The play didn't measure up, and unfavorable notices would have forced its immediate closing. Instead, the producer allocated additional money for advertising and publicity, and by the end of the first week, the advance sale was large enough to promise a run of at least three months.

Anne appeared on a number of radio and television

shows, plugging the play, and her relaxed, finishing school manner pleased viewers and production people alike.

"All this publicity," her agent told her, "is going to be very beneficial. Even without reviews, there's increasing interest in you. Two producers have inquired about your availability for next season, and I've had a feeler from a movie company."

They were having an early dinner at Sardi's following the matinee. By now, Anne had become accustomed to the stares of the curious, to the attention of other performers who frequently intruded to wish her well. So it was that she found it not unusual when the tall man appeared at the table.

Slender and handsome in a gray sharkskin suit, there was a familiar cast to his face, to the suggestion of a smile on the finely sculpted mouth.

"Miss Lockridge," he began. The voice was rich and cultured, but unpretentious. "You don't remember me."

"I'm sorry," she said, trying to recall.

"Harrison Gunther. We met at Dung Sa, last summer. In Vietnam."

She blushed, embarrassed that she had not remembered. She gave him her hand. "How nice to see you again, Senator." She introduced him to her agent, invited him to join them.

"No time. I'm in New York on business. Just a day or so. Did that play of yours ever open?"

He hadn't remembered, she thought wryly. Not the name of the play. Nor to seek her out, to find her. But then she had forgotten him, too. The agent said the name of the play.

"Of course," Gunther said. "Is it a success?"

"A personal success for Anne," the agent told him.

"I'm glad. I'll try to see it."

"That would be nice," Anne said carefully.

After he was gone, the agent turned to Anne. "Attractive guy," he said. "And a good Senator. First-class record."

She nodded absently, certain she would never see

him again. But three weeks later, on a Friday night, he came backstage. He complimented her on her acting, said that she dominated the play, was even more attractive offstage than on. He made a small joke about the similarity of actors and politicians, and she laughed too loudly when he delivered the punch line. He asked her to have a drink with him and she accepted.

He took her to an intimate place in the East Seventies and they nibbled at delicate crepes and drank Pouilly Fuisse. He pressed her to speak about herself.

"How did you happen to become an actress? No," he amended. "Not how. Why? That's the interesting story. Why a person does whatever he does. Becomes what he becomes. Myself, for example. I've always been predisposed to teach. A born pedagogue."

"You're not at all pedagogic."

"If not, mark it down to self-control."

"Tell me what it's like in the senate."

He scowled and rubbed his football knee under the table.

"Is something wrong?" she said.

He told her about the torn tendons, the surgery, claimed the knee was an excellent weathervane.

"Let me see," he said, appraising her. "You're not from New York . . . ?"

"No."

"Cleveland?"

"Well, yes. How did you know?"

"A guess," he admitted. "But there's nothing of the country girl to you. People like us, we're urban types in an increasingly urban world. The rural life, the small town, it's an anomoly in our time. You possess the best qualities the city has to offer."

She studied her glass which was half empty. He filled it.

"Do you find the Senate a rewarding place to work?" she said after a long, silent interlude.

"It's a place to get things done and things do get done. Not as swiftly as you might like. Not as totally as you might like. But then it isn't much different anywhere else. Short of a totalitarian state, all systems work deliberately and accomplish only small portion of what is actually required at any one time. It may not be ideal but it does damage to the fewest people."

It was past four when he returned her to her apartment. He took her hand and told her that it had been very pleasant being with her.

"I enjoyed it," she said.

"May I see you again?"

"Yes."

He released her hand. She expected him to kiss her and wanted him to. Instead, he frowned. "There is something you should know. I have a wife."

It seemed reasonable and she was neither surprised nor shocked. He was too attractive not to have married. Besides, a proper wife would be an asset for a politician. She thrust the thought out of mind, not liking herself for thinking it.

"There are no children," he was saying, "and there is little left except habit between Mrs. Gunther and myself." He hesitated. "I would like to see you. I won't make any apologies and I can't make any promises. If you said no, I couldn't fault you. In any case, don't answer me now. Think on it. I'll phone you one night for a dinner date and you'll answer then."

She thought about him often in the days that followed and was pleased at his reluctance to put her under pressure by insisting on an immediate answer. Over the telephone, she would be able to refuse him more easily.

She made up her mind. There was no percentage in becoming involved with him. He was too attractive, was too easy to like, to love. That would mean only disappointment and pain. For him, it would be ideal, an occasional evening or a weekend in New York. A convenient companion and bed partner. A free ride. For her, too much emptiness.

And there was Eric. Eric Frank, big and accommodating, easy to be with. Or without. Eric, always around when needed, ready to help rearrange her furniture or escort her to a party or to a movie. A satisfying if uninspiring lover, Eric made few demands, never intruded. She didn't need Harrison Gunther.

She was putting on her makeup at the theater one evening, when he phoned. She went out to the pay phone in the corridor feeling the draft from the stagedoor and said hello.

"I've been meaning to call before this," he said. "But this has been a rather busy time for us. Perhaps you've read about the investigation. Corruption in high places, that sort of thing. Very complicated, very messy. I think we've got it licked now."

She understood. She had been reading the political news since meeting him, telling herself that it was less his influence than a determination to know what was happening in the world. Her world. But she didn't believe it. Not for a minute.

"I'm coming up to New York this weekend," he said. "Could we meet after your show on Saturday night . . . ?"

She exhaled wearily. "Yes," she said, knowing that she had never seriously intended to refuse him.

Usually, after a performance, she was famished. But on Saturday night, she could not eat. Instead, she drank, three whisky sours, which seemed to affect her not at all. They spoke of nothing that was close to either of them during the evening, as if trying to avoid coming together, avoid any involvement. She was committed to treating this as a passing interlude, to allow it no importance, no real place in her life. As an adult woman, she owned certain needs, certain desires, and he was an attractive man who could provide what she wanted. It was that simple. Nothing more than fun and games, and when it ended, as it surely must, she would not grieve for what might have been.

He brought her back to her apartment, and she invited him in, gave him a brandy. She sat close to him on the couch and waited for him to make love to her. Instead, when he finished the brandy, he stood up, announced that it was time for him to leave.

"It's been very nice for me," he said. He kissed her tenderly and smiled wistfully. "Tomorrow, at noon, I'll come for you. I've rented a car. I know a restaurant on Long Island that serves a beautiful lobster . . ."

She agreed that noon would be perfect, and he left without kissing her again. She realized that she had no chance of resisting him.

It was two weeks before they met again, and then for barely an hour between shows on a Wednesday. The following week he was in New York for three days, and they saw each other whenever possible. On his last evening, they made love for the first time. It occurred easily, without urgency, normal behavior for them both. The experience was everything she had hoped for, and something more. He owned a gentle strength that aroused her and made her want to please him. Made her want as much of him as she could have.

Neither of them slept much that night. And when he left in the morning, he told her that she had rejuvenated his body, replenished his virility.

"I was sure I was too old for such a multiplicity of sexual activity," he said, kissing her eyes, her mouth, her throat.

"You're the youngest man in the world."

"If I am, it's thanks to you. I feel so physical. Totally muscular. Very strong. I could beat my chest and give out shouts of triumph." He laughed, a deep, free sound. "If you don't mind, I'll come back . . ."

He said it flatly, with a suggestion of smugness. Yet there was also a note of uncertainty, as if he feared she might close him out. Her arms went around his waist and she placed her cheek on his chest.

"I don't mind at all," she murmured. "Please come soon, Harrison. I'm not very good at waiting."

But waiting was what she did most of after that. With time, the lapses between his visits became more intolerable as her feeling for him intensified and grew.

Worst of all was the night of the convention, the

night he was nominated for the Presidency. She was ecstatic for him, sharing his victory; and horrified, for this meant the end for them. They would never see each other again.

She was wrong. He arranged for her to visit him twice during the campaign; and on election night, when it became clear that he had won, he called her from Kansas City and asked her to give up her career, to move to Washington, to be near to him, and available. She agreed, certain she knew what it would be like, but not knowing at all. Not knowing that the waiting would be worse than ever. Always waiting . . .

"I don't have to wait anymore."

She drained her glass and stood up, looked over at Pompey. "Another drink?"

"I'm doing fine, thanks."

She moved across the room to the bar with a delicate grace, the black sheath emphasizing the curves and the hollows of her body, buttocks shimmering. He wouldn't allow himself to watch her when she returned to her place on the couch. He had come only for information, and anything else would be too dangerous, too tasteless, under the circumstances. But he could not keep from wondering what it would be like to make love to her.

"I don't have to wait any more," she said. "Not for Harrison Gunther or anyone else." She eyed Pompey speculatively across her glass. "You have no idea what being in love means to a woman like me, how it takes hold and drives everything else out of life. I was born for love, to give it and take it, and that's how it was for me with him, and when it was over nothing was left."

"I'm sorry. I didn't mean to——"

She brightened perceptibly. "That's perfectly all right. I'm glad you came. I need no one to help me be unhappy. I manage that quite well by myself, thank you. You listen, that's all, and later you'll get exactly what you came after."

She finished her drink and stood up, took his glass, headed back to the bar, the thick female scent of her trailing behind.

"Shouldn't we go to dinner?"

"Not until I'm ready," she said coldly, then softly: "One more drink, please. After all, you mustn't expect a lady to go out before all her security shields are in place. It wouldn't be fair."

When finally they left the apartment, she held herself stiffly, clutching tightly to his arm, her occasional laughter too shrill, her words and gestures exaggerated, and as they walked her breast pressed against his elbow. His efforts to draw away did no good, and although the repeated contact was stimulating, it left him uneasy.

He chose a small French restaurant in the East Forties where the food was excellent and the wine list adequate; most important, it was protectively dim, a place for people who chose not to be seen and recognized. The conspiratorial nature of this meeting troubled Pompey. If word of it got back to the President . . . He shuddered.

"Harrison," she said, "never could take me to a place like this. Not any place. We always stayed at home."

He forced himself to concentrate, reminding himself why he had come. "Could we talk now," he said. "I thought there might be things you could tell me—about the private man."

It was as if she hadn't heard him. "This is a fine place for a man to take a woman, to woo her, to make love to her. That's so necessary, you know, to make love, I mean. So many men make only sex, all physical. But it's so fine when it's done with words and ideas that don't bear directly on the bed. Do you know what I mean, Mr. Pompey?"

"I think so."

She shook her head and drank the last of her wine and he refilled the glass.

"Of course you don't," she bit off, then smiling thinly. "Have you had many women, Mr. Pompey? Of course you have," she answered herself quickly. "You have the face and form that would draw them to you, and I'm sure you've been spoiled. Men like you are frequently good lovers, not that you care about the vessel for your sex, but because you fit the fanciful notions some women have about love." She looked around and smiled, gently hopeful. "This is a fine place for love-making. I must remember it, the next time I'm in the mood for some intensive wooing."

She drained half her glass.

"You would be surprised at the variety of men who have sought to woo me since I came back to New York, Mr. Pompey. Or perhaps you wouldn't be. All sorts, some so young and innocent in their arrogance, seeing me as lonely and aging, easy prey, but still good for an energetic roll in the hay." She laughed briefly. "Do I shock you? That sort of remark is out of character for me. Or is it? That's the way I feel right now, the way I've been feeling for some time. And there are older men, too, oh, so sophisticated and slick, full of little verbal tricks and tests, trying to find out what my intentions are in advance, seeking guarantees. Beggars, all of them, in one way or another, unable to deserve love and struggling so hard to deceive themselves that drenching a lady's insides is a badge of manhood."

She drank the rest of her wine and emptied the bottle, raised her glass in a silent toast.

"Yes, when I want to delude myself that it really matters, I'll bring someone here, and afterward I'll tell myself that he loves me and really wants me, and that it all means something besides a sweating obscenity . . ."

Pompey wanted to touch her, reassure her. He said, "A woman who looks the way you do——"

"Oh, shut up," she said quietly. "For God's sake don't be nice to me. I don't want that from you. There's too much pain, and being nice only makes it worse, reminds me of too many things." She took a cigarette and he lit it for her. "An article, you said. You must have a hundred questions prepared. All right, fire away." She frowned. "But I won't have what was between Harrison and me scandalized. Someday, when the burning eases off it will be a sweet memory to live with. So, even though it was not exactly a secret thing among people who make a point of knowing such things, I still wouldn't want it made into a tabloid feature story. You can understand how I feel."

"Trust me."

"No, I won't trust you. Nor anybody else. Not even myself. There is no good reason for me to talk to you about this. But then there is no good reason not to." She swallowed the remainder of the wine and leaned forward, and the swell of her breasts gleamed in the candlelight. He raised his eyes and thought he perceived an amused expression in her deep-set eyes. A moment later an opaque curtain descended and he couldn't be sure. "You'll see that Harrison is protected."

"Yes."

She made a small skeptical snuffling sound. "We'll go back to my apartment. It will be more comfortable there."

As soon as they arrived, she poured two Scotches, then settled on the couch, the bottle within arm's length, folding her legs under her, making no attempt to adjust her skirt. She drank rapidly, as if fearful she might be deprived of her rightful share of the bottle.

"I always thought that you and the President——" Pompey began.

She broke in. "Were a thing of lasting beauty? So did I. Or at least I wanted to believe it. How naïve of me. Nothing is forever. It's all transitory, especially human affection, and you may as well take what pleasure there is. He grew weary of me, I suppose, bored."

"I find that hard to believe."

"I expected it would happen one day, but I was sure I'd see it coming, see his love diminishing, feel his ardor cooling. Oh, damn!" She swallowed some Scotch and smiled a swift smile. "It wasn't that way at all. It was over so quick, so damned quick." She reached for the bottle. "But you're not interested in that."

"I noticed some changes in him recently," Pompey heard himself say. She changed her position and the short skirt rode higher up her thigh, and he was able to see above her stockings where the flesh met, and a thick knot lodged low in his gut. He made himself look up. "I thought he might be under some personal strain."

"Is he ill?" she said absently.

"No."

She swallowed some Scotch and patted the couch. "Come. Sit here, next to me. This way, you're too far away. It makes me tired to have to look over a great drinking."

He took a position alongside her, and she leaned against him, her breast on his arm. She laughed softly. "I like a man to be close to me, to know he's with me."

"When I learned you had left Washington," he said. "I wondered . . . and with this article on tap, and since I had to be in New York anyway . . ."

"Let's not talk about what's past, at least not now. It isn't flattering. The way you ignore me, it isn't at all proper. I'm not used to it. Men don't ignore me. I mean, the minute a man's alone with me he's usually all over me." She pressed herself against him, and a laugh sputtered across her full lips. "Wouldn't you like to be all over me?"

He wanted her, and knew it was as much for having been the President's mistress as for what she was as a woman. He shivered and she misunderstood.

"Patience, baby. I'll take care of you."

She placed her hand on his stomach and pressed firmly. "Flat. I like flat bellies. It makes it easier somehow." She allowed her hand to fall onto the inside of his thigh.

He bent to kiss her and she pulled back. "No. No kissing." She reached for his hand and raised it deliberately to her mouth, watching him all the time, slowly folding her lips around each knuckle in turn, lingering moistly. She took his thumb into her mouth, and an old familiar thickness came into his throat, a hollowness across his middle.

"Miss Lockridge . . ."

She turned her attention to the palm of his hand, her tongue marking a sensuous trail. Pompey's senses were thick and ponderous, and he saw it all as if from a distance, everything slow and full of wonder.

At once, there was movement, abrupt images flashing onto the screen of his mind, then gone, replaced by another visual delight. Garments fell aside and there, in soft focus, she stood naked, moved tantalizingly forward. He reached through the distance, anxious to pierce the shimmering murkiness, but she avoided his hands, knelt in front of him, fumbling with his clothes. Then her face was against his naked leg.

"You," she muttered into his flesh. "You mustn't do anything. Nothing at all. You aren't to touch me or try to please me. This is for you, for taking me to dinner, for giving me an excuse not to get drunk alone, for just being here with me." She shuddered. "It means nothing at all."

Her mouth found the inside of his thigh, biting wetly, moving always, eyes hooded, watchful, making sure that he was witness to it all, voicing a descriptive catalogue of what was to come.

"Both of us," she murmured finally, "both of us love him—"

"What?"

She made no answer; she couldn't.

He was jarred backward, into himself, alone and distressed, everything sudden, ended brusquely as if anxious to be rid of this moment.

She rose and left the room without looking at him. He stood up and dressed and lit a cigarette and took a long swallow of Scotch. He wanted to leave before she returned, but there were still unanswered questions. He drank some more Scotch.

When she came back into the living room, she was

wearing a floor-length hostess gown, and her manner was cool and distant. She smiled with proper restraint.

"I'd offer you some coffee," she said. "But it's late and I'm a little tired; and, of course, you have a long trip in front of you."

"I didn't intend for this to happen."

She stared at him with no change of expression. "Please. Just go. Isn't that what you came for, to make it with the President's ex-lover?"

"Oh, no!"

"That business about an article—I never believed it. Not really."

Something clicked into place in his brain. "It's true. There is an article."

"And you didn't get your story."

A vision of Ralph Jacobs faded into view, his expression frozen with disapproval. "It's important. Could you give me a few minutes more?"

She shrugged and turned away, lit a cigarette. "Why not? There's not much to tell. He simply stopped caring, lost interest. It's happened many times to many women. Inevitable, I suppose. The circumstances were impossible." She sucked on the cigarette. "Sometimes, when I think about it, which is almost constantly, it's so hard to understand. One night he was with me, tender and giving and gentle, not at all that fearful presence who lived in the White House and made monumental decisions. Just a man, my lover, often weary and afraid that he wasn't quite up to the demands of his job."

Pompey recognized the Harrison Gunther she described, that curious combination of strength and uncertainty.

She crushed out her cigarette, lit another one. "Without warning, he changed. The next time I saw him, a different man."

The pulse in Pompey's temple began to throb. "How do you mean different?" he said.

"Probably not at all. Just a man no longer in love and trying to make it easy on the girl. An abrasiveness, a harsh undertone when he spoke about people, condemnatory in ways he'd never before been. Harder, even physically, if that's possible." She gave a brief, nervous laugh. "But that's impossible, isn't it?"

"And he called it off between you."

"Oh, no. Not like that. I suppose he couldn't face a scene. There was a letter, in his hand, on plain paper, but unsigned, saying it would be profitable to us both for it to end now, practically ordering me to leave Washington, saying he would never see me again, warning me not to try to contact him, not to capitalize on what had been between us." She chewed her lip. "*Profitable to us both.* How unlike him, that phrase. To put it on some kind of a semibusiness basis, when all we ever exchanged was love. How quickly good things end."

"When did all this happen?"

"The letter? Not quite three weeks ago. But I must have sensed the difference earlier, must have anticipated the change. A month earlier, or more. I *must* have known. There was one evening when he came, the way he always did, without warning, and I was there waiting. I seldom went out. And it was different from that time on. So quickly over." A wry smile turned her mouth. "I did my best to keep him. Unfairly, I suppose. To excite him," she went on absently, remembering, her voice so quiet that Pompey had to lean forward to hear. "I knew how. But when he lost interest, when he stopped being gentle, turned hard and demanding, when I realized that I was losing him . . . there wasn't anything I wouldn't have done." She presented a wistful face to Pompey. "Nothing worked. That's when I knew it was truly over."

"Was there anything else, anything that made him special, something he particularly enjoyed?"

Her mouth worked soundlessly, and when she finally spoke her voice was trembling. "Get out, damn you! Go away and don't come back. Let me alone. You got what you came for, everything. What's left belongs only to me."

It was past two in the morning when Pompey arrived at Dulles Airport. He gave his address to a cab driver and settled back and closed his eyes. He was tired, anxious to get to sleep, but his mind refused to be still, ranging back over the evening. He felt guilty at having betrayed the President and at the same time took pride in what had happened. He longed to share the experience, to tell someone about it, someone who would understand, someone to assure him that he had done no wrong. And in that moment he realized that he had no one, no close friend in whom he could confide.

He opened his eyes and sat erect and tried to review what Anne Lockridge had told him. Was it possible that a stranger could have taken the place of her lover, and she not know? The changes she had mentioned—hardly dramatic enough to make her suspect such an outlandish act.

Reluctantly, he allowed himself to consider Gail's story. Twin brothers who had changed places at college, substituting for each other in all things. No one had suspected the truth. He leaned forward and gave the driver Anne Lockridge's former address in the Meridian Hill Park district.

It was one of those huge and expensive structures, a soaring, curved slab of concrete and glass, complete to an open driveway and a fountain in the front. A uniformed doorman stood in the doorway. Pompey walked around to the back and was pleased to see he had guessed right—the building had its own subterranean garage. He walked down the ramp. Inside, damp and chilled, despite the fine spring evening; the quiet was almost audible. There was no one in sight. He moved toward the elevators when he heard the tinny sound of rock 'n' roll music. He ducked between two parked cars and looked around. The music came from a glass-walled office along the far side. He spotted the attendant, seated with his feet up, engrossed in a paperback novel, a transistor radio blaring beside him. He never looked up as Pompey stepped into the elevator.

At the seventeenth floor, Pompey held the elevator door open, counted eight apartments, and located the fire door in the northwest corner. He ducked back into the elevator, pushed another button, and this time got out on the twenty-first floor. All the floor plans were alike. He tried the fire door. It was unlocked.

How easy it would have been! A few men, anticipating the President's coming, could have concealed themselves on the landing behind the fire door on the floor where Anne Lockridge lived. They would have waited until Harrison Gunther stepped off the elevator, until his Secret Service escort descended discreetly to the lobby, there to await his subsequent summons on the house phone. It would have been a simple matter to slug the unsuspecting President before he rang Anne Lockridge's bell, drag him into the fire exit and undress him. The double would have donned his clothes and, seconds later, be admitted by an unwary Anne Lockridge, to make love to her.

The other conspirators would wait until their colleague, now posing as the President, had departed, taking the Secret Service detail with him, before descending into the garage with their unconscious burden, by now probably drugged, to load him into a waiting limousine.

It could have happened that way, Pompey thought, riding the elevator down to the garage. Or similarly, at a dozen different times in a dozen different places. He walked slowly past the windowed cubicle; the attendant never noticed him. It would have been so easy, so easy, and no one need ever have known.

When he got back to his apartment, he went right to bed; but sleep wouldn't come. He couldn't make himself stop thinking about Anne Lockridge, about Gail, about what lay ahead if what he feared was so. He got out of bed, after a while and swallowed two Seconals. Just before he dozed off, he began to wonder what his punishment would be.

VII

Ralph Jacobs woke full of resentment. Sundays were always bad days. The tempo of the seventh day, leisurely and private, went against the grain. Even as a young man, he found Sundays slow, the day crowded with too many hours, each of them expiring with depressing reluctance. Others could find pleasure on Sundays, involved in family doings, playing, taking delight in time spent away from their jobs; not Jacobs. He resented the interlude. As a result, he came to save certain tasks for Sundays; and in Washington, he pored over reports and analyses, undisturbed in his Pentagon office.

On this morning, the huge building seemed particularly deserted, the guard's formal greeting hollow in the still corridor. Once in his office, Jacobs went right to work, but soon realized that very little was going to get done. Only one subject occupied his mind—the man in the oval room.

Everything about the affair troubled him. A crazy-quilt pattern was emerging, one set of facts contradicting another so that he was able to reach no satisfying conclusion. Complicating the situation was the hope that he was wrong in his suspicions; he *wanted* to be wrong, sought proof of his error. As yet there was none. He searched desperately for a thread of logic to cling to. Perhaps Pompey had found something in New York. He reached for the telephone.

The Press Secretary came on, voice thick with sleep. "Yes. Hello."

"Jacobs here. What happened in New York? Did you see the lady?"

There was a silent interval as Pompey made an effort to come fully awake. "Oh, yes. I was going to phone you later. What time is it?"

The battery-driven clock on Jacobs' desk read 7:42. "What did you learn?" he said.

Pompey swallowed an angry retort. He lit a cigarette and repeated his conversation with Anne Lockridge. When he finished, Jacobs considered the information, then: "A man grew tired of a woman. That kind of thing happens every day."

Pompey crushed out his cigarette. He wanted to shout, to slam down the phone. Not even his Cabinet rank gave Jacobs the privilege of acting in such a cavalier fashion. Then he recalled his survey of the building where Anne Lockridge had lived. He told Jacobs about it, offered his conclusions.

"Very good," Jacobs said when he finished, and Pompey was pleased at the compliment. "About Miss Sorrell. What did she learn from the President's wife?"

Pompey cursed himself. Under the pressure of the Baltimore trip, and the visit to Anne Lockridge, he'd managed to let that slide past. And Gail never thought to tell him. He spoke without thinking. "I guess nothing came out of it, or Gail would've told me."

"To hell with that!" Jacobs shot into the telephone. "Talk to her, dammit, and get back to me. Now."

"No," Pompey said. "Not now."

Jacobs hadn't expected any opposition. He was accustomed to acquiescence from Pompey.

"It's too early," Pompey was saying. "I'll call her later."

"Yes, of course," he said quietly. "I'll be in my office." He hung up, thinking that he might have to revise his estimate of Pompey upward.

Jacobs got out his notebook and entered a summary of Anne Lockridge's remarks. At first they seemed to support the theory of an impostor in the White House, but a closer study revealed that the evidence was too inconclusive.

He tried to consider the information in the notebook from a fresh point of view, as a disinterested observer might. It didn't work. An objective opinion was required. Pompey, like himself, was too much involved, and there was no one else. For the first time, despite the risks, he considered seeking additional help.

Harvey Gordon was the first name that came to mind. The DIA agent was trained to function well under pressure and could be trusted to remain cool and efficient no matter what was happening around him. Place Gordon in a given situation, give him an assignment, and he would carry it out. But there were limitations, too. He lacked imagination, could not go from the specific to the general, his potential circumscribed by a parochial frame of reference.

Jacobs went down a mental roster of his Washington acquaintances and colleagues. None struck his fancy until he came to Peter Street's name. What he wanted was a man who combined the qualities of both Street and Gordon, the man of action and the theorist. What a wide gulf existed between the two men! The one a competent extension of national policy, the other a self-destructive but imaginative drunkard. He reminded himself that he had sought Street's judgment during his meeting with Ambassador Sokoloff, had proceeded on that judgment. There was no reason why Street could not continue to be helpful; he owned a mind that, when sober, was still sharp and perceptive, and he had been close to Harrison Gunther in the years preceding his election.

Did he dare enlarge the circle? The risks, immense from the start, were increasing, heightened by Pompey's interview with Anne Lockridge and Gail Sorrell's questioning of the First Lady. Despite the danger, help was required, and the judgment of other minds.

At eleven o'clock, Pompey called back. "I spoke to Gail."

Jacobs turned to a clean page in his notebook. "Yes," he said.

"She had a long interview with Mrs. Gunther. In the Rose Garden, mostly."

"Get on with it."

"Mrs. Gunther indicated that the President has been much more attentive lately, much more *affectionate*. Affectionate was her word and she giggled a lot, Gail said."

"At forty-four that schoolgirl manner of hers loses something. What else?"

"She said the President had changed in the last few weeks, seemed more vigorous, more insistent, demanding, more passionate." He hesitated. "*Demanding*. Anne Lockridge used the same word."

Jacobs grunted. "Did she say anything else about changes in the President?"

"As a matter of fact, something interesting. The President has taken to combing his hair."

Jacobs suppressed a rising annoyance. "Is there a point to this, Pompey?"

"There is. Seems that when the President was a young man his hair was too thick to comb. He *always* used a brush. The habit carried over, and even after he began losing his hair he still used a brush."

"And now he's begun to comb it!"

"That's it."

That decided Jacobs. "I think it's time for us to bring in some other people, some expert assistance."

Pompey didn't like that. Other people would make them more vulnerable, and he said so. Jacobs swept his objections aside, emphasizing the need to determine the truth swiftly.

"Be at my house at 1 o'clock," Jacobs said. "Make sure no one knows where you're going. If you think you're being followed, don't come."

"Followed?" Cold seat dampened Pompey's palms.

"It's unlikely, but possible. I'll see you at 1 o'clock."

Jacobs wasted no time. First, he called Harvey Gordon, then Peter Street, asking each man to come to the house in Georgetown. Having committed himself, Jacobs felt better. Now there was no turning back.

Peter Street wanted Scotch, the others nothing. The four men were in Ralph Jacobs' study. After qualifying Gordon professionally, for the benefit of Street and Pompey who had never met him, Jacobs assessed the others. Pompey's handsome face appeared strained, pale at the corners of his mouth; Street was loose in one of the big leather chairs, toying with his drink, a vaguely amused smile on his fine mouth; and Gordon waited with no hint of emotion, his ferret features credulous and patient. Jacobs began to speak.

"Pompey and I have separately raised a ghost which has drawn us into collusion, a ghost which we've tried without success to lay. We've gone as far as we can alone, which is why I've asked you two men to come here. We need assistance, objective opinions, other skills and intelligences.

"I would warn you both that there are risks involved. Great risks. Your careers are vulnerable; perhaps your lives. If our suspicions are correct, all our lives may be up for grabs, gentlemen."

Street's smile widened perceptibly and he swallowed a mouthful of Scotch. It amused him to hear the usually imperturbable Secretary of Defense talk in such melodramatic terms.

The reaction was not lost to Jacobs. "Do I sound like a bad movie, Peter? Let me go on. The security of the nation is concerned here, the future of the world. Out of that belief, I have asked you here. Without telling you more, I suggest that now is the time to leave, if you so desire. If you leave, I will forget this visit ever happened, and you will do likewise. I hope you will both remain and help." He waited. When no one spoke or moved, he went on. "Perhaps the best way to do this is to present for your consideration all the information Pompey and I have gathered, withholding our conclusions until after you've been able to assess it. To begin, you're both aware of the radical change in the President's attitude toward the Mutual Defense Pact, a pact he conceived and fought for until . . ."

He spoke steadily and without emotion, occasionally referring to the notebook in his hand, omitting nothing, careful to interpret nothing. When he finished, Jacobs circled the desk and sat down, made an entry in the notebook. He looked up.

"All right, gentlemen. I'll entertain your reactions. Gordon?"

"Technically, an impersonation is possible. It has been tried elsewhere, at different levels."

Jacobs frowned. "Based on the evidence presented, what do you think?"

Gordon shrugged. "I'd want to be sure before I did anything."

"And you're not sure yet?"

"No, sir."

Jacobs made another note. "And you, Peter?"

Street finished the drink. He went to the bar, poured another. There was an indulgent smile on his face when he turned back into the room.

"Whatever my shortcomings, Ralph, I consider myself sane."

"You believe it's madness to entertain this possibility?"

Street resumed his seat, crossed his long, thin legs. "It's a fascinating intellectual exercise, Ralph. But to seriously consider . . ." He broke off and looked into his glass. After a moment, he glanced up, expression guarded. "Of course, that would account for a lot that's been happening. Ken MacMillan, for example. That never made sense to me, any more than the Bookman appointment. I *know* how Harrison felt about MacMillan. We both studied with him as undergraduates at Princeton. Political science. Harry always thought Mac was short in the brain department, considered his Marxist-rooted philosophies stupid. I never went quite that far myself, but Mac *is* pretty doctrinaire. Harrison was always convinced that Mac was a card-carrying member of the CP. It was his point that anyone who belonged to the party in the U.S. as late as the fifties, with the Soviet record of deceit and aggrandizement, was either a fool or a fanatic."

"And now we find this same MacMillan appointed to a sensitive government post," Jacobs said.

"Interesting," Street remarked.

"Would Gunther, the real Gunther, have appointed MacMillan?"

Street met Jacobs' eyes for a long interval, finally averted his gaze. "I must doubt it," he said quietly.

Listening to this exchange, Pompey found himself troubled anew. Street seemed to enjoy the situation, enjoy being part of something important once more, even something as charged with danger as this. To take even a small amount of pleasure out of the situation, indicated his unreliability to Pompey. He saw Street as a threat to his own welfare, a man without controls or prudence. He failed to recall his own pleased reactions at the moment Ralph Jacobs had given credence to his suspicions.

"Mr. Secretary," Harvey Gordon said.

"Yes."

Gordon glanced around. "Does everyone know about the 54-12 Group?"

"The basic unit of the control system that sits in on CIA operations," Jacobs explained. "They try to prevent some of those foul-ups, such as the Bay of Pigs."

Gordon assented. "Yesterday I learned that the President has replaced two of the men in the group. No public announcement, of course. But he won't be able to keep it quiet for long. MacMillan is one replacement and Edgar Bookman the other."

"They'll function as the White House representatives?" Jacobs asked.

"Exactly."

"Fascinating," Street said, the indulgent smile returning. "A peculiar tandem for Harry Gunther to ride."

"Does this influence your opinion any, Peter?" Jacobs asked.

"You make a good circumstantial case, but nothing I'd want to go to court with."

"Is it worth pursuing?"

Pompey saw the smile wash away, and at once those finely matched features paled, seemed to sag wearily. He sighed audibly.

"Yes, pursue it by all means, but God help us all if it's true."

"That's why I asked you and Gordon here today," Jacobs said. "Can I depend on you, Peter?"

"To do what?" Street's eyes darted from Jacobs to Pompey and back again.

"To help."

"I'll try," he mumbled into his glass.

"Gordon?" Jacobs said.

"Yes, sir, Mr. Secretary." He paused, lips pursed, thoughtful. "To pull off something like this would require a big organization, a lot of money, and time. A lot of time, and a tremendous desire to persist. The training that an impostor would require——"

"That reminds me," Street said. "You speak of time," he said to Gordon, "of the training required. Just after Gunther's election, a matter of days, Ken MacMillan disappeared. Dropped out of sight. He was still teaching then and he simply evaporated. Later, he claimed he had been sick and needed a vacation. Very sudden sickness. He was gone for about six weeks and no one ever found out where."

"What are you suggesting?" Jacobs said.

"I don't know actually. But it occurs to me that there may be some connection between MacMillan's disappearance and an impostor in the White House, if there is an impostor."

"Could be," Gordon said. "On this kind of a project, you'd start early. If you had a double for the President-elect, you'd begin training him as soon as your target got into office. You'd want to collect all possible information, information a former teacher might be able to supply in part."

Street lurched erect and headed for the bar again.

"Stay with us, Peter," Jacobs said mildly. "And stay sober." Street filled his glass and sat down again. "What we've got is this," Jacobs continued, his voice harsher. "A President who seems to be changing policy abruptly and for no good reason, taking on new and heretofore suspect advisers, a President suddenly militarily aggressive and politically unreliable, a President who has altered his personal life radically, appears to be a changed man in certain sensitive areas —with the dog, the way he combs his hair, the way he plays handball."

"And makes love," Pompey said.

"There's something else," Gordon said. "San Carlos."

"Go on," Jacobs said. "There are no secrets in this room."

The small dark face seemed to squeeze together even more. Gordon lived with tight security measures and this casual disregard for procedure troubled him. He chose his words carefully.

"My man in San Carlos doesn't like what's happening. He says that while it looks as if the Russians are supplying the rebels, it's not that way at all. He claims it's the mainland Chinese who are arming the rebels, doing it with Soviet hardware."

"What does it mean?" Pompey said.

Jacobs spoke slowly. "That this country is being maneuvered into a situation where we would be pitted directly against Russia. Someone is plotting to make the American people believe the Soviet Union is being militarily aggressive in the Western Hemisphere."

"Exactly," Gordon said.

"Oh, no," Pompey said. "What you're saying would be an international frame-up to involve the United States and Russia in a war."

"Right," Gordon said briskly. "Black operations go on constantly. Ours and theirs. Remember, during the fighting in Vietnam—in April of 1966, I think it was—the Russians spread the word to their friends in Europe that China was trying to push her into a shooting war with the United States.

"Two attempts were made. First, the Chinese tried to get the Russians to create an incident in Berlin, hoping to force us to withdraw troops from Asia. Moscow refused to have any part of it, claiming China hoped to provoke a shooting war. Subsequently, the Chinese harassed and delayed Russian arms shipments across the mainland to North Vietnam. They forced Moscow to transport by sea—again hoping for an incident, thinging some hot-headed U.S. destroyer captain might blast a Soviet freighter, forcing Russia to retaliate and so set off a big war."

Street chuckled into his drink. "Let's you and him fight. Divide and conquer."

"Is that all you have to say, Peter?" Jacobs said.

"Think of it, Ralph. The CIA and the Chinese Communists both working to stir up a shooting match in San Carlos. Enemies striving for the same result. Camus was right—about the absurdity of life, I mean."

"Can't something be done to stop it?" Pompey said.

Jacobs frowned in his direction. "These operations take on an existence of their own. The department of dirty tricks starts something, and soon it becomes national policy. That's what happened with the Bay of Pigs, with the CIA revolution in Guatemala in 1954, with other operations. If this affair in San Carlos is the work of the Chinese, and if the man in the White House is an impostor—one of their people—then we have to act promptly to reverse the flow of events."

"It all seems to hinge on the identity of the President," Street said. "Do you know Judy Chapman, Ralph?"

"Who is she?"

"She was a pretty thing, with a vivacious manner, very much alive. The kind of girl in a hurry to do everything, try everything. She was freshman at Barnard during Harrison's sernior year and he dated her on and off, saw her occasionally after that. It was one of those affairs, not going anywhere, but pleasant for them both."

"Get on with it, Peter," Jacobs said.

Street nodded amiably. "As Harry moved up the political ladder, he saw less and less of Judy. All of us did. She stayed on in New York and did some painting, studied at the Art Students League. Later she went to Europe, Florence mostly. Spent a couple of years in Algiers, I think. She showed up again about five years ago and three husbands later. I think Gunther took her to dinner once or twice. He was married by then and so, of course, it was all very hushhush."

"There is a point to this story?" Jacobs said.

"I think so. You see, Judy was in trouble. Too many men, too much liquor, and drugs, I think. Anyway, she needed money. Girls like Judy always need money and they usually find ways of getting it. She contacted me just prior to Harry's inauguration. It seems that she had been approached by some magazine published in Germany, one of those lurid picture-and-text books they do over there. Scandal stuff. They wanted an interview with her, about Gunther. Seems they had found out about her romance with him and were willing to pay quite well for it."

"Why did she call you?"

"For approval, I suppose. The poor creature had little strength left and didn't want to peddle her memories, but she was desperate."

"You told her to go ahead?" Pompey broke in.

Street turned to him, brows raised in polite surprise. "Why, of course not. Not that it mattered. She wasn't able to turn the offer down."

"I'd like to see that story," Jacobs said quietly.

"I can't recall the name of the magazine," Street said. "I never did see a copy."

It was Gordon who voiced it for them all. "Such an interview would be invaluable if you were collecting information about a man. It would have revealed a lot of personal material."

"Oh, Jesus!" Pompey said.

No one heard him. All eyes had swung to Ralph Jacobs, scribbling into his notebook. He looked up finally.

"Very well," he said. "Peter. Harvey. Will you now accept the premise that a foreign agent sits in the President's chair?"

Street clicked his teeth against the rim of his glass. "It's worth serious consideration."

"I'd like some hard proof," Gordon said. "Let's run a check on the man's fingerprints and a handwriting sample."

"I can get those for you," Pompey said. He shuddered. Both Street and Gordon, he realized, had been converted, at least to acceptance of the possibility. Where, he wondered unhappily, would all this lead? And wondering, he knew, but refused to think about it.

Gordon acknowledged the offer. He glanced at Steet. "Drugs you said. Let me check out this Chapman woman, too. With Narcotics. Maybe we can locate her. That interview intrigues me."

This was why Jacobs had wanted Gordon involved. His professional competence would make certain they omitted nothing, for he was a master of the techniques required in an investigation.

"What else, Harvey?"

"We've got to dig back. The President's friends, relatives. Has anybody been nosing around, asking questions? Starting about the time of the election."

"That's three years go," Pompey said.

"Not so long when you're working on something this big. Before we can take the next step, we've got to put the pieces together."

"I could take a trip back to Kansas City," Street said. "It's been years since I was home. I know people, Harrison's folks, old friends."

"When can you leave?" Jacobs said.

Street laughed. "Today, I suppose. It might even be fun, going back. But I doubt it." He took a long drink of Scotch.

"Be careful," Jacobs said. "All of you. No one must know what we're doing. Even the suspicion is dangerous to the country. And as soon as anyone finds out anything, he's to contact me."

"Speed is important," Gordon said in that flat, ominous, professional manner of his. "They must be aiming high, and we can't have much time left."

VIII

The next morning, Ralph Jacobs made a mistake.

He woke late—and that rupture of his self-discipline made him irritable—he had to hurry to get to the White House in time for weekly meeting of the National Security Council. He took his place at the coffin-shaped table in the Cabinet Room only seconds before the President entered, trailed by Kenneth MacMillan and General Quirk. Quirk saw the President more often these days than Jacobs did, another indication of the unsettling situation.

The meeting began with the usually vague and uninformative report on CIA operations by Daniel Crowell. They were prohibited from asking any questions of him and accepted his remarks for what they were—a verbal curtain behind which the activities of that agency were concealed. When Crowell finished, the President asked General Quirk for a status report on the readiness of the Armed Forces. A few eyes were turned toward Jacobs at this obvious affront; he kept his glance lowered, anxious to reveal nothing of his uneasiness.

Quirk concluded a rabling dissertation with the proud declaration that the Armed Forces were prepared for any eventuality. In the face of that, Jacobs could not remain silent.

"An amendment to the General's conclusion," he said, not lifiting his head.

"You have something to say, Mr. Secretary?" the President said.

"Our defense posture is now, and has been for years, shaped only for global war, a nuclear conflict. As was conclusively shown in Vietnam, we are not completely prepared yet to do battle except on ultimate terms."

"The Special Forces——" Quirk began.

"Your precious Green Berets, General," Jacobs went on, "are composed of little more than cadres at three bases, men who train draftees who serve their time and leave. We could not put a ready force into the field on short notice and expect affirmative results. I might also point out that we lack water transport to solve the logistical problems of any such endeavor."

"Nonsense," Quirk blurted out. "Ships are unimportant. The Air Force has the power and the will to supply any fighting force any place in the world. I've seen to that."

"I agree," Edgar Bookman said.

Jacobs stared at him until Bookman turned away. "Your pride, gentlemen, in the Air Force is commendable. However, it causes you to overlook one salient point—in order to land cargo planes, even the largest of helicopters, and *they* have limited range, it is helpful to have airstrips. Depend on this—any limited war that breaks out will occur in a dense jungle or mountainous area favorable to guerrilla bands, not in terrain designed for our air transports."

The President spoke in a thin, penetrating tone. "Your negative attitude disappoints me, Jacobs. You low-rate your own department. If it is in the sad condition you indicate, I, and the Congress, would be justified in wanting to know how this came about." He swung around to the Congressional representatives. "Let me assure you gentlemen that I believe otherwise. And you will be pleased to learn that in the future we will be getting more value with fewer dollars spent for defense. Mr. Bookman and Mr. MacMillan have evolved a plan, which I will shortly submit for approval, for a total reorganization of the military, a plan already considered favorably by the Joint Chiefs."

Jacobs felt his rage gather and intensify and set himself against it. He wanted to strike out, to denounce the man in the President's chair, to expose and destroy him. It was reminiscent of his youthful temper, of the quick flaring outbursts that had cost him so dearly so many times. He could recall easily the emotional storms that used to encase him—his being glutted with anger, blinded by swirling bloodied mists, the agony stabbing from deep in the back of his skull, driving him to boundless furies, to outbreaks of violence.

Once he had almost killed another man, a man who had merely questioned one of his decisions, a man in his employ. And afterward there had been conversations with lawyers and threats of jail and suits and finally a large cash settlement. What had remained was the lingering fear of what he had almost done, what he had ached to do, to kill, to destroy for all time another human being, to take a life. Even now the memory loosed a hollow flood of sickness behind his navel. He forced the memory into a dark recess and concentrated on what was being said around the Cabinet table, a slight figure who sat without moving, pale face expressionless, intent on every word spoken.

When the meeting ended, he moved swiftly to intercept the President. "I'd like to talk to you for a few minutes, Mr. President."

"A bad morning, Jacobs——"

"This is important. I *must* talk to you now.'

"Very well." The President gestured. "Ken, you and Edgar come along. You too, General Quirk." Before Jacobs could protest, the President left the Cabinet Room. He followed, aware of his returning rage, fighting against it.

In the oval office, Jacobs waited for the President to settle himself behind the big desk, then began to speak.

"Mr. President, I want it on record—I'm opposed to the policies you've embarked on at the moment."

"Continue, Mr. Jacobs."

The Defense Secretary stared at the other man. Was it his imagination, or were the features somewhat blurred, coarsened, no longer the aristocratic details of Harrison Gunther's face? He couldn't be sure.

"I believe you've set out on a course that will undermine our current defense structure, at the same time insuring that the Senate will not ratify the treaty. I have reason to belive——"

The President snapped his fingers, and Ketza pushed himself erect, lumbered reluctantly across the room. Jacobs saw the dog lift his head, exposing the sensitive underside of his throat. The President began to scratch his ears.

"You were saying, Mr. Secretary."

"I believe in the treaty," Jacobs heard himself say.

"So did I, until events proved me wrong." The crooked smile came and went. Was it possible, Jacobs wondered, to locate a man so identical, even to the angle of his grin? The mere idea was so far-fetched, so daring, so defiant of logic. Was he in fact wrong? And Pompey, too? His mind reached backward. Neither Gordon nor Street had offered any firm argument against the possibility. Yet now, looking at this man, was there any difference to be noticed, any definitive change?

An alteration in policy, no matter how mistaken or foolhardly, hardly indicated an international plot. Jacobs made a powerful effort to clear his mind. "To turn away from the treaty would be a tragic error, perhaps the last chance the world will have for peace."

"A matter of opinion," MacMillan said. "You're too dramatic, Jacobs. This country must move in such a way as to serve its own best interests."

"A treaty with Russia would do exactly that."

"No, sir, it would not, sir," General Quirk said. "The Russians have always been the primary enemy, the driving force behind the Communist threat, the core of the enemy strength. They've never changed."

"My sentiments," Bookman said.

Jacobs looked at one and then the other. And he doubted neither their sincerity nor his blindness. If an impostor had indeed been placed behind that big desk by China, then these two men, from their rigidly ancient political positions, did his bidding more effiiently than would a paid agent.

Jacobs glared at the Chairman of the Joint Chiefs. "You're out of step, General. Premier Grishin is not Joe Stalin, not even Nikita Khrushchev. He is a man deeply dedicated to the welfare of his people, and to him that means peace. The Soviet Union today is a middle-class nation with middle-class ambitions. These do not include war. China, on the other hand——"

"China," the President said, "Is still an emerging nation. A large one, I agree, but light years away from achieving a competitive level with the West. An unaggresive country, given, I concede, to making warlike remarks, but no hostile gestures."

"Not true," Jacobs retorted hotly. "You forget Tibet in 1950 and again in 1959. And the raids into Northeast India. And North Korea. Her active support of North Vietnam. She is an aggressive force politically, economically, idealogically and militarily."

The President spoke in a low, hard voice. "I suggest to you, Jacobs, that you get in line with this Administration's policies. Your negativism begins to wear thin, your constant objections, your carping."

"My job is to establish a defense community——"

"And my job is to do what I think best for the entire nation. You seem to favor the Soviets with an inordinate intensity, Jacobs. It makes one suspect all manner of things. Let me tell you, sir, that even now the Russians plot a rebellion in San Carlos——"

A glut of passion impacted Jacobs' throat. "Ginastera runs a dictatorship, and the CIA——"

"The Russians are attempting to establish a bridgehead in this hemisphere."

"And we don't intend to allow that to happen," Bookman said. Jacobs' head swung back to the President. The rage was everywhere, an advancing, ballooning thing, swinging pendulously in ever-widening arcs, breaking over him in smothering waves, slowing his thought processes. "That isn't the way it is." A crimson film lowered itself across his line of sight, and everything appeared blurred and distant, and he struggled to see clearly, to reassert his self-discipline, to swallow the emotion. It refused to be downed. "It's all a trick to make us believe the Russians are behind it. Peking is pulling the strings."

The President scowled. "You can't prove that."

General Quirk broke in, proper, yet somehow mocking. "The CIA has definite proof of the Russians' involvement, Mr. Secretary. Definite proof."

"You're in opposition to national policy," the President said, his voice reaching Jacobs through a muffling barrier. "My policy. Imagination, all of it. Fantasy. Chinese chicanery. Old wives' tales. Smarten up. Toe the line. We're about to assume a realistic national position from this time on. To turn our attack posture toward Moscow and put an end to this foolishness about China. As for Formosa, those people are on their own from now on. Peace is what we want and they're a constant thorn in our side. If the Generalissimo really wants to be unleashed, he now has his chance."

"This is insanity." Jacobs never realized the words were coming out of his mouth until he heard them, until the mistake was made, and compounded. It came through a distant roaring, a hollow echo. "You want to wreck every safeguard the nation owns, provoke an incident, thrust us into nuclear war. To resume U-2 flights over Russia at this time——"

"Who told you that?" the President burst out.

"Unnecessary, outdated, useless, flights serve no purpose——"

"I've heard enough, Jacobs. You're a sick man."

". . . Trying to start a war, a madman or a traitor . . ."

Through the heaving rage, the oppressive, obsessive anger, Jacobs knew he'd gone too far, said too much, but he was driven by a restless force that refused to be quieted. He made a gesture toward Ketza, lying now in a patch of early morning sunlight alongside one of the tall windows in the south wall of the office. "Not nearly thorough enough," he burst out. "For all the preparations. You missed the thing about the dog, about his throat, about rubbing his throat, not his ears."

It passed then, as swiftly as it had come, and he stood there, chest heaving, aware of what he'd done, yearning to correct it and knowing there was no way. He struggled to regain his composure. "I am going to oppose you," he said quietly, in a controlled voice. "In every possible way. Publicly and otherwise. I won't let you succeed." He slammed out of the oval room.

A long, uncomfortable silence was broken finally by General Quirk. "With all due respect to the Secretary, it looks to me like he's working up for a good-of-the-service discharge."

The President let that crooked grin tug the corner of his mouth upward. "The man has worked hard. Much too hard. The pressure sometimes grows too intense. Remember Forrestal." He lowered himself back into the green leather chair. "None of this is to go beyond these walls, gentlemen. I know you understand." The smile sliced higher. "Well, I imagine we've all got work to do. Oh, Ken," he called to MacMillan, "stay a moment. There's something I want you to do for me. . . ."

IX

Pompey was on the phone with the chief editorial writer of the San Francisco *Chronicle*, insisting that there were no plans for dropping the Vice President on next year's ticket.

"The President's convinced the Vice President is the most competent man ever to hold that office. He appreciates him personally and professionally, and considers him to be a positive asset to the Administration."

"My information says otherwise," the editor insisted.

The door to the office opened and Hank Luplow came slouching in. Pompey scowled and waved him away. Luplow grinned and arranged himself comfortably in a chair, heaving his long, narrow feet onto the Press Secretary's desk.

"Believe me," Pompey said into the phone, "if anything breaks I'll get back to you. And thanks for calling." He hung up and grimaced. "Get out of here, Hank. I've got too damned much work to do. I'm supposed to address the senior English students at George Washington University and I haven't even got my talk outlined. Why don't you do a speech for me?"

Luplow grinned smugly. "Forget it. I got troubles of my own."

"You don't know the meaning of the word."

Luplow drew his brow together and a deep, vertical crease appeared. He pulled at his long nose. He's got me baffled, buddy-boy. Figured I knew him. Figured wrong. He's done a complete turnaround—going all the way on the *Peace Now* speech—going the other way."

Pompey looked at the other man with what he hoped was a bland expression. "Okay, Hank," he said with contrived lightness. "What is it this time?"

Luplow's long face lengthened and he began to speak in the middle of a sentence, ". . . a strong public endorsement of the treaty, a public plea for the voters to pressure their Congressmen to ratify. Bit by bit he forced me to water down the speech. The tone changed and soon it contained harsh criticisms of the Russians, thinly veiled threats. Well, he has come full circle. He's coming out *against* the pact, claiming he made a mistake, claiming that ratification would be bad for national interest."

Pompey wanted to cry out, to protest, to gather Luplow into the bosom of the conspiracy. Instead, he forced himself to remain calm. He tried to placate Luplow, which only aroused the speech-writer.

"Stop apologizing for Gunther," Luplow burst out.

Pompey raised his hands in mock surrender. "Okay. You win. Tell you what, Hank. Let me have a copy of the first draft you wrote. Maybe I can persuade the President to ease off a little, to revert to the original concept."

Luplow's skepticism was evident. "You think you could?"

"I'll try. No guarantees, but I've gotten to him before."

Luplow heaved himself erect. "Okay. What've we got to lose, except World War III? You'll have it today."

As soon as Luplow left, Pompey put in a call to Ralph Jacobs. He was not in his office, wasn't expected for the remainder of the day, couldn't be reached. Pompey hung up, annoyed and resentful. The Defense Secretary should have been available. He was their leader, the core of their strength, and they depended upon him. Pompey told himself that, had their situations been reversed, *he* would not have disappeared. As if to underscore Jacobs' failure, Gordon contacted Pompey that afternoon and forced him to assume an authority he did not want, to make a decision.

"The material you supplied," the agent began, "worked out fine. There's only one trouble—everything checked out."

Relief mingled with apprehension in Pompey. What a preposterous fantasy they had cococted, complete with spies and murder and international plotting. All the product of their unsettled imaginations, his and Ralph Jacobs. This information ended all speculation; it meant that the President was in fact Harrison Gunther, the rightful occupant of the oval room.

"The prints matched those in the FBI files," Gordon said. "And the handwriting sample. It was compared with a specimen made prior to the election, a copy of a letter he wrote. My graphology expert didn't know whose writing it was, and he estimated the probability of both samples being for the same band at about ninety-eight percent."

That did it. Pompey had seen the variations in his own script from day to day and he supposed that such long odds could not be improved upon. He said so and Gordon agreed.

"My expert," he went on, "says that the sample was of a man of increasing purpose and zeal. A deep dedication."

Qualities, Pompey reflected, that a successful politician would possess. As would any man capable of enacting such a bold and dangerous impersonation.

"I suppose that does it," he said, a vagrant doubt flickering.

"Not much point in going on, in the face of that," Gordon agreed. "Too bad, because I located that Chapman girl Mr. Street mentioned."

Pompey wanted to let it go, finish it here, to accept the obvious. But the doubt grew stronger, refused to be quelled.

"Gordon, if you were running this show, if you had planted a man in the White House, wouldn't you have taken steps to make sure the official records jibed in order to protect your agent?"

"I'd have tried." There was a long, thoughtful interval. "To pull this off, the people had to be pretty good, damned good, with a lot of contacts, secondary agents in key positions. A switch of print cards in the FBI files? Why not? It could have been done a long time ago. Passports, identity cards, the works. There was never any reason to question them."

"And the handwriting?"

"No problem for a trained hand, especially one practicing every day for a couple of years."

Pompey experienced the flush of personal triumph, aware that he had approached the situation in the same methodical manner as Ralph Jacobs, cool, intelligent, logical.

"Nothing has changed," he said. "We'll proceed on our original assumption."

"Whatever you say, Mr. Pompey."

Pompey allowed himself a small smile. Gordon might have been speaking to Jacobs, the same suggestion of deference in his voice, the same silent patience as he awaited his next task. And what was that? What would Jacobs have done?

"The Chapman girl," Pompey said, the steadiness of his voice a pleasant surprise.

"She's in Mexico, one of those way-out places on the west coast. No telephones. No way of contacting her, except to go there. I guess we'd better wait and let Mr. Jacobs decide."

Resentment came swiftly, salted with anger. Where was Ralph Jacobs?"

"Someone should talk to the girl," Gordon said without emphasis. "She might be able to confirm some things, clinch it."

Little time remained to them. The *Peace Now* speech was to be delivered on Saturday, would end for all time the chances for the treaty. It was vital that they arrive at a decision before then, that they act before then. And in that instant the awful burden of responsibility, heavy and insistent, bore down on

Pompey. He yearned for the dark and comforting oblivion of sleep.

Instead, his brain functioned with brisk competence. Judy Chapman would have been able to provide a catalogue of vital data to people plotting an impersonation, necessary information otherwise unavailable. How else to fool Gunther's wife, and Anne Lockridge? And no one had actually seen the German magazine article. He reached a decision.

"I want you to go there," he said to Gordon, "to this place in Mexico."

"Yelapa," Gordon offered. "It's near Puerto Vallarta. I could."

"Today?"

In his usually thorough way, the agent had inquired about the flight schedules. There was a night plane to Mexico City. "It makes connections with Mexicana to Puerto Vallarta in the morning."

"Be on it." It was an order, allowing no room for refusal, and Gordon accepted it without question.

As the day progressed without word from Ralph Jacobs, Pompey grew increasingly alarmed. He began to imagine that something serious had happened to the Defense Secretary. He kept calling until, at ten o'clock that evening, Jacobs finally answered his phone. Relief washed over Pompey and he identified himself.

"What do you want?" An alien apathy in Jacobs' voice flattened it, caused a notable absence of vitality and authority.

"There are some things you should know. It might be better if I came over."

"As you wish." He hung up.

Pompey found Jacobs in the third-floor study, slumped in one of the maroon leather chairs, staring into the cold fireplace. Even in that dimly lit room, Jacobs appeared paler than usual, the narrow face drawn, the normally alert eyes sunken in their sockets.

"Mr. Secretary, I've been trying to get you all day."

Pompey was unable to disguise the reproach in his voice.

Jacobs gave no indication that he noticed. "I went for a drive. Alone. I don't like driving much, but this was pleasant. A nice day, soft and warm, and I toured Washington and saw all the monuments and then went into Virginia, deep in the countryside. The trees are almost fully leafed out, and the air was clear, and I sat and watched some horses as they grazed. And I tried not to think about anything very important."

Again resentment came to life in Pompey's middle. Jacobs had no right to indulge himself this way. Without him this matter would never have gone this far; it was his duty to see that it was properly terminated. Pompey shifted his position, allowed his irritation to show.

"I spoke to Harvey Gordon. You weren't available."

When Jacobs said nothing, Pompey repeated Gordon's report.

"I told him to go to Mexico," he ended, "to speak to the Chapman woman."

"You did well, Pompey." Jacobs glanced up.

"And now the President intends to come out openly against ratification. I read the original speech—it's difficult to believe the same man could even consider both positions."

"If our premise is correct, the same man is not involved." An indulgent expression came onto Jacobs' face. His eyes seemed to soften, turn inward and he spoke quietly, without animation, as if considering some abstraction of the mind. "Saturday is our deadline. There is no going beyond it. Once the President speaks in opposition to the treaty, Armageddon will be close at hand. Perhaps we deserve no better than annihilation. All man's conceits of religion and philosophy, and we still seek mainly to destroy and kill. Finally we have the means to do so with a rare completeness, to kill so effectively that all further killing will be unnecessary. Impossible, in fact." A sound came from the back of his throat, mournfully harsh.

Pompey shivered. The Defense Secretary was laughing.

"Mr. Jacobs, are you feeling all right?"

Jacobs lifted his head and stared at him coldly. "Understand, Pompey, those people are not fools. They are shrewd and determined. Ruthless."

"Yes, sir."

"There is danger now, immediate danger to us all. I made a mistake today."

Fear, moist and expanding, blocked Pompey's throat. A scream of terror lodged in his chest. How had this begun? By what madness had he allowed himself to become involved? This was no element of his. He was an ordinary man meant for milder endeavors, the competition of business, the wheelings and dealings of daily life in twentieth-century America. He marked himself as unfit for intrigue and danger and the rising threat of instant vaporization. Yet he *was* involved and would continue to be.

"I lost control," Jacobs was saying. "I let it happen. It was coming on and I saw it, but failed to take hold. Self-indulgence. I allowed the rage to build up, to concentrate, until it overflowed. Like a petulant child, I was compelled to strike out. I told the President that I was aware he had ordered the U-2 flights resumed, and *I wasn't supposed to know.* And I mentioned the dog, about his throat." A long breath came out of him. "Only that. A small mistake, but damaging enough." He looked up and his eyes were clear, shining hard, unblinking, a trace of amusement on his bony features. "To think that a dog is the key to it all, the weak link."

"What are you going to do?"

He shrugged. "*I* am going to do nothing, Pompey. Street went to Kansas City and Gordon to Mexico. Perhaps when they return we'll be certain. Until we are, we must wait. . . ."

Jacobs remained in the big chair for a long time after Pompey left. The stillness of the house seemed to press down on him, to isolate him further, to separate him from the world outside. There was no one to whom he might look for comfort. He considered that fact of his life.

How had it come about? Why? What implacable authority had directed him onto this path of solitariness? A grim smile flexed his lips. He knew how people viewed him—tough and demanding, dedicated only to efficiency. It was true, as far as it went. But who considered his feelings, his human desires? True, he had labored over the years to subdue his passions, to conquer and control his weaknesses. Still, he was a man. And there were interludes when he was tired and afraid, lonely.

His mind reached back to the circumstances that had shaped his life. The people who had mattered. There had been his aunt, and there had been Mendelsohn. After them, who? He struggled to clear his mind. A vision drifted to mind. A bright-eyed girl with a short, tilted nose and a mouth that never quite closed over slightly protruding white teeth.

That mouth. Those teeth. Kissing had always been a problem. A man could get bitten to death, he used to tell her, and both of them would laugh, and he would kiss her teeth, touch them with his tongue. It was one of those private jokes that they could share in public, something special that existed only between them. He remembered warmly how her upper lip was never still when she laughed, lifting and descending over the fine, white teeth.

Margaret Theresa Mary Katherine Donahue. Product of the schools of the Brooklyn Diocese. Taught by the nuns and thin-lipped priests, tugged and pushed into a preconceived mold, her mind and emotions prodded and shaped. Her father had wanted to send her to Manhattanville, or one of the other good Catholic colleges for women, but she went to City College at night where she met Ralph Jacobs. He called her Peggy.

He spied her the first day of the new semester in English Lit. She was more than just pretty, with an expression both bold and wary, the kind of clean-cut features you found in movie stars or models, but with a sensusal promise that excited and attracted him.

He warned himself that he didn't have time for a girl. Not even one as appealing as Peggy Donahue. There were his classes, the time needed to study, the accountancy firm. He didn't need Peggy Donahue. But he wanted her. Very much.

Jacobs recalled what Freud had said: When you understand the problem, you can deal with it. The way to deal with Peggy Donahue, he decided, was to confront her, discover her failings, recognize that she was no different than other girls, and thus get her out of his system. He approached her one evening after class and introduced himself.

She studied him frankly. Jacobs was only slightly taller than she, slender, his features concentrated, his eyes steady, far-seeing. She had noticed him, recognized that he was different than most of the other students. He seldom spoke in class, except to ask a question. And frequently the instructor had no answers for him. It occurred to her that Jacobs knew more about English Literature than the teacher.

"I'm Peggy Donahue," she said.

Jacobs knew her name, of course, and all the rest would come in time. "There's a concert at Town Hall Saturday night. I have two tickets. Brahms. I hope you like Brahms."

"Are you asking me out?"

He flushed. "I'm sorry. I thought I made that clear."

"It sounded as if you were telling me what I'm going to do on Saturday night."

He nodded briskly. "You're right, of course. Will you go to the concert with me? I should be very pleased . . ."

"If I don't go, I suppose you've got three or four other girls you can ask."

He spoke quickly. "No other girls. None at all. Besides, it's you I want to take. Only you."

"You must be pretty conceited."

"It isn't like that at all. I'm not very good with girls. I thought it all out, how to perform most efficiently in this situation. So I went out and bought the tickets and . . ." He shrugged. ". . . And I'm asking you to go with me. If you'd rather not . . ."

"What makes you think I'd rather not?"

A sense of confusion returned.

"Do you like music?"

"I like music."

He nodded solemnly. "Will you go with me?"

"Yes."

He smiled, sobered quickly. "I'd take you to dinner first, but I'll be working all day. You see, I have this business and——"

She interrupted. "What time will you call for me?"

"Then you'll go!"

"What time?"

She lived in one of those two-family brick houses in Queens. Her father had bought it three years earlier, renting the apartment on the second floor.

Her father admitted Jacobs. John Donahue was a big man with powerful hands and bulky shoulders. He ushered Jacobs into the clean, neatly furnished living room. Mrs. Donahue appeared to offer refreshments and say something about the weather. Jacobs agreed with her that the weather was good and refused her offer. She withdrew.

"Sit down," Donahue said in a voice that indicated he was used to being obeyed.

"This is a very nice house," Jacobs said.

"I own it," Donahue said. "Anyway, I will when it's paid off."

"A good investment. Property values are bound to go up in this area."

Donahue eyed him skeptically. "What makes you say so?"

"The city is spreading out of Manhattan. Property is limited, and in time only the very rich or the very poor will be able to live there. Queens, Staten Island, Long Island. These are the places where people will have to live. They'll work in New York and commute."

Donahue grunted. "The city's changing. It ain't like when I was growing up."

Jacobs decided not to pursue that.

"Margaret says you have a business of your own," Donahue said.

"I'm an accountant."

"And you go to night school. That's the way. I'll say this for you, you know the name of the game. Get an education and make the loot. That's what it's all about. Margaret didn't want to go to school at night, but I insisted. This way, she'll have that degree. Never can tell when it comes in handy."

"Yes," Jacobs said.

"My old man should've made me go to school. I'm with the department—the cops. Just an ordinary cop on the beat. Maybe if I had a proper education, I could've passed their lousy examinations, know my way around their lousy politicians."

Peggy came into a room wearing a simple pink dress and a matching ribbon in her fine hair. Jacobs tried not to show how much she affected him.

"I'm ready," she said.

Donahue accompanied them to the front door. "What time will you be home?"

"Not late, Papa."

"What time?"

"The concert should be over by eleven or so," Jacobs said.

Donahue figured silently. "You'll need time to eat something and get to the subway. 1 o'clock."

"Oh, Papa."

"1 o'clock."

The concert ended early and they were both hungry. She suggested the Stage Delicatessen. "I like Jewish food," she said.

"Full of garlic," he said, trying to keep his manner light. "It doesn't encourage kissing."

"Listen, Ralph. I don't know what kind of girls you're used to, but I'm not like that. I'm a good girl."

"I know, I know. It was a bad joke."

He extended his hand formally when he took her to

her door, but she lifted her mouth to him. His kiss was perfunctory and badly aimed, landing mostly below her lips. She giggled. "You don't even know how to kiss. For a smart man, you're awful dumb sometimes." She placed her mouth carefully on his, lips soft and agile. He was careful not to allow their bodies to touch, embarrassed at his swelling crotch, disappointed in his lack of control.

"Don't you enjoy kissing me?" she said.

"I like it very much."

"Maybe it's the corned beef," she teased.

He shook his head. "Will you go out with me again?"

She hesitated. "All right."

"What is it?"

"Well, next time, I'd rather go to a movie. All right?"

"All right."

They saw each other every Saturday night after that. Occasionally they had dinner together, and once they went to the theater, and another time to the circus. But mostly to the movies, one of the big theaters in Times Square, or to Radio City Music Hall. They would hold hands and sometimes kiss, and there was one evening when his hand came up against her breast for a single, extended second. Then she altered her position, and it was over. Neither of them ever mentioned it, but Jacobs thought about that brief contact frequently, and with the memory came a hollow sensation in his stomach, a reminiscent movement between his legs.

His experiences with women were limited mostly to prostitutes, who asked nothing in return, except their standard fee. As a rule, women unsettled him, made him unsure, afraid that he would not be able to please them, fulfill their expectations. And so he had kept his distance. But it was different with Peggy. He did not want to remove himself, did not want to stop seeing her. But she appropriated too much of his time, particularly when they were apart. She intruded constantly, capturing his attention, his imagination. Steps had to be taken. He vowed to exercise the same discipline toward her that he owned in his work and his studies.

He failed. That Saturday, when he took her home, he pressed against her desperately and felt for her breast. She made no response, and he was encouraged and tried to put his hand under her sweater. She broke away.

"Stop that!"

He pulled away as if struck.

"I won't have you mauling me."

"I'm sorry," he murmured, unable to look at her.

"I'm not that kind of a girl."

"I love you," he said, and was awed by the sound of the words in his own ears.

She gazed at him searchingly. "You really mean it?"

"Yes," he said, surprised at himself. "I mean it."

She laughed softly. "I've never had a man love me before. Boys, nineteen, twenty, but no one almost thirty. Tell me again."

"I love you, Peggy. I really love you."

"In that case," she said, coming closer. "I guess it's all right, a little . . ."

They kissed and she curved into him, belly moving in a tight little circle. She laughed against his mouth. "I like to be loved." She put his hand on her breasts.

"You don't know how I feel," he managed.

She pressed her thigh against him. "Oh, yes, I do."

They kissed again, and after a while he slid a hand onto her firm bottom. She leaned back and looked up into his face. "I'm a good girl, Ralph. A virgin. That's important, to be a virgin for my husband."

He couldn't speak. The idea of marriage was terrifying. Marriage meant being like Mendelsohn, frustrated and bitter. It meant being trapped physically and emotionally in one place, unable to advance through life. It meant an end to the dreams and to accomplishments. It meant a commitment to another person, and a family, to time. It meant a surrender of too large a portion of himself.

"Would you like to kiss me again, Ralph?"

Her lips parted and she accepted his tongue for the first time. He reached for her breast and suddenly the tumescent nipple was under his palm. Her hand came to rest on his hip. It drifted across his groin, came to rest on his penis. He quivered, made a sound back in his throat.

"Quiet," she warned. "You want my father to know we're back? Just be still and I'll do you . . ."

Her fingers opened his trousers with practiced ease and she reached for him. It was over in moments. She removed her hand.

"There," she said. "Better fix yourself."

He felt peculiar. Pleased and at the same time discontented, irritable, anxious to be away from there.

It became a routine. Every Saturday night, after returning from the movies, she would repeat the ritual. He looked forward to it eagerly and was disappointed with himself afterward. He felt despoiled and used, cheated. He wanted more and told her so one night.

"Well, that's just too bad!" she shot back. "Because you aren't going to get any more."

"I love you, Peggy."

"That's your problem."

"Next week, let's go to my apartment."

"Not a chance."

He took a deep breath. "I love you, Peggy. I want to marry you." It was done. All the concern, the fear, was still present. But it was of no account. He had to be with her, to have her always available. They would marry, live together,and he would make whatever adjustments were required.

"Well," she said. "I do appreciate your asking, Ralph. Honest. But I don't want to marry you."

"I thought you loved me."

She laughed, a brittle sound. "Where'd you get that idea! I never said it. Listen, Ralph, I liked the idea of running around with a guy like you in the beginning, but you're really kind of dull, you know. Besides, you're not the only fellow I'm dating."

Desperation lodged in his throat, a thick wet glob. "Please, Peggy. I love you. Marry me and——"

She flushed and her mouth tightened. "I told you I wasn't going to. Now stop being a pest," she said; then, more kindly: "Why, Ralph, I could never marry a Jew, even if I wanted to. My father would kill me. I shouldn't even be dating you."

He froze in place, unable to think, unable to speak, his emotions roiling wildly. Terror came, and the desire for revenge. And at last the sharp pain against which there was no defense. He turned away.

"Ralph," she called after him. "What time next Saturday?"

He made no response. He never spoke to her again. And in class he refused to aknowledge her. By the end of the following school year, he was unable to remember her name, or precisely what she looked like. But the pain lingered, and no amount of emotional scar tissue could make him ignore its deep prick.

Now, slumped in the big chair in his study, calling it all back, he wondered about his reactions to Peggy Donahue. Other men had been disappointed in love, discarded for one reason or another. He was dull, Peggy had accused. He was a Jew. A breathy sibilance trickled out of him. He confessed to both crimes, knowing that if neither had been true, she would have found another excuse.

Thinking back, he could not delude himself. If he had been done damage by Peggy, he had also accepted her refusal with marked relief; he had not truly wanted to marry her, had not been willing to pay the necessary price for the pleasure of her flesh.

Nor had he ever chosen to pay that price, to abdicate his freedom to be alone. There had been other women over the years. Other opportunities. He remembered one woman fondly. She had been soft and gentle of touch and spirit, as much mother to him as she was lover, with two children by a former marriage. Sophisticated and lively, she had been a rewarding companion in every way, and he had enjoyed her company as much as anyone he'd ever known. But he knew from the beginning that he wasn't going to marry her, wasn't going to take on the responsibility for her existence, and the existence of her children. And when she began to get too close, he stopped seeing her.

The contradiction was striking. Ralph Jacobs, who had sought greater and greater responsibility in his public life, had assiduously avoided it in the private areas.

Most men acted otherwise. Even those without families tended to fill their days and nights with something other than work. Hobbies. Athletics. They went to the theater or listened to music or were dedicated readers. They took mistresses. Jacobs had turned away from all of these, learned to function within himself, to find everything he needed within his own skin. The self-sufficient man.

It railed to ring true.

He gazed around the room, at the objects with which he had surrounded himself, material rewards of his success. For the first time he wondered if there was any meaningful value to such trappings. And even as he allowed his mind to drift, he recognized how unusual such introspection was for him. He was a man directed outward, impatient with the wasteful internal meanderings most men indulged in. Action solved problems. Action always obtained the things he wanted. Action always took him where he wanted to go.

He estimated the worth of it all. This house, the money accumulated, the companies saved or created, his holdings, a considerable personal fortune, a fortune he alone was responsible for, belonging only to him. A troublesome thought crossed his mind. What would happen to it all when he died? Who would get it? The answer was startling, frightening. There was no one. No relatives. No wife. No children. No close friends. He straightened up in the chair. Something had to be done. Death was inevitable and he was no longer a young man.

Men, his age and younger, died of heart attacks, men like himself, with no history of such trouble. And there were stories of such men dying alone. It was a distressing thought and he forced it out of his mind.

A grim smile lifted the corners of his thin mouth. Never before had he dwelled on his morality, on the nearness of death. He wondered what made him think of it now and, wondering, determined to do something about it. A will was called for, a precise disposition of his money.

Who would he leave it to? A charity, a home for abandoned children? No, better than that. He would establish a scholarship fund that would include money to live on while at college. For boys without parents. They might not get affection, but at least they could have a decent education. It was settled then, and he made a determined effort to turn his mind to other things, warning himself against the dangers of self-pity. He was Ralph Jacobs, and he had always done what had to be done. He would do so now.

He had always sought responsibility, had met every challenge, anxious to test himself, to prove himself. And now this terrible burden, more oppressive than any he had ever carried. Some relief was needed, some way to ease the constant pressure, someone to talk to, a sympathetic listener, someone to trust. To care.

Pompey had many likely qualifications for the role, but he had come seeking support, not yet able to give it. Jacobs wished the younger man had stayed longer; there were so many things to discuss, pleasant things, and in time they might even have become friends. He found that thought wryly amusing.

For him, there were no friends, never had been, only equals and subordinates; and Pompey, while striving for the former, was still among the latter. Jacobs found it interesting that at the very moment he had noticed a certain forward movement in the Press Secretary, a mounting strength, Pompey should have failed him most. A faint craving was born in Jacobs' loins and he struggled to ignore it, to turn it aside, only to have it become more insistent, giving life to old, familiar tensions.

A vision of the woman at the Lincoln Memorial came into view, that generous face warmly inviting. What a fool he had been that night, and all the other nights, the slow, lonely, dark hours. No one had ever demanded that he live such a Spartan existence, except himself. If only he had been man enough to share his life with someone, a woman, to enjoy the rewards that might have come his way.

He took the notebook out of his pocket and began to read the entries. Halfway through he stopped. Every phrase had been implanted deep into his brain and was unforgettable. Very carefully, neatly, he removed the appropriate pages. Next, he searched the big center drawer of his desk until he found a packet of matches.

He went into the bathroom, dropped the pages into the sink and put a flame to them. When the pages had been reduced to ash, he turned on the hot water and washed it all away. He sprayed the air with a pine-scented deodorant and left the bathroom.

He went downstairs and got into the Buick. He took a pair of large dark glasses out of the glove compartment and put them on. He drove toward the Lincoln Memorial, the craving more insistent, loathing himself for succumbing to weakness. He wanted her to be there again, and at the same time hoped she wouldn't be. He pressed down on the accelerator, the need expanding, wanting somebody to be there. . . .

Pompey strolled aimlessly after leaving the house in Georgetown, trying to assemble his thoughts. This last encounter with the Defense Secretary had stirred him deeply. He had always viewed Jacobs as a dynamic and dominant force, strong in every way; to see him depressed and remote had affected Pompey strangely, as if discovering human weakness in the Defense Secretary made him better able to accept his own limitations and to recognize his own strength.

He thought of Gail and a surge of guilt passed

through him. He had not spoken to her in two days. He owed her better than that. He went into a phone booth and dialed her number. There was no answer. He looked at his watch. Where was she at this hour? He remembered the tall man who had brought her home that night and a wave of jealousy washed along his nerves. Her recovery, he told himself bitterly, had been amazingly swift.

His reactions puzzled him. There was relief that she had not answered, that he had not been forced to talk to her; and at the same time he wanted her more than ever, couldn't help wondering what it would be like being married to her.

He began to walk briskly. There was no sleep in him, his mind ranging actively. He decided to return to his office, spend a few hours clearing his desk.

There was a deep quiet to the West Wing at night, a kind of eeriness that this apex of executive power could be so tranquil and without activity. He reviewed the transportation ordered for the members of the press who would be traveling up to New York on Saturday. This done, he checked the seating arrangements in the Peace Now Foundation ballroom. The Foundation people were dealing with the television networks and he made a note to look into it on Saturday. He also had to make sure Hank Luplow completed the President's speech in time to have copies mimeographed. The jangling of the telephone startled him. Who would be calling him at this hour? Who knew his whereabouts?

"Yes," he said.

It was the operator. "Is that you, Mr. Pompey?"

He recognized her voice. Elizabeth Burke, a pleasant woman with a broad New England accent. "Yes, Liz. I guess we're both slaves to the system tonight."

She laughed, a high-pitched sound. "Yes, sir. There's a call for you, Mr. Pompey. Long distance. From Kansas City." She pronounced the name of the city with typical Eastern disdain for any place west of the Hudson River. "You want to take it?"

"Put it through," he said, trying to remain calm. A

moment later he heard Peter Street's voice, thin and taut over the wire, and he was instantly afraid.

"Hello. Hello, is that you, Pompey?"

"You shouldn't have called me here."

"Thank God I got through to you. I'm in trouble, Pompey. I need help."

Pompey straightened up in his chair. "What are you talking about?"

"I've been arrested. It's a mistake, you understand. A mistake. But the police—you know the police mentality. They won't listen. They refuse to acknowledge their error."

"What did you do?"

"Try and understand. I talked to everyone out here. All the people that might help. It isn't that I can't be depended upon, you see. And then I had hours to kill, all of tonight. I'm flying back in the morning. So I went into this bar across from the Muehlebach Hotel and had a few drinks. Not drunk, you understand, only a few drinks. And the cocktail waitresses were so lovely, provocative——"

"What did you do?"

"Nothing, you see. That's just it. I'm innocent. I decided to go to a movie, to keep my mind off things, to drink only a little. After all, I do have a sense of duty, a responsibility toward my mission."

"For Chrissakes, get on with it."

"There was this girl. At the candy stand. So pretty and mature. You must understand, she seemed quite grown up. And I sat near her and after a while I spoke to her. Something about the movie, an innocent remark. Innocent——"

"And you're in jail?"

"The police refuse to understand."

Pompey fought against the burgeoning panic, struggled to order his thoughts. Too much had been said already. For all he knew, Liz Burke, bored at this hour, might be listening in. No, White House operators were too well trained for that, understood the consequences of such transgressions. Thank God this President had ended the old system of recording all incoming calls. He wished he were no part of this, that Street had not turned to him for help, that no connection existed between them. But there was a connection and he was unable to break it.

"Do the police know who you are?" he asked.

Street spoke quietly, as if trying to keep from being overheard. "Not yet. It cost me twenty dollars just to get them to let me make this call. There's a pay phone in the station house and an officer in watching——"

"All right. Listen. Don't give them your right name. If they insist on a name, lie, but don't identify yourself. Can you do that?"

"I'll try."

"Stall as long as you can. I'm going to do my best to get you out of there somehow. But nobody must know why you're out there, or about us. You're not to phone me again. *Nor anyone else.*" A hard edge crept into Pompey's voice, a tempered element never present before. "Do you understand me?"

"Yes," Street said. When he spoke again, it was with gruding admiration. "You're coming along fine. Just fine."

Pompey asked for the precinct number and wrote it down. "Hang up," he said, "and keep your mouth shut." He replaced the receiver in its cradle, made himself think, consider all the possibilities, before reaching for the phone again.

"An outside line, Liz," he said with forced lightness. "I'll dail this number myself, to protect the lady's reputation."

"Men," the operator clucked. "All alike." The dial tone was reassuring.

Pompey called Jacobs at home; there was no answer. He tried the Pentagon; not there either. Pompey swore. What the hell was wrong with the man? He *should* be within reach in case of trouble. Pompey resented having to salvage Peter Street. He searched his brain for a solution, silently excoriating Jacobs for not choosing more reliable confederates. He flipped through his address book until he came to the name he wanted, dialed swiftly. A servant answered.

"Mr. Hepburn, please."

A moment later the Chairman of the National Committee came on, his manner bright and cheerful. "Charley Hepburn here."

"This is Pompey, Charley."

"What a nice surprise, Guy. I didn't realize you were this political, phoning an old backroom hack like me at this hour. What are you after, Guy?"

"Somebody's in trouble, Charley. It could be dirty."

Hepburn grunted and Pompey visualized that bony, thrusting face, the eyes lively, the mouth pursed thoughtfully. "You want to give me a name?"

"You know him, Charley. Right now he's in Kansas City. He's been arrested. Something about a young girl in a movie."

"I see," Hepburn said. There was a brief silence. "Maybe the time has come for this particular person to take it on the chin." All the lightness had washed out of his voice.

"I'd like to protect him," Pompey said carefully. "I imagine the man who used to be his friend would feel the same way."

"I suppose you're right," Hepburn said after a moment. "Does he know about it?"

"No one knows. And I think it should stay that way."

"Okay. What's the story?"

"I don't know and it doesn't matter. But I want to get him out. Can it be done, Charley?"

"Was the girl hurt?"

"I don't think so."

"He deserves to rot." He fell silent and Pompey waited. "Oh, all right. I'll call a friend in Kansas City and he'll take care of everything. What do you want done with him when he's sprung?"

"Put him on a plane and send him back here. And, Charley, this is off the record."

"Sure, friend. That's my business, favors for people.

Someday, you'll have to explain your concern for this man. Now I'd better get to work."

Pompey clicked off. He felt drained, wanted to rest, and knew that there would be little real rest for him for a long time. Well, at least one good night's sleep was in order. A couple of Seconals would guarantee that. He stuffed papers into his briefcase, and as an afterthought, Hank Luplow's original speech. He rose to leave when the phone rang. He hesitated, picked it up. It was Lou Wallace, night editor of the *Post.*

"I tried you at home, Pompey," Wallace said in that gruff manner of his. "Then I figured maybe you'd still be down there. I suppose you heard?"

Pompey froze. It had all been for nothing. He'd been too slow getting to Charley Hepburn. Someone in Kansas City had identified Peter Street, had broken the story. He sagged back into the chair. Now there'd be hell to pay.

"What've you got, Lou?" he said wearily, postponing the inevitable.

"Does that mean you don't know, Pompey?"

"Know what?" There was little point in continuing this charade.

"About Ralph Jacobs."

"What?"

"They found him about twenty minutes ago. Near the Lincoln Memorial. Walking, the way it looked. The cops say he was drinking, reeked of booze. Hard to imagine, Jacobs drunk, I mean. Anyway, he's dead. . . ."

Four

The Only Thing to Do

I

The plane flew low over the mountains. The country below was rugged and, looking down, Gordon could see that the overland journey would have been long and arduous. Dangerous, too, he assumed, visions of white-clad Mexican bandits coming to mind.

The plane began to lose altitude and soon they were over the Bay of Banderas, circling toward the airstrip. Gordon managed to be the first one out of the plane. He strode through the small, hangar-like terminal building to where jeep-taxis were lined up. He addressed one of the drivers in Spanish.

"I wish to go to a place called Yelapa."

The man looked off to the southwest. "Yelapa is on the point of the bay and a jeep cannot go there. The authorities construct a road now in that direction, mainly so that more rich Americans can build their houses away from the village and near to the water. But it will be a long time before one can drive to Yelapa."

"Are boats for hire?"

"At Playa de Los Muertos."

The Beach of the Dead. Gordon smiled grimly and hoped the name was only symbolic.

The driver motioned for Gordon to get into his jeep. "I will take you. My cousin, Orlando, owns a boat which is for hire. If he is not already employed taking tourists fishing, he will take you to Yelapa."

They bounced along the narrow two-lane highway past a succession of beach-front hotels, past an expensive-looking restaurant, and Gordon knew that this place was on its way to becoming another Acapulco, a brassy playground.

"Many more tourists will soon come," the driver said. He laughed happily. "They will bring much money."

They entered the village and the driver slowed the jeep, tooling his way past elderly men in straw sombreros straddled comfortably on gray burros, past thin-shanked dogs, past a family of hogs rooting in the gutters, past half-naked children at play. They rolled along the waterfront, the street lined with souvenir shops and narrow-fronted bars. To the left, the village climbed the hillside, a mosaic of pink stucco and red-tile roofs, broken only by a golden-domed cathedral. They rolled past a tree-lined plaza along narrow, cobblestone streets and turned left to a bridge.

"The River Ameca," the driver said.

Here the women of the village were doing their laundry, beating the clothes against rocks. A weekly ceremony. Above, was Gringo Gulch, the hillside studded with expensive homes built in the Mexican manner by movie stars and businessmen, and occasionally occupied.

At Los Muertos, the driver led Gordon across the palm-shaded sand, past bikini-clad sunbathers. It was hot and Gordon took off his jacket. He was grateful when the driver led him into a small frame house, dark and cool. They advanced along a hallway lined with skindiving equipment to a back room, where a stocky Mexican in bathing trunks was eating an avocado, washing it down with dark beer. This was Orlando. The driver spoke to him and when he was finished, Orlando nodded, turned his attention back to the avocado.

"My cousin will take you," the driver said, "for six dollars American for each hour."

Twenty minutes later, Orlando and Gordon stepped into a *ponga*, one of the dugouts used to bring ashore cargoes from the freighters that put in at Puerto Vallarta. The *ponga* carried them through the surf to where Orlando's motor launch was anchored. Minutes later, they were bouncing toward Yelapa.

Off Los Arcos, three great sentinel rocks which had been tunneled through by centuries of pounding waves, they slowed. Gordon was impressed, but he had no time for sightseeing and said so. Orlando shrugged and shoved the throttle forward. They sped on past thin strands of bleached coral.

Less than two hours after leaving Los Muertos, they entered the *boca* leading to Yelapa. The view was lovely, the wide, white beach, a river tumbling down the verdant mountainside, a fresh-water lagoon. On the slopes, horses and burros grazed peacefully, and the thatched huts of the villagers stepped upward in no particular formation.

A few words to some native children brought Gordon a team of chattering guides. He followed them past the lagoon, up a narrow, twisting trail through a stretch of jungle that opened finally into a clearing. A single, thatched-roof house with open sides stood at the far end. At one side of the clearing, a Mexican youth lay in a grass hammock suspended between two trees. He watched Gordon out of lidded eyes, but made no move.

"Here, señor," the children insisted. "This is where Señora Chapman lives."

The houth in the hammock offered no confirmation. Gordon distributed a handful of silver to his guides and watched them disappear into the jungle. He moved toward the house, and the boy in the hammock allowed his eyes to close.

Gordon mounted the five wooden steps that led onto a wide porch. The front door was open. Inside, it was surprisingly cool and Gordon credited the practicality of the open architecture. Slatted walls provided the illusion of privacy and divided the house into separate living areas.

"Miss Chapman!" Gordon called. There was no response and he said her name again, louder. This time, a stirring from behind the house.

"In back," came a throaty summons.

Gordon picked his way toward the voice and found himself on an open deck shaded totally by the encroaching jungle. Here, spread-eagled on an old Army cot, propped up on pillows, was a woman. She wore a huge straw hat, a flowered skirt and a soiled white blouse. She peered up at him suspiciously, eyes laced with crimson, yellow hair streaked and without luster. Here skin was brown in that way that blondes get, wrinkling and mottled, looking older than her years. Her lips pulled back in what passed for a smile. Her teeth were stained.

"Miss Chapman?"

"Who're you?"

It was difficult to imagine her young and attractive enough to interest Harrison Gunther, though there still remained a reminiscent beauty. Her thickened features were in balance, her eyes large, her bones fine and well shaped. He introduced himself and said that he had flown down from the States just to see her.

That made her laugh. "Men used to do things like that for me. Lots of them. Once, a papal prince came to see me when I was living on Ibiza. He stayed two weeks, which is a lot of time for a papal prince." She frowned. "Nobody comes anymore."

"I did."

She picked a tall glass off the floor. "You want one of these? A *coco-loco*. It's got everything in it."

"No, thanks. I want to talk to you, Miss Chapman."

"Judy," she corrected, and giggled. "You're kind of nice-looking." She scowled when he made no response. "Not that I need a man, you understand. You see Beauty outside? He belongs to me. I practically own him and he's something special. I taught him everything I ever learned and that's considerable." She giggled again. "You'd be surprised what a good student he is." She sucked *coco-loco* through a straw and squinted at Gordon. "What are you after, mister?"

He told her that he was an editor for a New York publishing company, that he was researching Harrison Gunther's early years for a biography. "The story led me to you, Miss Chapman. You did know him rather well."

She laughed raucously and scratched her cheek. Gordon noticed the track of needle scars on her forearm. "Hell, yes, I knew him. For a long time and as good as a girl can know a man. And he knew me too, in a sense, if you get my meaning.

"Perhaps you could tell me about it. We'd pay, of course."

She measured Gordon. "The last time I was interviewed about Harry they paid. Big, too. Five thousand dollars American. Cash, too. That seemed like an awful lot to me, but I wanted that money."

"That was a German magazine," he prompted.

"How'd you know?"

"I'd like to see that article. It might be helpful."

"That's a laugh. I talked to those people for a week, a full week, and you know what? They never printed the story. That's the funny thing. I tried to find out about it. I even wrote the publisher."

"And?"

"And he wrote back, said he didn't know anything about it, that they weren't planning any story on Harry." She shrugged. "Well, I thought that was funny, but as long as I got the dough—that five grand—it bought me this place here and a little bar in the village that pays my way. The tourists come over from Vallarta and I hit them with Stateside prices for gin and tequila. I make out okay." Her manner changed abruptly. "You don't think much of me. I don't blame you. But what the hell, a girl's got to get along as best she can. In every way. That little Beauty, a real Mexican jumping bean, if you know what I mean. I found him over at Los Meurtos selling it to those nice ladies who come down from California for two weeks without their husbands. I offered him steady work at good wages. So he came over here. He's wearing thin by now, beginning to bore me. Most of them last about six months. And then I have to find another one. You gotta admit it's better for them than cracking their nuts lugging cargo around or farming for a living."

Gordon allowed her to go on, certain she eventually would come around to Harrison Gunther. He was right. Soon she referred again to the magazine interview. "I told those people all about me and Harry. Everything, almost. Listen, a man like Harry, the world should know about him. I never knew another man so gentle and sweet, and I would've married him, if he wanted me. But I was never for marriage. Something always drove me, kept me on the move. Oh, listen, mister, it's been a lot of laughs, and you better believe it."

"I believe it."

"Sure," she said. "Harry never hit me, like some of the others. And how many girls can say they made it with the President of the United States, even if he wasn't President in those days?"

She rambled on, and Gordon picked out those bits and pieces of information that might be relevant. She described every detail of the youthful Gunther's body, every turn of muscle, every blemish, every physical idiosyncrasy. "I remember when he hurt his knee playing football and they had to cut him open. His right knee on the outside. They cut him—like a half-moon with a tiny hook at the top of the crest. And it never tanned in the sun, always that little white arc." She sucked on the straw. "They should have printed that story," she said petulantly. "They should have. People are entitled to know what a fine man Harry is in every way."

Gordon was disappointed. She had revealed nothing that would be helpful. The football scar; there was no doubt that the man in the White House, authentic or not, possessed such a scar. It was too obvious to overlook and too easy to reproduce. He glanced at his watch. If he was going to make that afternoon plane back to Mexico City, he had to get started. He gave her $250, money from his contingency fund. She walked down to the beach with him.

"Listen," she said. "I'm not so bad. I mean, living

here this way. Who do I hurt? I mean, I made my mistakes. So now I do the best I can." She glanced sidelong at him. "That interview—I didn't tell them everything. Not everything. But I'll tell you, because you're a nice guy. You'd like to know, wouldn't you?"

"If you want to tell me."

"It was a private thing," she said, the raucous quality gone from her voice. "A private thing. A place behind his upper lip that used to excite him. When he was a kid he fell and cut himself, on his teeth, and it was always extra sensitive, tender. A girl could always get to him there, excite him, I mean, if she knew about it." She leaned closer to Gordon and placed her hand on his arm. "Listen. Why not stay a couple of days? This is a good place for a vacation and I'm a pretty good cook. I could send Beauty away and you'd like it. I'm sure you would."

"I'm sorry. I have to get back tonight."

She removed her hand. "Sure. Have to get back. Hooked by all that civilization crap. Hooked worse than I am. Go on, get out of her. Go back to your jungle. None of you know what it's all about. None of you."

Gordon climbed into the motor launch, and Orlando eased it into the deep water and turned toward Puerto Vallarta. Gordon never looked back; he had what he came for.

II

A nice day for a funeral, diamond-hard, bright and cloudless. The scent of freshly cut grass made the rolling lawns of Arlington a pleasant place to be. The coffin containing Ralph Jacobs was lowered into the grave and a rabbi prayed in Hebrew.

The President stood next to the rabbi, head bowed, the aristocratic face handsome and suitably solemn. Here and there among the dark-clad mourners, Pompey recognized Secret Service agents of the White House detail, heads alertly up, mouths set, eyes searching. There were other familiar faces, White House staff, Senators, members of the House of Representatives, Cabinet officers, Ambassador Sokoloff, other foreign emissaries, military men. And toward the rear, inconspicuous in the crowd, Pompey picked out the squeezed-together features of Harvey Gordon, the expressionless eyes fixed on some point in space.

The rabbi tossed a handful of dirt onto the open grave and an honor guard fired a salute. It was over. There was a scraping of feet and the mourners returned to their limousines. Pompey peered across the grave to where a line of visitors were shuffling toward the grave of John F. Kennedy. Someone spoke his name and he turned. A Secret Service agent approached.

"The President would like you to ride back with him, Mr. Pompey."

With the President in the bubble-topped limousine was the First Lady and Kenneth MacMillan. Pompey took his place on the jump seat.

"Poor Mr. Jacobs," Mrs. Gunther said, as the car began to move out of the cemetery. "Such a nice man. A little shy, I thought, but always very proper. I'm a firm believer in good manners."

The President ran his strong fingers through his thinning sable hair. "Jacobs was a good man. Sad that he should go so suddenly."

"I didn't know that Mr. Jacobs drank," the First Lady said. "A nice man like that, a secret drinker." She sighed. "Had he been sober, there might have been no accident."

Pompey held himself very still. His mind was a kaleidoscope of thoughts, jumbled and confused. Twist, and a changing image came into sight, another disturbing vision, a different idea. Ralph Jacobs was not a man to whom accidents happened. Ralph Jacobs controlled his environment, shaped his destiny, managed events to his own ends. He wanted to say so, to deny that the Defense Secretary allowed himself more than a single brandy in any twenty-four hours. He made himself keep silent.

Ralph Jacobs had made one mistake. Ketza. That single reference in the President's office. A wrong word and he was dead. His suspicions revealed, he had been killed. Murdered. Pompey stared at the Chief Executive and hoped that what he felt did not show in his face.

"I'm sorry about Ralph," the President said. "However, he's gone and the responsibility for governing remains with those of us who still live. I'm appointing MacMillan here to take over as Secretary of Defense——"

"Congratulations, Mr. MacMillan," Mrs. Gunther said happily.

"Thank you, ma'am."

"Get out a story today, Pompey. Later this afternoon, I'll meet with the press. About four o'clock. In my office, I think. No TV. At a time like this, I don't want the defense establishment to be run by some Under Secretary."

Pompey listened with only a portion of his attention. He was assailed by guilts that Jacobs was dead while he still lived; at the same time he was glad to be alive, glad to be able to see and hear and smell, glad that the years still stretched before him. His joy was brief. Apprehension forced it aside, his confidence dissolving with the sudden realization that Jacobs' terrible burden now belonged to him. He felt inadequate to the task, poorly equipped by training or temperament or experience. He longed for Jacobs not to be dead, to return and take his rightful place.

He tried not think about what had to be done, to concentrate on the details of being Press Secretary. It was impossible. During the remainder of the day, everyone who called, everyone talked to, mentioned Ralph Jacobs, always in theatrically sepulchral tones. Everyone but Hank Luplow. He slouched across Pompey's desk and winked long and knowingly.

"Those quiet ones, every time," he drawled, "I mean, that Jacobs, he must have been a real swinger."

"Shut up, Hank."

"Strait-laced, square, is the way I figured him. A quiet drinker? Never. I bet he was on the prowl for some action. Old Jacobs must have liked a little nooky as much as anybody. . . ."

Pompey stood up. A faint trembling took hold of his knees. "Hank. Get out of here or—get out. I mean it."

The remainder of the day drifted past unnoticed, unmarked, Pompey reacting reflexively, anxious not to think, not to consider what had to be done. Gail had asked him to visit her after dinner, and that loomed as an odious chore, oppressive, and he considered begging off, going home. Instead, when nine o'clock came around, he presented himself at her apartment.

She gave him a drink and sat across the room from him, her attitude distantly proper and they exchanged the amenities with no particular interest.

"How are you feeling now?" he said.

She arranged a cool smile on her generous mouth. "Oh, very well. My doctor says everything is perfect. I came through in fine style. A very professional job, he says. There's nothing to be concerned about. I went to work today and I'm not even tired."

Her attitude still puzzled him. He couldn't understand how a woman could undergo such a traumatic experience and display so little emotion. Since their return from Baltimore, she had become increasingly aloof, removed from what had occurred, as if it had happened to someone else. He had expected tears, regret for the lost baby, and part of him resented her detachment.

She broke into his thoughts. "What are you going to do now, with Jacobs dead, I mean?"

"There's nothing to do," he said automatically. "It's over. I'm only a public relations guy, out of my element. They killed him."

She shook her head slowly from side to side. "No," she murmured. "Not like that. Not killed. Jacobs died in an accident. A hit-and-run driver. It could have happened to any one of us. An accident, that's all. It wasn't deliberate. It wasn't."

"It was murder——" he began.

"No! It couldn't be. Can't you understand that it *mustn't* be. It's too fantastic and I won't believe it. The way you have it, Harrison Gunther isn't in the White House and that means the President is an impostor." A low, tragic note echoed in her voice. "Don't expect me to believe that. I won't. I can't. And neither should you. Put it out of your mind. Don't think it again. Don't say it again. Not to anyone. It's mad and will only make terrible trouble for you, for us all. Forget you ever thought it."

"I want to."

"Then do. Believe that Jacobs died accidentally. There's nothing you can do about it anyway."

"Yes," he murmured. "There's nothing I can do. You're right. We'll never talk about it again. Never. I'm going to forget about it. Everything. And you must too."

"Yes." She stood up and took a step or two away, then swung back to face him. "I want you to know that I loved you very much, Guy, loved you so much and for such a long time."

"I know that. I loved you, too."

"But now it's over between us."

It came as no surprise. Only the abruptness, the curt announcement, the disposition of three years. Just like that. He stared up at her. "You don't mean that," he heard himself say. "After what's happened——"

She shook her head in stubborn rejection. "It's been over for a long time—before the abortion."

"No," he said, glad it was, yet compelled to protest, to act out his chosen role.

He started toward her and she backed away. "Try to understand, Guy. You and I aren't after the same things. I want to face life squarely, to risk whatever's involved. You insist on turning away, on playing it safe. I can't live that way."

"You want to get married?"

"It's not that simple anymore. I want to marry a man I can love and respect."

"And I'm not that man?"

"I'm sorry, you're not. The abortion was the end of it, Guy. I guess I knew it then, perhaps before, but that finished things for us."

"It doesn't have to be that way."

She settled into a chair and tried to smile, to soften the words. "You didn't love me, Guy, not enough. And you didn't want my baby." He saw the Tartar eyes grow moist and he almost reached out for her, hoping to soothe her. He made no move.

"I still love you, Gail. More than ever."

"No. It isn't true. And even if it was, I must stop seeing you, for my sake. I must take care of myself, give myself a chance to get what I want out of life, what I need."

"I thought you could help me," he said, not wanting to let go of her. "I can't handle this thing with Jacobs gone."

"No," she burst out. "It's over, you said. Just a crazy

idea of yours. We were going to forget it, forget you ever mentioned it. Both of us."

"I can't do that!"

Her mouth tightened. "Don't tell me again. This madness. Nothing has happened. It's all in your imagination and you can't separate the fact from the fantasy."

"It isn't like that."

"I won't listen anymore. You never told me anything about it. Nothing. None of it occurred, and no matter what you do or say I won't remember any of this, won't know about it. Go away, Guy, and take your madness with you. Go and don't talk to me again."

"I need your help."

"No, not here. No help for you here. Can't you understand? I have nothing left to give you. It's all gone, withered, used up. This terrible idea, I won't let you put it on me. I reject it. I don't believe it. Stay away from it, Guy. It will lead to disaster."

"I can't stop now."

She turned away and he could hear the sound of her breathing. He wanted to reach out and touch her, make her understand, to accept him and help him. He did nothing.

"Please, go now, Guy."

It was remarkable. He could think of nothing to say. Three years, and it ended like this. A word—*go!* And no longer did they play a part in each other's lives. It seemed strange, a part of himself swiftly and unexpectedly chopped away, leaving him deprived, flawed, empty. He searched for some appropriate final phrase that would stamp finish to it, allow him a dramatic withdrawl. Nothing came. He stared at her, blinked once or twice, and left, went back to his own apartment.

Once there, he vowed to close it out even as she had, to exclude her from his thoughts, to feel nothing. There wre other things, more important considerations that required his attention.

He thought about Jacobs. Certainly *he* had

believed that the man in the White House was a foreign agent, else he would not have become so agitated, would not have lost control. Now he was gone and no one suitable remained to take charge. Someone strong, intelligent, daring, was needed, a man able to see what needed doing, and do it.

But who? Peter Street? Hardly. He was weak and unreliable, a man who long ago quit on himself. Harvey Gordon? A specialist, a technician only, adept at executing orders, a man peering through the wrong end of the telescope. There was no one left but himself.

And he was mortally afraid.

III

Peter Street arrived first, eyes red-rimmed, speech slurred, apologetically humorous. Pompey ushered him into the living room and offered some coffee.

"I'd prefer a drink, if you don't mind."

"I do mind," Pompey said calmly. "I want you sober." He saw Street recoil and felt shamed, but he was determined to show no weakness. "My nerves are shot, Peter, and I don't want to talk about what happened in Kansas City, except as it affects this business. The rest is your own affair. But don't expect me to honor you for it."

They sat in silence until Gordon arrived. Pompey brought coffee for them all and waited until the agent was settled before he began to speak.

"I believe Jacobs was murdered," he said. "He made one mistake, gave himself away. Except for his nighttime brandy, Jacobs never drank. But there's no way to prove it, and if there was I'm not sure it would help. So let's go on. I want to know what you two found out. Peter, you first."

Street spoke haltingly, straining for words. The once delicate face was rutted, lumpy, and there was a defeated slump to his shoulders. It seemed to Pompey that he was too small for the tweed suit he wore.

He reviewed his experiences in Kansas City, his conversations with friends and relatives of Harrison Gunther. "All of them told me the same thing. Between the time Gunther was nominated until about three months after the election, they were all subjected to interviews, ostensibly for magazines and newspapers, here and abroad. Whoever's behind it, they were very thorough, missing no one who ever knew him. A lot of people are still angry at what happened. Marv Lyons had some photographs stolen, pictures of him with Harry when they were counselors at a boys' camp in Michigan. And Joan Keefer had some letters Harry wrote her from Korea. They were taken, too. The big haul came from his parents. They're both pretty well on in years and not too alert. So robbing them was no trick. It happened two days after the election."

"What was taken?" Pompey said.

"A set of scrapbooks which they had faithfully kept from the day Harry was born. The books contained mementos—official records, newspaper stories, photographs, school records, birth certificate, stories of his athletic exploits. Name it and those books had it."

"The kind of thing a professional would go after," Gordon put in.

"Did his parents report the theft to the police?" Pompey said.

"Yes. Nothing was found."

"Anything else?" Pompey said.

"I don't think so," Street replied softly. The sound of relief was in his voice. He leaned back and allowed his eyes to roll shut. "No. Nothing else."

Pompey turned to Gordon. His manner was brisk, authoritative, and he was already filing away Street's report, arranging it sequentially with the other information he possessed. "Did you speak to the Chapman girl?"

"To call her a girl is wrong. Her girlhood is long past."

"Never mind that. Get on with it."

Gordon nodded and delivered a concise report. "Two points stand out in my mind. One: the German interview was a fraud, never published, never intended to be published. Two: she referred to an erogenous zone behind his upper lip. If we could check that out . . ."

Pompey reached into some recess of his brain. There had to be a way. He went into the bedroom and closed the door and placed a call to Anne Lockridge. He recognized the risk in what he was doing, but told himself it was worth it.

"This is Guy Pompey," he said, when she came on.

"No," she burst out. "You're to let me alone, I told you. I meant it. You had your night of fun."

"Listen to me," he said aggressively. "I want to know something and only you can tell me."

"I'm going to hang up."

"If you do, look for me on your doorstep, lady. I mean it. This is the easy way, believe me."

He listened to her breathing. It slowed and finally she spoke in an almost inaudible voice. "What do you want from me?"

He talked rapidly, wasting no time on niceties. When he finished, there was a long, crackling silence.

"I'm not at all certain I care to answer that question, Mr. Pompey,,' she said at last. "This is becoming too personal."

"It's very important."

"I don't see why it should be."

He plunged ahead. "I believe that Gunther did have such a sensitive area, Miss Lockridge. When you said you tried to reach him, tried *everything*—I want to know whether you tried to excite him in that way."

He could hear her breathing. "Yes, Mr. Pompey." Her voice was biting. "That way and every way. But it didn't work. It was as if he no longer responded in that place. Or anywhere. I loved that man and I wanted to keep him. I would have done anything. And you must admit I'm good at what I do. But nothing helped. Nothing. Does that satisfy your curiosity, Mr. Pompey? Your editors should be very pleased with the kind of information you're accumulating. It should sell a lot of magazines." She hung up.

Pompey forced the echo of Anne Lockridge's scorn out of his mind and returned to the living room. He told Street and Gordon what he had learned.

"That cinches it," Gordon said.

Street straightened up, eyes darting. "Can we be sure? Even such a personal thing——"

Pompey cut him off with a gesture. "Let's review what we know," he said. He began by recalling the way in which his suspicions were aroused, and those of Ralph Jacobs, bringing them to that point where each of them had become involved. Next, he attempted to develop a logical understanding of the impersonation, how it came into being and was advanced.

"Somewhere along the line, somebody, the Chinese, we're assuming, came across a man with a close physical resemblance to Gunther. This must have occurred prior to the nominating convention. Remember, Harrison Gunther was already a nationally known personality and there had been considerable speculation about his chances of being President."

"The resemblance is perfect," Street protested. "Too coincidental for my taste."

Pompey hesitated, disturbed by the logic of Street's objection. It was Gordon who provided perspective.

"The resemblance was undoubtedly strong," he said. "But in the beginning it needn't have been perfect. Cosmetic surgical techniques are fantastically advanced and a skilled surgeon could have completed the resemblance. Ears could have been adjusted, a nose shortened or reshaped. Even his eyes might have been changed."

"What about that grin?" Street said. "That crooked grin."

"Easy enough. A muscle cut and shortened from inside of the cheek. Quite possible. Electrolysis could have removed excess hair, or drawn a new hairline as needed, thinned it out."

"The handwriting?" Street said.

"Practice. As for the rest, they acquired a body of knowledge that could have been committed to memory. If I'd headed the project, I'd have had my man studying every word Gunther ever wrote, every speech, every article, until he learned the verbal patterns, the word frequencies. Television and radio tapes would have provided the key to expression and mannerisms, gestures. And even if someone noticed a slight change in him, a new line or two, a slight difference in posture or position—so what? We all change with time. And in *that* job you can always put it down to pressure."

"They were able to approximate most things," Pompey said. "But not all." He mentioned the change in Gunther's handball strategy, his frequent rudeness to subordinates, the new, tough way he made love, the way he combed his hair.

"And his rejection of Anne Lockridge," Gordon said. "She was too intelligent and perceptive, too liable to see through him, so he turned back to the First Lady. It was safer."

"Whoever's behind this," Pompey said, "missed some key points. They never learned about the erogenous zone behind Gunther's lips so that their man failed to respond to Anne Lockridge's attentions."

"And the dog," Gordon said.

"Yes," Pompey agreed. "The dog. They blew that one, Ketza's predilection for having his throat rubbed."

"What irony," Street murmured. "All the foresight and attention to detail, the cerebral shrewdness, the intellectual effort—only to be betrayed by sensuousness, that of a man and his dog."

There was a brief, silent interlude, then Street spoke again. "Is this information enough to go on? Would it stand up in a court of law?"

"There won't be a court of law," Pompey said. He was equally concerned about the circumstantial nature of what they knew, about the gaps that existed, but he was convinced that no hard evidence would be forthcoming. They were dealing with shrewd people, thorough and careful, and if mistakes had been made they would be of omission rather than commission.

The killing of Ralph Jacobs—that had been a mistake, making it appear as if he had been drinking and thus fair game for a hit-and-run driver. Pompey knew that it was murder, a murder to eliminate the one man considered strong enough to be a dangerous opponent. But it was something he would never be able to prove.

A frightening thought: suppose they had learned that he and Jacobs had been allied? Perhaps even at this moment plans were being made to kill him too. He set himself and forced the idea out of his mind; there was nothing he could do about that either. "What we know," he said slowly, "was sufficient to convince Secretary Jacobs. And that's good enough for me. Now let's go on."

"But the substitution," Street protested. "Could such a switch have been successfully made? The Secret Service——"

Gordon spoke in that mechanical way he had, the words coming in a flat, expressionless sequence. "Most laymen give the Service too much credit. Security is good, but not perfect. This is particularly true when they have to deal with an energetic President.

"Gunther used to work out at the Spartan Club. The switch might have taken place there. Some unguarded moment, in the shower or one of the small gyms. Or that time he vacationed on that island in the Caribbean. Those runs along the beach. He'd outdistance all his guards, was often alone for long stretches of time. Or the trip to Chicago to study that pilot slum-housing project. Or his visits to Camp David. Or —oh, let's face it, you've got to give your enemy credit for being at least as smart as you are, and maybe a lot smarter."

"It might have happened in any of those ways," Pompey said with certainty, thinking back to his meeting with Anne Lockridge, recalling her words, her remark about the abrupt change in Harrison Gunther's attitude toward her. Pompey felt sure he knew where the substitution had been made.

"I lean toward one particular possibility," he said. He described the survey he had made of Anne Lockridge's Washington apartment house.

Gordon grunted questioningly. "Why there especially?"

"It makes sense," Pompey said. "Here was the dark

portion of the President's existence, the truly private part of his life, offering times when he was alone. The Special Agents escorted him up to Miss Lockridge's floor, but that's probably as far as they went. He stepped out alone and they returned to the lobby to await his signal when he was ready to leave. That left him unguarded and vulnerable. It would make sense for the switch to be made there. Remember this, even the President's closest associates, men who undoubtedly knew about his affair with Miss Lockridge, ignored this aspect of his life. It was never spoken about around the White House."

"Okay," Gordon said quietly. "It makes sense. I buy it. And on the night of the switch, after it was done, after the impostor left the woman, after he left the building with the Special Agents, his colleagues simply removed the body of the real Harrison Gunther and later disposed of it."

"Body?" Street said breathily.

"Yeah," Gordon said. "They would have killed him right away. Getting rid of the corpse would be no problem. They might have dismembered it, or used chemicals or a used-car press. No sweat there."

"I guess that once you accept the premise of an impostor," Street said slowly, "it makes little difference how the substitution was made." He took a deep breath and tried unsuccessfully to smile. "Suppose we did nothing, just waited to see how——"

"No," Pompey said quickly, fighting back the uncertainty in his gut. "If the man is an impostor, an enemy agent, then we must assume that, at the very least, murder was done twice—Gunther and Jacobs both. And what lies ahead would be worse. I'm convinced that we're dealing with the people in Peking, that they intend to literally take over the Government of this country."

Street resisted. "There's no proof, no solid proof."

"This is not an orderly affair," Pompey said tightly. "For Christsake, man, wake up to what this is all about."

"But how——?" Street began.

"A few key appointments," Pompey said, remembering that Kenneth MacMillan was the new Secretary of Defense. "Agents in strategic posts, a few alterations in policy, in defense planning. It could be done."

"The San Carlos affair," Gordon said quietly. "We can be reasonably sure that the Chinese are behind that, trying to drive a wedge between this country and Moscow. The situation is perfect for them. Look at our national response—Pavlovian."

"If they do have a man in the White House," Street said, "isn't all the scheming elsewhere unnecessary?"

Gordon supplied the answer. "They can't be sure their man won't be found out. They're moving as fast as they can toward their goal, knocking us out as a military and economic threat."

"It makes sense to me," Pompey said. "If a shooting war does not commence between the U.S. and the Soviets, the Chinese still have their operative pretending to be Harrison Gunther, acting in their behalf. And, unless he's exposed, it's a fair assumption he'll be returned to office at the next election to continue doing his job for four more years."

Pompey's eyes went from Street to Gordon and back again. They were watching him warily, expectantly, and in that moment he knew that he had often looked at Jacobs that same way, awaiting his decision, willing to act in accord with his desires. A quick flash of panic came and went, and he spoke, voice steady.

"We all agree then there's a strong probability that the President is an impostor?"

"Yes," Gordon said.

"If we're going to act," Street offered reluctantly, "it will have to be done soon, before he makes that anti-treaty speech this Saturday."

"I agree," Pompey said. "Let's explore the choices open to us. We could denounce the President publicly as an impostor. Announce what we know and hope it stands up under examination. But it won't hang together, not under any kind of a structured investigation. Chaos would follow. People would panic and it might very well result in a suspension of the democratic process. And power would remain in the hands of the man in the White House. No one would question his right to declare a state of emergency, institute martial law. We'd have accomplished his work for him. All faith, domestic and foreign, in the Government, would be undermined. The country would be torn apart, and opposing factions would spring into action—a polarization of political extremes."

He paused, organized his thoughts. He was pleased to be so calm, his confidence spreading.

"Where does that leave us?" he asked rhetorically. "Can we go to the government agencies established to handle subversion? The FBI, for example? I imagine that at best we'd be laughed out of court. More likely we'd find ourselves charged with conspiracy to commit treason." The echo of Ralph Jacobs' clipped tones came back to him as he advanced that thesis. "Mr. Marshall would undoubtedly question our sanity, and with apparent cause."

He refilled his cup with coffee, primarily to allow the others time to digest his words, to ready them for what was still to come. "There's another course available. We could prevail on some member of the Senate to move for impeachment. Could we convince a two-thirds majority of the Senate? Doubtful. So again we'd fail and be worse off than before, the country fragmented, our case dissipated. Let's face one fact—any President is entitled to change his policies, alter his political philosophy.

"Here's another alternative. We confront the impostor directly. Tell him what we know, threaten to expose him, demand he resign. But, Street, what would you do if you were President and so confronted? Let me tell you. You'd laugh your accusers out of the White House, or have them charged; or perhaps you might arrange to have them killed, as Ralph Jacobs was killed."

Pompey found himself breathing hard, imagined he could hear his heartbeat. He lit a cigarette with trembling fingers, but when he resumed speaking his voice was quiet and steady. "There are only three of us, and we're weak and vulnerable. We're conspiring against the apparently legitimate Government of the country. We are the outsiders and history would surely judge us accordingly."

As he spoke, Pompey tried to think as Ralph Jacobs might have thought; and he knew that Jacobs would have insisted that history never learn of their activities, for—right or wrong—the foundations of the Republic would be weakened if what they suspected was made public. A rebellion, a military takeover, a surprise attack from without against a nation sundered by internal confusion, a diminishing of constitutional government—all were possible.

His mind ranged ahead. Once the San Carlos situation broke out in the open, apparently the work of the Soviet Union, the United States would likely intervene. At the very least, the two countries would confront each other indirectly, with a head-on military clash a distinct possibility. And that would eventually mean nuclear war.

Time was running out. Action had to be taken, and soon. Street and Gordon were waiting, waiting for him to decide, waiting to be told what to do. He snubbed out his cigarette and spoke with calm certainty.

"We're going to do it," he said. "We're going to kill the President."

Five

The Outsiders

I

"I need a drink," Peter Street said, after an interval.

"There's no time for that." The words were spoken with blunt authority. Seconds passed before Pompey recognized the sound of his own voice, and the confidence in it pleased him. This new strength—there was a familiarity about it, as if it had always been a part of him, but ignored. He accepted it now, put it to work. His eyes assessed his two listeners. From the way they held themselves, watched expectantly, he knew that they had accepted his decision without question, were awaiting his next move. He filled his lungs with air. "We must decide how we're going to do it, and where."

A spasm of terror broke over Peter Street. "Do we have to discuss it now? There's plenty of time."

Pompey stared at him. Clearly, Street's usefulness was over. Too much of his manliness had been eroded by the facts of his life to allow him to act with courage and determination. Whatever occurred, he would be only an appendage. Nevertheless, he was privy to it all, and therefore a danger to them all, a danger that sooner or later would have to be faced and dealt with; but Pompey still needed him, hoped to utilize him as much as possible. He arranged an encouraging smile on his full mouth.

"Plans must be made carefully," he said. "Our deadline is Saturday iight, before the President delivers the *Peace Now* speech. That gives us less than seventy-two hours to decide what to do, and do it. We've about run out of time. The President mustn't be allowed to make that speech on Saturday."

"But to kill the President . . ." Peter Street murmured.

Pompey ignored him, directed his attention to Gordon. The decision made, the means of killing had to be worked out. To that end, the DIA men was valuable. Pompey looked at him, hands plucking at each other, at his tie, fingers combing through his thick black hair. The ferret face, however, showed nothing. Pompey supposed that it was the face of a man who had killed often, and the fact of Gordon's presence was testimony to his competence.

Pompey addressed him without special emphasis. "In professional terms, assume you were assigned this job officially. To assassinate a head of state. How would you go about it?"

Gordon tugged at his nose, pulled at his ear, cupped his chin in one hand. A soft baritone rumble sounded back in his throat, thoughtful and appreciative. "Been thinking about it. People try that sort of thing a lot. Kings, Presidents, Ministers. Some pretty bizarre attempts have been made, successful and otherwise. Toward the end of World War II, some German Army officers tried unsuccessfully to blow up Hitler in a bunker. And some anti-Communists went after Fidel Castro, parked a car full of explosives alongside his car; that one failed too. In France, a group of Algerians took a crack at De Gaulle with machine guns; it backfired."

"You make it sound impossible," Pompey said, masking his fear behind a flat, cold voice.

Gordon laughed briefly. "Not so. These were all excellent ideas, failing in execution only. The difference between success and failure in these affairs can be very thin. A number of attempts were made to kill the Dominican dictator, Trujillo, until finally he was brought down by some effective machine-gunning while out driving one afternoon."

In the silence that followed, Pompey thought rapidly. The examples given by Gordon hardly seemed to apply here. Each of them had been devised not only to remove a head of state, but to bring about a total change in government. His aim was opposite—in no way to disturb the existing form, to create a minimum of turmoil.

"Two things," he said. "First, nobody but the President is to be killed or injured. We're after only one man."

"That inhibits us severely," Gordon put in.

"That's how it has to be." When there was no further objection, he went on. "Second, we must kill the President without allowing the real reason for our action to come out."

To Street, that was a glimmer of hope. "That's impossible," he blurted plaintively. "A thing like this can't be concealed. The President is someone special in our society." He straightened in his chair and his pouchy face seemed to rearrange itself, firm up, his eyes brighter as he reached into himself, into some deep reservoir of energy and of strength. "Not only is the President the embodiment of our power, but of our integrity. The President *may* not be killed," he said pedagogically, then softly: "And if he is, the explanations must be clear and unquestioned. People want it that way. When Lincoln was shot it was generally agreed that John Wilkes Booth alone was the killer. Today we have had enough experience to know better."

Pompey broke in. "Granted, Street. Our institutions make an investigation in depth mandatory if a President is murdered. Therefore it's up to us to arrange matters so that any investigation will be limited in how far it *can* go."

"The assassin," Street said, "he'll be able to tell them."

Pompey stared at him. "There isn't going to be an assassin to be questioned."

Gordon uncrossed his legs, straightened the seams of his trousers, and crossed his legs again. He adjusted the knot of his brown knitted tie. "You're making it difficult," he said.

Pompey shook his head from side to side. "I want the assassination put down to a fanatic, a man with a personal grudge, perhaps—but with no evidence existing that would support any political theory. If the truth came out, confusion and terror would result. Factions would spring up and there would be demands for immediate war with China."

Street paled. "You're right. It's reasonable to assume there would be a radical change in our form of government, a military takeover perhaps."

Street's political assessment strengthened Pompey's resolve. No nation could stand idle when attacked from without at its apex.

"It's an interesting problem," Gordon said. "What would the Soviets do under the circumstances if we were to attack China? Which of us would they side with? Or would they simply stand by and watch?"

Pompey stared at the agent. He was enjoying this, enjoying the technical problem involved, able to perceive almost all the ramifications; but he was unmoved by them. The ultimate progmatist, considering all problems with cool detachment, solving them if possible, leaving them behind if not. This detachment troubled Pompey and he wondered what Gordon would do if left to his own devices with this situation; and, wondering, he knew the answer—nothing. The DIA operative would act only when ordered to do so by someone of authority.

"No one must ever learn of the impersonation," he said. "Once the President is assassinated, that will be the end of it. The question is—how do we kill him?" He turned to Gordon.

The intelligence officer shrugged. "Considering the limitations imposed, the simplest way."

"And that is?"

"When he's alone and most vulnerable. Least protected. In his office, at the White House."

A convulsion rippled through Pompey's bowels. The total insanity of this moment, of three men—educated, soft-spoken, mild of manner, comfortable in a quiet Washington apartment, plotting to murder the President of the United States. Even more, the savage recklessness of what Gordon proposed—to perform the act in the President's own house—it was an obscene violation of that traditional place.

"It can't be done," Peter Street objected in a voice weak and hopeful, voicing Pompey's own thoughts. "The Secret Service."

Gordon lit a cigarette and Pompey saw that his hands were steady. "It can be done," he said with quiet confidence. "The Special Agents wait outside his office, never intrude unless invited. As for the uniformed police on the grounds of the White House, they pose absolutely no problem."

Street leaned forward, hands spread as if pleading. "But whoever shoots him would be caught."

"There are other ways than shooting," Gordon explained patiently. "Better methods exist for these conditions."

Pompey put the question. "How?"

"Poison's a possibility. But it leaves too much to chance. Explosives, I think. A timing device. An item concealed in the office and set to go off at an appropriate moment. When he's alone. That way the man who places it would be long gone and no suspicions would be directed toward him. At least none that could be proven."

There was a nightmarish quality to all this for Pompey. His brain turned slowly, his thoughts ponderous, appearing as massive words trailing across the screen of his mind. Gordon was talking about *him*, for no one else in their tiny group was so advantageously placed, with easy access to the oval room. He wanted to cry out in terror, to protest, to retreat from all the risks.

Nothing of what he felt sounded in his voice. "Can an explosive be placed without subsequent detection?"

Gordon smiled thinly. "More than four thousand people with security clearances work in and around the White House. There are the guards, the Secret Service, gardeners, cooks, valets, cleaning people, secretaries, housekeepers, officials of one kind or another, chambermaids, all sorts of visitors, carpenters, painters, messengers. And more. Many of them have access to the President's office, at least long enough to plant a bomb. Such a device could be set to explode hours after it had been placed—days, if necessary. So you can see that there's no great risk involved for you."

Accepted. By them all. Pompey would execute the deed. He would transport a murderous container into the oval office, would deposit it there, would wait in some safe place for the explosion. For a man to die. He would become a murderer, an assassin. The thought diluted his resolve, gave rise to questions, equivocation; he cleared his mind. Doubt would lead to vacillation, too expensive a luxury. There was a job to be done and he was going to get it done. His mind ranged ahead. No matter how crowded the President's schedule, there were always gaps when he was alone, time used to study reports and proposed legislation, time to think, to sign bills into law.

"It must be arranged so that no one else gets hurt," Pompey said again.

Gordon extracted a pad of paper from his pocket. "Can you give me the approximate dimensions of his office?" He wrote down the figures Pompey supplied and made a few rapid calculations. He looked up. "I suppose he spends most of his time behind his desk?"

"Yes."

Gordon considered for a moment. "Is there an overhang on the desk, on the side away from where he sits?"

"No. But there is a kneehole, a recess to allow a secretary to take dictation."

"That's better. We'll put the device there." He tugged thoughtfully at his lower lip. "I'll make the mix strong enough to take out the desk. That way we'll be sure to get him. Wouldn't want a sloppy job. We'll need his schedule in order to establish the time of the shoot."

"I can get that," Pompey said.

"Meanwhile, I'll put the thing together, a molded job, shaped for maximum effectiveness."

"There'll be evidence," Street protested weakly. "Pieces of metal, other things——"

Gordon laughed without humor, and it occurred to Pompey that this was the first time he had seen the agent laugh. "Leave that to me," he said with professional pride. "There will be nothing to trace. Nothing." He turned to Pompey. "How frequently do you get to see the President on a given day, inside the office, I mean?"

Pompey stared at Gordon. "Twice, maybe three times. Sometimes more. It depends. Special assistants go in there four or five times, if something's going on that concerns them. If it involves the press, he calls me. Friday, there are things to be settled before the weekend, especially with the President going up to New York. It's going to be a full day."

"Good," Gordon said. "That means a better cover for you."

"Yes," Pompey said. He had accepted it. Completely. Up to now it had been sort of a game, a near-childish fantasy. But all at once the game was over. This was real and dangerous. He was going to kill the President of the United States. That was decided. All the rest was detail.

Gordon was talking in his unleavened, professional voice: "You'll activate the timing device just prior to placement. I'll make that part simple. Just fix the bomb to the underside of the desk, as deep in the recess as possible. The package will be small enough to be concealed and I'll use a special adhesive." He considered the matter and brightened. "That's all there is to it."

"Suppose I can't place it?" Pompey said.

Gordon scowled. "That's your job. You'll have to find a way. No one can help you there. Do you ever carry anything with you when you visit the President?"

"Yes. Releases, clippings, all sorts of things."

"That'll make it easy to conceal the bomb until the time comes to plant it. Once it's made, I'll arrange to get it to you, Mr. Pompey. After that, we shouldn't be seen together any more than is absolutely necessary. And when this is over, we barely know each other."

They stood up, three men ending what might have been a pleasantly fraternal evening. They shook hands.

"We're lucky," Street said, his relief apparent. "To be able to do it this way, the easy way."

"Not easy," Gordon put in. "An assassination is never easy. No matter how well planned, things can go awry. The attempt on Hitler's life—they were careful, made allowances for every eventuality, and still it failed. Unforeseen events crop up and a plan, no matter how thorough, can't account for them." He looked at Pompey. "Stay alert for accidents."

Pompey breathed out audibly. "Yes."

Street cleared his throat. "I'm supposed to attend the Foundation dinner. I'm a member, you know. I was going up to New York Friday. I don't want to miss Henrietta's party tomorrow night. There doesn't seem much point in making the trip now."

"Make your plans and let people know about them," Pompey said flatly. "All of us must continue to act naturally until this is over. Do nothing to break your normal routine, nothing that might draw suspicion afterward."

"Yes," Street said. "You're right, of course." He wanted very much to be away from Washington at the moment it happened.

Alone in his office the following morning, Pompey reached for Friday's schedule of Presidential activities. His eyes dropped down the list.

7:00 a.m.	Kenneth MacMillan	breakfast
7:30 "	Sarah Harris	office
8:15 "	Don Levinson, writer (Pompey)	office
9:00 "	Nat'l. Security Council	Cabinet Room
Noon	Review *Peace Now* speech (Luplow, Pompey)	office

1:00 p.m.	Lunch: Chilean Ambass., Sec'y. Keefe	2nd Floor Dining Room
2:30 "	Dedication New Wing—Smithsonian Institution	
3:30 "	Report from Sec'y. Knoop on Nat'l. Parks	office
4:00 "	Free time	
4:45 "	Meet 4-H Prize-winners	Rose Garden
5:00 "	Congressional Briefing	Cabinet Room
7:00 "	Summary of Press Reports (Pompey)	office
8:30 "	Dinner: C. Hepburn & Members of Nat'l. Committee	2nd Floor Dining Room

4 o'clock. Free time. Forty-five short minutes. That was when it would happen, ordered by Guy Pompey—the death of a President.

Pompey struggled to immerse himself in his work. His concentration faltered and he was unable to wash away a spreading sense of doom. Fear was no longer an abstraction, for now he was involved, about to kill a human being who might or might not be Harrison Gunther. He fought against the doubt, refused to let it take hold. And in the end he knew it didn't matter; he was totally committed, perhaps for the first time in his life. The intercom buzzer interrupted. He flipped a lever.

"Yes, sir."

"Come in here, Pompey." It was the President's voice.

Sarah Harris sat across from the President at his desk, her legs tucked primly into the deep well. The President leaned back in the green leather chair and grinned at Pompey.

"I want to go over the *Peace Now* details with you." He snapped his fingers, and Ketza shuffled over to him. The President stroked absently at the dog's throat. Pompey felt his joints lock into place. It was crazy, all of it, and here was the proof, Gunther caressing the dog's throat. Then Pompey remembered

Ralph Jacobs' mistake and, remembering, knew there would be no turning back.

"Sit down, Pompey." Sarah Harris rose to go. "Stay, Sarah. This will only take a few minutes." Pompey watched as she seated herself again, adjusted her knees in the desk-well. It was shadowed enough, deep enough, to conceal a lightweight parcel, a proper hiding place for a bomb. He pulled a chair up to the desk and sat facing the President.

"We'll be going up to New York in Air Force One, landing at Kennedy. Then a helicopter into Manhattan, the Pan Am Building. Julian is arranging the details of the police escort from there. I've decided to go up in the morning, spend some time with Felix Wagnall at the U.N.—I want to talk with the Secretary General. It's about time he knew my exact thinking concerning the Russians and the way they're acting these days. It seems he needs reminding about just how much money this country puts into that organization of his. Maybe I'll lunch there, too, then spend a couple of hours at the Warren House on Madison Avenue. Bill O'Brien can fill you in."

Pompey made a note. The President usually stayed at the Waldorf Towers. He wondered about the change and asked.

The President shoved Ketza aside. "It's closer to the Foundation Building. Only two blocks. Maybe I'll walk over and give the voters a thrill. Man-of-the-people kind of thing." The crooked grin tugged at the corners of his mouth and Pompey smiled back reflexively. "Me and Harry Truman."

"Anything else?"

They went over the press coverage at the dinner, and Pompey pointed out that the networks were pooling camera coverage as well as crews would go on the air only a minute or two prior to the President's speech.

"Good," the President said. "Check with me on all of this Saturday morning before we leave, in case there are changes. Now let me get back to work."

Back in his own office, Pompey tried to reach Gordon; he had not yet arrived at his office.

"May I ask who's calling, sir?" Gordon's secretary said.

Pompey hung up without identifying himself, trying not to worry. Twenty minutes later, Gordon phoned him.

"I've been trying to get you," Pompey complained.

"I was busy. Making something."

"Oh," Pompey said. "Of course."

"Can you get away from there? Now."

"I think so."

"Meet me in Meridian Hill Park, in thirty minutes. The upper portion, at the statue of Joan of Arc. And bring the schedule."

The park was peaceful at midday, sunny and hopeful. The fragrance of wisteria and dogwood sweetened the air. A trio of pretty girls crossed Pompey's path, giggling, eying him covertly. Off to his left, a couple sat on the grass beneath a shade tree, and the young man kissed his companion's neck, and she laughed, a clean open sound. An old man fed bread crumbs to a flock of pigeons. A squirrel assessed the scene warily, scurried away.

Pompey saw none of it. An emotional shade had been lowered into place between him and the rest of the world, and he operated sluggishly behind it.

The area around the statue was deserted when Pompey arrived. He lit a cigarette and circled the monument, puffing nervously until Gordon appeared. His squeezed-together features were solemn.

"Let's not waste time," he began. "It would be better if we aren't seen together." He tapped his breast. "The toy is here, a real prize. When it detonates, it's going to take that desk apart and anyone in that room. You needn't worry though, the walls will contain the explosion. People in the adjoining offices will be safe enough."

"How can you be sure?"

"In my business, you learn to be sure. This is what is commonly called a plastic explosive. It was used as far back as World War II—composition C-4. I used a somewhat refined version—more sophisticated, you might say—and certainly more powerful."

"You're certain it'll work,"

"I'm certain."

"No one else must be hurt."

Gordon grunted noncommittally. "About the schedule. What time do you want it to go off?"

There it was. When did Pompey want it to go off? Ultimately it came to that, *his* decision. He visualized the schedule. MacMillan, Sarah Harris, Don Levinson, the members of the National Security Council, Hank Luplow; any one of them, or someone else, might carry a small bomb into the President's office, leave it there to explode at a predetermined time. Time. What time?

Free time.

He spoke slowly. "Between 4 and 4:45. He'll be alone then."

"Right. Can you arrange to be with him some time earlier?"

To review the *Peace Now* speech with Hank Luplow. The President would be fully occupied with the contents of the speech, and Luplow would be no less involved, alert to the most subtle reactions.

"For about an hour, starting at noon."

"Good. I'll supply you with a delayed triggering device. It'll set the thing off about four hours after——"

"*About!* What are you saying? We must know exactly. It has to go off while he's by himself. Suppose——"

Gordon frowned and tugged at his nose and shuffled his feet. "There's nothing to suppose, Mr. Pompey. The firing device will go off *exactly* four hours after you trigger it. *Exactly*. You said you'd be with the President for about an hour. Very well. Set it off at 12:15. Fifteen minutes headroom. It will explode at 4:15, when he's alone."

Gordon reached into his pocket and came up with five brass tubes of varying lengths, each the thickness of a small caliber bullet. They glittered dully in the sunlight. "Triggering devices." He removed the third longest, returned the others to his pocket. "To initiate the firing train, you merely bend the tube, making certain to crack it."

"The firing train?"

"This device contains a chemical, an acid, that will eat through a seal, and in turn set off a blasting cap which will immediately ignite the explosive. The entire procedure is called the firing train. Very simple. Almost foolproof."

"What if something goes wrong?"

"In that case, interrupt the firing train. Separate the fuse from the blasting cap, or the cap from the main explosive charge. Afterward, dispose of the material. The plastic has a high safety factor and is easily gotten rid of." He withdrew a six-by-nine manila envelope from inside his coat. From it, he extracted a smaller rectangle of brown paper, unobtrusive and innocent, no more than an inch in thickness. A blasting cap jutted out of one corner. "Insert the timing mechanism into the cap," Gordon explained patiently. "Secure it with tape before you place it. To fasten it into place, just press either of the flat surfaces of the package against the underside of the desk top. Apply pressure, and the adhesive element on the paper will take hold. Then, break the fuse. The acid will do the rest. Okay?"

Pompey slipped the package into one pocket of his jacket, the fuse into another. "And if I'm unable to place it?"

Gordon stared off into space. "There are other ways."

"I suppose there are," Pompey said. It occurred to him, as he walked away, that the other ways would be harder. Much harder.

Pompey drove along the curving streets of the garden-apartment complex until he came to the building where Gail Sorrell lived. He had been drawn inexorably to Alexandria, though not invited, not expected, owning no reason to believe she'd be waiting. Still he had to come, anxious to talk to her. It was with relief that he heard her coming to the door in answer to his ring.

"You shouldn't be here," she said at the sight of him. "I told you it was over." She started to close the door, stopped, measured him. He was sallow, drawn, an uncertain look in his almost black eyes. "Oh, why don't you leave me alone?" She held the door open. "You're here, you might as well come in."

She went into the living room and sat down, reached for a cigarette. He dropped onto the couch, an arm's length away.

"What do you want, Guy? Why did you come?"

His brain was a disordered confusion of cravings and thoughts, blurred, all motion and blinding color. Tell her everything, he ordered himself. Blurt it all out, the fears and regrets, the poorly defined aspirations, the hope for the future. A placebo of love and compassion was what he craved, the warming reassurance of her firm, soft flesh. He lifted his hand to her cheek and she turned away.

"What do you want?"

"To see you." Words bounced around the inside of his skull, skidding from crest to crest, words and unframed thoughts which, if structured, would convey knowledge and ideas too fearful to entertain. *We're going to do it!* was what he wanted to shout at her. *To kill the President.* And that silent formation of words caused all strength to ooze out of him. *I'm going to kill the President of the United States!*

She stared at him for a long time. "Oh, Guy," she said at last, said with compassion and wonder and nostalgia, "what's going to happen to us?"

It came to him slowly, moving into place piecemeal, in harmony, settling down as if grateful to rest after a long journey, startling, fear-making, but strangely gratifying.

Guy Pompey, he thought. *Public Relations Counselor First Class. Press Secretary. Man of accomplishment and stature. Important in the scheme. The finger on the trigger. The strength and the purpose.*

The font of all power, the source, the egg and the sperm. Creation and life and death. Oh, baby, baby, baby. And the tough spine to make it happen. Guy Pompey. Me, me, memememememe.

He studied it from every angle and accepted it, convinced there was no choice. But without comfort.

"I wanted very much to see you," he said.

"Leave me alone," she said softly. "I don't want to see you. Find someone else. Talk to someone else. You only bring me anguish and I don't want that." She slumped forward and when she spoke again, it was with an imposed patience. "There is nothing here for you, Guy. You don't have me anymore. You're alone now."

Yes, he thought, the way Jacobs must have been alone. Absolute isolation, no other human being admitted, and what a terrible condition that was. No one could help. His brain seemed to lurch, to swell against the confining tissue, anxious to break free of its moorings.

"I've submitted my resignation at the paper," Gail was saying. He forced himself to listen. "I'm leaving Washington," she said.

He felt impelled to persist. "Stay. We'll begin again. Try again. I'll go back to New York, to the agency. We can make a good life together, raise a family."

The green eyes clouded over. "Oh, please, don't. Understand how I feel. No babies for us, Guy, not us, not together. We had our chance and we killed it, both of us; and what's left in me must go to someone else. Can't you see, it ended for us in Baltimore."

"I'm not the same man," he persisted.

"Nor am I the same woman. Now go away and don't come back. I don't want you anymore."

He stared at her, indecision mingling with a ballooning anger. If not for her, he wouldn't have been in this situation. She had worked on him, influenced him, forced him to get involved, making him feel guilty, obligated. This wasn't his business.

It wouldn't wash. This was very much his business,

had always been, and no one had talked him into it. It was much deeper than that, the way he felt about Ralph Jacobs and his dying, and about the country, about what was happening. A man didn't get talked into something like this. He felt it was right, or he did nothing. And Pompey was sure he was doing the right thing.

He stood up and looked down at Gail. It *was* over between them, and in time he would reflect on it and grow from it. But not now.

He spoke to her without emotion, without emphasis. "If at any time you're questioned about me"—she glanced up, eyes wide and glazed—"you might be, then say only what you must say. Don't invent anything."

"Oh, God!" she managed to say.

"Don't try to conceal anything. But don't mention our conversations concerning the President, about his being an impostor. Never talk about that part of it. Anything else is all right. Is that clear?"

She could only nod.

"As for why we broke up," he said, "in case anyone cares, tell the truth—that I wasn't man enough for you."

Then he left.

II

He woke feeling out of place and threatened. A moan trickled across parched lips, out of a throat thick and glutted. He had dreamed and it lingered at the fringes of his memory, vague and unsettling. He made no effort to bring it into focus.

Pompey sat up. He lit a cigarette and coughed. He switched on the radio and padded into the tiny kitchen, put water on the stove, and filled a glass with orange juice. He went into the bathroom and began to shave. Half-finished, he returned to the kitchen and made some instant coffee. A voice on the radio cheerfully forecast an unspringlike day, ominous, with increasing cloudiness and reports of rain.

He finished shaving, then showered and dried himself vigorously. In the bedroom, he sipped coffee, lit a second cigarette, and studied his wardrobe. He decided finally on a navy blue suit of lightweight hopsacking, a blue button-down shirt and a navy blue knit tie, and black loafers.

He contemplated his image in the mirror on the closet door. Navy blue dramatized his swart good looks, accentuated his leanness. Gail had made a mistake in turning away from him. She should have been more patient. Her actions confirmed a suspicion he had long held—she fell short of his standards, his needs—he had been right not to marry her.

He swallowed the last of the coffee, now dank and bitter. There was a girl in Treasury—cute and very blonde, with exceptional hips. What was her name? She was young and receptive, and could be depended upon to be grateful for any attention paid her by the

Presidential Press Secretary. The name would come before the end of the day, and then a phone call, a drink, some dinner.

She would offer a transition, a change, turn his mind outward, away from the terrible burden he carried. But not tonight. Tonight there was something else. He struggled to remember. Maggie would know. She knew everything he was supposed to do.

He carried the empty mug into the kitchen and rinsed it, lit another cigarette, and left the apartment. A man and woman, married, of course, were in the elevator as he rode down to the lobby. He'd seen them before. Both wore that strained, artificial look that signaled growing discontent with each other. He knew the look well, knew the feeling that gave it life, remembered it vividly from all those years with Betsy. Perhaps it would have been the same with Gail, always at each other, the carping, the shrill demands, the oblique attacks, the emotional bloodletting increasingly painful.

The elevator door slid open and the couple stepped out. Pompey watched them move through the lobby, eyes straight ahead, careful not to touch, each shielded by invisible barriers. Not with Gail. It might have been different, good, and he had a sense of loss, of deprivation.

The doorman opened the heavy glass door for him.

"'Morning, Mr. Pompey."

"Good morning, George."

"No raincoat?"

Pompey looked up at the lowering clouds and clucked disapprovingly. "You figure it's a sure thing, George?"

George nodded solemnly. "I'd give long odds, Mr. Pompey."

Pompey rode the elevator back upstairs and hurried down the carpeted hallway to his apartment, located the Burberry. He started out when he remembered Harvey Gordon's package. Sweat broke on the palms of his hands. He had almost forgotten. He went to the closet and reached behind the storage boxes on the shelf.

It was difficult to believe that this ineffectual looking package, so bland in its plain brown wrapping, could cause any damage. He put it in the pocket of the Burberry. In the bedroom, he located the fuse between the handkerchiefs and the socks in the top drawer of his bureau, then set out for the White House.

Traffic was heavier than usual that morning, at least it appeared so. The air was thick, oppressive, smothering the city in gray gloom. Suddenly Pompey wanted out, out of government, out of Washington, and he wondered how much time must pass before he would be able to make a safe and proper exit.

At the East Gate, he responded automatically to the greeting of the uniformed White House policeman and nodded at the Secret Service agent on duty. What was his name? Oh, yes. Paul Frede. A pleasant man with a boxer's face, wide-boned and flat, able to absorb a considerable amount of punishment. Pompey wondered what Frede would do if he should learn about the contents of the flat package in his raincoat pocket? He envisioned swift violence, a torrent of hard blows, or perhaps Frede would simply shoot him on the spot. A titillating consideration, a small, not unpleasant game.

During his almost three years at the White House, Pompey accepted the security regulations as routine, paying little attention to the men who enforced them. Now all that was changed. He saw each uniformed guard patrolling the grounds, holstered pistol powerful and close at hand; and the Special Agents on post in this corridor or at that doorway, quiet men with an animal tension waiting to be unleashed.

The nightmare quality increased, all of it irrational. To think that he could assassinate the President and expect to escape unpunished was total madness. Surely Jacobs would have understood that and put an end to such an absurd adventure before it had progressed even this far.

A uniformed guard, recognizing Pompey, greeted him by name and smiled. A Secret Service man nodded and looked at the wall ahead of him, bored already, his day just begun. The man reminded Pompey of Harvey Gordon, so casually professional; and he understood that what they were about to do was more than merely possible, that the very daring of their scheme went far toward insuring its success.

The click of his heels on the tile floor of the West Wing corridor was reassuring; it was the walk of a man who knew what he was doing. He wanted very much to believe that.

Margaret Reilly reached for the morning mail when he entered her cubicle.

"A couple of minutes," he said.

She sank back in her typing chair. "Coffee?"

"Please."

"Some breakfast?"

The thought of food was repellent and he told her so. Alone in his office, he placed the brown package on his desk, fascinated by its pacific appearance, by the explosive power he knew it contained. He sighed and slipped it into a large yellow file folder, deposited that in the center drawer of the desk and locked it.

He looked at the President's schedule. Don Levinson of *Newsweek* was due in the President's office in forty-five minutes, and so was he. That would provide an opportunity to study the office, the desk, time to decide where to position himself in order to fix the bomb in place quickly and unobserved. When that time came, it would be vital that the President's attention was directed elsewhere.

That brought him up short. The plan called for him to set the explosive, trigger it at the same time, during the noon review of the *Peace Now* speech. Possibly circumstances then might deny him the chance. Could he afford to risk everything on that one visit? His mind worked quickly. It might be better, safer, to place the bomb earlier, while Levinson interviewed the President, igniting it during his subsequent visit to the oval room. That seemed to make sense and he unlocked his desk, opened the drawer. At that moment, Reilly appeared with his morning coffee. A despairing cry lodged in his throat. He forced himself to slide the drawer slowly back into place slowly, very slowly, and smile up at her with practiced ease. But his heart leaped wildly in his chest, and his hearing was muffled.

"Ready for the mail?" she said.

"Give me a few more minutes, Maggie."

"You're due in with the President at 8:15," she said, the rebuke implicit.

"God will forgive me."

She sniffed and left him alone. When the door closed behind her, he took out the bomb, positioned it on the desk so that the blasting cap was directed at him. Very carefully, he inserted the timing device, securing it with transparent tape. Satisfied, he replaced it in the file folder, sandwiching that between reports and files that he would be using throughout the day. He leaned back and studied the low pile of documents, an innocent assemblage that would arouse no suspicions. He drank some coffee, then rang for Reilly.

The mail was routine. The usual requests for information from editors around the world, for White House correspondent accreditation, for interviews with the President, for special tours of the second and third floors of the Executive Mansion, areas generally prohibited to the public. Most were easily disposed of. Then it was time to go.

He rose and reached for the stack of papers. He didn't want to be late. The President had been reluctant to grant this exclusive interview to Levinson, had done so only at Pompey's urging. He clicked along the corridor and into Sarah Harris' cramped quarters."

"Levinson here yet?" he asked.

"And in good spirits today," Sarah said, standing. "He hopes to be able to go to the party."

"Party?"

"Henrietta Birdsong's. You are going?"

Of course! That's what he had forgotten. It was to

be one of the social events of the season. Each year, Henrietta gave a party. They were famous, her guests coming from all over the world. This one was in costume, and Pompey reminded himself that he had failed to make suitable plans. He smiled at Sarah Harris.

"It slipped my mind."

She nodded agreeably. "You want to see if the boss is free?"

Pompey squinted through the Judas hole in the door. The President was alone and he said so.

"I'll fetch your Mr. Levinson," Sarah said.

Pompey opened the heavy door and entered the oval office. The President sat hunched over his desk, engrossed in the editorial page of that morning's *Times*. He looked up from under his brows as Pompey entered, face dark, his annoyance evident.

"The *Times*," he let out thinly. "Sometimes I wonder whose side those people are on. Everybody's for peace, but at what price? There is such a thing as national pride, as national self-interest, as a moral position."

The words were well chosen, the ideas they expressed proper and fit; Pompey was forced to remind himself that this man was not Harrison Gunther, but a foreign agent determined to bring down the Government of the United States.

Moments later, the corridor door swung open and Sarah Harris appeared with Don Levinson. He was a lanky man with sparse, close-cropped hair and high shoulders that made him appear deformed. He moved into the office with a jerky stride, all angles and protuberances, disjointed and distracted. Pompey knew him to own a quick mind, a storehouse of political information, and a keen understanding of people.

The President rose and Pompey made the introductions. During this, he maneuvered himself squarely in front of the big desk. And when the President invited Levinson to sit, he automatically moved to the chair at the far corner of the desk. Pompey sat down and arranged his knees inside the secretarial recess, the collection of reports and files resting on his lap. He drew a long breath.

"I understand you're doing a book on all the Presidents," the President began. "It sounds interesting."

"I hope it will be, sir," Levinson said. "But it isn't only the Presidents, it's this house itself, and what it's like to live here, to work here. It's the personal touch that I'm after. I've already spoken to one of your predecessors and I've read everything pertinent that I could get hold of. What I want is your reactions, both affirmative and negative.

The President laughed softly. "A tall order, Mr. Levinson." He stretched his long legs and rubbed his football knee. "I'll do what I can to help."

They began to talk and Pompey cautioned himself to remain alert, ready. All at once he stiffened, berated himself for being a bungler, an incompetent, a man not up to the terrible task at hand. He had failed to devise a scheme for diverting attention from himself, from the desk, a way to guarantee that brief moment of privacy necessary to place the package safely. He cursed himself and strained to conceive some plan, but every idea seemed flawed to him, obvious, too larded with risk.

It was the President who provided a solution.

He heaved himself out of the green chair and crossed to the tall windows behind the desk. "Have you ever seen this view, Mr. Levinson? Few people have. Come, look. It's something to cherish and remember." The writer stood alongside the President, almost as tall, but lacking his breadth and that easy, casual stance. "Look out there. What do you see? A fine expanse of lawn, some trees. It's so much more than that. Off to the left, the big American elm. Put there by John Quincy Adams. And those two Japanese maples, just this side of the fountain—Grover Cleveland's trees. The history of the nation is in that soil and in this old house. It makes the man who holds this Office aware of the trust placed in him."

With uncertain fingers, eyes fixed on the men at the windows, Pompey reached for the bomb. For a single, suspenseful moment it seemed to avoid his grasp. Seconds later it was in his hand and he thrust it into the well, shoved it up against the underside of the desk top. Hard. He removed his hand tentatively, apprehensively. The package remained in place. He sat back and forced himself to concentrate on what the President was saying, waiting for his heartbeat to return to normal.

The interview continued. Levinson's questions were designed to keep the President talking, and they did. His own comments were provocative and it was evident that he had come well prepared.

Pompey made himself listen. Looking across the desk at the President, at those familiar aristocratic features, hearing those cultured tones, the Missouri drawl almost lost under the refinement of four years at Princeton, Pompey was forced to remind himself this was all part of a disguise shrewdly and laboriously worked out. What was going to be done here today had to be done.

He checked the time. Not yet nine o'clock. The explosion would not occur for some seven hours. So much could happen during that span of time. Someone, Sarah Harris for example, might absently reach into the well, discover the alien package. Or perhaps the adhesive might weaken, allow the bomb to drop to the floor. So many things could go wrong.

Placing it so early in the day was suddenly a personal threat, a mistake that must be corrected. But how? There was no way of retrieving the package without being seen. Soon the interview would be over and he would be forced to leave. He searched for a solution to the problem. Outside, rain had begun to fall, beating a light tattoo on the French windows.

"A bad day," he murmured.

The President glanced at Pompey, but made no response, returning his attention to Levinson. Pompey persisted.

"It ought to please Mrs. Gunther."

"And why is that, Pompey?" the President said, his impatience apparent.

"The rain, Mr. President. For the Rose Garden."

He hoped the President would invite Levinson through the French doors into the covered colonnade that faced the Rose Garden. The President made no move.

"Yes," he said without enthusiasm. "Too bad I can't take you out there right now, Levinson. A lovely garden, Mrs. Gunther's pride and my deep pleasure."

Then it was all over and the President was guiding them into the corridor, past the warrant officer seated there with the black code box, thanking Levinson for his interest. Pompey made a conscious effort to keep from going back after the brown package. He escorted the writer to the West Wing lobby.

When Pompey returned to his office, he had a headache, a persistent throbbing above his right eye. He swallowed two aspirin. They did little good. The throbbing worsened, the pain more acute than ever.

Time. It expired reluctantly, oozing past with excruciating slowness, clinging with fierce dedication. Pompey found it impossible to ignore his wrist watch, convinced that the message of its delicate arms were part of some insidious deception.

Resentment traveled along his nerves, a sense of apartness, of being the sole defense against complete disaster. He wanted to share the burden, to distribute responsibility, to diminish the fear.

There was no one to turn to. No longer was Gail part of his life—gone when most needed; and he no longer dared contact Gordon through the White House switchboard; Peter Street.

Pompey's bitterness grew more acute. He loathed Street for being out of it, for being too weak to assume his rightful burden.

The morning went slowly.

A few minutes before noon, Hank Luplow appeared, draping himself over one corner of Pompey's desk. He propped his chin in his hand and gazed steadily at the Press Secretary.

"Good friend and companion," he began with exaggerated sonority. "Art thou ready to face thy Master who awaits with the Judgment of the Age?"

Pompey cautioned himself to react in kind, lightly, to conceal the raw state of his nerve fibers. He arranged a small smile on his mouth and reached for his papers.

"Let's go," he said.

They entered the oval office through Sarah Harris' cubicle, stepping across the Great Seal of the United States in the green carpeting. The President was studying his copy of the speech, pen in hand, making notes as he went. He motioned for the two to take seats. Pompey quickly established himself in the chair nearest the secretarial well.

His watch read 12:04.

The President made a steeple with his fingers, peered over it. "The speech, Hank," he said. "Still not precisely what I want."

Luplow grimaced. He'd been working on it for nearly three weeks and suspected that he'd become too involved, cared too much, losing all objectivity along the way, all perspective. Too many changes had been requested; too damned many made. Someone else should have been assigned to it, someone more inclined to the President's recent point of view.

"I've done my——"

"Your best," the President interrupted. "I know, Hank. Sadly, your best hasn't been consistent with the high standards of this Administration." The cultured voice was low and, Pompey decided, ominous. "Your concepts of excellence seem not to jibe with my own, which is the reason for this meeting, the reason I was forced to set this period aside while there's still time for you to correct certain errors, time to emphasize that which needs emphasizing." He swung around to Pompey. "Which brings us to you, Pompey. My feelings must be made clear in this matter, crystal-clear, so that no doubt exists as to where this President stands. Tomorrow night, with this speech, I intend to come out directly against the Mutual Defense Pact.

Foursquare, the reasons spelled out in simple, no-nonsense language."

Shock traveled along Pompey's limbs in successive waves, though he had expected no less. There would be no ratification, and no treaty, a massive public slight of the Kremlin leaders with whom the Pact had been negotiated. Such a destructive move was horrifying and he almost said so. Again, he had to remind himself that this man was not Harrison Gunther, was not the President of the United States. He kept quiet.

Luplow was unable to do the same. Words came tumbling out of him. ". . . Is this course prudent? Can you expect such an act to possibly lead to lasting peace——?"

"You write the speeches, Luplow," the President said hoarsely. "I will speak them, when I so wish. Remember this, young man, the words I read tomorrow night will in fact become my words, my ideas, my policies, and you will therefore put them down as I dictate."

Luplow paled, but refused to retreat. "I can't believe that Secretary Keefe goes along with this, or the other members of your Cabinet——"

"Mr. Keefe is an appointed adviser to the President, nothing more. The ultimate authority rests in this office, at this desk, with the man who holds the job. I am that man, sir, a fact you seemed inclined to overlook."

Luplow hung his head, but there was still a ring of defiance in his voice. "If Mr. Jacobs were still——"

"Mr. Jacobs," the President said thinly, "is not around; nor would he be, were he still alive. Not for long, I can assure you."

The President rose, went to the windows, standing between the American flag and the banner bearing the Seal of the Chief Executive. His hands were clasped behind his back as he gazed across the President's Park to the south. Luplow automatically placed himself at the President's shoulder.

"This is a rotten day, Luplow," the President said, after a moment, voice soft now, ingratiating. "Look at that rain. It's with us for the remainder of the day. Don't make things worse by arguing with me. This speech is a simple thing—you know what I want and I expect it from you."

Luplow began to respond, haltingly, searching for the right words that would influence, modify, convince. Pompey's attention was riveted to the exchange. Gradually, after a few moments, from some gray area of his brain, a faint memory sparked into being. It sharpened and took hold. The timing device! The two men at the windows; at any moment they would turn, the opportunity lost forever. He drew air into his lungs and reached into the secretarial well. His fingers found the package, traced along its edges until he located the brass tube. He took it firmly between thumb and first two fingers and squeezed—hard. Nothing happened. The long festering terror erupted in his bowels. He fought against it. His eyes rolled upward and he imagined he saw the President begin to turn around. Sweat made his palms slippery. He manipulated the brass cartridge until it was angled between his fingers for maximum power, then bore down with all his strength. Seconds later there was the feathery crunch of metal tearing. The time was 12:14.

In four hours, the President would be dead.

In the corridor, afterward, out of earshot of the Secret Service agent on duty, Luplow leaned toward Pompey, spoke in a hushed, strained voice. ". . . Gone absolutely berserk, that man has. He's about to set the world aflame with this speech. Doesn't he realize——?"

Pompey cut him off. "Dammit, Hank. He's the President, not you, or me. He can make the speech he wants to make, anything. Be for or against any treaty he wants. The people elected him and he's supposed to know what he's doing."

Luplow raised his hands in mock surrender. "Okay. No harm meant. I know he's your boy, but he puts his pants on the same as I do. He can be wrong. Look, baby, try talking to him, convince him that he's about to blow the whole thing."

"Why should he listen to me?"

"You're his Press Secretary. You're supposed to have your finger on the pulse of the nation, know what's happening. Tell the man the voters want this treaty."

"He wouldn't listen to . . ." An idea was born in Pompey's mind.

It would mean work. He would have to find an opportunity to use the mimeograph machine unobserved to run off copies of Luplow's original version, the one favorable to the treaty. It would be difficult, dangerous in fact, but it could be done. It had to be done.

"You could try."

"Well, I could try."

"Sure. You've got the original speech. Make him read it."

"I'll talk to him," Pompey said quietly. "This afternoon, at the press briefing."

Luplow brightened perceptibly. "A winner, baby, that's you! Tell you what, let's celebrate. I'll blow you to lunch and a couple of martinis at Duke Zeibert's."

Pompey refused the invitation, claiming the press of work. When he got back to his desk, it was 12:55; three hours and nineteen minutes to go.

He reached for the President's schedule. At that moment, the President was at the South Portico, along with Secretary Keefe, welcoming the new Ambassador from Chile, receiving his credentials, escorting that gentleman to the small elevator, up to the second floor dining room. Pompey asked Reilly to order some lunch from the Navy mess in the basement.

He couldn't eat. The food, normally well prepared and tasty, seemed lifeless, unappetizing. He pushed it aside and tried to edit a release; he read the same sentence five times and gave up. His mind kept returning to the brown package fastened to the President's desk.

After a while, he began to feel that his skin was too

tight for his bones, a swelling internal pressure struggling to break out. He left the White House.

It was raining steadily, a thin slant of moisture, insistently penetrating. He turned up the collar of the Burberry, but water trickled down the back of his neck. He walked swiftly, around the President's Park, past the Ellipse. In good weather it would have been alive with people sunning themselves and children playing. He strode past the statue of General Sherman and, face set against the rain, moved along E Street, past the Commerce Building onto Pennsylvania Avenue. People hurried by, anxious to get back to their offices, to escape the rain. When he reached the old Department of Justice building, he headed up 9th Street.

There was a coffee shop across from the Palace Theater. He went inside and ordered scrambled eggs and coffee, picked at the food without enthusiasm. The clock on the wall read 2:30. The President would be arriving at the Smithsonian, to dedicate the new addition to the American History Wing. It was the sort of ceremony Harrison Gunther enjoyed, being something of an historian himself. *Was,* Pompey amended silently. *Used to be.* He paid the check and went back to the White House.

Reilly shook her head in disapproval when he appeared. She trailed him into his office with a fresh, white towel.

"Dry yourself," she commanded.

He obeyed silently, combed his hair.

"Catch cold and you'll be sorry," she said. "Spring colds sometimes last all summer."

"Thank you, Maggie."

She left and he studied the schedule. Next: Interior Secretary Knoop. The discussion about National Parks should be brief and to the point. Though considerable lobbying had gone on to open the national lands to commercial development, the President had shown no inclination to do so. Pompey reminded himself that Knoop was a persuasive talker, could be very amusing. What if their meeting ran long, extended into the free time?

Uncertainty took hold and Pompey berated himself for not allowing for a greater margin of error. He had been too tense, thoughtless, anxious to get it over. That someone other than the impostor might be killed sent a flood of guilt surging through his middle and he tortured his brain seeking a solution to the problem. None came. He rolled some copy paper into his typewriter and tried to write a release about the extension of all Social Security benefits to people reaching their fifty-fifth birthdays. It was one of the President's pet projects.

No good. Nothing of value came. He tore the paper out of the machine, balled it up, and heaved it at the wastebasket. It missed. He lit a cigarette and checked his watch. 3:38. Secretary Knoop was in the oval room now. Or was he? Perhaps the weather had delayed the Smithsonian ceremonies. Perhaps the President had not yet returned. Perhaps the oval office would be unoccupied when the bomb exploded. He rang Sarah Harris.

"How did it go at the Smithsonian, Sarah? Everything smooth?"

"Just fine, Mr. Pompey. Mr. Paine, the Secret Service agent in charge, said the President seemed to be in very fine spirits, despite the weather."

"Good," Pompey said. "Secretary Knoop in with him now, I suppose?"

"Yes, sir. Did you want to see him about something? There is some open time and I could talk to Mr. O'Brien."

"No, Sarah. Thanks. There was something about the New York arrangements," he made himself say casually, wanting to make it clear that he was thinking beyond 4:14, a fact bound to be noticed afterward. "It'll keep until I see him at seven."

"Whatever you say, Mr. Pompey."

His eyes were drawn back to the schedule. "Those 4-H kids," he said. "Let me know when they arrive. I want to arrange some pictures for the wire services, the home town papers."

She laughed in that private way that most women laugh when concerned with children. "Oh, they're so adorable, so clean and healthy-looking. They arrived about thirty minutes ago. The weather, you know. Poor dears, it spoiled their sightseeing. I arranged for them to take a special tour of the White House. I imagine they'll be coming back any minute now. Do you have any idea what I should do to entertain a dozen energetic teenagers until the President can see them?"

He made a facetious remark, but already doubt was gnawing at him. Something was wrong. It was a visceral reaction, without proof of any kind, and he ordered himself to stop worrying, to stop anticipating trouble. It was 3:47, and Knoop was with the President. The bomb was firmly attached to the desk, the acid eating its way toward the blasting cap, and time was running out. Nothing could go wrong now. Nothing.

The haunted feeling remained. He began to pace the office. Finally he made himself sit back down, to stare at the list of that day's appointments, as if the cause of his anxiety was rooted there.

It was no use. He was out of his element, dealing in black areas not usual to ordinary men, areas where governments schemed and plotted against each other, where the life of a single person was held valueless and men died or lived according to political necessity.

But how had he arrived at this point, how had he been sucked into this vortex of deceit and death? This was an alien world to him.

What inexorable power had drawn him into this, step by blind step, from that initial uneasiness that eventually led him to Ralph Jacobs and to this dismal day? That visit to Jacobs' house—suppose he had not gone?—that confrontation, corroboration for them both, so that neither of them could turn away. Poor Jacobs. Pompey shuddered as he considered the finality of death. He raised his left wrist and the numerals on the dial of his watch faded into focus: 4:01.

He listened to his heartbeat, loud and fast, and admonished himself to keep calm. Soon it would be over. He lit a cigarette. Some coffee, strong and black, was what he wanted. He rang for Reilly. No response. He rang again. *Where the hell was she?* No one was ever around when he needed them. He tried not to think.

"They're so cute."

It was Reilly, beaming in the doorway.

"I wanted some coffee."

"The boys and girls from the 4-H. What a fine group! Sarah introduced me—just before they went in to see the President. I'll order coffee."

A silent shriek went leaping across the poles of his brain, a searing cry of despair. *The rain.* The rain had brought them to the White House early. The rain had left them with nothing to do and the President, with forty-five free minutes, had decided to see them early. And the rain meant that the awards would be made in the oval office, not in the Rose Garden.

And afterward the President would still have time to prepare for his five o'clock meeting with the Congressional leaders in the Cabinet Room.

But there would be no Congressional meeting, and the awards would be a memorial for all those young people.

What was it Gordon had said? *When this package goes up it will kill whoever is in that room.* All those children were going to die.

Pompey wanted to protest, to cry; but there was no time. He made a powerful effort to clear his mind. He checked his watch.

4:07.

He came erect, eyes darting, straining for a solution. On the far side of his desk, the pile of papers he had carried into the President's office earlier, the now empty folder still among them. He gathered them up and stood wondering on what pretext he could return to the oval room, and once there, what he could do.

He reached for Hank Luplow's original speech and stepped out into the corridor. His heels were loud on the tile floor. Someone brushed past, offered a greeting that he didn't hear. Pompey turned into Reilly's narrow chamber.

She was standing in the open doorway, looking into the President's office. That made it easier. She saw Pompey and smiled, moved aside so he could have an unobstructed view. Inside, the President was seated in the green leather chair, and clustered around him were the 4H prize-winners, faces glowing as two photographers from the press pool snapped away. Pompey moved forward.

The President frowned. "What is it, Pompey?"

Pompey forced the corners of his mouth upward. His cheeks felt stiff and brittle. "I thought I might be able to help." He looked around, and in that millimicron of time he imagined he could hear the ticking of his watch, each second bringing them all closer to death.

"Oh, I can handle these youngsters," the President said, with forced joviality. "Don't you agree, people?"

"Yes, sir," came the response.

Pompey tortured his brain. "I also wanted to discuss the Foundation speech with you," he said. "Something I overlooked."

"There's nothing more to be said."

Pompey shivered, and his eyes came to rest on Ketza sprawled out beneath the windows. He snapped his fingers and the dog came unhappily to his feet, lumbered forward. "What about a couple of pictures with Ketza, Mr. President? You, and the boys and girls. In front of the fireplace. Everybody likes dog pictures."

A chorus of approval went up from the young people, and they began to shuffle toward the fireplace. The President scowled but made no objection. Pompey backed toward the big desk.

"I'll let you boys set it up," he said to the photographers.

The time, he thought frantically. How close it must

be to 4:14 He inched backward, another step, another, finally coming to rest against the desk, eyes riveted on the people across the spacious room. No one paid him any attention. He reached quickly, feeling under the desk. Nothing. He extended his joints to their limits, and a little beyond. The package! Fingers searched for a grip, found it and pulled. It wouldn't come loose. He pulled harder and at last it came away in his hand. Turning quickly, using his body as a shield, he sandwiched the flat brown charge in the stack of papers.

He knew that not enough time remained for him to make a graceful exit and defuse the bomb in privacy. Gordon's cautionary words came flooding back: *You must interrupt the firing train.*

His hand felt for the bent brass tube. He manipulated it, struggling to work it free of its moorings, to separate it from the blasting cap. Nothing happened. He closed his eyes, and applied as much force as he dared. The brass tube came away in his hand. He dropped it into his pocket and faced about. Later, he told himself. Later he would dispose of it, break it into small pieces, flush it out of existence. Later, when it was safe. He looked at the photographers snapping their pictures.

"That should do it, fellows," he said, with professional heartiness.

"Just one more," the photographers said.

The President nodded in Pompey's direction. "My Press Secretary is right. Afraid I must cut this short. There's a busy afternoon in front of me."

"If you'll all step this way, please," Pompey said, ushering the 4-H delegation into the corridor to the West Wing lobby. He looked at his watch. It was exactly fourteen minutes past four. He walked slowly back to his office, one recurring thought sounding in the hollows of his skull.

The President still had to be killed.

III

The rain stopped falling about nine o'clock and the city, slaked and cool, stirred under a deeply speckled sky. In Meridian Hill Park, the night fragrance of damp grass was heightened by the scent of forsythia and pink magnolia. Here Pompey waited, pacing a short span of concrete path until Gordon materialized out of the darkness, pinched face expressionless. Pompey fell into step beside him.

"What happened?" Gordon said.

"I had to stop it," Pompey blurted out, anxious that Gordon understand and approve his action. "There were people, boys and girls. In the office with him."

"You said he'd be alone for forty-five minutes."

Pompey felt compelled to explain. "He changed the schedule without notice. Invited these 4-H people after I set the charge. I had to do something or they'd all have been killed."

Gordon pulled up and stared up at Pompey. In the darkness, his face, cramped and wrinkled, assumed a new hardness. His black eyes were small and penetrating. They showed no compassion.

"You should've let it blow."

Pompey shivered. "Those children——"

"There was a job to do," he said in a voice almost inaudible. "Did you expect it to be easy?"

They walked again. Pompey's eyes were hot and moist.

"I couldn't kill those innocent kids."

"Shit."

It was said quietly, without emotion, adding to its impact. Pompey had never heard the agent swear before, and the expletive made it clear that in Gordon's view he had committed the unforgiveable sin, had botched an otherwise perfectly planned assignment. That single word contained all the logic that Gordon might have directed at him, the rationale for killing the 4-H prize-winners, their deaths nothing when compared with his failure to do his job.

Pompey resented the criticism, wanted to believe that Ralph Jacobs would have understood. But he knew differently. Jacobs would not have allowed emotion to rule when a tough discipline was required. Jacobs would have cared about those young people, but he would have done what was necessary, allowing them to die, mourning them afterward.

Was extravagant killing required, Pompey silently asked, in order to achieve his end? And asking, he knew the answer; this was command, the ability to do whatever was necessary, the awful and total responsibility to a given purpose, the courage to fulfill his responsibilities. Weakness had prevented him from killing that afternoon, the same weakness that had caused him to kill the child he had fathered. He wanted to explore these thoughts, to parse the elements and consider each, but there was time now only for certainty and action. He stepped across the line.

"It won't happen again," he said.

Gordon grunted, already seeking some way to rectify the situation. "The idea of using the bomb," he said after a while. "It's neat, leaves no meaningful evidence and there's virtually no chance of a finger being pointed at anybody."

An apology rose up into Pompey's throat. He suppressed it. "There isn't time for that now."

"In the morning, before he leaves for New York?"

Pompey considered. "No. He'll be seeing only a few people, for one thing. For another, with a trip planned, the Secret Service will be all over the White House."

"Okay," Gordon said. "We'll have to figure a way.

Tell me everything that's planned for tomorrow, right through the dinner. Schedules, places, everything."

Pompey recited the information without emotion. At 6:45, the President would rise, breakfast in his quarters with Charley Hepburn, who would accompany him to New York. At 7:30, he would be in his office, to complete the remainder of the week's work with Sarah Harris. Two hours later, he would depart by helicopter from the South Lawn for Andrews Air Force Base and the short flight to Kennedy Airport aboard Air Force One.

At Kennedy, the President and certain members of his party would be transported by Army helicopter into Manhattan, landing on top of the Pan Am Building. High-speed elevators would take them to the street where limousines and a police escort would be waiting.

"Anything else?" Gordon said.

"Like what?"

"Like weak spots. Flaws in security. I'd prefer to pull this off and get away without a scapegoat."

Pompey's mind reached back to the Kennedy assassination. That's what Oswald had hoped to do, kill, then flee safely and without a trace. He didn't make it. Fear, the anxiety to escape punishment, panic; these made mistakes inevitable.

"What else?" Gordon said.

From the Pan Am Building, the President would go directly to the United Nations where he was to confer with Felix Wagnall, the United States representative to that body; the rest of the day was to be spent at Warren House, studying his speech.

"I guess that's it," Pompey said. "One more thing. He mentioned that he might walk from the hotel to the Foundation. It's only a couple of blocks. That might give us a chance——"

"Not likely. Too many unknown factors. He could change his mind and come by car, for example. If he walks, will he come down Madison or cut over to Fifth Avenue? And walking, he'll be surrounded by security people, though that might not be a deterrent.

It would have to be done with a rifle from long range, and where would the sniper position himself? What is rooftop security? No, that won't work."

Neither man spoke for a long interval, both reviewing the next day's activities, seeking the soft spot, that single moment when the President would be most vulnerable, could most easily be destroyed. It was Gordon, conditioned by experience to measure risk against opportunity, who found an opening.

"I think I know how. But I'm going to want some help. You'll be with him, I suppose?"

"I'll be at the Foundation most of the time."

Gordon tugged at his nose, scratched his ear, and shoved his hands deep into his pockets. "I guess Street is my man."

Pompey stopped and Gordon turned to face him. "He's a drunk. Can we depend on him?"

Gordon shrugged. "There's no choice. I'll need someone."

"His plan is to go up to New York in the morning."

"Contact him. Tell him to meet me. At exactly ten o'clock in the morning. On the northwest corner of Third Avenue and 36th Street. I want him on time and sober."

Street would be at the party. He would talk to him then. "Is there anything I can do?"

"If I want you tomorrow, you'll be at the Foundation?"

"Or the Warren House."

"If this comes off okay, you'll know about it. In that case, you and I are not to talk again. Never."

"I understand." He paused, then: "And if it doesn't come off?"

Gordon stared up at him. "You tell me, Mr. Pompey."

He never hesitated. "We'll have to find another way." "It'll be tight, real tight." His manner changed, became brisk, businesslike. "Let's hope this works. There's one more thing. When it's over, Street will be a threat to us both, a weak spot. Drunks talk too much. He should be killed."

Gordon nodded slowly.

"No!" Pompey burst out. He clutched Gordon's arm; the small man was all hard muscle and bone.

The agent disengaged himself. "Dead, Street can be helpful. Alive, he's a danger and always will be." A brief humorless smile fanned across the thin mouth. "But suit yourself, Mr. Pompey. I'm just an instrument of policy. This is your show."

Pompey discovered that he had been holding his breath. He allowed himself to exhale. "Let's see what happens."

"Whatever you say. Anything else?"

Pompey offered his hand, and Gordon took it. "Good luck."

Pompey watched the DIA man disappear into the darkness. A random thought drifted to mind. He knew that since 1965 a formal agreement had existed between the Defense Department and the Secret Service to remain in close contact and so insure the exchange of pertinent information concerning threats against the person of the President. The agreement had been made after the Warren Commission had submitted its report. And now, a Pentagon intelligence officer was abroad, determined to kill the President.

Pompey went back to the Mercedes, relieved that it was now out of his hands. He drove until he came to a phone booth, called Peter Street. There was no answer. Pompey swore. He didn't trust Street to follow orders. He climbed back in the Mercedes.

Back in his apartment, Pompey showered and shaved, found the costume he had worn to Bette Swarthout's party last summer. It was a British Guardsman's uniform, complete to the black beaver hat. Finally dressed, he put on his Burberry, then drove out to Chevy Chase.

Henrietta Birdsong lived in a mansion that dated back to the late 1700s. Renovated and expanded over the years, it boasted twenty-seven rooms, rolling lawns and gardens, an indoor swimming pool, and a huge greenhouse. Henrietta, widow of Nathaniel Birdsong, who had made his fortune in shipping and lumber, enjoyed entertaining on a lavish scale. Such parties had to be plotted and planned, the logistics complicated, giving her something to do.

Pompey turned the Mercedes over to a uniformed attendant and went inside. A pretty black girl took the Burberry and said she'd remember him, directed him to the central foyer. Here, dramatically placed in front of the wide marble staircase, Henrietta Birdsong, dressed as Little Bo Peep, complete with shepherd's crook, greeted her guests.

"Darling," she gushed, kissing Pompey's cheek. "A uniform becomes you. Never take it off, except in bed, darling." In her fifties, and looking a decade younger, Henrietta Birdsong lived accordingly. Since the death of her husband, she was seen only with men much younger than herself. She patronized all the discotheques and nightclubs and never missed a party. Since she contributed lavishly to the election funds of both major parties, she was invited everywhere. She leaned toward Pompey. "Is your boss coming to my party, darling? I do hope so."

"I wish I knew, Henrietta. You know his fondness for surprises."

She sighed. "Well, go on inside, darling. The liquor is limitless, and the place is loaded with pretty girls just waiting for you to seduce them."

Pompey found the bar and got a double scotch and looked around. He imagined close to one thousand people were present, drifting from room to room, out onto the wide veranda that circled the mansion, and into the gardens. The costuming was brilliant. A profusion of military uniforms and sultans and dancing girls and cyclists in black leather, and elderly ladies dressed as young girls, and young girls dressed as boys. There were streetwalkers and baseball players, Indian princesses and cavemen, African chiefs and Eskimos, spacemen and spacewomen. There were the usual number of George Washingtons, and Pompey counted three Lincolns and two Teddy Roosevelts.

He wondered what Peter Street was wearing, if in fact he had come. There was a good chance that Peter, ignoring orders, had gone to New York tonight. That would complicate matters. Pompey picked his way through the crowd searching for the tall man. He considered asking for him, but decided against it. He was anxious to display no unusual interest in Street, to do nothing that might later connect them in anyone's mind.

"Pompey!"

He turned and saw Senator Lucas Abernathy coming toward him, a generous smile on that pink, fat face, the great white mane flowing in studied disorder. The Senator wore the white suit and broad-brimmed Panama of a plantation owner, his usual garb at such affairs. Trailing close behind him was a pretty girl in diaphanous pantaloons and a bejeweled red vest that barely covered her breasts.

"Pompey," the Senator enthused. "It is sure good to see you, son. Distressing," he went on, the voice properly funereal, "about Ralph Jacobs. One fine fellow and a superb public servant, no matter how much we differed as to methods. I shall miss him."

Pompey said something suitable and the Senator smiled, beckoned the girl closer. "Pompey, I should like to introduce you to Miss Jeanette Millard, from my home state, appropriately bearing the title of Miss Missouri. Miss Missouri is pretending to be some kind of a potentate's plaything this evening, I reckon. This is Mr. Guy Pompey, my dear, Press Secretary to our revered President. A man of great accomplishments, he happens to be unmarried."

"How nice for me!" the girl cried. "It restores my faith in the divine order of things, to meet a handsome man who is also unattached, Mr. Pompey."

Pompey watched the Senator disappear into the crowd. Pompey wondered where he could deposit Miss Missouri.

"I'm not a potentate's darling," she was saying brightly. "I'm a dancing girl. I suppose I should be wearing a veil, but I didn't want to hide my light under a bushel basket, you might say."

Pompey glanced at the deep cleavage, the breasts swelling out from under the crimson vest. "There's little chance of that."

"You don't think I'm too forward?" she said. "I mean, I was brought up to avoid coarseness and vulgarity in all things. My mama is a very proper lady. But after all, Mr. Pompey this is the latter portion of the Twentieth Century, and this is a costume party. I mean, we are all playing different roles, aren't we? I mean, if a party isn't for having fun, what is it for?"

"It's for having fun."

"I knew you'd see my point." She placed a hand on his chest for emphasis, and the gesture caused the front of the vest to spread. Her breasts rode incredibly high on her chest. He lifted his vest. She continued to chatter happily. "I knew, at first glance, I knew you were simpatico, if you know what I mean, amigo. You and I are going to be friends, I just know it. I'm remaining in our capital city for four more days, and that can be a veritable lifetime to a young girl alone and in dire need of the companionship of a handsome male such as yourself, Mr. Press Secretary."

"Call me Guy."

"How sweet! You're an Italian, I take it. Pompey is an Italian name. I've always had a weakness for things and men Italian. All that Latin passion, you know. I have always hungered to visit Rome, to see where they chewed up all those Christians. The lions, I mean, not the Romans. Is it true about Italian men? All that pinching and being outstanding lovers?"

"Outstanding."

She measured him deliberately. "I bet you are."

"I think it's time for another drink."

"I say yes to that. Yes to everything, I would say. But only an itty bitty drink, Guy, 'cause whiskey tends to make me feel—you know, passionate. I wouldn't want to be taken advantage of. That is, not unless I was aware of what was happening to me. I don't want to miss a thing." She looped her arm through his, her breast flat against him, and together they went to the bar.

The advertising executive was dressed as Paul Revere. Charley Hepburn, in a conservative gray business suit, sipped a whiskey sour and listened attentively, shutting out all the sound and movement of the party around him.

"In every campaign," the advertising executive said gravely, "television has had an increasing impact on the American voter. I can deliver that voter to the Party, Charley. Selling a candidate is no different than selling a new car. The right packaging, the right appeal, push the right buttons. I can do it."

"How?"

"I hire the best people—writers, directors. I say, *Boys, this is what I want.* Then I pull back, stay the hell out of the way. And they produce. If they don't, they're out, but quick. Quality is what I'm after, and what I get. Quality is what I deliver, Charley."

"What about costs?"

"Charley, everything costs."

Charley Hepburn wanted another whiskey sour.

General Quirk wore the armor of a Roman centurion. He cradled a plumed helmet in his brawny right arm and smiled at the ladies who surrounded him. They had come as a team—all costumed as Betsy Ross, all sewing stars on a single huge American flag.

"Ladies," Quirk said kindly. "I've always held that nuclear bombs are just another weapon in the fighting man's arsenal. To be used as strategy dictates. If the Commies make trouble for us, I'd go in and clean 'em up, use whatever's necessary, finish what Karl Marx started. Face it, ladies, we Americans have always believed in victory."

The ladies voiced their approval and kept stitching stars.

A small woman with bright eyes and quick movements, dressed as Peter Pan, and drinking vodka on the rocks—she was the National Committeewoman of the opposition party in Delaware—managed to isolate the two young Congressmen on the veranda beyond the huge, blue-and-white striped tent that had been erected as a precaution in case of rain. Her abrasive voice sliced through the din of the party.

"Something must be done, gentlemen," she shrilled, "to counter the President's attitude toward the stock market. The people of this nation demand a free marketplace. They are sick and tired of controls and more controls. Restrictions and prohibitions! Why should some bureaucrat, who could never make a decent living in the outside world, tell us how to invest our money? He shouldn't."

"Mrs. Merrill——"

"I say it is vital that we lower stock commission rates. And more. There must be a complete revision of the rules on mutual funds. Believe me, I know. Mr. Merrill has operated in the Street for years and is in constant touch with people who matter, who really count."

Peter Street, looking elegant and vaguely debauched in his J. Press dinner jacket among the colorful costumes, downed his second drink, helped himself to another. Reasonably braced against the hazards of the evening, he went looking for a sympathetic face.

The lobbyist for the oil company wore the flowing robes and burnoose of a Bedouin shiek. He spoke earnestly to the Congressman from Louisiana.

"There's a great deal of unhappiness, Fred, about this proposed foreign trade zone up in New England. My people have a great deal of money invested and they would be very unhappy if profits were suddenly siphoned off to another section of the country."

The Congressman, in faded jeans, a long wig and dark glasses, was imitating a hippie. "What would you like me to do, Chandler?

"Stop the project dead in its tracks."
dead in its tracks."

"But how?"

"That's what we pay you for."

The Congressman's eyes skittered around, afraid someone had overheard. Suppose I accuse the New England people of trying to bribe me? That ought to do it."

"Can you make it stick?"

The Congressman laughed cheerfully. "Oh, that doesn't matter, once I make the charge. That'll finish them off with the boys on the committee."

"Good. Do it."

An amplified rock group blared out its charged sound in the dining room. The floor had been cleared and was alive with movement as Ambassadors and Secretaries, businessmen and ladies of no visible means, Cabinet members and their wives, jerked and twisted, hopped and swayed, eyes fixed in space, faces grim and concentrated.

News photographers snapped pictures, their flashbulbs blinding. A clutch of them formed a wall around a tall brunette of dramatic proportions. She was wearing a jump suit made of transparent plastic. And nothing else. Under the glistening costume, her breasts shimmered and shook as she leaped and stomped to the driving beat. Her partner, an economist from Interior, kept his eyes averted, fearful of what his wife was going to say.

"That," Hank Luplow said to Guy Pompey, "is the true source of power. Or do I mean corruption?"

Pompey grunted and turned away. Luplow, dressed as an Elizabethan poet, went after him. "What happened to that beauty I saw you with? She was constructed for comfort and action."

"I delivered her to Dan Crowell."

Luplow cackled happily. "Now there's a combination I'd like to see making it. Crowell the Puritan and that pair of hot pants. Crowell will probably investigate you for subversion in the morning."

Pompey stopped a passing waiter and exchanged his empty glass for a full one.

"Later," Luplow was saying, "there's going to be a party. A really swinging affair. Anything goes, Guy. The best looking females in this town. It should be—"

"No, thanks," Pompey said, absently, searching among the guests for Peter Street.

"Congressman," the lawyer from International-American Fruit & Vegetable said soberly. "Something has to be done about conditions in the orchards."

"I'm certain you're right, son."

"We have *outsiders* stirring up our working people. Our fruit pickers are good folks as a rule. Same as their fathers and their fathers before them. And we want them to stay that way."

The Congressman, ranking member of the House Un-American Activities Committee, swallowed the last of his drink and headed for the bar. The lawyer followed, waited until the Congressman held a glass in his fist before going on.

"Some of those long-haired union organizers are coming into our orchards."

"Hippies!" the Congressman sputtered.

"An investigation might be in order."

"Time is running out," the ranking member agreed hotly. "How many more chances are we going to have to stop the liberal politicians that are leading this great nation down the garden path directly to socialism and communism?"

"I've asked myself the same question."

The ranking member finished his drink and signaled to a red-jacketed waiter. The waiter went in another direction. "Talk to my executive assistant. Give him the names of those anarchist bastards. I'll fix 'em good. Now let's get us another drinkypoo."

She was the wife of a minor official at the French Embassy. Very beautiful, very chic, very French. She had come as Joan of Arc, hair cut short for the occa-

She stood in the center of the small upstairs bedroom and waited. After a few minutes, the man came into the room.

"Lock the door, please," she said, her accent charming.

He did, turned to face her. He was an importer from Berlin and looked the role. Short, stout, red-cheeked. He watched with a rising passion as she undressed. Naked, she was all he had supposed. Slender, with the kind of round breasts that so excited him. She lay back on the bed.

"You are ready?" she asked pleasantly.

He dropped his trousers and went over to her.

"The money," she reminded him, regret tingeing her voice.

He made a thick sound and dug into his pocket, counted off fifty dollars, placed it in a neat stack on the night table.

"There, my sweet," she said, smiling. "Now we make an alliance, for the moment, at least."

The man with the cold blue eyes and the bullet-head led the big-shouldered youth across the veranda to the spot where a tall man in an impeccably tailored Western suit and cowboy boots waited.

"Son," Blue Eyes drawled. "This here is Senator Joe Don Longstreet, senior Senator from our great state of Texas. Senator, makes me proud to introduce you to Leslie Lee Wister, finest passing quarterback the high schools of our great state have ever produced."

The Senator, lean and weathered, looked the youth in the eye and took his right hand in both of his own.

"Leslie Lee," he drawled sincerely. "It's fine to meet you, son. I have heard only the best things. The *very* best." He measured the boy, gripping his hand tightly. "There's the look of a natural leader to you, boy."

Leslie Lee nodded agreeably. "Sure hope so, Senator."

"Word I heard is you're the best thing Texas has turned out since Sammy Baugh."

"Sure hope so, Senator," Leslie Lee said.

"Better believe it," Blue Eyes put in. "Every college in the country is after Leslie Lee. Every bird dog has been camping on his tail. That's why I brought him up to Washington, D.C., Senator, to talk to you. Back home, you're still The Man, Senator, the hardest-nosed running back that ever performed at Central High."

"They still got your picture on the wall outside the varsity lockers, Senator," Leslie Lee said.

"That's mighty nice of the folks, to remember, I mean." The Senator looped an arm around Leslie Lee's shoulder. "Boy, I know what you're going through. Those people from Notre Dame and U.S.C. and 'Bama—they come sniffing after me in my time, apromising and awooing, offering me all kinds of things. Don't you listen to those people, Leslie Lee. You're a Texas boy and Texas boys should stay back home and play Texas football."

"That's the gospel," Blue Eyes said. "Come to U. of T., I told Leslie Lee, and he won't suffer none when it comes to benefits."

The Senator laughed. "Son, I happen to know you can have your pick of sports cars and we have a hell of a lot of doorknobs at Texas need wiping for good money. And, boy, have you ever seen the likes of those Texas fillies? The prettiest, most agreeable gals——"

"Amen to that," Blue Eyes intoned.

"I been thinking ahead," Leslie Lee said slowly. "After school, after pro ball. I been thinking it would be nice to have a spread of my own, breed some cattle . . ."

The Senator turned up his hands. "Now, Leslie Lee, that ain't going to be difficult to fix. George," he said to Blue Eyes. "You have Edgar Lee in my office first thing tomorrow. Old W. D. Spence himself will be there and we'll arrange matters. W. D. is an old home boy himself and he owns some of the best breeding stock around. I reckon we can set things up right now. Do we have a date?"

"Reckon so, Senator."

"Well, good." The Senator slapped Leslie Lee on the back. "Now, George, I got me a little secretary gal who's very partial to good-looking young football players. Let's dig her out of this crowd and turn her loose on Leslie Lee. A healthy boy needs to dip it regular."

Edgar Bookman laughed and tapped General Quirk on his armored chest. "You're going to miss Jacobs, aren't you, Arthur?"

The general scowled that famous scowl of his. "You know what I think? I think he was peculiar. After all, a secret drinker. They're all a little peculiar. If I had my way, none of them would be in government. Jews, Niggers, Catholics, queers. I don't trust one of them."

Omar Hassid was head of the history department at his country's leading university right now he was on sabbatical and making a round-the-world trip. In his early forties, his dark handsomeness and brooding eyes had already caused considerable unrest among the ladies in Washington. But at the moment, he had other concerns.

Henrietta Birdsong had permitted him to use her library for this meeting with Mike Andrews. The book-lined room was softly lit and quiet, and smelled of old leather. Omar sipped brandy and smoked a Turkish cigarette.

"My government feels itself threatened, Mr. Andrews," he said at last.

Andrews was a fleshy man with a faintly quizzical expression, a man who had learned to believe little of what he saw and almost nothing of what he was told. He held a glass of Irish whiskey in his hand, but did not drink.

"Someone is about to invade your country, Professor Hassid?"

Hassid allowed himself a tight smile. "Countries, like people, are constantly beset by dangers. My government is concerned with its security, the security of the people. To that end, I am authorized to purchase certain armaments. Armored cars, machine guns, automatic rifles, anti-personnel grenades, some helicopters, perhaps."

Andrews raised his brows. "Those don't sound like the kind of things needed in case of an invasion."

Hassid shrugged. "Allow the generals of my country to make their own strategy, sir. In any case, it is rumored that you have access to such goods."

Andrews stared into his glass. "Such equipment comes high. It's not readily available. Deals must be made with people in government, clearances arranged, military approval obtained, shipments scheduled and——"

"Any trouble you go to could be made profitable."

Andrews looked up. "I never doubted that for a moment."

A thread of spittle dribbled from the corner of the mouth of the ranking member of the House Un-American Activities Committee. He swayed toward Jeanette Millard, peering closely at the rise of her large breasts under the jeweled red vest.

They were deep in the gardens behind the Birdsong mansion in a corner of the maze, Jeanette backed against the hedges.

"Man," the ranking member sputtered. "You are the juiciest piece I seen in a long while. I was just waiting for a chance at you . . ."

"I should go back inside," she said. "Somebody's waiting for me." He came closer and she smelled his rancid breath. She averted her face. Some men.

"Say, those bazzooms of yours. Are they really real?" She tried to move around him, but he cut her off. "Let's have a look!" He plucked at the vest. She tried vainly to push his hands away. "Oh, sweet Jesus, ain't that a sight! You got the greatest titties I ever did see. Give us a taste of that mother's milk." He lunged at her, mouth gaping, his sharp, little teeth closing hard. She shrieked and struck at him. He staggered and fell to his knees. "Come on," he muttered.

He reached for her leg. She kicked out hard and he went over backwards. She ran away.

He tried to call out, but made only thick, unintelligible sounds. He fell back, moaning softly, aware of the mounting pressure in his bladder. He ordered himself to rise, to relieve himself, but was unable to move. He dozed and, after a while, became aware of the warm dampness spreading across the groin.

Paul Taylor owned three automobile agencies, a trucking concern and a string of service stations in the Midwest. He was a generous contributor to the party. He was the kind of man Charley Hepburn paid attention to.

They were standing on the veranda, under the striped tent, eating sliced turkey and bits of Polish ham off paper plates drinking German beer.

"This boy of mine, Charley," Taylor said. "He needs a job. He made it through law school and—"

"Failed the bar exam, Paul. In three states."

"Lots of kids have that trouble."

"In three states, Paul?"

"The boy has to have a job, Charley. One of those Congressional committees that's always investigating things. Charley, my boy would make a fine investigator. Another Roy Cohn. Another David Schine."

Charley Hepburn said nothing.

"I'm prepared to deposit a substantial amount of cash into the party coffers. Say, ten thousand dollars."

Hepburn shook his head slowly from side to side.

"How much then?"

"You tell me."

Taylor made a face, started to speak, thought better of it. "All right. Fifty thousand."

Hepburn sighed. "I'll arrange it."

"You won't be sorry, Charley. Come on, I want you to meet my son."

"Hell, no! I don't want to meet him. What I want is a stiff drink."

Pompey discovered Peter Street watching the rock

dancers. His fine Ivy League face had sagged perceptibly and his eyes were puffy, moist.

"We have to talk," Pompey began. "Meet me in the garden, beyond the maze."

"Later," Street replied uncertainly. "I want to—"

"To hell with what you want! Meet me. In five minutes."

Street was already behind the maze when Pompey got there. He held a glass.

"Christ," the Press Secretary ripped out. "Can't you stay off the stuff for one night?"

"You mustn't talk to me that way. I am—"

"Shut up and listen. Thre's something you have to do."

Street paled. "What do you mean? Everything was arranged. What happened? What went wrong?"

"Never mind that now. It still has to be done. Tomorrow. In New York. And you've got to help."

"Oh, no. I can't do that." A shrillness came into that cultured voice, a rising hysteria which, if it took hold, Pompey feared, would reduce Street to total uselessness.

"Shut up!" The words were sharp, piercing, leaving no room for argument. "You listen."

He could hear Street's breathing and after a while he heard an assenting sound.

"All right," Pompey said. "Our friend—you know who I mean—will be there in the morning. He's got a plan and he needs your help."

"Oh, no. You mustn't ask me. I can't do that sort of thing. I'm not constituted that way, for violence."

Rage stirred in Pompey's gut, rage that this had happened, that so much depended upon a man like Peter Street, that so much depended on a man like Guy Pompey. He wanted to close it all out of his mind, to find a quiet place in the sun and not think. And wanting, he knew that for him such a place no longer existed, might never exist. There was too much to do. He softened his voice, tried to reach Street.

"You can do *this.*"

"Please don't ask me. It's all a mistake."

"We need help. *Your* help. Hold our friend's coat, so to speak. That's all you're being asked to do. Is that too much for you?"

"I won't have to *do* it, to actually do it?"

"Just help him. He'll explain exactly what's necessary."

"What does he want?"

Pompey smiled. Not knowing what Gordon intended was better than knowing.

"He'll tell you at the proper time. You're to meet him on the northwest corner of Third Avenue and 36th Street at ten o'clock in the morning. Is that clear?"

Street repeated the instructions in a voice thick and distant.

"I don't want you drinking any more tonight. You must be sober tomorrow."

Street's voice rose resentfully. "You don't control my life, sir. You assisted me once, and I appreciate that, but you have no right to insult me."

Pompey felt vaguely reassured, the unexpectedly strong reaction suggesting that enough pride remained in Street to make him dependable.

"I apologize," Pompey said. "We're all a little edgy."

"I'm not equipped for this kind of thing."

"None of us is. But it has to be done. You know that. Two men are already dead—Ralph Jacobs and the real Harrison Gunther—two important men, and you know what will happen if we don't act at once."

"If only I were as certain as you are."

That brought Pompey up short. He hadn't felt *that* certain, hadn't realized he sounded so sure of himself, so confident. Yes, he thought, in surprise and pleasure. *He* was doing it. *He* was the driving force behind it now. *He* had taken charge, filling the vacuum left by Ralph Jacobs. *He* was going to get the job done.

"There's an inevitability about all this," he heard himself say in a crisply metallic voice. "And we can't escape it. This is our responsibility, yours and mine. Our friend will expect you in the morning. I know you won't disappoint him."

Street said, "I'll be there."

"At ten o'clock," Pompey said. "And don't worry. Everything will be all right."

Street left first and Pompey allowed him ten minutes. Then he started back toward the house by a different route. In the dark, he stumbled over something. He looked down and saw the ranking member lying on the ground asleep and snoring. Pompey stepped over him and continued on his way. Inside, he sought out Henrietta Birdsong and thanked her for inviting him, said it was a lovely party.

"You tell Harrison that I'm annoyed with him," she said petulantly. "He should have come."

"Big day tomorrow," Pompey said. "The trip to New York, the *Peace Now* speech. A big strain."

"I know."

"By the way, there's a drunken body out in the garden. An old friend."

"Oh, *him*," she sighed. "I'll send somebody along to clean up the mess."

Pompey went out to the parking area, found the Mercedes, and got in. Jeanette Millard was curled up in the front seat.

"I've been waiting for you, sweetie," she simpered. The prettiest man I found all night. Take me home with you and make me happy." She took off the jeweled red vest. "People've been grabbing and clutching at them all night, sweetie, but they belong to you."

He was tempted. But he thought about the kind of day tomorrow was going to be. He reached across her and opened the door. "Out," he commanded. "I'm tired and I'm going home to sleep."

She pouted and climbed out, breasts gleaming in the moonlight. "Oh, shoot! I was looking forward to it." She watched him drive off, then started back up toward the house. Surely she'd be able to find someone else, even if he wouldn't be as pretty. It wasn't unt she noticed one of the parking attendants staring at her, that she remembered to put the red vest on again.

Later, in bed, Pompey's mind ranged restlessly backward and forward in time, assessing what had passed, what still was to come. Reluctantly, he came to understand that Gordon was right. Peter Street was a dangerous luxury. He had to be killed. Having decided, Pompey rolled onto his side, closed his eyes and went to sleep.

IV

After leaving Pompey, Gordon drove carefully back to his home in Bethesda. It was a modest frame house painted white with an enclosed porch in the front, not much different from the other houses on the street. He'd put in a lot of work on the house, making improvements himself, though some of his friends warned him he was throwing away money. Perhaps they were right, but he enjoyed the work and neither he nor Maryse intended to sell.

Gordon left the car in the driveway and went inside. He tried to be quiet but Maryse heard him. He wondered if she ever went to sleep before he came home. She called his name.

"I'll be right up," he replied.

"Want something to eat?"

"Nothing. Go to sleep."

He switched on the basement light and made his way down the narrow, low-ceilinged staircase. Half of the basement area was finished, a game room; the remaining portion was Gordon's private preserve. Here, there was a workbench, outlets for power tools, a welding setup. About six feet of the workroom had been walled off, its precincts forbidden to other members of the family. A heavy combination lock enforced the rule.

He opened the door, and inside an overhead light came on automatically. Here the walls and the door, reinforced with sheet steel, formed a virtually impregnable vault. A tall steel cabinet stood in one corner. He unlocked it and withdrew a battered brown suitcase. From the shelf, he took a snub-nosed .38-caliber Smith & Wesson revolver set on a thirty-two frame. A reliable weapon, it was extremely accurate at close work. He had appropriated it from the corpse of a Nazi agent in San Diego toward the end of World War II, taken by the German, undoubtedly, from someone he had killed.

He flipped open the cylinder and, using cotton patches, swabbed out the chambers and the bore. Satisfied, he loaded a short round into each chamber and snapped the cylinder back into place. He slipped the .38 into a small belt holster, locked the cabinet and, carrying the old suitcase, left, locking the door behind him.

He climbed quietly to the second floor, stepping over those steps that creaked, padding past the children's room. In the bedroom, he put the suitcase behind the door and removed his jacket, placed the revolver on the bureau. Maryse spoke his name in that contralto sleep-voice of hers.

"Let me look at the kids," he said. "I'll be right back."

The boys were asleep, Terry curled onto his side, his bony bottom shoved high in the air under the blankets; John spread comfortably on his back, one arm hanging off the side of the bed. Gordon gazed at them for a long moment, then withdrew.

Maryse turned on the night lamp and sat up. She watched him undress.

"Are you going away?" she said.

"It's nothing. Routine. Just a few hours to talk to a man, get some information."

"It's Saturday."

"I know. These desk jobs. All that paperwork. One mistake, and none of those computers will work. Have to check something out. It shouldn't take long."

Her expression never altered. They didn't discuss his work, not in eleven years of marriage, except that one time. He had told her that he was a soldier, that he was on constant call for assignment, though he never wore a uniform. He told her that there would be occasions when he'd have to go away, without explanation, often without advance notice, that she was never to question him or to talk about his work with anyone. He also told her that, if anything ever happened to him, she would be taken care of.

She had cried at that and said she didn't want to be taken care of, except by him, and he soothed her and afterward they made very good love. But then it was always very good between them. She had never mentioned his work again; but whenever he left her, she existed in a kind of suspended condition until he returned. She realized that the work he did was dangerous, and that frightened her.

She loved Gordon with a desperate intensity. She was terrified of doing or saying anything that might cause him to consider her or the children when he should have been attending to his job, fearful of what such a lapse in concentration could mean.

"Just a few hours," she said.

He slid into bed beside her. "That's all. To Cleveland. First thing in the morning." He set the alarm clock, an unnecessary precaution. He would wake up before it went off. "I should be back in the afternoon, maybe in time to do something with the boys."

"That would be nice," she said, and turned out the light. They lay quietly for a while, and then she moved against him, hands roaming over his finely muscled body until he began to respond. When it was over, he went to sleep right away and that pleased her. It was important that he be rested and alert. As usual, she lay awake for a long time, wondering—as she so often did—if this was the last time for them.

A surging restlessness kept Peter Street awake. His mind refused to be still and his right leg kept jerking reflexively. There was a half-bottle of good Scotch on the bureau and that would help him to relax. He got out of bed and reached for the bottle, when he recalled the conversation with Pompey.

He pushed the bottle aside. He dressed hurriedly and went out. A long walk might help ease the tensions.

There were still people in the streets, couples strolling arm-in-arm, here and there a man alone, or a woman. There was that about New York. No matter the hour, life was always on the move, even when it was of a kind he found distasteful.

He walked north on Lexington Avenue to 42nd Street, turning west. At Fifth Street, he paused to gaze at the big library, its pillared façade illuminated by concealed floodlights. All those books and knowledge, the issue of the best minds of the ages. He was stirred by nostalgia, regret. It had been a mistake to give up teaching. Within the limits of that prescribed existence, he had been sheltered, among people who understood him, people who never made demands he was unprepared to fulfill. His entry into politics had been unwise, for in that arena his shortcomings could not be concealed and his dark cravings made him too vulnerable.

Tomorrow frightened him. All the tomorrows, the oncoming hours fraught with danger. That visit to Kansas City. How close to disaster he had come, the little he still possessed almost taken away by his terrible need. Without Pompey, he would have been lost. The thought of public exposure, of the shame and humiliation, unloosed waves of terror in him.

How far he had fallen. Once there had been so many friends anxious to assist a man of his distinction, his promise, a man with an unlimited future. So much had been there, the talent, the quick, active mind, the charm, the appearance. At college, he'd been a superior student to Harry Gunther, and more popular, twice president of his class, participating in a variety of activities. In those days, people reckoned Street would travel much further than Harry Gunther. Where had he gone wrong? At what point had he been diverted, turned in the wrong direction, set on that long downhill slide?

Not even the ascendancy of his best friend to the Presidency had advanced his lowering estate. And tomorrow he was going to help to kill Harry Gunther. No, he reminded himself. Not Gunther. Gunther was already dead, his body hidden, or destroyed. And a stranger sat in the White House, a mounting danger that had to be removed.

An icy bead of sweat trickled down his side. How odd, he thought with some bitterness, that he who had always owned such an intense and quiet patriotism, that he who had been so often castigated for the direction of his thinking, for his refusal to conform, that he who had wanted only to help fulfill the high promise of the Constitution, how odd that he was about to help to murder the President of the Republic.

He walked across Broadway toward Eighth Avenue. The air was corrupt here, the noisome odor of pizza and stale beer, the lights glaring, the amplified sound intruding, the people equally obtrusive. His senses were battered and he set himself against the sights and the smells and the sounds.

His thirst grew stronger. He hesitated, looked blankly around, not seeing the small, quick man who had been watching him, who was now moved forward.

"Hey, friend, a slow night."

Street turned awkwardly, uncomprehending. "What?"

The man eyed him curiously. "Interested in some action, friend? I mean, real sweet *action.*"

Street stared at the man, trying to clear his brain, to understand.

"Check the teenybopper over my shoulder," the small man said, narrow face insinuating great and tasty rewards. Street looked. In a shadowed doorway, a young girl. She wore a tight white dress emblazoned with a black-and-red parallelogram, the skirt ending halfway up her fine strong thighs, her feet thrust into calf-high white boots. She stared at Street through large dark glasses, face smooth and unlined, expressionless, framed by long, straight blonde hair, breasts peaked high, heavy. Her mouth was a moist pout.

"A pretty girl," Street murmured.

"Fantastic, I tell you," the small man muttered, leaning forward confidentially. "First-rate merchandise. Those boobs—real, and she's wearing nothing under that dress."

Street straightened up and turned away, telling himself to be offended by this blatant approach. "I'm not interested."

The small man sidled alongside. "Listen, friend, where you gonna find better? Check her again. This is young stuff. Sixteen, only. And just come into town today, I tell you. From Altoona. I'm trying to help the kid out. She don't know her way around. She only wants to make enough bread to stretch until she can locate a square job. Understand?"

The man continued to talk, the words running into each other. Street no longer listened. His eyes returned to the girl. From where he stood, he could make out the flare of her young bottom, the roundness of her belly. He craved the taste of that firm flesh, to sink into it, to be surrounded by it.

"Stay all night," the small man murmured. "Use my place, if you want. Nobody will bother you. I mean, I got a late date myself, friend. And the price is right. Only fifty bucks and you can hang around until tomorrow."

Street listened.

Gordon's eyes snapped open and he was instantly awake. He turned the alarm off before it could ring. Very carefully, he eased himself into a sitting position, trying not to disturb Maryse. A futile effort.

"I'll make some coffee," she said.

"Go back to sleep. I'll do it."

She got out of bed and into her robe. It was old, frayed, and he made a mental promise to buy her another one. She went down to the kitchen and he moved to the window, checked the sky. Bright and clear. Good flying weather. He went into the bathroom.

When he returned to the bedroom, he found a large tumbler of freshly squeezed orange juice sitting on top of his bureau. Next to it were four vitamin pills, his daily quota. He washed them down, began to dress.

He chose his clothes carefully. He wanted nothing to attract attention to him and made his selections accordingly: a muted gray herringbone jacket, a gray knit sports shirt and flannel trousers. He put on crepe-soled desert boots; should any running be necessary, he wanted a sure footing. A soft cloth sports hat completed the job.

He checked his reflection in the bureau mirror, approved of the way he looked. Rather innocuous, with no outstanding features, he might have been a Frenchman or an Italian or a Greek. Once, he had lived as an Arab in Tangiers for three months without detection. He slipped a pair of dark glasses into his breast pocket and reached for the Smith & Wesson, adjusted it into place on his belt, buttoned the jacket. There was no bulge. From his drawer, he took a pair of unlined soft leather gloves and a small leather case containing burglar tools. He put some cash in his pocket, bills, but no silver; and nothing that would identify him. He picked up the battered suitcase and went downstairs.

The coffee was hot and strong. She reminded him that he had promised to do something about the dandelions that were spotting the front lawn, and he agreed to see to it the next day. He finished the coffee and stood up.

"See you later," he said.

She put up her face and he kissed her mouth. "Shall I tell the boys that you'll do something with them this afternoon?"

"Sure," he said, matter-of-factly. "Why not?"

He drove toward National Airport, careful to stay within the speed limits. There was no need for excessive speed; he had allowed plenty of time. He parked the car in one of the lots and made his way to the Eastern gate where he got on line for the 8 a.m. shuttle flight to New York.

Once aboard the plane, he found a seat in the rear,

away from the noise of the jets, fitting the suitcase under the seat. He fastened his seatbelt, adjusted the seat, and closed his eyes. In the lidded darkness, he began to review his plan, hunting for flaws. Street might create a problem. If so, he'd deal with it at the time. As for the rest, chance played a larger role in the operation than he liked, but there was no choice. He estimated that, when it came, the opportunity would present itself for no more than seven or eight seconds. That should be time enough. With any kind of luck, he would be on his way back to Washington by noon.

The plane touched down at Kennedy at 8:50, right on schedule. Gordon put on the dark glasses and averted his face as he passed the stewardess who favored each passenger with an official smile. He made his way to the taxi stand and gave the driver an address in the Rego Park section of Queens.

He sat back in the cab, the suitcase at his feet, and smoked a cigarette. When they arrived at the Rego Park address, a red-brick apartment house in a street of red-brick apartment houses, Gordon tipped the driver enough to satisfy him, but not enough to cause him to remember the quiet passenger in gray. He started toward the entrance of the apartment house. With grinding gears, the cab drove off. Gordon stopped to watch. When it disappeared, he strode swiftly up the street in the same direction.

He turned into a tree-lined street, deserted at this early hour, stopped alongside a parked car that satisfied his professional taste—a two-year-old beige Mercury hardtop. A single glance revealed the street was empty and he reached for his burglar tools. The door lock came open with no difficulty, he slid behind the wheel. Using the same instrument, he turned on the ignition. Moments later he was driving along Queens Boulevard toward Manhattan.

V

Pompey arrived at his office in the West Wing early on Saturday morning. Work demanded his attention from the start. Some last minute changes, a request from a Boston columnist for a ticket to the dinner, a reshuffling of the seating arrangements on the dais to accommodate Senator Abernathy, who had decided to make the trip. In the midst of this, Reilly interrupted to inform him that the President's speech had been mimeographed, the copies collated and wrapped for shipping.

"Right," Pompey said. "Send them over to Andrews and make sure the driver puts them aboard Air Force One himself."

"Yes, sir."

After she left, he thought about the copies of the original version which he had locked in the tall gray file cabinet. He would arrange to destroy the anti-treaty press copies. Later he would distribute the version favorable to the treaty.

Five minutes later, one of his assistants was demanding his attention, wanting accreditation for a correspondent from Nigeria for the dinner. Routine duties kept Pompey occupied; but as the morning wore on and the time of departure came closer, tension bubbled under his skin.

At exactly 9:30 the President came out of his office, looking alert and refreshed. The Secret Service agent on duty at the office door stood straighter, and the President greeted him by name, asked about his son, in his second year at West Point.

Sarah Harris, standing behind the President,

watched him with pleasure. He was in high spirits, seemed to be anticipating this break in his routine, and that was a good sign; she worried about him, about the strain of the job. He swung around, grinning. "Well, Sarah, it's about that time. Is everybody ready?"

"Yes, sir. Mr. Hepburn's gone down to the helicopter with some of the others."

"And Mrs. Gunther?"

"Still upstairs. Shall I ring her to come down?"

"Do that, Sarah, and send Pompey in. Also, make sure I haven't forgotten anything—like the studs to my dress shirt."

She smiled smugly. She had checked carefully. "All packed," she said.

He winked at her and she pulled back into her office. She felt good about this trip, about the way he was acting, more his old self again.

At her desk, Sarah Harris notified Holly Price, Mrs. Gunther's personal secretary, that the helicopter was ready to depart. This done, she rang Pompey.

The President was still in the corridor, talking to the Secret Service men and the warrant officer on duty, when Pompey appeared. The three men were laughing.

"Ready to go, Mr. President?" Pompey said.

The President looped an arm across the younger man's shoulder, guided him back into the oval room. "Just about, Pompey. You'll be coming along with me in Air Force One. But when we get up to Kennedy, I want you to head directly into town, make sure things are A-OK. Okay? Check the hotel and the Foundation. See that the press boys are set up right, and the radio and TV people, too. If anything's wrong, let's get it corrected before I hit the air. Clear?" He signaled for Sarah Harris and she appeared, notebook in hand.

"Sir?"

The President snapped his fingers and Ketza responded sluggishly. The President stroked the underside of the dog's throat.

"Leave word that Ketza is to have a good meal this evening, Sarah. A little extra meat, and some of those dog biscuits he likes. And after I've left, he can be turned out on the lawn." He laughed quietly. "No reason why the President's dog shouldn't enjoy the President's Park." He straightened up, manner crisp. "All right, Sarah, you better hustle or I'll leave you behind." She ducked back into her own office and the President grinned at Pompey. "Let's get it started. I want to be at the U.N. before noon."

The President led the way through the French doors to the colonnade and onto the lawn. A handful of Special Agents, who would make the trip under the command of Julian Dawson, fell into step around him. To Pompey, they all managed to look alike, though the physical differences among them were marked, and one of their number was a Negro. As they approached the big Army helicopter, twin rotors limp and still, the First Lady, escorted by Holly Price and two Secret Service men, came from the South Portico, and the President moved to join her.

Beyond the iron gate, on East Executive Avenue, tourists gathered to watch; and a spontaneous burst of applause brok out, was sustained, and spread. The President waved and the First Lady smiled timidly. Minutes later, they were all inside the helicopter. The plane began to vibrate as the rotors spun noisily above them. The vertical lift-off was smooth. Pompey sat back and tried to relax.

Peter Street arrived at the northwest corner of Third Avenue and 36th Street a few minutes before ten. Traffic sped uptown, a cacophony of screeching low-pressure tires and blaring horns. A young mother, shopping cart bulging with laundry, approached, her daughter clinging to her skirt. The woman glanced idly at Street, who averted his face. He focused on the window of the antique store on the corner.

At two minutes after ten, a beige Mercury pulled

up to the curb. Gordon was behind the wheel. Street climbed in and they continued up Third Avenue.

"What are we going to do?" Street asked at once.

Gordon concentrated on the traffic. "I'll explain as we go along. First, we're going to park this car, some place near the Chrysler Building." Then, as an afterthought. "You can drive, if necessary?"

"Yes, I can drive." He hesitated. "You must understand that I'm not a violent man. The idea of killing another person——"

"*You* won't kill anyone."

They found parking space on 44th Street, facing east. Gordon maneuvered the Mercury so that it wouldn't be boxed in by another vehicle. "Remember where the car is. We are going to be in a hurry when we come back."

"Yes. What happens now?"

"Come with me, and if there's any talking to be done, leave it to me."

They walked down Lexington Avenue to the 43rd Street entrance of the Chrysler Building. They paused on the sidewalk.

"This is where we'll come out later, and from here back to the car. No matter what happens, don't get confused. Do you remember where the car is?"

"I'm not a child," Street said testily.

Gordon stared him down. "And this is no child's game. Where is the car?"

"44th Street."

"Okay. We go in now. There'll be a man on duty, the elevator starter. Ignore him. Act as though we belong, as if we've done this a thousand times, as if we work here. The starter can't possibly know every tenant in a building of this size. Let's go."

Gordon led the way to the express elevators and as they swooped upward, he donned the leather gloves. They got off at the 68th floor. No one was in sight, the silence serving to heighten Street's apprehension.

"Won't you please tell me what we're doing here?"

"This isn't quite high enough," Gordon said. "I've had this kind of thing in mind for a long time. I walked through it once about a year ago, to see if it would work. It will."

"What are you talking about?"

"The footage per floor is about the same in both buildings, so we've got to go higher. I wanted to play it safe, in case the starter noticed which floor we got off at on his signal board. Follow me."

The emergency staircase was locked but the latch gave way easily under Gordon's burglar tool. The stairwell was dimly lit and cool as they climbed, Gordon allowing a respite at each floor for Street, already breathing hard.

"All right," Gordon said at last. "This should do it. Let's hope our luck holds. We need an empty office, one facing in the right direction. This way."

The corridor was still and they moved swiftly toward the northwest corner of the building. Gordon paused in front of a double glass door. Gilt lettering indicated that these were the New York offices of a national woolens company. Gordon went to work on the lock.

Once inside, they passed through a reception room into an area divided by panels into small cubicles, all deserted. Along the far wall were the permanent offices. These too were unoccupied.

"We're in luck," Gordon said. "Nobody's here."

"And if someone comes?"

Gordon shrugged. "Let's hope that doesn't happen." His eyes raked over the offices. "The one in the corner. That should do it."

Obviously this was the workroom of a senior executive, luxuriously furnished with an unobstructed view to the west, the city glittering in the early sunlight like a million sparkling facets.

"What a magnificent sight," Street enthused. "It's almost as if you can reach out and touch the Pan Am Building."

Gordon grunted. He swung the old suitcase onto the polished rosewood desk, then went back outside. Street watched the agent brace a chair under the knob of the door to the reception room. When he returned, Gordon explained.

"This is a selling office. I doubt that anyone will show up on Saturday. But if they do, I want some warning."

Gordon opened the suitcase and felt along the inside of the top. He found what he was searching for, a shred of loose fabric. Very gently, he exerted pressure, pulled. The lining came away in his hands. The suitcase had a false top. Gordon reached inside and brought out a blue steel barrel nearly fourteen inches long. No more than half an inch across at its mouth, it widened gradually to about twice that size at the base. Street could see three small holes in the butt.

Again Gordon reached into the top. He yanked hard and the flat metal frame supporting the suitcase came away in his hands. With practiced skill, he twisted it to shape and quickly fastened it to the bar rel-butt with tiny screws. Finished, he tested the fastenings. They were solid and for the first time Street realized that Gordon was assembling a rifle, the suitcase frame forming the shoulder stock.

He moved to a more advantageous position and saw that the false top of the suitcase was fitted to accommodate various items. Next, Gordon snapped the chamber and trigger assembly into place. And the bolt. He cocked the piece and squeezed the unguarded trigger. The firing pin shot forward with a dull click. Satisfied, Gordon attached a telescopic sight to the barrel, tightened the lockscrews.

"A thirty-power lens," he explained. "At a thousand yards, I can tell you the color of a man's eyes."

"With that rifle?" Street asked.

Gordon hefted it admiringly. "A lovely piece. Made it myself. The barrel is cut down from an Army Springfield '03, also the bolt and chamber. Refined, of course. The stock is my own doing, and so is that suitcase. I can transport this piece anywhere in the world." He went to one of the windows and opened it, stepped back and sighted on some distant target. "Perfect," he said with quiet pride. "Perfect." He reached back into the suitcase and came up with a single .30-caliber bullet, slid it into the chamber and slammed the bolt shut. He placed the rifle on the desk and made himself comfortable in the big swivel chair, facing west.

"It's five minutes before eleven," he said. "Within the next thirty minutes, the President will be coming from Kennedy Airport by helicopter. He's going to set down on top of the Pan Am Building. When he gets out of that plane, I'm going to shoot him."

Street's eyes swung to the helioport on the roof of the gray, coffin-shaped structure. He wet his lips and rubbed at the nerve which had begun to leap about in his thigh. "It's so far. Can you do it from this distance?"

"It's a clear shot. As long as nothing gets in the way, this rifle and I can hit anything within range. And that building is within range."

Street was appalled. "What about afterward? The city will be a madhouse. And we're more than seventy stories up. How will we get away?"

"That's why you're here," Gordon said easily. "When the helicopter comes into view, you're to go out to the elevator bank and get a car up to this floor. When it comes, you'll keep it until I get there."

"What if someone wants to use it?"

Gordon's expression never changed. He reached for the snub-nosed Smith & Wesson, handed it to Street. "You won't let that happen."

Street paled, gazed at the weapon with distaste. "I could never shoot anyone."

Gordon stared at him. "Do whatever is necessary, Mr. Street, as long as that elevator is waiting when I come. Because when I do, I'll be coming fast." He pivoted around to face the Pan Am Building. "Now relax. It'll all be over in a few minutes."

Six

—

The Fifth One

[illegible] During the ride into Manhattan [illegible] to
[illegible] his increasing [illegible] admiration [illegible] be
[illegible] that Gordon [illegible]

I

Pompey went from Air Force One to a waiting limousine, ordered the driver to take him to the Warren House. During the ride into Manhattan, he tried to suppress his increasing agitation, now wished he knew what Gordon's plans were.

At the Warren House, there was the normal amount of nervous anticipation occasioned by a Presidential visit. The various suites had been prepared for occupancy by the members of the President's party.

"Would you care to inspect them, Mr. Pompey?" the manager asked.

"No, thanks, I'm sure everything's all right." An electric clock on the wall of the manager's office told him that it was a few minutes past noon. Whatever Gordon had in mind, must happen soon, before the President arrived at the United Nations. Pompey arranged a smile on his face. "I have to be at the Foundation. If there are any calls, please refer them to me." Surprisingly, his voice as quietly controlled, his manner relaxed, confident.

"Yes, sir."

Pompey walked, the probable route the President would follow—two blocks south on Madison, past shop after chic shop, and half a block to the west.

Headquarters of the worldwide organization were contained in a row of ancient, architecturally impressive buildings, galleried and pillared, bayed and shuttered, sheathed in marble and accented with gargoyles. The main entrance was in the building nearest Fifth Avenue.

Pompey made his way toward it, striding swiftly

along the gracious street lined by leafy trees. Already police barricades had been erected at both ends of the quiet block to exclude unauthorized traffic.

The Foundation, organized only three years earlier, had made rapid progress, becoming in that comparatively short time the most influential group of its kind. Its roster listed some of the most famous and honored names in the world: diplomats, businessmen, artists, writers, university presidents, people of every station and every interest, joined by a common desire to establish peace as the normal condition on the planet. To this end, the Foundation was actively supported, richly endowed, able to dispatch representatives to the capitals of every nation, to influence policy, to lessen international tensions, to cool national angers. Heads of state made themselves available to Peace Now ministers, and Peace Now embassies had been established in the capital city of every major power.

There were exceptions, of course. Both China and France claimed the organization was a front for the American CIA; and in the United States itself there was a movement to have the Foundation investigated by a House committee with powerful support in Dallas and Los Angeles.

But the Foundation continued to prosper and grow, its influence more pronounced each year. In order to accommodate the swelling staff of workers, the separating walls of the four buildings had been penetrated and the internal structure altered as needed. The result was a maze of corridors and stairways, of private offices and meeting rooms, of lobbies and terraces, of landscaped gardens and blocked portals. It was generally agreed that sooner or later everyone working at the Foundation lost his way, and it had been suggested that kegs of brandy be mounted on the walls instead of fire extinguishers.

At the main entrance, a policeman checked Pompey's credentials, waved him inside. Up five, low, white-granite steps, through massive doors, black iron lacework and glass, into an airy, ornate reception foyer, the lofty ceiling carved, supporting a crystal chandelier, and curving to the left a red-carpeted stairway.

A detail of Secret Service agents was working to find some logical architectural pattern to the sprawl of chambers and hallways that would allow them to protect the President with reasonable efficiency.

Once recognized, no further attention was paid to Pompey, and he made his way to an ante-chamber just behind the third floor ballroom where the dinner would take place. This was his press room, and here he found the packages containing copies of the President's speech. He put them out of sight, making no effort to unwrap them, reluctant to take even that step toward making known the sentiments they contained.

With the help of a Foundation functionary, he went over the seating plan. He checked off Peter Street's name with no show of interest. This done, they compared press lists; there were three additional names to be added, foreign journalists. Finished, he looked at his watch. It was 12:23. Surely now now.

Fred Vogel, Assistant Chief of the White House Secret Service detail, appeared in the doorway of the press room. An anticipatory tension oozed into Pompey's extremities. He forced himself to greet Vogel affably. The Special Agent looked at him glumly.

"What a mess," he muttered. "This joint has got more exits and entrances than a museum. With twice the men, I wouldn't rest easy about this job.

The Foundation man arranged his pale features in a pleased expression. "Each of these four buildings was at one time a private residence, and each was constructed to the particular specifications of the family involved. So, you can see——"

"Yeah," Vogel muttered unhappily. "I can see okay. And, like I said, it's a mess. Wait'll Cchief Dawson gets here. He's going to have a large fit."

Pompey was commisserating with Vogel when the telephone rang. The Foundation man answered, offered the instrument to Pompey.

He said, "The city room of the *Times*."

Vogel turned away disinterestedly as Pompey took the phone. "Pompey here," he said. It was Gordon's voice he heard, low and unmistakable.

"Listen to me. The job still has to be done. You understand?"

"Yes," Pompey heard himself say. "But there are no more places available at the press table."

"Do we make another try at ti?"

Pompey hesitated. Nothing had changed; the need to act still existed. "The question," he said in a mild voice, "is where would I seat another man?"

"We'll work it out," Gordon said. "I hate to do it, but we better meet again. I'll name a spot—and if it's agreeable, say yes. If not, I'll pick another." There was a long silence. "Somewhere in the open. Central Park, I think. North of 72nd Street, the statue of the Alice in Wonderland characters. Do you know it?"

"Yes."

"In one hour?"

A suite of related images went romping across Pompey's mind. He was free to come and go as he wished, but to do so might cast later suspicion on himself. It couldn't be helped. "That'll be fine," he said with contrived brightness.

"I'll have our friend along and I'll keep moving, so don't worry if I'm not there when you arrive. I'll show by-'n'-by. Now say something appropriate and hang up."

Pompey listened to the phone go dead. He made himself laugh. "Sorry. I'll do my best to squeeze your man in, but don't count on it. It's a full house for this one. Thanks for calling."

"Everybody wants a piece of the action," Vogel said glumly.

Pompey grunted his assent and turned to the Foundation man. "Let's get with it. It's too nice a day to spend in this place."

II

Pompey walked swiftly up Fifth Avenue. At 72nd Street, he swung into the park and made his way down the slope to the sailing pond. A variety of model boats plowed through the water to the urging of a small army of onlookers. Pompey circled the pond, hurried to keep his appointment.

The Lewis Carroll characters—Alice, the March Hare, the Mad Hatter, the Cheshire Cat—drew children and parents alike. Mothers rested on nearby benches while their offspring expended energy clambering over the weathered, bronze figures. A father deposited his young daughter in Alice's lap and began snapping pictures.

Pompey looked around There was no sign of Gordon or Peter Street. He swore silently and checked the time. A chocking sense of frustration took hold of him, and he fought against it, directed himself up the path for a few hundred yards, turned back. Still no Gordon. He settled onto a bench and stared at the children playing around the statue and puffed on a cigarette until it was too small to hold. He vowed to quit smoking and lit another.

Gordon and Street appeared in the distance. Pompey watched them come closer. His eyes met Gordon's. There was no recognition in the agent's glance. Pompey waited until they had passed, then followed.

Across the roadway that twisted uptown through the park, alongside the lake, outside the boathouse, among the lovers and the cyclists, he found them waiting. Gordon was holding two cones of soft chocolate ice cream. He handed one to Pompey. It had begun to melt.

"Very good," Gordon said.

Pompey tasted the ice cream. "What went wrong?" he said. The ice cream was good.

"Let's walk," Gordon said.

They walked, Pompey between the other two, attending their ice cream, commenting on the sights and sounds of a Saturday afternoon in Central Park. Around the lake crowded with rowboats, to the Bethesda Fountain, and the café, up the broad, stone terrace steps that led to the Mall. In the band shell, some singers were rehearsing an opera. A soccer game was in progress on the Sheep Meadow, the action flowing continuously with liquid grace. At a point some yards beyond the near goal, Gordon seated himself cross-legged on the grass and the others did likewise.

"This is a good place to talk," he said. The pinched face opened in a silent laugh. "Three middle-aged soccer fans watching a game."

"For Chrissakes," Pompey burst out. "Stop playing games and tell me what happened."

Gordon finished his ice cream. "The odds were in my favor. I recognized the chance of failure, but it was worth taking. It didn't pay off." He pulled out his handkerchief and used it as a napkin. "I was going to pick him off when the helicopter landed on top of the Pan Am Building. From the tower of the Chrysler Building."

"That's crazy!" Pompey said.

"Not at all. The odds were good that the 'copter would set down with the exit facing in my direction. I could have gotten him as he moved into the doorway. Instead it was turned, slightly, but enough. I still had a chance at him, as he headed across the roof. It just didn't come off. Too many people around. Mrs. Gunther and a Secret Service agent screened him from me. I followed him through my sight until he disappeared, zeroed in on his shoulder." He shrugged. "Not much point in just nicking him."

Pompey envied the DIA agent his detachment. To him, this was merely a detail of a job that hadn't come off. A bit of bad luck, worthy of no further consideration. That the impostor was still alive and functioning, and all the terrible implications of that fact, appeared to have left Gordon untouched. Not so Pompey. He kept thinking about the speech that would be delivered in the Peace Now Foundation dining room that night, a speech designed to create chaos and war.

"It still must be done," Pompey said.

Street protested. "No. We did our best. Twice. Men can't be expected to do more than their best."

Pompey looked out at the soccer field. A blue player was dribbling the ball, managing to avoid those who would have taken it away, his movements quickly deceptive, strong when he had to be, swift. A large red player angled in front of him, and it seemed as if Blue's run on the goal had been ended. He thought otherwise. A feint to the left, a convincing dip of his left shoulder, drew the red player forward. A sudden acceleration, and Blue was free, the ball an extension of his flashing feet. The goaltender came out to meet the threat, defensive, alert, sure of himself. Blue hesitated, waited, poised on his toes, and the goalie committed himself. Blue spun back into action. The goalie, faked out, tried to recover too late. The ball went flashing by him. A score.

"We're going to kill him," Pompey said, "before he makes that speech."

"No," Street muttered.

"How?" Gordon said.

Pompey went over the President's schedule for the remainder of that day. No way existed of getting the President in Gordon's rifle sight with any certainty. And this time they had to be sure.

"We've got to do it at close range," Pompey said. "So close that there can be no mistake."

Gordon agreed amiably. "Get close enough and we've got a sure thing."

"The Secret Service," Street said, a rising note of anguish in his voice.

Pompey looked at Gordon questioningly.

Gordon shrugged and adjusted the knot of his tie. "There's no stopping a man, if he's determined to pull it off. Oh, if it happens in the open, someone trying to get at the President through police lines or from across a hotel lobby, he'd be dead before he could pull the trigger——"

"You see!" Street said hopefully.

Gordon kept talking as if there had been no interruption. "The thing about the Secret Service, they're supposed to protect him from crowds mainly, to keep him from getting hurt if people get unruly. But if anybody wanted to shoot the President, all he has to do is take a pot shot at him with a rifle."

"We tried——" Street muttered.

"A rifle's out now," Pompey said. "The route's too uncertain and he might even come by car. That bubble's bulletproof."

Gordon said, "Up close. In a crowd, pushing in tight, using the other people to mask your intentions. That way it can't be stopped. The security people would be helpless. Before they could act——"

Pompey made up his mind. "At the dinner," he said. "Before he delivers the speech. In the ballroom."

"Oh, no!"

"It's possible."

"It's our last chance," Pompey said.

"Is there a dais?" Gordon asked.

"Yes. He'll enter from the right side and as he approaches the microphones he'll be exposed to the audience, the television cameras."

Gordon tried to visualize the scene. "Procedure is for the Secret Service people to scatter themselves around the room. They'll be posted at the exits, and a few more will be spaced out in front of the dais."

Street leaped on that point. "You see, it can't be done. Not that way. Guards everywhere. They'd stop a man with a gun." The aristocratic face was mottled and puffy, the eyes unsteady.

Gordon ignored the interruption. "You said television coverage?"

"Yes," Pompey said. He wanted Gordon to digest all the information, the problems and the advantages, to estimate the odds, to feed back a satisfactory answer.

"Where will the cameras be placed?"

"Two of them. One on the ballroom floor, on a dolly, in the center aisle, free to move in and out as needed."

"The other?"

"On a small balcony on the wall facing the dais."

"The easy way," Gordon said. "Right up that center aisle, in front of the TV camera. Dawson's people will be off to either side, out of camera range, and the avenue of approach will be wide open. A quick move and that's it."

They sat quietly for a long interval and watched the soccer game. The small blue player seemed to dominate the action. Pompey decided that it was less his natural talent that brought this about than his need to triumph.

"We'll require a pistol," Pompey said.

"I have one," Gordon said. "It can't be traced." He hesitated. "It's simply a matter of execution. He'll have to approach the President from the front. No one will be able to get through from behind."

"I'll be on the dais," Pompey said. "Near the entrance."

Gordon looked at him. "Will you do it?"

Pompey tried to imagine what it would be like. The crashing shots, the confusion, the swelling fear, terror overflowing, paralyzing.

The *speech!*

That sinister confluence of words. It was vital that they not be made public, that no one see them, that the intent of the President be buried with him. Only Pompey could do that, and now he knew why he had brought Luplow's original version along in his attaché case. He alone could effect the transfer. And he alone could keep the mimeographed copies of the deadly speech out of the hands of the newspapermen.

And more. Once done, the assassination would trigger a massive investigation. The investigators had to be supplied with a satisfactory reason for the killing, one that would close the file on it. Pompey, as the assassin, would raise more questions, create doubt and uncertainty; he was determined that the truth about the impersonation be concealed forever.

He began to speak in a halting voice, to explain to the others that not only must they kill, but that they must do so in a manner consistent with the national good.

"We're agreed that none of this can be made public," Pompey said. "The truth must be buried." He lit a cigarette with steady fingers. "Nobody must ever learn what happened. History must record that it was the real Harrison Gunther who was killed on this day. Otherwise, this is all futile."

Street said weakly, "How can we be sure of what will happen afterward?"

Pompey spoke softly. "We've got to give them somebody."

Gordon stared at him, the pinched face blank, its very lack of expression knowledgeable. He felt an increasing admiration for the Press Secretary, the reluctant admiration of a professional for a skillful amateur.

Street began to sputter his protests. "This is ridiculous. It will take time to arrange matters properly, a suitable cover story, time to find someone to do it. Such matters can't be done on a moment's notice."

"We need someone who in his own person provides a solid motive," Pompey said. "Someone who might want the President dead, might view him as a personal threat, an enemy, someone who might seek revenge on the man."

Street struggled to his feet. "Where are you going to find such a man?"

"Sit down, Peter," Pompey said. His voice was serrated, edged with authority, demanding obedience.

Street hesitated, stared sightlessly, and wearily lowered himself to the grass, his breathing audible.

"There will be things to do afterward," Pompey said. "Things that only I am in a position to do. Also, I lack a motive, a built-in motive. So does Gordon. That leaves you, Peter."

Street's eyes rolled wildly in their sockets. "No," he muttered. "No, no."

"There is no else," Pompey said flatly. "You have a perfect right to be at the dinner, you're a member of the Foundation. You're invited and will be comfortable among those people."

"Oh, I couldn't do it. I won't."

Pompey looked at Gordon, who returned his glance steadily, expectantly, and in that brief moment Pompey knew that at last the responsibility was totally his own. For now more than a decision to act was required, Peter Street had to be convinced to commit murder, to perform in a manner that was contradictory to the values by which he lived, had to be convinced to risk his own life in the doing.

"No one else can do it, Peter," Pompey said. "You will do it."

"No."

Pompey felt unusually calm, his breathing regular, his heartbeat steady.

"You and Gunther were friends," he said. "He rejected you."

"Gunther's dead," Street protested.

"To the world, he's alive."

"Nobody would believe that I wanted him dead."

"You *do* want him dead, Peter. You hate him, resent his success, his popularity, the way he's treated you. He turned away the moment you had any trouble, left you beyond the pale of polite society, undercut your political career. He left you with nothing."

"People don't kill for that."

"*You* do, Peter. You kill when the bitterness piles higher than you can bear. You kill when existence becomes too difficult, too painful. You kill when there is no hope."

"I don't feel that way."

Pompey stared at Street and he turned away.

"I feel resentment," Street muttered. "Yes. I admit it. Harry and I were good friends. He might have helped me, extended a hand. I was hurt and I wanted to hurt him, but that was long ago and it's all over. I hold no grudge for what he did. Not anymore."

"You've spoken against him all over Washington."

"That doesn't matter. I embarrassed him, and in politics that's the kiss of death. It was logical that he drop me. I was a liability."

"You criticized his Administration in print and in person." Pompey leaned forward and spoke with quiet intensity. "You were a man with a bright future, and Harrison Gunther wiped it out. He left you nothing, not even a second chance. All doors were closed to you in government. There's been no place for you in Washington."

"No. People called on me from time to time. For advice, for suggestions. My opinion has always been solicited. My opinions still have value. Ralph Jacobs——"

"Jacobs is dead."

Street looked around, eyes lighting nowhere. His cheeks were flushed and his lip trembled. "I couldn't kill. I couldn't. I–I've never used a gun. Never!"

"No problem," Gordon said. "The pistol I gave you. It's simple to use. Five shots. Point it and pull the trigger. Thirteen pounds of pressure does the job, and if you cock it first only two and a half pounds. Hardly any kick at all. No sweat. Just aim and let go."

"You see?" Pompey said.

Street began to perspire. He squinted off at the skyline to the west. A kite soared and stunted. Without warning, it dived out of control, crashed.

"I don't want to die," he moaned. His soft eyes were misty and the blurred features seemed to run together. "I want to help," he murmured. "To do what's right. I haven't always been smart, but I wanted only more for my country, only better. But this–I'm so afraid, so afraid of dying. Please, try to understand."

Pompey desperately sought the ultimate persuasion. To get Street to agree was not enough; he had to sustain the commitment for the next seven hours. He dropped his hand on Street's arm, squeezed reassuringly and allowed a small smile to turn his finely sculpted mouth. "This talk of dying, Peter. That's your imagination at work." He laughed shortly. "Nothing so dramatic is necessary. Isn't that right, Gordon?"

"That's right."

Street looked from one to the other. He said nothing.

Pompey laughed again, warmly reassuring. "Forgive me, Peter, for not making all of it clear. The pressure on all of us." He let it hang.

"Yes," Street agreed quietly.

"You know the Foundation Building," Pompey said, "better than I do. There are dozens of exits."

"Yes," Street said.

"When I was there earlier, I noted the precise placement of every Secret Service agent. Let's face it, Peter, those men are human. They make mistakes."

"Make a book on it," Gordon said. "Look at the record."

Street eyes Gordon speculatively; then to Pompey: "I don't see how——"

"The balcony," Pompey said. "The balcony overlooking the dais. Only the TV camera and the operator. No one else will be up there. And the stairs will be unguarded. There's no reason to post a man there." Street started to speak but Pompey went on. "The balcony overhangs the ballroom, looks down on the dais, no more than twenty-five feet away."

"An easy shot," Gordon said.

"I never shot a gun."

"It's easy," Gordon said. "Just aim." Using his forefinger, he demonstrated the technique. "Support your forearm on the balcony railing and brace the gun with your other hand. Squeeze off the shot, a couple more to be sure."

"Then back down the steps before anybody can move toward you," Pompey added.

"There'll be time," Gordon said.

"Once the shooting starts, that ballroom will be a mass of people rushing around, trying to find cover. Any security agents outside will come busting in to see what's going on. You'll have plenty of opportunity to get away."

Street wet his mouth. "And then?"

Pompey smiled confidentially at him. "There's an old fire door on the same floor, no more than thirty feet away, at the east end of the corridor, around the corner, concealed behind some drapes. Since it's never used, it's been barred from the inside, and is easily opened. Through there and down the fire escape and you'll be in the back yard of the adjoining apartment building. Keep on going into the alley until you exit on the next street, near Fifth Avenue. Gordon will be waiting for you with a car. As simple as that."

"But everybody will know what I've done. I'll never be free, always hunted."

"I know a place where you can hide out," Gordon said. "Right here in New York. I've used it before. You'll be safe for as long as you have to stay."

"When things calm down," Pompey said. "we'll get you out of the country."

"No point in kidding you," Gordon said matter-of-factly. "It won't be easy. Your life will be different, radically different, hell, perhaps; but you will be able to survive, to exist—and be able to start a new life somewhere. Argentina will probably be the best place. No extradition treaty exists with the United States, and I've got some good contacts who will be able to smooth the way. Yes, Argentina. We'll create a new identity for you. The necessary papers, your appearance altered . . ."

Street stopped listening. He was torn as never before. The President had to be eliminated, had to be killed, and perhaps Pompey was right in saying he was the only one who could do the job as it had to be done. He *wanted* to do it. Wanted to act in a proper fashion for a noble motive, to take pride in at least one single moment of his life, a moment that would cancel out all the wasted years, all the futility.

If only he were able to suppress the roaring, despairing, ill-making terror that slithered along his nerves. He told himself that it would be the way Pompey said, simple and precise, an esoteric ballet choreographed to the smallest detail, its patterns unknown to those who might cause him harm, its end product the most good for the most people. He wanted very much to convince himself.

Pompey helped.

"I'll unlock the fire door myself," he said. "You can depend on it. Just go onto the balcony, do the job, and get out of there."

A thought flickered at the periphery of Street's brain. "The television cameraman?"

It was Gordon who replied in that mild professional manner of his. "I'm afraid you'll have to take him out. No trouble, he won't be expecting it. One good belt with the gun butt from behind."

Street frowned but said nothing.

"Once it's done," Pompey said, "everyone will put it down to personal revenge, and the truth will never come out."

"The agents," Street said. "They'll shoot at me."

Pompey spoke quickly. "No, Peter. Not in that crowded room with all those important people. They can't risk it. They'll want to take you alive. You can understand that." Pompey looked into Street's puffy face, empty and weary now, drained of emotion. "You'll always know, Peter, that what you did was an act of supreme patriotism."

The corners of Street's mouth lifted slightly. "Your single-mindedness, Mr. Pompey. Your dedication. Your strength of purpose. So impressive, all of it, so worthy of admiration. But at this moment I can only despise you." He turned to Gordon. "I've always been afraid of guns. . . ."

III

They walked in a great circle, keeping to the grass, away from other people, seeking privacy for what they said. Pompey and Street pooled their knowledge of the Peace Now Building and framed each move that was to be made.

"When I get back," Pompey said, "I'll make another check. If there's been any change in security arrangements, I'll find out."

"How?" Street asked.

"Stay in your hotel room. Get some rest. I'll contact you there."

Street sucked air in through his teeth. "Yes," he said. "Of course. I'll be available when you call." Then, with a rush of apprehension: "The gun, what about the gun?"

A warning glance went from Pompey to Gordon. He didn't trust Street to keep the gun for the rest of the day. It would serve as a prod, a constant reminder, increasing the pressure on a man already unstable. Gordon understood the silent message.

"No point in any of us carrying it around," he said. "Why take chances? Not that anybody is going to search anybody. But why take chances?"

"Then how——?" Street muttered.

"After the Foundation has been checked out, it will be easy for somebody to bring in a gun, hide it some place safe where it can be gotten to when you want it."

"Ah," Street said. There was a tired slump to his shoulders, and his eyes were cloudy and lifeless.

"We'll make it easy," Pompey added. "I'll bring the

gun in, hide it. Later, when I phoned you, Peter, I'll tell you where it is. Okay?" Street offered no response. Pompey leaned forward. "Did you hear what I said?"

Without looking up, Street spoke, resignation in his voice. "I heard."

"And I'll pick up another car," Gordon said. "Once we have you tucked safely away, I'll ditch it. This place, Mr. Street, you'll be comfortable there. Plenty of books and television, and lots to drink and eat. You won't shave. Let's see what a beard does for you, or a mustache. Trust me. I've done this sort of thing before."

"This is going to work out fine," Pompey said.

"Yes," Street said.

"Now," Pompey said. "Go back to your hotel. Gordon will go with you. Keep you company."

"No," Street's head came up. He spoke with quiet emphasis. "Nobody. I want to be alone." A mocking light materialized in his eyes, was extinguished quickly. "I insist on that much privacy."

Pompey hesitated before agreeing. "You'll wait for my call?"

"Yes."

"We're depending on you, Peter. All of us."

"Yes," he said. "Of course."

They watched him shamble off across the lawn, stooped, immersed in his own thoughts. They waited until he turned onto a path that took him out of sight before they left the Sheep Meadow and angled across the Mall. Much time passed before either of them spoke, and then it was Gordon, crisply professional, concerned with the technical aspects of the job.

"Where will you hide the gun?"

"What do you suggest?"

Gordon had thought about it. "There'll be a final security check. In the late afternoon, most likely. Some time after that."

"No problem. I'll get there early, before the President, and I'll have time to hide it. The question is where."

"Keep it simple. Street is pulled up tight. It wouldn't surprise me if he cracked. Let's make it easy for him. An air-conditioning vent is a possibility, if it's accessible without too much strain."

"No good. The buildings are old and each room is cooled individually. Window units. Why can't I pass the gun to him sometime during the evening?"

"Too risky. The gun might be spotted and, also, you shouldn't be seen talking to Street. Let's see . . ." They walked down a flight of stone steps alongside the bear pens. In the zoo, they picked their way past playing children. Gordon bought a box of Cracker Jack from a vendor and deposited them one at a time in his mouth, chewing with careful precision. The sweetish fragrance offended Pompey and he looked away. "The john," Gordon said.

Pompey tried to anticipate him.

Gordon continued. "It's an old building, you said. That means paper towels in those wall containers. Or one of those infinite cloth rolls. It's easy to open those containers. A coin will do it. Place the gun there. At a convenient time, Street can get it out."

"I wish I was more confident about him."

"You don't have much choice." Gordon stared at Pompey. "That fire door," he said in a dead tone. "You'll never be able to unlock it. There'll be a guard."

"I know." Pompey gazed straight ahead. They were out of the zoo now, past the children's pony ride. "There's no need for you to get a car, or make any other arrangements."

Gordon gazed admiringly at him. "I wondered if you'd come around to that."

Pompey jammed his hands into his pockets. The palms were moist. "Street," he said, "he's got the motive. It's got to end with him."

Gordon finished the last of the Cracker Jack and dropped the empty box into a trash basket. "You've got my vote."

"Afterward, with the confusion, with the swearing-in of the Vice President, with all that will be happening, no one will ever think to question the identity of the dead man."

"Right, they'll check everything else, but not that. To all intents, Gunther will have been assassinated."

Pompey lit a cigarette and coughed softly. "After Street does the job, it would be better if he died too. The Secret Service—can we be sure they'll shoot him?"

"They'd like to take him alive. But that's under ideal circumstances, which of course never exist. Those agents—well, when guns start going off, people, no matter how well disciplined, get nervous. My guess is that somebody will let him have a few. A reflex action. Bet on it, Mr. Pompey. They'll shoot."

"I hope so."

"I want to compliment you," Gordon said. "You handled Street very well, getting him to agree. Very professional."

"It had to be done."

"You did what was necessary." He paused. "You know, there may be more. If things don't go exactly according to plan, you won't be able to depend on Street to follow through. Reliability is not his strength. Be ready for anything."

Pompey made an assenting sound in the back of his throat.

They walked outside the park and stood alongside the high, dirty stone wall that separated it from Fifth Avenue, their backs to the traffic. Gordon acted with smooth efficiency. He covered one open palm with a clean white handkerchief, reached under his jacket. A moment later Pompey took the handkerchief, now concealing Gordon's .38, placed it under his belt with a nonchalance he did not feel.

"I may as well head home now," Gordon said. "I've got two sons. I'd like to spend some time with them."

They shook hands.

Gordon pursed his lips and tugged at his ear. "Street mustn't be allowed to talk," he muttered. "If the agents fail to kill him, you must do the job yourself."

"Yes," Pompey said gravely. "I will."

Pompey wasn't ready to go back to Warren House. Something vague and disturbing held him out; he moved south on Fifth Avenue. The sun, warm on the back of his neck, was soothing, yet he felt no comfort. The fountain in the plaza at 59th Street was flowing; people perched around its white granite lip. He settled into a space between a hulking red-bearded man with a camera dangling from his neck and a lean youth engrossed in a paperbound copy of *The Hobbit.*

Pompey adjusted his jacket, making sure the .38 was concealed, and allowed his eyes to rake over the Saturday afternoon strollers. There was that about New York, a fine place for walking, always interesting shops, and the people, so many of them, the variety startling. A rueful smile fanned across his mouth. He couldn't remember ever walking when he lived in New York, surely never for pleasure, only when hurrying from place to place. Once he had believed he knew the city, that he was wise in its ways, but at this moment he realized how little knowledge he really owned about it. The most expensive restaurants, the bars, the chic and glossy places so suitable for impressing a client or influencing a contact—these he knew. But the same could be said about Los Angeles or Chicago and, he supposed, Washington. It occurred to him that always he was in a city, but seldom a part of it, never a part of anything, functioning too often on the fringes propagandizing the creative efforts of other men, men like Harrison Gunther, the real doers of deeds.

He heaved himself erect and moved into the stream of pedestrian traffic. Faces came into view, each person concerned with his own affairs, oblivious to him and his problems, to what was happening. A cry of despair and frustration came into his throat; he ached to shout out what he knew, to warn them of the danger, of the monstrous marriage of events that endangered each of them, to force them to assume their share of the burden, to shock them out of their self-absorbtion, the smug certainty that someone else would act when action was called for, that someone would always be able to protect them.

The light changed and he crossed Fifth Avenue. Were they right? Was there always someone to do it, to take care of them? It seemed so. There were men to assume the risks that accompanied power, men like Gunther and Jacobs. He looked into the window of F.A.O. Schwartz, seeing his own toy-shadowed reflection in the glass. Men like Guy Pompey, he told himself. It was a terrifying thought, and at the same time it fortified his pride.

He walked slowly. The .38 was a mind-prodding drag at his waist. He swung into 57th Street, a man and his wife separating to let him pass. He paid no attention to the glossy shops or the art galleries or the antique stores or the people brushing past. He struggled to isolate his thoughts, to find the hard core in this looking-glass world, plumbing the convolutions of his brain for the neat order of things. Perverse and thin, life was out of sync, a wild put-on, yet rooted in the reality of pain and blood, the more insane for that.

People hurried on their way—a trio of laughing men, blond-helmeted girls, all frowns and deep concerns, then shrieking loudly, a pair of matrons gossiping out of tight mouths. Was this all of it, transient, hollow, a matter of kicks and rewards, of places and things? Was there nothing to believe in?

Didn't anyone care?

An oath died behind Pompey's clenched teeth. He thought of Jacobs and knew that he never had to ask such questions. He knew the answers, what mattered in life, had been born knowing. It was unfair, Pompey decided, that he had to struggle so to make sense out of what could have been simple and pleasurable. In dying, Jacobs had left a void, a singular loss. They might have been friends, Pompey silently suggested. Now that he had entered the breach. Now that he had taken command. Now that he was doing what needed to be done.

A cold spasm caused his sphincter muscle to tense. Keep a tight ass-hole, they warned in combat. It was no idle remark. That kind of fear took hold of him now, that kind of separateness. Only more so. He was isolated as never before, and no sanctuary existed. And in that split second he knew it all, everything: that the people in the streets, the millions more all across the country—they *were* depending on him to protect them. It had always been that way. Men like him doing what was necessary, what was expected of them. This was what it was all about, the authority of high office, responsibility, the time when a man earned his pay.

He headed back to the hotel, past a vendor selling chestnuts, past a Salvation Army band playing *Onward Christian Soldiers,* walking faster. He knew exactly what he was going to do.

IV

There were Secret Service agents all over the Warren House, out front and in the lobby. Guarding the back entrance and in the kitchen, Pompey supposed, and probably patrolling the basement. When the elevator reached his floor, a tall Negro agent named Ferguson who worked the night shift at the White House, said, "Hello, Mr. Pompey," politely but without friendliness.

Ferguson's eyes were wary and made Pompey acutely conscious of the revolver in his pocket. He returned Ferguson's greeting and strode rapidly down the corridor to his own room. Farther along, two more agents were stationed at the entrance of the Presidential suite. Pompey waved and ducked inside his own room.

He locked the .38 inside his overnight bag and placed the case deep in the closet. At least it would be safe from the prying eyes of the chambermaid.

This done, he called the President's rooms. Sarah Harris came on.

"When is he due back from the U.N.?" he asked.

"He's on his way now, Mr. Pompey. He intends to spend the rest of the day working on the speech."

"I want to talk to him. I'm going to be over at the Foundation most of the afternoon. I'll check back with you later."

She hesitated. "I'll do what I can for you, but you know how jittery he gets before a public appearance. Nerves, I guess. You would think a man in his position would be used to it, get over his stage fright. But he never has. Such a sensitive man."

Finished, Pompey stripped off his jacket and shirt. In the bathroom, he washed his hands and face. He studied his face in the mirror. A complex of tiny lines was visible beneath each eye, time marking his skin. It was nothing, he told himself. He still looked good, younger than his years, and he felt fine. He had retained all his hair, and his stomach was flat and comparatively hard.

Gail had always liked that, the tautness of his body. Gail, gone now, lost to him forever. A sentient stirring made him wish she was there with him, and with the wish came the memory of what it had been like to make love to her, the taste of her, the delicate female fragrance of her. He had never desired her more than at that moment, and at the same time he conceded that she had been right to turn away from him.

The phone interrupted. It was Sarah Harris.

"He just came in. You can have a few minutes."

"I'm on my way."

He dressed swiftly and hurried into the corridor.

The Presidential suite faced southwest, a complex of large, white-walled chambers trimmed with gold and decorated with French antiques. The President was in the sitting room with Mrs. Gunther.

"Okay, Pompey," he began, obviously in good spirits. "Unless you've got some pleasant news for me, I'm not interested. I had a very nice lunch with the Secretary General and Felix at the U.N. I want to treasure the mood."

"Oh, yes, Mr. Pompey," the First Lady said in that whispery voice of hers. "Only pleasant conversation. Sometimes I wish Harry was back in the State House, many fewer problems there. While in Washington," she laughed, the sound of old crystal crumbling, and brightened perceptibly, "I must confess Harry appears to thrive on difficulties."

Pompey waited until she was finished before turning back to the President. "Wanted to be sure there was nothing you wanted."

"Nothing, Pompey."

"I'm going over to the Foundation early, to stay on top of things."

"Good thinking. These damn liberal groups are never very competent. Full of love of mankind and anxious to do good, but never quite sure how to get things done. By the way, I've decided to skip the meal. Convey my apologies."

Pompey froze. Dinner was scheduled for eight o'clock. That meant two more hours before the President arrived, two more hours for Street to sit and wait, for the tension and the uncertainty within him to gather and expand. To explode.

"Is that a good move?" Pompey began.

The President frowned. "That's the way it has to be. I want to make some changes in the speech. Luplow seems to have lost his flair for *le mot juste,* as the French say. Also, I want to add a few phrases about San Carlos. The Russians are going out of their way to force us into an armed confrontation——"

"Wouldn't it be better to placate——?"

The President pushed himself erect. "No, it would not." The words came out dry and flat. "You know my intentions and nothing has happened to make me change my mind. Now just trot over to the Foundation and keep those newspaper boys content, and make sure they've got those TV cameras cranked up. You take care of those things and leave the thinking to me, Pompey. I still run the country."

The First Lady giggled nervously. "Mr. Gunther and I are going to dine together, Mr. Pompey. Here. Just the two of us. We have so little time to ourselves. You do understand?"

Pompey made himself smile at her. "Yes, of course," he said, then to the President: "The speech is scheduled for ten o'clock."

The President grunted and deposited himself on the couch, absently stroking his football knee. "I imagine they'll wait, if I'm a few minutes late. I *am* the star attraction."

Dismissed, Pompey went back to the Peace Now Foundation. In the lobby, in the shadow of the great, curving staircase, there were three phone booths. He called Peter Street. The hotel operator rang his room.

"Sorry, sir. Mr. Street does not answer. Is there any message?"

"None."

Street should have been in his room. It was his responsibility to be there, to wait for instructions. A vein pulsed erratically in Pompey's temple. Three time during the next few hours he called Street with identical results.

Fear triggered Pompey's imagination. Nothing Street might do would have surprised him. At that moment, with so much dependent upon him, he might be lying somewhere in a drunken stupor. Or be in some other kind of trouble. What if he failed to show? The possibility made Pompey weak and afraid.

Pompey returned to the Warren House. He showered and shaved and brushed his teeth, then stretched out on the bed and tried to sleep. It refused to come. Each time he dozed, something would jar him awake, his mind reaching for some elusive thought. Finally, he rose and put on his tuxedo.

This done, he retrieved the revolver from its hiding place. He hefted it, enjoyed the virile power in his hand, the feeling of strength it provided. He sighted at a lamp across the room. Not since the Army had he fired a weapon. He flipped open the cylinder; all chambers were loaded.

He stood in front of the mirror and placed the stubby muzzle against his forehead. One pull of th trigger and oblivion. Peace. A simple procedure. Doubt entered his mind. He had heard stories of would-be suicides who failed. He supposed they hadn't really wanted to die. He didn't want to die either, but should it become necessary he wanted it to happen quickly. He placed the barrel in his mouth, metallic, passively violent, cold against his tongue, yet strangely satisfying.

He put the gun on the bureau.

He took four Band-Aids out of his toilet kit,

stripped away the protective covering, and dangled them from the edge of the bureau top. This done, he rolled up the silk-striped left leg of his trousers and, using the Band-Aids, anchored the .38 behind his knee. He adjusted the trouser leg and studied himself in the long mirror on the closet door; there was no bulge.

He picked up the attaché case. In it was Hank Luplow's original version of the *Peace Now* speech, calling for immediate Senatorial ratification of the Defense Pact. It was protected by a black, spring binder, a duplicate of the one the President had. Pompey took one last look at himself in the mirror. His face was pale.

Outside, on Madison Avenue, it was pleasant, the shadows of the tall buildings bringing on an early dusk. An anticipatory excitement filled the air, and people were collecting already behind the police barricades, uniformed officers posted every few yards. Pompey walked slowly, carefully, afraid he might jar the .38 out of its perch.

Pompey went into a drugstore and bought some cigarettes. There was a phone booth at the rear. He dialed Street's hotel. This time he answered.

"Where the hell have you been?" Pompey began harshly, keeping his voice down. "I've been calling all afternoon."

A disturbing silence followed.

"Street?" he said, afraid the other man had hung up. "Are you still there?"

"It was impossible to stay here," Street said, voice relaxed, casual. "Have you ever been in the 42nd Street library, Pompey? What a magnificent treasure it is! Not only the millions of volumes, but the structure itself. It has the grace and permanence of an era when men found time for contemplation. That's where I belong, Pompey. Always have."

"Are you ready to leave?"

Street laughed, a soft, not unpleasant sound. "You needn't worry, Pompey. I'll be there. And in plenty of time."

"Of course. I have confidence in you. I'm on my way over to the Foundation now myself."

"How will I know," Street said, "where *it* will be?"

Pompey discovered that he was holding his breath. He released a slow, controlled exhalation. "I'll have to contact you again. Wait for my call."

"I will."

"You mustn't leave before I call."

"I said I'd wait." A peevish element seeped into Street's voice. "Is there anything else?"

"Yes. *He's* going to eat at the hotel. He'll arrive about ten."

"I understand."

Street's restraint troubled Pompey. Had their positions been reversed, he would have been agitated, anxious, emotions close to the surface.

Pompey walked very carefully to the foundation.

On the third floor landing, at the head of the central staircase, he met Julian Dawson. The Chief of the White House detail wore a worried frown.

"You don't look happy, Jules," Pompey said.

"What would I be happy about?" He waved one big, fleshy hand. "This place," he snorted. "They ought to demolish it. Everywhere doors and passageways. A man could get lost here and never be found. I tell you, Pompey, Congress ought to pass a law forcing the President to spend his term of office inside the White House. It's a miracle we're able to protect him as good as we do."

Pompey commiserated with the security chief. "If I know you, Jules, you've got every entrance and exit blanketed."

"Bet on it."

"Are my TV people cleared?"

"Yeah." He swung around and waggled a thick forefinger at Pompey. "But I'm telling you now, my men got their orders—nobody gets into that ballroom without a ticket." His face was flushed, the blue eyes cold. "That ballroom, and that lousy balcony. Should've been torn down years ago. All of it. I'm taking no chances in this museum."

Pompey went to the ballroom. Television technicians were working over a camera on the balcony, and another team was busy in the center aisle. Waiters arranged place settings, and Secret Service agents stood guard at each of the doors. They appeared relaxed and unconcerned. A temporary condition. Their alertness would increase as the day wore on.

Pompey sought out the television director and made the usual reassuring offers of help that would never be required and listened to the usual complaints that would never be answered. He went back out into the corridor and glanced down the long hallway to where the heavy iron fire door was concealed behind maroon draperies. The door, he knew, would be locked and barred, checked frequently during the evening by a member of the security force. No one would leave by that exit. He walked in the opposite direction, toward the lounge.

His eyes raked over the small, tiled men's room, empty and sparkling clean. Congestion gathered in the cavities of his skull, and his vision blurred. There was no towel container. Instead, a warm-air drier had been installed in the far corner.

He tried desperately to clear his mind, to consider the problem. He needed Gordon, his experience, his cool competence. But the agent was back in Washington by now; there was no one to help. He made a concerted effort to throw off the inhibiting fog which encased his brain.

And he succeeded.

Three booths lined the wall opposite the sinks. He went into the first one, locked the door, and sat down. He stared at the brightly polished paper container briefly, then, using a dime, unscrewed the cover, lifted it away. The container was newly filled with neat, rectangular tissues. He removed half their number and flushed them.

He rolled up his trouser leg and removed the .38, flushed the Band-Aids, and situated the revolver on top of the remaining paper, depressing the spring until it was secured. Satisfied, he replaced the container cover, tightened the screw. He stood up, adjusted his trouser leg, wiped the container with his handkerchief. He flushed the toilet again; he wanted no Band-Aids to come floating back into view.

He went down to the main lobby and called Peter Street from one of the booths under the stairs, telling him where the gun was concealed, how to retrieve it.

"I understand," Street said. "I'll get it a few minutes before he arrives."

"Don't cut it too fine."

"I suppose you're going to have to depend on my judgment from now on."

"And I do," Pompey heard himself say. "We both want things to go right, don't we, Peter?"

After a short silence, Street said, "What about the other arrangements, the transportation?"

"All taken care of," Pompey said without hesitation. "There's nothing to worry about." The next words came gushing out before he could stop them. "And no drinking, Peter. You've got to be sober."

"You needn't have said it," Street said in a distant voice. "You might have given me that much." He hung up.

Pompey went back up to the third floor to his press headquarters. He draped his dinner jacket over the back of a chair and sat down to wait. There was nothing else to do.

V

A bar had been set up in the ballroom along the wall adjoining the entrance to the kitchen. It was a simple affair—four tables butted together and covered with white tablecloths. A trio of bartenders dispensed liquor freely, drinks included in the entrance fee. It was all tax deductible.

The attraction was irresistible to the newsmen covering the event, and they came early and drank hard. It was one of the fringe benefits of having press credentials. A few of the more dedicated types found their way to Pompey's headquarters to inquire about copies of the President's speech. Pompey put them off, claiming the copies had not yet arrived, directing them back to the bar.

"Don't worry," Pompey told them. "I'll see that you're all taken care of."

"Jesus, I hope so," the man from the *Daily News* said. "If I have to make notes with my handwriting, I'm in trouble."

Pompey went back into the ballroom. Guests were beginning to arrive—people unknown to him, minor functionaries of the Foundation, or precinct political figures, or supporters of the President's party whose contributions fell into that middle area, deserving of some attention, but not too much.

But no Peter Street.

Pompey looked at his watch; not yet eight o'clock. Still early, but he could not help worrying. There were so many reasons to distrust Street, so many reasons to believe that before this night was over, his nerve would go and he would fail them all. Pompey returned to the press room and phoned Sarah Harris.

"How are things going, Sarah?"

"Lovely, Mr. Pompey. The President and Mrs. Gunther are about to have dinner in their suite. They both look so handsome, all dressed up. It's so nice to see them this way, caring about each other, I mean. For a while, I used to think there was something the matter between them. But I was wrong, you see."

A vision of Anne Lockridge came floating to Pompey's mind. He supposed she would be at home on this night, along, waiting to watch the President deliver his speech on television. She had not stopped caring for Gunther and would be interested in what he had to say, how he looked. Pompey refused to consider her reaction to what was going to happen. If it happened.

He kept his voice casual. "A busy afternoon, Sarah? I imagine people have been in and out of his suite."

"Happily, you're wrong. It's been kind of quiet. He wanted the time alone, to polish the speech. No visitors, not even any phone calls."

Pompey made a small joke about the food at Warren House being superior to that at the Foundation. Sarah Harris laughed dutifully and said she was happy not to have to attend the dinner. Pompey agreed that such affairs were tiresome. He gave her the number of the press room telephone.

"Call me, Sarah," he said, "when the President leaves. "So I can alert the television people."

"Yes, sir."

He hung up and tried to sit quietly, to wipe all thoughts from his mind. It was impossible. He went back into the ballroom. People were arriving in increasing numbers. A festive atmosphere filled the big room with its high, vaulted ceiling, an intramural gaiety, for these were people whose long efforts to achieve world peace seemed close to fruition. Ratification of the Mutual Defense Pact, they were sure, would introduce a new and lengthy era of good fellowship to the world, and the President was going to insure that ratification.

Pompey watched them, faces glowing, eyes sparkling, confident that this night marked a major milestone in their efforts. He greeted people he knew, exchanged polite remarks, always searching the swelling crowd for Peter Street.

Eight o'clock came and went. No Peter Street. Panic was born behind his navel. He fought to keep it localized, to clear his mind. He felt uncoordinated, detached from reality, alone. His mind turned to the Smith & Wesson .38 resting so passively in that shiny container in the men's room. If Street failed to come for it—a shattering idea—then he, Louis John Dominic Gaetano Pompey would have to act in his place, do what was required. And for the first time in twenty years he contemplated Jesus and death and a life beyond this one.

Street had always taken pleasure in the way he looked in black tie. That pale and lean, slightly effete indolence that marked him, that men like himself and Harrison Gunther seemed to possess from birth, complemented the dark severity of evening dress.

He was particularly fond of this dinner jacket. Not quite two years old, it draped off his bony shoulders with a casual indifference that bespoke its rightness. And by that rightness, it managed to veil the evidence of disintegration—the tracery of red veins in Street's eyes, the pouchiness of his face, the soft sag of his paunch—all were rendered nearly invisible.

He slouched uptown in the last light of that mild spring day, oblivious to the complimentary glances of passers-by. He walked east to the river and watched the tugs muscling coal barges upstream, enjoying the slow-flying grace of the river gulls as they circled. When this palled, he crossed the footbridge spanning the East River Drive and resumed his walk. Two young girls approached, voluptuous and provocative in short skirts, eying him surreptitiously, whispering to each other. He admired the freedom with which they moved, self-consciously aware of their bodies and at the same time free from restrictions, reveling in their youth and beauty. It would have been nice to sit with these two, to listen to them laugh and talk, to talk to them, to allow the warm desire to build up in his loins.

As they came abreast of him, he nodded with exaggerated formality. "Good evening, ladies," he said.

The girls giggled, hesitated, and moved on, glancing back. He watched them go, smiling wistfully.

That made him feel better. He increased his pace, walked with a new briskness. So many young girls, he thought, so much pleasure, so many good things to enjoy.

Street moved past the Waldorf and over to Fifth Avenue before continuing his advance uptown. A clock in the window of a travel agency told him that he was late, and that amused him briefly. He imagined Pompey anxious, worried, not knowing what to expect. His merriment was brief. Pompey had done well. No one would have done it better. Not even Jacobs.

They seemed to have much in common. Pompey and Jacobs, a hard core of strength and determination, and if the Press Secretary lacked that same internal discipline, he was moving steadily toward it. After all, Jacobs had perfected his artistic vision of himself before arriving in Washington, was complete, ready for anything. Not so Pompey. He had come blurred and without form, was still learning, still reaching. After tonight, he would be much closer to fulfillment.

Street began comparing himself with Pompey. For him, there had been so many advantages, of appearance, background, education. Everything had been given to him, everything but the ultimate gift, that singular ability to shape the raw material of life into a worthwhile construction. Into a work of art, a productive thing of beauty. Into a man.

He considered what lay ahead, the ultimate test. His mouth went dry, and a pervading thirst lined his throat. Just one drink, he told himself.

One.

VI

Pompey stepped out of the phone booth. Street wasn't in his hotel room. At that moment he was somewhere in the city streets, and that worried Pompey. For Street temptation waited on every corner, and disaster. Pompey closed out the thought and went back upstairs.

The ballroom was crowded, a babble of sound rolling around under the ceiling. Table number 11—Street's chair was empty.

At the press tables, the reporters were busy eating, joking, talking among themselves, unconcerned about the evening's assignment, confident that an experienced and reliable Press Secretary would supply an exact copy of the President's speech on which they could base their stories.

On the balcony, a cameraman stood impatiently alongside his camera; and on the floor below, two technicians talked with the floor manager.

Four muscular young men in tuxedos moved into place in front of the dais, spacing themselves at irregular intervals. They were members of the Secret Service detail. Other agents were situated around the ballroom.

Pompey had started toward the press room when Peter Street appeared. Street moved gracefully across the floor, stopping at his table, not twenty feet from the dais, lean and handsome, an arrogant smile slicing across that aristocratic face as he greeted the other guests. He sat down and Pompey went back into the press room to wait for Sarah Harris' call.

VII

Street ordered a Scotch on ice. When the drink came, he put the glass to his mouth and allowed the liquor to dampen his lips. He swallowed none of it. The taste intensified his craving and he forced his attention elsewhere, talking to a manufacturer of leather goods on his left.

"This is great," the manufacturer said. "This peace thing, I mean. I mean, what the hell is more important than peace, y'know. I got a son in college, and if there's anything I want to leave him it's . . ."

Street arranged a half-smile on his mouth and nibbled at his grapefruit and amused himself by anticipating the man's words.

At the same time, he began a covert survey of the ballroom. The balcony. It hung off the back wall fifteen feet up, ten feet wide and no more than four feet deep, rimmed by a waist-high railing.

The cameraman was a slender young man, balding and sallow with no particular distinction, now talking into the microphone around his neck to the director in the control truck parked in the street below. Street made a mental note not to hit the man too hard, only enough to render him inoperative.

He anticipated no trouble. The cameraman would be peering through his viewer, concentrating on the President, when Street stepped onto the balcony. It would be a simple matter to come up unnoticed and slug him. This done, he would kneel at the railing, steadying his right hand with his left, cock the pistol, take aim and fire. Two shots at most, and then he would leave, gone before the realization of what had happened could penetrate, before anyone could act. Seconds later he would be down the corridor, through the fire door, on his way to meet Gordon.

His eyes continued around the ballroom. There were more Secret Service men than he liked, but surely they anticipated no trouble in this select group.

He studied the agent in front of the dais, boyish almost, his face unlined, with close-cut brown hair and watchful eyes, a generous mouth. The dinner jacket he wore made him appear slender, delicate, but the thickness of his neck was evidence of concealed muscularity. Street warned himself to shoot accurately; it was important not to hurt the young man.

He brought the Scotch to his lips, returned it to its place without swallowing any. The game was entertaining and he repeated the process from time to time, pleased that he was able to resist temptation.

Time passed unmarked. Unreal. Suddenly busboys were clearing the tables and coffee and dessert were served.

Pompey appeared, crossed over to the press table. From where he sat, Street could see that some of the reporters were agitated, that Pompey was trying to placate them. After a few minutes, Pompey picked his way back, turning at the entrance to the press room. Their eyes locked and Street knew that Pompey was trying to reach across the space that separated them, seeking reassurance. He looked at his wrist watch. It was eighteen minutes before ten. He excused himself and stood up.

"That's right," the leather manufacturer said in a raucous voice. "Do it before old Gunther gets going. Nobody's gonna leave the room once he starts talking."

Street slouched out of the ballroom looking neither right nor left. He was aware of his body as never before, increasingly sensitive to the conditioned air cooling his fevered cheeks, the numbness in his extremities, the deep nausea oozing through his gut, the congestion in his throat. His heartbeat was an insistent thumping, its echo in his skull. No longer was this a charade to be enjoyed in the privacy of his mind. This was real and he was on his way to fetch the murder weapon. He pushed into the men's room and wanted to laugh.

Or cry.

The booth, the first booth. It was occupied.

His mind raced wildly and he fought a rising hysteria. He sucked in great drafts of air. No tolerance remained for indulgence. All of it had funneled down to him, the vital cog, and there was no allowance for failure. Pride and terror mingled in his blood as he picked his way out of the emotional sump.

He took off his dinner jacket, hung it on a wall hook. Slowly, very slowly, he opened his cuff links and rolled back each sleeve. He washed his hands. The booth remained closed. He washed his hands again. Thoroughly. He washed them three times more before the man in the booth stirred.

At the sound of the flush, laughter filled Street's throat. He forced it back down. How absurd, he thought, that he, a man so socially proper, so cultured, so exquisitely educated and groomed, should be reduced to waiting for some stranger to relieve himself.

The man came out. He was stocky and florid-faced, and wore a very bad toupee. Street washed his hands and the man did likewise. Street insisted that the stranger use the hand-drier first. He did, finally left. Street took his jacket and went into the booth and locked the door. He sat down and reached into his pocket. He found a dime.

And dropped it.

He searched with trembling fingers, couldn't find it. He swore again and again went to his pocket. No more dimes. He tried a quarter and then a nickel. Neither fit, both too thick for the slot of the screw head. At once, what had been a faintly ludicrous situation lost all its humor. He carried no pocket knife, no nail file, no other device that would turn the screw. Nor did he dare go outside in search of a dime.

With mounting desperation, he went to his knees,

began feeling for the elusive dime. Those restricted confines had not been designed for a man of his proportions, and he moved with great difficulty, his long legs getting in the way as he strained to reach behind the commode. He began to perspire. His breathing was labored, the beat of his heart more rapid. He extended his fingers, felt along the cold tile. Nothing. He swung his hand to one side and back again. As far as he could reach. Still nothing. He shifted position, reached out. Ahh! At last, something. *The dime.* He closed his eyes and forced himself to inhale, exhale, a succession of long, regular breaths. He gathered his resources and stretched as far as possible.

With one finger, he managed to draw the coin closer, to squeeze it finally between thumb and middle finger, to grasp it firmly in his clenched hand. He felt weak, helpless, and a number of minutes passed before he was able to climb back up to his feet, knees trembling, the fibers of his nerves rubbed raw. A swirling faintness drifted under his skull as he sat down.

Finally it passed and he turned his attention to the container. It took a long time to loosen the screw, a painfully long time to remove the revolver, to replace the chrome cover.

Fighting for air, waiting for his heartbeat to slow, the gun in his lap, he sat back and closed his eyes. Eventually his strength returned, and he opened his eyes, hefted the pistol. It felt heavy, larger than he remembered, alarmingly cumbersome, and he wanted to return it to its nest, to forget it ever existed.

He stood up and slid it into the waistband of his trousers, under the cummerbund. He sighed and stepped out of the booth.

He gazed at his reflection in the mirror. All too apparent was the encroaching dissolution in his face, the coarsening of skin, the ruptured veins, the pouches beneath his eyes. But nothing to signal the fear he felt. Nothing to give him away. He wet his crusted lips and calmly walked out into the corridor.

And saw the Special Agents.

Two of them. Alert, wary, balanced athletically on the balls of their feet. One man, sinewy and glowering, guarding the balcony entrance; the other, bulletheaded with no neck, solidly planted in front of the fire exit. The man at the balcony door glanced at the Street, measured him coldly with detached professional interest, then turned away.

And in that suspended fraction of time, Street was sure he was going to be sick.

VIII

Think!

His mind was a seething pit, of distorted and ill-defined images, snatches of faintly recalled lessons, fragments of experiences long forgotten, of questions without answers, of childhood prayers. Of regret. Relief. Confusion.

Of fear.

The fear was worst. An overwhelming storm that enveloped him, hoisted him high into swirling currents, battered him mercilessly, depositing him helpless, frantic, choking. An enervating cloud smotheringly, caused his heart to skip. The hard bulge of metal against his middle was painful, terrifying, and he yearned desperately to rid himself of that awful burden.

He made a powerful effort to strip away the emotional fog, the fear, to find some order in himself.

His first impulse was to go back into the men's room, to return the .38 to its hiding place. But to his cluttered mind that seemed an obvious subterfuge, one inclined to draw the interest of the Secret Service agents in the corridor, to alert them to his purpose. There had to be another way.

Leave.

Run away. Walk out of the Foundation Building without a word to anyone. Once outside, it would be easy enough to dispose of the gun. A trash basket or down a sewer. Anywhere. Later, should anyone inquire about his sudden departure, he could claim illness. No one would care. Not really.

Except Pompey.

And himself.

Time was what he needed. Time to consider, to displace the confusion, to take charge. He thrust his shoulders back and forced himself to ignore his fluttering heartbeat. He walked toward the Secret Service agent at the balcony door.

At close range, a very impressive man. The facial bones were broad and heavy, close to the surface, the neck corded, the shoulders high and muscular. He looked at Street with pale eyes.

"Excuse me," Street said. He cleared his throat and made himself smile. "Is there a pay phone?" He gestured toward the men's room. "None in there."

The bony face showed nothing. It swung toward the other agent, the one guarding the draped fire door. "Hey, Marcus. Any telephone around? This gentleman wants a telephone."

Marcus considered. "Downstairs," he said. "On the main floor. Under the steps."

"Under the steps," the first agent echoed. "Downstairs."

"Thank you," Street said.

Pompey stood alongside the bar. The ballroom was a mélange of sound—voices, silverware clinking against china, women laughing, deeper masculine tones. And of constant movement—the industrious flow of waiters and busboys, disinterested in the people they served, anxious to get on with it, to return to the private sectors of their lives.

Pompey stared across the room to table Number 11. Street's chair was empty. A chill caused him to shiver before he remembered the gun. Of course! Street had gone after it.

He went back into the press room, fighting against his increasing agitation. The phone rang. He picked it up, anticipating Sarah Harris' voice.

"Pompey," Street began.

The Press Secretary felt his joints lock into place. "Where are you?" he husked into the phone.

"Downstairs, in a phone booth. Listen to me. Something's happened. Gone wrong."

"What are you talking about?"

"The balcony, it's guarded, and the fire exit. It can't be done. We've got to forget about it."

Through the door and the wall, the sound of the ballroom carried to Pompey, filtered and purified, a distant buzz of life, remote and beyond comprehension. A fusillade of negative images bombarded his brain. All those men who had assassinated American Presidents–Booth, Czolgosz, Guiteau, Oswald–all were made of the stuff of martyrs. So too was Peter Street. He was *needed*, the one man who could kill the President, and in being killed terminate the crisis in which an unknowing world found itself. The Indispensable Man. Necessary. Vital.

"You must do it," he said. "You *will.*"

"I can't. Not now."

Pompey sifted through the cerebral clutter. He spoke with more confidence than he felt. "There's still a way, an easier way, a more certain way."

"No," Street said instinctively.

"In the ballroom, when he comes in. Just walk up to him and do it."

"No."

"It has to be done, Peter. Tonight. You know that."

"No. I won't."

It was all there in Pompey, anger and hope, dismay and relief, fear and a kind of tortured joy, resentment that it had come down to this, to Peter Street. To himself. To strike out, to cause damage, to punish this man who opposed him, took hold. Peter Street, the vital element. What a bitter, unfunny joke! A shadow without substance, a suicide taking an ungodly amount of time to finish the job, imposing on the world.

A chilling reminder filtered through the swirling emotions: if Street failed to complete his assignment, it would mean the end of everything for Pompey—sooner or later *he* would be killed. He began to speak, softly but intensely, through the thickness that lined his throat.

"Listen to me, Peter," he said, struggling against the swinging terror he felt, keeping his voice gentle and reasonable. Oh, sweet reason. "We've gone over it in detail. Think about it, what will happen if it isn't done and done tonight. We're depending on you, Gordon and me. Everybody. You know what he is, Peter, who he represents. Think, Peter."

"I'm frightened."

"Of course. But you agreed. You agreed and we believed you. We could have made other arrangements, if we'd known earlier. Now it's too late. Too late."

Street's voice was small, almost inaudible, childish. "I'm so frightened——"

"Yes. All of us. I am. Not to be would be unnatural. But it can't stop us, Peter, this fear. It mustn't. This is too vital. Listen, Peter," he said, plumbing his brain for the thought, the words that would convince, support, direct the wavering instrument at the other end of the line. "This is our last chance, Peter. I spoke to him earlier and he demanded my resignation."

Street gasped. "He suspects you! My God, he knows about us!"

A mistake, to add another worrisome detail to Street's already intolerable burden. Pompey sought to correct it. "He knows nothing," he said. "But if I'm no longer to be in the White House, we lose our primary advantage. You see that, don't you? So you must understand how important it is—that we act tonight, before the speech is delivered. We *must* go through with it!"

A distant sound of protest came over the wire, a whimpering sound, pathetically weak; and Pompey knew he had failed, failed to rouse Street's diminished manhood to action. It was all over. He started to hang up, hesitated. Not yet. No. It couldn't end this way, a feeble capitulation.

Street's face came into being on the screen of his mind, rutted with indulgence, bagged with self-pity, formless in its corruption, the eyes turned inward in defense, fading swiftly across a great void. There had to be some way to span the chasm, to reach him, draw him back, convince him. Pompey stirred the dark reaches in a desperate search for an effective prod. What would Jacobs do? Gamble, he told himself. There was nothing to lose: he was teetering at the outer limits of risk. All at once the bright, cold flame of hate flared in his frontal lobes. He made his last bet.

"You disgust me," he said tightly.

"You mustn't say——"

"Loathsome and gutless, without manhood."

"That's not fair——"

"Fail is all you know how to do."

"I tried."

"Ho, never! Now is the time to try, when things are rough, with the pressure on. You've never tried, not anything."

"I don't want to die——"

A harsh laugh broke out of Pompey. He sustained it. "Why so squeamish about dying? You've been killing yourself for years."

"That's not true——"

"Hear me, Peter. You're finished. One way or another. Today or some other day. You stopped being a man a long time ago. All that talent and intellect. You gave it away because you never had the guts to face up to your life. There's nothing left for you now, Peter, an empty past and a dark future, all shadow and no substance, Peter. You drenched your good brain in alcohol for so long that it's of no value to anyone, least of all yourself. You're a drunk and always will be."

"You have no right——"

"Don't talk to me about rights! You abdicated your rights every day of your life. Make a list of your contributions, Peter to the world, to yourself. You come up empty. A blank. Peter Amory Street, cipher. Weak and afraid, quitting every step of the way, the way you're quitting now."

"I won't listen——"

"You've never been a man, Peter. Not even for a woman—just for little girls who don't know better. That way you don't have to come through, don't have to pay off——"

"You bastard!"

"Feeble and perverted. One of the walking dead. Lie down, Peter. Die. Die now."

"Oh, you bastard, you rotten bastard——"

"Only make it count. Do good for someone, finally, for the world, for your country. You want to be a part of it—well, here's your chance. The last chance. Go out in glory, Peter, a proper finish. Show us your balls, Peter, show us——"

Street hung up.

IX

It was ended.

Street wasn't going to do it, had never owned the resources needed, and Pompey blamed himself. He should have recognized the truth from the start. Jacobs would've known, would have made some other, more certain arrangement. He considered hurrying downstairs, finding Street and taking the gun from him, doing the job himself. It was too late even for that. Street would be gone, lost in the avenues of Manhattan. Pompey knew he had failed, and he was terrified.

The phone rang. It was Sarah Harris saying that the President and the First Lady had just left the hotel.

"Is he walking?" Pompey heard himself ask.

"They're using the limousine. They'll be there in a matter of minutes."

"Thank you for calling."

Pompey returned to the ballroom and waved to the television floor manager, a prearranged signal. Then he went up onto the dais to the place where Jay Peterson, Chairman of the Board of the Peace Now Foundation, was seated.

"The President is on his way," he said. Peterson nodded agreeably.

Pompey walked to the far end of the dais, to the Secret Service agent guarding the entrance to the waiting room into which the President would be brought.

"They're on their way," Pompey said.

"Okay, Mr. Pompey. Thanks for telling me."

Pompey turned back to the ballroom and saw Peter

Street making his way back to his table. Street moved with a kind of casual disregard. He was seemingly at ease in these surroundings, comfortable, relaxed. He paused before sitting, looked up. Their eyes met and Pompey read the accusatory expression on that weary, but still elegant face. Somebody at the table said something, and Street sat down the the accompaniment of laughter, the butt of the joke.

Street couldn't hate Pompey. The Press Secretary had come a long way and was, after all, only getting done what needed doing. This, Street thought wryly, was the American Way, detached competence under pressure, the end-product the only concern.

Success.

His glance wandered to the television balcony. And at once he understood that Gordon would not be waiting with an escape car, that it had been intended all along for him to die an assassin's death under a hail of Secret Service bullets. Part of him yearned to protest, to sound his fury at this betrayal; but there was no anger left in him. His admiration for Pompey increased. The whole affair had been handled very well, a neatly structured design, advancing methodically toward its inevitable end. Jacobs would have done it this way, and Street tried to tell himself that he would have too.

His eyes fluttered up to the dais, ranged over the handsome, confident people seated there. These were the doers, the people who mattered, the men and women who accomplished things, lived worthwhile lives. The Contributors. He ticked them off: the Vice President, Jay Peterson and Jonas Keefe, Louis Malamud and Dolly Quentin, Mac McClintock and Charley Hepburn, Felix Wagnall, Kennety MacMillan . . .

His glance fell away and came to rest on the young agent standing less than a dozen feet from the Seal of the President of the United States. His pleasant face was masked, the eyes alert, far-seeing. Street wondered what he was paid for this duty—nine, ten thousand a year? No more, surely. Not much money considering the risks and the responsibility. This young man, was he married, a father? What plans did he have for the future? Was there a son to follow in his image, or did he own greater aspirations for his offspring? This one, Street determined after a moment. This pleasant-faced young man was the one who was going to kill him.

Sudden movement drew all eyes to the dais. Pompey disappeared into the wings, and the agent on duty stiffened alertly. Excitement rippled through the ballroom, and as if on signal people put aside their utensils and silence descended in layers upon the hall. A man rose in order to see better, and another, another. Throughout the room, people were standing.

Jay Peterson left his seat and strode toward the waiting room at the end of the dais. Moments later he returned, smiling, taking his place in front of the microphones, holding his hands aloft for quiet. When he got it he began his introductory remarks, speaking for less than a minute.

"Ladies and gentlemen," he ended. "Without further delay, I give you the President of the United States!"

On the television balcony, the red light on the camera glowed, and people in living rooms across the nation watched.

Applause crashed out and was magnified. Street rose to his feet.

Julian Dawson was first out of the waiting room, his policeman's face wary, set, eyes raking the scene. Next, the First Lady, and behind her the President, smiling and waving, carrying the black-bound copy of his speech. That crooked grin, the stooped style of the man, the shy charm. And that familiar gesture, the clenched fist pumped high in the air. The applause grew louder.

Nothing had changed, and everything. Street remembered every word Jacobs had said, remembered his suspicions and his fears, the way he had died, remembered that chaos and terror and death would be the result of the words spoken by this man on this night.

The crowd pressed forward. Splendidly tailored men and stylish women crowded toward the dais to be nearer the President, to call out their good wishes, to urge him on in the struggle for peace. Street allowed himself to be carried forward by the flow. He remembered the untouched drink on the table and regretted not finishing it. One last drink would have been so very nice.

The excitement subsided and gradually people began to retreat, returning to their seats. But not Street. Laughter formed on his lips as the stepped forward—What a strange thing for a patriot to do.

Pompey saw it all.

Street appeared out of the mass of white shirts, hand extended, inviting. The President reacted instinctively, reaching for the hand. Flashbulbs exploded and recognition came onto the President's face, an expression of dismay. He stepped back, tried to disengage himself. Street hung on.

The pleasant-faced Special Agent, brow grooved, watching, recognized the President's displeasure, moved to help.

Street, skin sallow and stretched tight, eyes almost squeezed shut, tugged hard on the President's hand, pulling him off balance.

Two shots sounded. A collective intake of breath. The ballet continued to unfold. A woman's shrill peal. It was choked off. A masculine oath. An angry cry. The crowd fell back, and as it did another shot sounded, heavier, coarser. Another. Still another.

Sound rose up and the pattern of movement was destroyed. People scrambled for the exits, most unaware of what had happened, infected by a spreading hysteria. Others froze in place. Cries of dismay went up, screams, protests, shouts of anger.

Grim men with big shoulders shoved toward the dais, and Julian Dawson, gun in hand, barked out orders. "Seal off the building. Goddammit, nobody leaves!"

Ferguson, the big Negro agent, wrapped his arms around the Vice President, using his own body as a shield, bulldozing him into the kitchen. Two others, guns drawn, covered the retreat.

"An ambulance!" someone yelled.

Pompey viewed it from the periphery of his retina, a happening in grotesquely slow time, and distant. It was difficult to refocus, but he managed. He surveyed the narrow dais. At last he picked out of the confusion the raging urgency, out of the tumultuous shuffling—the black-bound copy of the *Peace Now* speech. He stepped solemnly past the First Lady sobbing in Jay Peterson's embrace, past the cluster of men around the fallen President, to the spot where the speech lay at the rear of the dais, partly concealed by the curtain masking the rear wall. He put his back to the ballroom, and swiftly made the substitution.

His mind reached out to the mimeographed copies in the press room. They would have to be destroyed, replaced with the copies in his office file cabinet. And the stencils—Reilly always kept them. An exchange would have to be made for those locked in his desk drawer. He breathed deeply. In the confusion, no one would think about the speech. That would make it easier to put things right, tidy up. Any discrepancies remaining afterwards would be marked down to the turmoil, the emotional blur of this moment.

He straightened up, face blank, eyes opaque. No one had noticed the exchange. He looked back to where Peter Street's body lay on the floor, one leg twisted unnaturally. Two Secret Service men stood over him, guns pointed as if fearing further violence. But Street was dead, no longer a threat, safe finally.

Pompey turned away and started toward the kitchen and the Vice President. He would be a deeply troubled man, fearful of the terrible burden that had been thrust upon him, anxious to do his best for the country in the uncertain days that lay ahead.

Pompey meant to help.

These men died by an assassin's bullet while serving as President of the United States:

1. Abraham Lincoln
2. James A. Garfield
3. William McKinley
4. John F. Kennedy
5. Harrison L. Gunther